I0819926

to never take for granted

Self-defence is not revenge

Adzumi
Aislinn
Gasha
Karla
Kysa
Nadira
Ramona
Sheila
Susie Cross
Tanisha
Ye Myo Tun
Zoe Wilder

Heinz G. Ross
Gold Coast, Australia

to never take for granted

to never take for granted

by
Heinz G. Ross

2023

Copyright Notice:

'to never take for granted' is a work of fiction, partially based on the book 'Barren Seed', written by Heinz Ross and originally published in 2008. However, it incorporates additional twists and features renamed characters, 200 added illustrations and substantial re-edits. The following notice is provided to clarify certain aspects of the content within:

Characters Resemblance: Any resemblance to real events or of the characters portrayed in this book to actual persons, living or dead, is purely coincidental. The author has taken creative liberty in crafting the characters and their characteristics, and any perceived similarities to real individuals are unintentional.

Fictional Nature: The events, situations, and dialogues depicted in this book are entirely fictional. While they may draw inspiration from real-life experiences or historical events, they have been embellished, modified, or entirely fabricated for dramatic effect and narrative purposes.

Imagery: The book contains AI-generated character images that complement the text and enhance the reading experience. The rear of this book offers further visual aids to assist readers in grasping the intricate web of characters and their dynamic evolution over time. They are all original illustrations created specifically for this book. The images should not be construed as representing real people, objects, or events unless explicitly stated.

ISBN: 978-0-6459281-8-1 (Hardcover print, colour)
BISAC code:
FIC009020 (FICTION / Fantasy / Epic)
FIC044000 (FICTION / Women)
FIC002000 (FICTION / Action & Adventure)
Thema notations:
FLQ, JBSF, JBSF1, FYS, FXS, FXN, FHM, FBFV

Disclaimer:

This book includes references to several real countries, cities and places as a backdrop for the fictional narrative. While the names of these countries are used, the events, characters, and circumstances depicted within this book are entirely fictional and do not represent actual events or individuals associated with the mentioned countries.

The author acknowledges that any country or region mentioned herein holds its own rich and diverse heritage, and the usage within this book is not intended to misrepresent or disrespect their culture or peoples.

Please note that all details and descriptions related to medical practices, procedures, treatments, or assumptions are entirely fictitious and should not be considered accurate or reflective of real medical knowledge or practices. Readers should consult qualified medical professionals or authoritative sources for any medical-related enquiries or concerns.

This book is a creative work of intellectual exploration, crafted to inspire thought and ignite the imagination. It challenges perspectives, provokes introspection, and encourages readers to form their own unique interpretations. Please note that all actions depicted by the characters in this work are purely fictional.

The true value of this book lies in the transformative journey it invites readers to embark upon. Let your mind wander beyond familiar boundaries, allowing the seeds of inspiration to take root. May this book serve as a catalyst for profound insights, personal growth, and the pursuit of knowledge and understanding.

Tiny are the seeds of life
in abundance everywhere
fragile each and precious all
to never take for granted

Table of Contents

Preface:

In a world where voices often go unheard and grievances are dismissed, there exists a collective power, an unyielding determination that refuses to be silenced. Within the pages of this book, a diverse array of characters comes to life, each contributing to the tapestry of the narrative. A multitude of supporting characters infuses the narrative with depth and nuance. However, it is the twelve main protagonists who step onto the grand stage, propelling the plot forward and embodying the very heart of the story. Within these pages, an extraordinary tale unfolds a testament to a group of women who, defying indifference, rise above the constraints imposed upon them. Their audacious quest for a fairer society resonates throughout this captivating narrative.

Their stories, woven together in these pages, are a testament to the resilience of the human spirit and the transformative potential that lies within each of us. They are stories of strength and vulnerability, of courage and doubt, as these women confront the barriers that confine them and the prejudices that confound their progress.

Ignored warnings echoed in their minds, urging them to rise above complacency and undertake a bold endeavour. The path they chose was arduous, leading them into uncharted territory where uncertainty loomed, but where the seeds of change could finally take root. Their journey was not solely for their own liberation but an endeavour that promised to reshape the lives of everyone around them, in particular future generations.

In the realm of this narrative, barriers crumble and traditions are re-imagined. It is a realm where the power of empathy and compassion become the guiding forces, where justice and equality form the bedrock of society. As these women venture forward, they carry with them the hopes, dreams, and unspoken aspirations of countless others who yearn for a fairer world.

Through the rich tapestry of their experiences, we witness the struggles and triumphs that mark their path. The characters that inhabit these pages are not mere figments of imagination, but reflections of the diverse voices and experiences that shape our reality. In their stories, we find our own, for their battles mirror our collective quest for a more equitable existence.

It is my humble endeavour, as the chronicler of their tale, to shed light on the untold stories that often remain hidden in the shadows. To illuminate the intricacies of their journeys, I have sought to craft a narrative that captures the complexities of their emotions, the depth of their convictions, and the profound transformations they undergo.

This book serves as a clarion call, resonating with the voices of those who have been silenced for far too long. It challenges prevailing norms and urges us to question the status quo. It invites us to imagine a society where the shackles of inequality are shattered, replaced by the bonds of unity and shared prosperity.

As you delve into these pages bear witness to the profound narratives that unfold. In the stories of these remarkable women, may you find inspiration, empathy, and the resolve to be agents of change. Although the writer does not condone the solution presented by the characters, it is important to remember that this is a work of fiction. Its purpose is to provoke contemplation and encourage readers to consider alternative, less dramatic approaches to addressing grievances. By exploring unconventional paths, this story sparks thought and invites us to seek peaceful resolutions to complex challenges.

Together, let us embark on this transformative journey, forging a path towards a fairer world, where every voice is heard, every grievance acknowledged, and the collective power of compassion and justice reigns supreme.

In all forthcoming works, I will unequivocally employ the name Heinz G. Ross, adorned with my unique HR logo, to differentiate myself from the numerous authors and artists who share the name 'Heinz Ross,' while also emphasizing my location as Gold Coast, Australia.

Heinz G. Ross

My grandchild and my sister

Myanmar (Burma), A remote Village located in the jungle

Aye Ye Mya turned five two days ago. Now her dark-brown eyes are vacant with an empty stare, reflecting the scene in front of her. Her mother is being raped by men with guns who arrived in the village this morning. Her wrists and ankles tied to a wooden pallet, her body stripped bare of all clothing.

Ye Myo Tun

Thankfully, Aye Ye Mya's mother passed out after the fifth of the men was finished. Many more would rape her unconscious body. Aye Ye Mya's consciousness cannot absorb the brutality unfolding. She stands frozen in shock, unable to move. The sacred body of her beloved mother used for a purpose she cannot comprehend. She is unable to scream, to run, seek help or defend her mother. A temporary paralysis overcomes her entire being. The only sign of life in Aye Ye Mya's face is the blood seeping from a deep, almost vertical gash on her forehead.

The flowing blood creating a narrow stream which runs along the side of her nose, like a red coloured line that divides her face into two parts. The flow bridges her lips to continue down her chin, following the path of gravity.

Despite the shock shielding the young girl, she cannot prevent absorbing the smell of urine. Her eyes cannot shut the vision out. Her ears do not stop the screams from all around her coming in. She will carry this weight into her future. For three more minutes, the sounds, smells and sights are entering her body. She did not hear the jeeps start their engines. She collapsed long before that. It saved her life. She never heard the gunshots. She never saw how the truck laden with soldiers drove over her mother's tied remains.

Two hours later, heavy rain saturates the village, trying to keep the flames of burning buildings in check. This is the worst Sunday she had ever experienced in her short life.

Ye Myo Tun and Nyein

Aye Ye Mya woke up to find Nyein kneeling on the ground. Her face was in pain, buried in her hands. Rain forms muddy puddles. Aye Ye Mya inched forwards, as in a trance, reaching for her grandmother's shoulders with shivering hands. Nyein turned, relieved to find at least one remaining member of her family. No one counted the dead that day. Only a very few members of the village survived. Nyein and the child hid in the jungle.

"From this day forward your name shall be Ye Myo Tun," said Nyein. "You will forget this Sunday ever was. I have now changed your name. Your new name will change your destiny."
Aye Ye Mya, born on a Sunday five years ago had lost her name forever. All trace of Sunday wiped from her name.
"Ye is for being brave. That part of your name you shall keep, because you will always be brave. Myo is for relative, and that you are to me. We are from one blood. My blood runs in your veins. You are my grandchild and my sister. Tun, so you shall succeed."

"Ye Myo Tun hear this: You must claim your own freedom. No one else can free you. You and only you have the strength to do that. Stay clear of hatred and guard from evil."

"The time I have left is short. I can do little for you. I can take some more steps with you. The rest of your path you will need to walk on your own."

"Ye Myo Tun, the strength of your name is within you. Never do forget these words."
What the fires could not claim of the village, the insects and the jungle would. The surviving villagers had long dispersed. No one could live in a place that had seen so much carnage. Five years later, the once village would be covered in green. Fifteen years later, it would become as the jungle had always been.

We need to go back

Venezuela, River Delta

José Julio Câmara de Sousa

José Julio Câmara de Sousa sits at the stern of the dug-out canoe to join the Indigenous one last time. Moyo, his 'Shadow', sat near the bow urging him to catch up to the others. Five canoes, each carrying two men, set out in the search for crabs, coming in from the beaches to the large river delta. August is a time to feast in the delta. The men are singing songs to ward against evil spirits, monsters of the sea or any ferocious animal that may be lurking in the trees or beneath the waves.

José, an anthropologist, lived amongst many of the Indigenous tribes for a good part of three years, most of it in the Amazon basin. The last six months of his stay spent in Venezuela, amongst a peaceful people. History here had many dark hours, slavery, relocation, smallpox, cholera, some tribes extinct forever, no trace remains. Big business is on the move in, to explore, extract, exploit.

Six months living in the river delta flew by so quickly. The natives live in houses built high on stilts, some in trees, to weather the tidal rise of the waters.
Children learn swimming before anything else; their dark eyes, olive skin, black hair, and teeth as white as snow when they smiled had all taken José into their lives. José and Aaron were part of an expedition, covering parts of the Amazon from western Guyana to

eastern Venezuela. José left that group a year ago to venture on his own.
Half a year of fish, berries and crabs, the delta's rich orchid provides all that one needs to live.

Moyo

Moyo, six years old, adopted José almost on day one when she saw him near the village. She was hiding behind a tree, watching him try to catch fish. With each failed attempt, she giggled more. She threw small lumps of mud near José to splash up the water, confuse him, and play.

Despite the giggles, José played along, knowing all too well that two eyes were watching his moves. Moyo led him to the village, which consists of 21 buildings with thatched grass roofs. None of the houses had walls. Hammocks were tied between the trees, and dugout canoes rested near the edge of the water.

In slow strides he paddles, looking at Moyo, her arms never still. "Oh, what will happen to you, little Shadow?"

She fiddles with her small woven pendant, symbolising the mother of her people, the forest. The father is symbolised as the river by the line across the forest. In that, she carried her parents, worn on a braided string of grass around the neck.

"Everyone came to rob your people and more will come in time," he says, but Moyo does not speak his language, she turns to nod and smiles.

“They took your pearls, and then sold your people into slavery. Whatever they’ll find, they will take again,” he says. José had learned that Moyo’s parents had taken ill, one died of pneumonia, the other from tuberculosis, when she was three. No matter how many songs the tribe sang, illness took many more lives. For six months, day in, day out, Moyo would shadow him everywhere.

Some clouds formed to cover the sky. Through a gap in the clouds, the sun’s rays shone through. José calls out to the others “Look, look up there,” his hand pointing to the hole in the clouds.
“Look Moyo, there, the legend says your ancestors come from there.” Moyo smiled.

“Moyo, look, the hole in the sky, whenever you need to make a decision chose the one that is higher, the one you need to climb. Climb high, reach upwards. The heavens are the home of your people.”

“Escalada para cima, alcança altamente,” he says in Portuguese, “Climb high, reach upwards.” Moyo nods and points at the rays shining through the hole, but she does not speak English or Portuguese, she smiles in her language, anyone can understand.

The hand-woven baskets were filled to the brim with crabs, enough for a feast to feed all in the village, José’s last meal with the group.
Next morning helping hands were assisting to haul the suitcases onto the waiting boat, to take José out to deeper waters. The clouds gathered, reflecting José’s mood.

"Moyo," he calls out, "I got to go. Moyo, come out to say good-bye."
The villagers searched too. She may be sensing his leaving. Time is pressing the crew urging José to come aboard the boat. "Moyo, thank you," the last words he could call before the engine drowned the sound of his voice.
Most of the villagers waved from the riverbank, Moyo not amongst them. Twelve canoes escorted the boat along the mangroves downriver into the ever-widening delta. The boat opened throttle to leave a world of long ago behind. "Sr. Câmara de Sousa, we need to depart a little sooner than we thought. There is a storm approaching," says one of the crew. They reach a larger vessel and transfer the suitcases and chests across to the ship.

"Welcome aboard, Sr. Câmara de Sousa. I am Captain Garcia da Costa. We need to get away. I don't like those clouds one bit."
"Antônio, show Sr. Câmara de Sousa to his quarters."

The vessel powers ahead clearing the delta then heading northeast. José is sorting his clothing in the small wardrobes then heads up on deck. The sky had turned dark quickly. Half an hour later rain lashes the vessel, swells rising. Within an hour the winds came, whitecaps on the ocean.

"Sr. Câmara de Sousa," said the Captain, "you better get some sleep while the ocean is calm." José grins, calm he calls this, the vessel rising with each peak, then diving to whip up the spray in the troughs. During the night the pounding and noise would not allow anyone any sleep, least of all Moyo, who is still locked in José's largest suitcase. Her cries draw his attention.

"Oh dear Moyo, what are you doing in there?"
He pulls her out of the suitcase and she becomes ill. José heads up to the bridge, "Captain, I need a bucket."
"Did you have a little accident?" he asks, "No, not I. We need to go back to Venezuela."
"Did you forget your pipe or tobacco?" asks the Captain.
"No, we have a little stowaway aboard and need to turn around to bring her back."
"Oh, that's good," says the Captain and laughs.
"What's so funny, Captain."

He laughs even louder, "You owe me another fare, Sr. Câmara de Sousa, that's what's so funny."
"We will talk about this, but first we need to turn around to get her back to her people."
The Captain laughs again, steering the helm to ride another wave. The bow digs in again, covering the whole fore-deck in spray.

"Sr. Câmara de Sousa, you may not have noticed the slight breeze we have out there. It is a little bit of a hurricane that is heading westward, probably the last of the season. We are south of the storm's centre and the wind is up our tail. It is pushing us eastward, exactly where we want to go. Now I am not going to turn this ship around and head back into it. Please understand, I am responsible for 22 lives aboard this vessel, no, 23."

"But Captain, you don't understand, she is just a 6 year old kid. She is a native, she is an Indigenous girl."

The Captain laughs, steering to ride another wave, "Sr. Câmara de Sousa, I have a soft spot for kids. You owe me only half the fare. For the kid the trip is just half price."

"Antônio, Sr. Câmara de Sousa needs a bucket and some extra blankets. Antônio, tomorrow morning make an extra breakfast, half portion, for Sr. Câmara de Sousa's guest. See that you find an orange."

"She needs to go home, Captain." José says.
"That's where we are heading, Grand Canary Islands is home, dead ahead."
"How am I going to get her off the ship and explain this to my fiancé?"

"Have you ever seen one of those pirate films, Sr. Câmara de Sousa, the ones where they wear a wooden leg, a parrot on their shoulders and a big patch over their eye?"
"Yes."
"Well, I don't have a wooden leg yet. My parrot may still be screeching in some gale-force storm, but I do have one of those patches somewhere. When we get to Canary Islands, remind me to wear it. It helps me not to see with one eye."
'What am I going to say to Angela?' José wonders.

How can she be so big already?

Las Palmas, Grand Canary

The ship reached Canary Islands before he had figured the answer.
"Captain Garcia da Costa, it's time for the eye patch. It might help if you have two," says José. "See the one over there, waiting for me, she has no idea."

Angela

The captain laughs, slaps him on the shoulders, "All the work's been done for her. She should be happy with the little surprise, Sr. Câmara de Sousa."
"Wait, here is the fare you gave me for the girl, get her something nice. Farewell and good luck."

"José, José," the voice of Angela. "I'm here, José," her arms waving in anticipation.
"I can see you," he calls out. Moments later he steps down the gangway, his Shadow behind.
They embrace, "I missed you, José. Oh I missed you so much."

José looks up to the captain, who grins and shuts both his eyes, cupped by two big black patches.
"What have you brought me, José?" Angela asks. The captain turns away in laughter. Whatever appropriate words might have been for such a moment, they failed José miserably. His Shadow is close by,

holding firmly onto his trousers. The captain's enthusiastic encouragement is of little help, but his laughter infectious.

José steps back, guides Moyo to the foreground, "How about this, Angela?"
"But you've been gone for only three years. How can she be so big already?"
The captain still watching raises his thumbs.
"This, Angela, is Moyo, a stowaway who hid in my trunk. When I found her, we were in a gale and the captain would not turn back. She is from Venezuela. I got to take her back."

"But not today, you won't," says Angela, "Hello, Moyo, welcome to Las Palmas."
"She lost her parents three years ago," he explains.

"And she's just found them again," Angela replies, "You know I can never have children. This is the most precious gift you have ever brought me, thank you, José."

She turns to the child and says, "Você é assim bonito, Moyo."
Moyo is shy, feeling safer with José.
"She does not speak our language," he says.
"Not yet," Angela smiles.

José rolls his eyes, then asks. "Has Aaron returned?"
"Yes, a week ago," she says.

Those are all songs from her people

Cascais Harbour, Portugal

Aaron Cross

Within a month, José and Aaron meet on José's ketch in the harbour of Cascais, east of Lisboa, Portugal.

"She's a beauty, José."

"Glad she is finally in the harbour. Sloop, yawl, schooner, ketch, I'm glad I went for a ketch. The smaller sails will make it easier to handle, as we're not getting any younger. A lot is changing in Venezuela."

"But also in the Amazon basin," says José. "I did collect many blood and sperm samples. Perhaps at sometime in the future we are able to backtrack, dissecting the DNA, to recreate the Indigenous that have been extinct. It is difficult to find a clear line."

"Poverty, illness, logging, all leaves its mark on the people."

"More than a mark," adds Aaron, "it kills them."

"Some groups just count a few hundred. A simple cough, a virus, anything can make them disappear overnight and no one gives a damn," he adds.

"A very fragile balance," says José. "There is no balance anymore, perhaps there never was," says Aaron, "the strong push the weak out of their spaces, kill the men, rape the women and sell the rest into slavery. Another takes over, pushes them to the edge of the fertile grounds, then some sickness decimates them to the brink of extinction. The pearl diggers, gold robbers, foresters and energy giants move in to clean up the rest. What does one expect?"

“The desolate ones try their luck in the cities, they get lost in it, become abused, a minority group without hope, to wither in the slums of towns.”
“You wait and see, the tourists come next, as long as there is one native standing, someone will find a way to make the money go ‘round.”

“How is the little one, José?” asks Aaron.
“She’s like a fish in the water, an expert swimmer for her age. At least here she doesn't have to worry about piranhas anymore. She is with Angela in town, getting provisions. We will be sailing out. Moyo might as well learn all about sailing.”

“Angela and I will get married next month. All the paperwork is done. We’ll adopt Moyo and have an instant family.”

“What’s that singing?” asks Aaron.
José laughs, “Those are all songs from her people. Moyo knows most of them. We try to keep her in touch with her heritage and hope she does not forget her language.”

I want to die

Chicago, USA, Samuel's Department Store, down town:

Ying An Jia's twin

On December 2nd, the 500th book published by the small Chicago publishers, 'S & C Ryder, Publishing House', hit the shelves. The cover of the book shows a young Chinese girl of exceptional beauty. She looks straight into the camera with her large eyes. Her head slightly bowed. The sadness in her eyes is beyond description. The title of the book 'I want to die.' When I saw that picture, I became violently ill, that is all I remember.

"Mrs. Snyder, hello, Mrs. Snyder, can you hear me?"
"Mrs. Snyder, you are in a hospital, can you hear me?"
"I am a Doctor. I'm Dr. Novak."
"Hello."

Somewhat dazed Mary Snyder regains visual focus.
"Hello, Doctor, why am I here?"
"You had a seizure, Mrs. Snyder."
"What day is it?"
"It is Wednesday, Mrs. Snyder, the 15th of December."
"But..., but how...?"
"But..., I missed my son's birthday. How is this possible?"
"Mrs. Snyder, you were found in a shopping centre. You collapsed. You were holding this book in your hands."
Mary Snyder's body twists in agony as soon as she saw the book's cover.
"Nurse, sedative, quickly."
"Mrs. Snyder, I'm giving you a needle to calm you down."

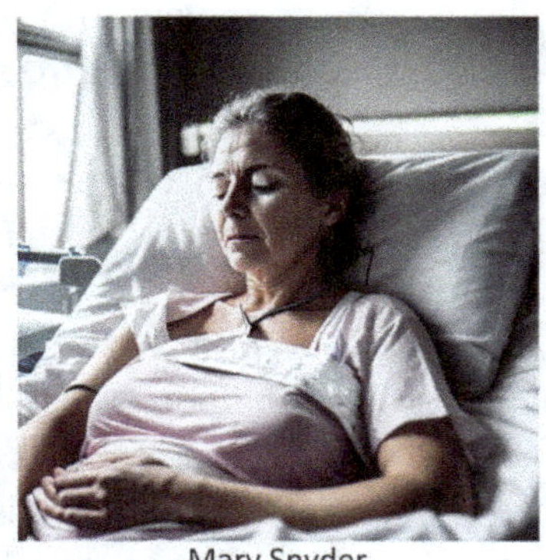
Mary Snyder

I woke up next morning, still heavily sedated. What is it with this book that makes me react this way, I wondered. As slowly as I could, my hand reaches towards the dresser. I touch the book with just one finger. It is enough to make me reach for the bag, just in case I might throw up. Perhaps ten minutes later, I try again. This time, the finger could touch the book without causing a fit. I ask myself, 'Why?' I know nothing about this book. All I have seen is the cover picture and the title. That is all I know, no more than that.

Is it my disgust with the publisher to stop at nothing to make a dollar? Is it my anger with the author, to exploit the misery of a young girl, to become famous? Is it in the story, which I not yet know? Is it my own past that this book writes about? Is it in the picture or is it the title?

I realise, that my whole hand has been resting on the book all along. I am still under the influence of some strong sedative, but my faculties are there. I can think. I do not understand what is happening to me, but I am calm and brave enough to find out.

Reality check 1: Who am I? Mary Snyder, I am 40 years old, have two children, am married for 15 years and I live in Chicago.

Reality check 2: The hospital's wristband states that I am Mary Snyder. If it is good enough for them, it is good enough for me. That is who I am. I am sane, just under sedation.

I am now holding the book in both hands with my eyes still shut. I will look at this book and I will remain calm. I peek through my eyelashes at the book. I will remain calm and will face whatever it is. I will not react to what I see. Being a bit lofty in the head might be a good thing at this moment. It is my intention to remain calm and uncover why I reacted to this book.

The book shows a beautiful young Chinese girl with big eyes. I can now see the cover. The title reads, 'I want to die.' I take a breather. I am still calm. Yes, I am... I am calm.
The author is 'Ying Kim Xia'. I do not know the writer. Is the writer male or female? I have no idea. All I can feel now in constant self-analysis is the powerful combination of image and title. It is very subdued, very simple, very sobering mood. It is brilliant by its punch. It hits very hard. It is as if I had already read the book.

Despite the sedative anger wells again. Stay calm, Mary. Where is the anger coming from? I am calm. I am calm. I just want to smash someone in the face, but I am calm. Why am I getting angry? I am full of assumptions, preconceived ideas. My anger is with the marketing people. Such a brilliant combination used for the sole purpose of making money. No, I want to slap the author in the face, for thinking up the title. I want to slap the photographer for telling a young kid to look miserable and taking that picture. I am angry with the supermarket for selling such confronting stuff at 50% mark-up or more. Money, money, money, I feel like burning it all.

Reality check 3: Of course, Mary, you are not thinking straight this minute, and that is OK. Mary, I love you. Mary, remain calm. I am. I am Mary. I am calm. Do not judge a book by its cover. OK. I am calm. I am in control.

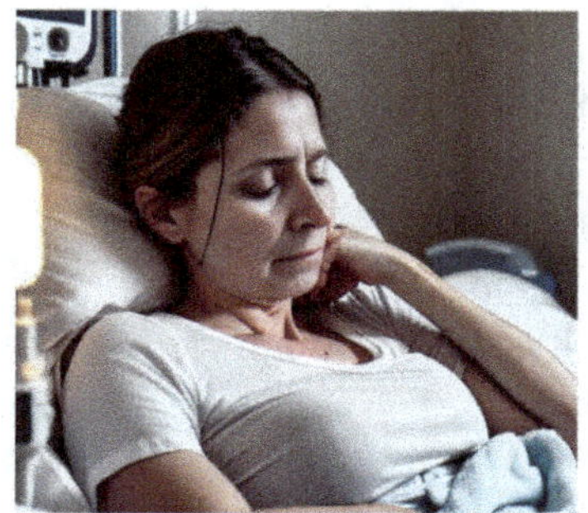

Reality check 4: Could I be pregnant? That does not make sense. You do not fall into a coma from that. Anyway, I would not want to curse a new life with the thought of death in my head before it has seen the light of day.

'About the author,' I am afraid to read further. Why am I afraid? It is just a book. Mary, face your fears, Mary, continue. I am calm.

About the author: I am Ying Kim Xia, the only daughter of Ying An Jia. I am not really a writer, and this is my mother's story. It is the only story I have ever put on paper. The girl on the cover was my mother's twin sister when she was 17 years old. The picture was taken after my mother had been missing for a year. There are no pictures of my mother. Ying An Jia, my mother, is dead. I was going to name this book 'Who is my Daddy?" as I could potentially have a thousand daddies or more, but I do not care about him.

I never had a father and certainly do not know what a 'dad' is. I am 21 years old and have spent three years of my life trying to piece this story together. There is a lot that I do not know about my mother's life. All I know is that her only crime was to be born with exceptional beauty.

You are about to read the true story, as far as I could establish, about my mother, Ying An Jia. I wrote this story because I can no longer carry the pain. It is with much regret that I cannot wish you to enjoy the book because it is so terrible. Please forgive me for that.

"Nurse, quickly, over here!"

Twelve minutes later, Dr. Novak reaches for the telephone.

"Hello, Mr. Snyder."

"Yes."

"I'm Dr. Novak, from the hospital."

"Yes, Doctor, what is it?"

"Mr. Snyder, I have bad news..."

The goldmine

Chicago, USA

M-Kay Y News Channel

Dulcie Nielson

An incoming phone call: "Is this the M-Kay Y news desk?"

"No, Madam, but you have reached the M-Kay Y News channel, not the news desk. How can I help you?"

"I may have a story that you find interesting?"

"What is your name, Madam?"

"I am Dulcie Nielson and I'm seventy-three years old."

"Thank you for thinking of us. What story do you have, Mrs. Nielson?"

“Well, that depends on what you pay me for this information, young man.”
“I’m sure we can work something out, Mrs. Nielson, as long as the story is worth it.”
Three hours later, at M-Kay Y News Studio, Newsroom: “In this hour, learn how to stay slim and keep staying slim. How can you stop your husband from cheating on you? What are the telltale signs to be aware of? But first, a story that is just breaking. We switch to our reporter, Tim Sorrens, who is covering part of the story. Are you there, Tim?”

"Yes, thank you, Jenny. We are outside the cemetery. Out of respect for the people concerned, we will not reveal its location or intrude any closer. Behind us is the burial ceremony for Mrs. Snyder. Three days ago, Mrs. Snyder was a healthy woman, 40 years old. Today, she is dead. Many people die all over the country every day, and you may wonder, Why is this newsworthy?"
"It seems there is some type of mystery surrounding this death. Back to you, Jenny."

"Thanks for that, Tim."

“With me in the studio is Mrs. Dulcie Nielson. Welcome Mrs. Nielson.”
“Oh, thank you, please call me Dulcie.”
“Mrs. Nielson, hmm ..., Dulcie, what can you tell us about this case?”
“I have been in the hospital for six weeks. You know, the circulation is a bit of a problem, but the doctors are ever so kind to me. But it will come...”
“Sorry for interrupting, Dulcie. What can you tell us about Mrs. Snyder?”
“As I was saying..., it will come good, so the young doctor told me.”
“That is wonderful, Dulcie, what happened with Mrs. Snyder?”
“I hope so too. My sister had all the veins replaced in her legs and I don’t....”

Inside the control room News Editor Roland McGuire becomes impatient, “Cut camera 2, switch her microphone off and improvise.”

"Thank you so much, Dulcie. Well it seems that Mrs. Snyder suddenly died by touching a book. With us via video link-up is Professor Edmund Fryer, who is an expert in the paranormal. Professor Fryer, is it possible to die from touching a book?"

"Hello, Jenny. That is a loaded question."
"We know about the terrible things that occurred with the opening of tombs and curses ..."
"Yes, Jenny, there is truth to that."
"So would it not be possible to die from a book?"
"I hope you don't expect a scientific analysis based on that question? Forgive me for laughing, people can die from anything."

"I'm telling you, one minute she was alive, the next minute she was dead."
"Thank you for joining us, Dulcie. Tell us, what did you see? What did happen in that hospital?"
"I watched her, there is little else to do in a hospital, you know. It can get so boring; you wished there were some flies to watch."
"About Mrs. Snyder, Dulcie? You were the only witness. How did it happen, Dulcie?"
"I am not deaf. I will tell you all about Mrs. Snyder, just as soon as the young man gives me the money he promised, $50 and gets my steps fixed."

In the control room, Roland instructs the camera operators: "Switch to camera 4. Could someone get her OFF the set, she is driving me nuts."
"We must interrupt for these short commercial messages, don't go away."
"Mrs. Dulcie Nielson, here is $50, as agreed and we are in the process of getting your steps repaired. When you get home all will be fixed."
"Why thank you, young man. Why didn't you do that in the first place, when I asked you?"
"I am sorry, Madam."
"In the next set could we have your co-operation in answering some questions about Mrs. Snyder?"
"That's what I'm here for, am I not?"
"Thank you."
"She's all yours, Jenny."

"And welcome back, viewers."
"Dulcie is about to tell us her side of the story."
"Thank you, is it Jenny?"
"Yes."
"And thank you for the $50 and getting my steps fixed."
In the control room: "Lord, give me strength."
"Yes."
"A few years ago one could buy a whole house for that, almost."
"Yes, Dulcie."

Roland McGuire

In the control room, Roland becomes agitated: "Help, I'm going nuts, what the ___ is going on today?"
"Let me tell you about Mrs. Snyder, OK, are you ready?"
"Yes, we are ready, Dulcie."
"Which camera you want me to talk to?"
"It doesn't matter, Dulcie, they will pick it up."
"I need to know which camera?"
In the control room: "Someone, get me a rope, I need to hang myself," Roland's patience is thinning out.
"It's that one, Dulcie."
"Do I look good in it?"
"Yes, you look wonderful, Dulcie."
"I was asking the man behind the camera over there, how would you know?"

In the control room: "My blood pressure is reaching bursting point. Camera operator 4 is that you, Tom? Tell her how great she looks, do anything it takes to get this wrapped up."
"Relax, man, she's a goldmine, look at the ratings. Channel 17 and 4 just rang, they want in, milk it, man. Golden Goose right there."
"Really?"
"Yep."
"She says a lot, reveals nothing, that's called suspense."
"Yes, Dulcie, Mrs. Nielson, Madam, you do look wonderful," says Tom, from behind the camera.
"Ah, you're a real smooth talker, but I like you."

Roland's voice, from the control room barks through the headsets: "Tom, you get in the chair, Ted, take over camera 4. Jenny, off the set. NOW! Tom, you ask the questions, go, move it."
"Could you tell me what happened?"
"Where?"
"In the hospital?"
"Certainly."
"What?"
"What, what? What do you mean?"
"Young man, 'where' and 'what' is not a sentence. A sentence needs some more ingredients. Add at least one subject and an object."

Control room: "Will this day never end?"
"Please tell me what did happen to Mrs. Snyder in the hospital?"
"She died."
"Thank you, Dulcie. That will be all."
"Not so fast young man. You paid good money, well not you, but the other man, I forgot his name, but I feel I owe you more."
"Please go ahead."
"Mrs. Snyder came to the hospital on Tuesday, at 12:27pm. She wore a red dress with white buttons. She was unconscious. Many doctors fussed over her behind the curtains and I do not know what they did. I remember that she was clutching a book in her hands. Her fingers were white."

Roland's voice renews instructions from the control room: "Tom, thanks buddy, let her run with it."
"She was in a deep sleep for many days, thirteen days, to be precise. During all this time she was hooked up to all sorts of gadgets, drips and drops and Lord knows what."
"They must have fed her through all the tubes she was on. At precisely 9:15am she woke up."
Control room: "Roland here, announcement: Ratings are climbing through the roof, 17 and 4 are on copy, two more channels want in, she's money in the bank. Let's hope she has substance."

"Doctor Novak came at 9:17am. I thought it rather strange how quickly he showed up. It took a little longer before she came to her senses. She said that she had missed her son's birthday, as she slept all this time, you see?"

"Dr Novak explained that she had been found in a shopping centre holding a book. He showed her the book, the doctor."

Dulcie slows her voice, bows her head forward and leans towards Tom. "Can I tell you what happened then?"

Tom's eyes are fixed at Dulcie. He swallows and nods.

"Then her whole bed rattled. She twisted in agony. Three nurses and two patients had to hold her down; otherwise she could have done all sorts of damage to herself."

"All the tubes and gadgets flew around the place. What an ordeal she must have gone through, poor thing."

"When they all had her pinned down, the doctor gave her an injection of clear liquid, it looked clear, but I didn't have my other glasses with me, so it may have been a little yellow, perhaps white, I am not so sure on that one. In any case, that calmed her down."

"It was 4 hours later, correction, that is a lie. It was 4 hours and 6 minutes later and then she woke up again. This time she was sedated and she opened her eyes very slowly."

"Sorry, we must interrupt Dulcie for a minute and bring you this report from the cemetery."

"The body of Mrs. Snyder laid to rest... the funeral is over. The husband is distraught and we spoke to some relatives of the late Mrs. Snyder. All are at a loss of explaining this sudden death that has tragically come to this family. Back to you."

M-Kay Y News, Executive office:

Jerry Baxter, Director of M-Kay Y News, "Give me the control room."

"Roland, whatever you do, do not, I repeat, do not broadcast the title of the book, the publisher, or the name of the author. We are in negotiations and need another three or four minutes before we have an agreement. This scoop is turning into a small fortune. It is our story. We have the exclusive, drag it out."

In the studio, on the set:

"And that was Tim Sorrens, live, from the cemetery," said Tom. "Recapping the News, if you have just joined us.... just a moment please."
Tom is holding the earpiece, listening to the station's instructions.
"Welcome to our viewers on channel 17 and 4, who have also joined us in covering this story. Three days ago, a woman has died. Excuse me please..."
Tom receives another message through the earphones.
"This is M-Kay Y News, now broadcasting live to the whole northeast. Welcome to this exclusive story unfolding right in front of our eyes. A perfectly healthy woman has touched a book. Now she is dead. The only eyewitness to this event is Mrs. Dulcie Nielson, who is in our studio right now."

M-Kay Y News, Executive office:
Jerry Baxter orders, "I want viewer participation, polls, feedback, something along the lines of 'curse' and comparison with the Egyptian mummies, do some research and think of something. Also, get the same stuff on the websites. I want the phones ringing hot. Hang-on..., turn up the volume."

The monitor in the office shows Dulcie.
"... oh yes, she bought the book in ..."
Jerry Baxter, "No, don't say it."
"...downtown, at Samuel's Department Store," Dulcie continued, "You know, the one with nice coffee shop."
Jerry Baxter barks, "Shit, shit, shit, why didn't I think of that, missed it, damn. Get them on the line and let us see what we can salvage. Who is this idiot? Does he not know the rules? Do we have a new reporter? We don't give free publicity to anyone."

"That is Tom, Sir. He's a camera operator but he can make her sing," says Roland, editor in the control room.
"Somebody give him a tie and a jacket so he looks the part. Give us another few minutes and we'll be live nationwide."
Jerry Baxter ends the call and dials a new number.
"Garry, where are you now? Have you found the author?"
"I'm on the outskirts of Hong Kong. It is pitch black and we're nearly there."
"Garry, don't tell her anything. I want everything live. Not a word to her as to what this is about, unless it's live."

"Yes Sir."

Meanwhile at Samuel's Department Store in downtown Chicago, the last of the copies sold out.

From the control room, Roland calls the executive office, "Sir, when do we get a copy of the book?"
"Don't we have one?"
"No, Sir"
"What the hell is going on? We are covering a story and no one has the goods?"
"Jim said they sold out."
"Then get one from the publisher."
"They don't have any."
"Why aren't they printing a new run, don't they know how to make money?"
"They cannot print any more books."
"What?"
"They have no rights. The girl only printed 5000 copies and paid for them out of her own pocket. She has copyright, not the publisher."
"For crying out loud, then find a customer and pay whatever it takes. Get in touch with the crew. They're at the store now."

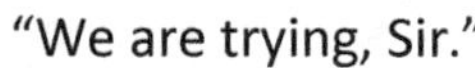

"We are trying, Sir."

"Don't try, deliver."
"Yes Sir."
The News crew in downtown Chicago could only film the empty stand where moments before all the books had been stacked. One of the crew noticed a customer sitting in the café with the book next to his cup.

"Sir, we would like to buy this book from you."
"I haven't read it yet. I just bought it myself. Go over there, that's where they sell them."
"Sir, they have all sold out. I need this book. I pay whatever you want."
"You are keen."
"OK, it's yours for a million dollars."
"But it only costs $4.80, Sir."

"That maybe so, but you offered to pay whatever I want. I want a million dollars. If you want it bad enough, then that is a bargain."
Phone call from the crew to the executive office:
"We found the book."
"Good, bring it in."
"The man wants a million bucks for it."
"Someone please, kick me, I think I'm dreaming. Is the world made up only of vultures?"

The executive looks around the room and asks, "Can we afford to spend a million bucks?"
"What for?"
"The book."
"If we have to, we can spend 5 million, Sir. We made more money in the last hour, than in the whole of last year."
The executive continues on the phone, "Write him a cheque. Yes, a million, if you have to."
"Yes, you heard me, give him the money, but get the book."

All the while at the News desk, Dulcie is still talking live about her experiences.
"Is that the book there?" asks Tom, "The one in your handbag?"
"Yes. That is the book Mrs. Snyder had."
Roland calls the executive office again, "Can we show the book?"
"Is it here already?"
"She laid another egg, she had it all along."
"Somebody, stop that cheque," Roland yells out, "Cancel it, we don't need his book. Sorry, yes, go ahead spill the beans, we are live, nationwide and ratings have gone through the sky."

Phone call from the News crew to the executive office, "Sir, we couldn't stop it, we got the news too late."
"What are you on about?" asks Jerry.
"The man insisted on cash. He is walking down the road with a million dollars in his bag, all in cash."
"What? Didn't I tell you to write him a cheque?"
"Yes you did, Sir, and you also said to give him the money."
"Easy come, easy go."

"It could be another story, Sir, something along the lines of highest price paid to an unknown author, first edition scoop etc."
"Do you take me as an idiot? You think I want the whole world to know about this?"
"Did he sign a non-disclosure agreement?"
"Who?"
"The million-dollar-bag-man?"
"No, Sir, we didn't have any with us."
"Can you still see the man? Get him to sign something along those lines. If the other stations get wind of this, I'll be the laughing stock in the industry."
"Sorry, too late. He left in a taxi a minute ago."
"Then go to his home and sort it out."
"We don't know who he is, Sir."
"I hate setting my own time bombs."

You are going to be a very rich woman

Heidelberg, Germany

Ye Myo Tun is now 23 years old. She is on a short stay in Heidelberg, a small town in the south of Germany, with plans to travel on to Basel, Switzerland, in the coming weeks. Her TV-set is on, showing the cover of the book for the first time. She sits down.

The image of the girl on the cover visibly affects Ye Myo Tun.
She swallows. Tears begin to well in her eyes. As the camera slowly zooms in on the title, she is overcome by the pain these images project. Tears stream down her face. She absorbs the full essence of the unread content in one second. Ye Myo Tun becomes ill and spoils the table in front of her. Despite her becoming ill, she turns the volume up.

"We are now crossing live to Hong Kong, where Garry Stoner has located the author of the book, 'I want to die'."

“I have just been informed that we are now broadcasting across the globe, and welcome to all our viewers. Are you there, Garry?”

“Yes, I can hear you loud and clear. This is Garry Stoner for M-Kay Y News. It is 3 a.m. local time, and I am at the outskirts of Hong Kong. Next to me is Miss Ying Kim Xia.”
Even in the harsh spotlights of the cameras, the somewhat bewildered face of Ying Kim Xia bears a remarkable resemblance to the picture on the book’s cover.
“Hello Ms Xia, oh ..., please forgive me, Ms Xia”
“Please, call me Kim.”
“Hello Kim, and welcome to the programme. How does it feel to become famous overnight?”
“I don’t know what you mean. I am not famous.”
“Oh yes, you are.”

Ying Kim Xia

“What are you talking about, what do you want from me? What is all this, cameras, lights, what is going on? It is 3am, what is all this?”
“You have a bestseller on your hands.”
“Which hands, what bestseller? What are you saying?”
“You are going to be a very rich woman, Kim.”

In Heidelberg, Ye Myo is trying to get her emotions under control, watching the News. She lets out a sigh, “You have the sensitivity of a jackhammer, Mr. Stoner."

“Kim, you might not be aware of this, all your books have sold within 30 minutes. The publishers have run out of stock. You are famous,” said the voice from the TV-set. Frightened by the overpowering experience, Kim asks, “Which book?”
“The book with the girl on the cover, ‘I want to die’.”
It is now that Kim is beginning to understand. With both hands, she clasps her mouth.

"Please, tell the viewers about the curse of the book."
"Curse...?"
"What? I do not understand."
"A woman in Chicago bought your book. When she touched it, she died."
"No, no, no."
Kim becomes upset, agitated, out of control, screaming the word 'No' consistently. Within moments she is hysterical and breaks down in uncontrollable crying, mixed with outrage and physical gesticulations. Distraught, she runs into the darkness.

At M-Kay Y News, Executive office:
Roland has a grin from ear to ear, as the drama is unfolding. "This gets better by the minute. I wish I could dream up a script like that. The joys and surprises of live TV. I can hear the money coming in."

Tom

In Heidelberg, Ye Myo Tun notes down the title of the works and the author's name, as it flashes across the screen. Despite her emotions overcoming her body, she searches the Internet for the title of the book and the author. She does find a listing for Ying Kim Xia, which includes an email contact. She composes a short message.

Dear sister,
I too can feel your pain.
You are not alone.
Together, the weight is less.
Love, Ye Myo Tun

News desk:
"Thank you, Garry Stoner, for this short report. We will now go to Tom, who is in our studio with Dulcie Nielson. For those of you who have just joined us, Dulcie is the only eyewitness to the death of Mrs. Snyder, who died 3 days ago by touching this book. We have reports coming in from Chicago, where several people, 5000 to be exact, had purchased the book this morning. Many have reported strange things happening."

"In Chicago, please use our hot-line number, shown on the screen now. If you have come into contact with this book and find some strange things occurring, let us know. Please, as M-Kay Y News is the first to bring this event to your living rooms."

At M-Kay Y News, Executive office:
Roland on the phone, instructing, "I want panels of 'experts' examining what comes in, reports of reactions to the book, sick people, dead people, whatever you can find. I want lively discussions with lots of viewer feedback and involvement. We make the News, we need to feed it."

News desk: Tom is now dressed with a tie and jacket and somewhat uncomfortable, tries as best as he can to play the part of a seasoned reporter.
"Hmmm, yes, thank you, Jenny for that."
"Don't be like that," said Dulcie, "I like you the way you are."

"Thank you."
"Dulcie, how did you get hold of this book?" asked Tom.
"I hope you don't do me in, but I took it from Mrs. Snyder's bedside table. You see, I didn't mean to take it, but when I thought about it, I said to myself, I said, 'Dulcie,' that is what I said..., I said, 'why not'?"
"You know, when you're alone, there is no one to talk to, and you learn to talk to yourself. And so that you are not so alone, you must answer yourself also. Otherwise, it is just a monologue, which it is anyway, I guess. But it keeps me occupied, you see."
"But weren't you afraid of the curse?"
"I wished it had a curse. You see, young man, say, what is your name?
"I'm Tom."
"As I was saying, Tom, I like that name. It suits you, Tom. It goes with your chin and the 'T' also goes with your bone structure."
"Thank you, Dulcie. You wished it had a curse. Why is this?"
"I am a lonely woman, Tom. I ache for my husband. He passed away, God bless his soul, let's see, hmm..."

"He passed away nine years ago, two months and four days, that's how long ago it was."
"No, that's a lie, I forgot about the leap years."
"Anyway, before I touched the book, I was fully aware that I could drop dead on the spot. But it didn't happen, as you can see, me talking to you right here and now."

"But I remember Mrs. Snyder didn't actually die just by touching the book, no, no. It was not like that. She opened it and read something. Now, I do not know which page she was on, but it must be somewhere on the right side. So I was thinking that there may be some sort of instructions of how to die in the book. When I find them I will let you know."

"Ha, well maybe not, and I don't mean to be funny. After all, if it kills me, I might not be able, or be in a position to tell you about it, will I?"

"But Tom, you see, I am so very tired of it all. I wished it were I instead of young Mrs. Snyder. I want to die. She has a young family and they will surely miss her. So when I took the book, and in the light of what happened to Mrs. Snyder, I thought it was an instructional book on how to die. I was not afraid at all."

"I did not really take the book away from anybody; after all, Mrs. Snyder was finished with it. I mean, when I die, I will leave everything behind as well, it is not going to be of any use to me over there, you see."

"I still have some jumpers from my husband and if you want, I take them in a bit and you can have them, Tom."
"That is very kind, Dulcie."

"Don't mention it, dear. I would love to do it. May I please have a glass of water?"

Harmony and balance

Czech Republic, Prague
Art gallery in the inner city

Felicia Fodor

Felicia Fodor looks like a fiery gypsy queen straight out of a movie set, dressed in a colourful wide flowing skirt with a matching embroidered blouse. Her black braided hair sat well on her shoulders. The clicking sounds of her boots on the tiles announced her arrival everywhere, but even if she were barefoot, she would be noticed anywhere. Felicia Fodor is an event in itself.

"Hungarian born, age 25, I hope I got this right, single, I hope? I didn't have the opportunity to meet up with you sooner, but welcome to our 'Golden City', a place rich in art, music and poetry. Thanks to your contribution, this remains to be so."

"And who might you be?" Felicia asks, "No, let me guess. By your appearance, I'd say you're the legendary El Dorado, Golden Boy."

A golden tie and an ostentatious heavy linked golden chain, worn on a dark plain sweater, three golden rings, securely locked by swollen fingers, all caught Felicia's eyes at once, she adds, "Perhaps some powder missing, gold of course."

Honza Horák

The man grins, revealing two gold-capped teeth, "Oh forgive me, Ms Fodor, I am only the director of this gallery. It was I who commissioned your exhibition."

"My name is Honza, which means 'Gift from God'. I'm Honza Horák, to be precise."

"Ho, Ho," Felicia lets out a loud shriek of laughter that echoes throughout the gallery. She slap's her knees. The explosiveness of her laughter took everyone by surprise.

"Oh, Gift from God, forgive this outburst." She slaps Honza on the shoulder. "I like you, Horák, you are straight to the point, and you are so humble, we will get on well. At last we finally meet, face to face. Honza Horák may not have the same ring to it, but you make up for it with those," she points to his fingers and grins.

"I'm just Felicia, and that means 'lucky' and as you can see, I am," she said, with a heavy eastern European accent that increased her attractiveness even more.
"Felicia also means 'success', and seeing the large crowd here, it looks like a good turn-out for our joint venture."
"My Father had a warped sense of humour," said Horák.
"Your mother must have as well," she responds.
"I have been a Gallery Director for the past five years. May I call you Felicia?"

"You call me anytime you like," responds Felicia, with a low voice, a wink in her eyes and slight tilt of the head.
"No, no, I meant, can I address you as Felicia, but thanks for the offer."
"Gift from God, you call me anything you want," she says, as she slaps him again, this time on the chest and another outburst of laughter bounces off the walls.
"About my statistics, yes, I'm Hungarian, born in Budapest, 25 years ago, but that doesn't mean my age is 25."
"For each year, I age three and based on that I am a seventy-five-year-old woman. Oh, not on the outside, but deep in here, deep in my heart, I am an old woman, dear Horák," she said, and her eyes revealed a depth that was quite different to her apparent exterior. But within a second she changes and bursts out, "In other words, I am, I suppose, 20 years older than you, but I am also an enigma, definitely complicated, vibrant, vivacious, volatile and ..., beware, ... highly explosive."

"That you certainly are, and I would gather you are a whole lot more than meets the eye, Felicia." Honza's eyes slowly wandered towards Felicia's low-cut dress.

"I can sense a little devil hidden in the Gift from God. You better watch where you point those eyes," Felicia lowers her voice and

head, casts her eyes on his and then lowers them, to look at her own cleavage.
With her head bowed low, she flicks her eyes to look into Honza's eyes, a slight grin that left Honza wondering, would this preying manta bite his head off before or after. With a cautious grin, Honza takes a few steps back, then claps his hands together. He calls out with a loud voice, "Distinguished guests, ladies and gentlemen, could I have your attention please. Please gather 'round, thank you." He is waiting a moment for the visitors to assemble.

"On behalf of the gallery, let me welcome you all to this, Felicia Fodor's third exhibition of outstanding works. All based on the theme, 'Harmony and Balance'. I am Honza Horák, the Gallery's Director."

"You may remember, two years ago, Ms Fodor showed her 'Love and Passion' collection, right here, which resulted in excellent reviews. Last year, we were fortunate to exhibit the 'Love and Nurture' art works, a set of 21 beautiful oil paintings, which I believe all sold out during opening week."
"Today Felicia Fodor presents us with 23 oil paintings, based on the theme 'Harmony and Balance'. For those of you, who might not be familiar with Felicia Fodor's work, let me tell you that she is an extraordinary artist with a depth of perception that is beyond her years. She always digs deep and she finds. She has the gift, an uncanny artistic ability to bring it to the canvas. And, yes, I can see some of you have recognised her already, ladies and a gentleman, Felicia Fodor is right here among us."

He steps towards Felicia, holds her hands, "Welcome Felicia Fodor and thank you, for honouring us with your presence."

After the applause died down, Felicia smiles, "May I thank all of you, for such a warm welcome and thank you, Mr. Horák, for the introduction? Also thanks to the gallery, for being so supportive over the last years."

"Yin / Yang, hot / cold, in / out, black / white, male / female, we have grown to believe that these elements are needed to balance, and that balance should lead to harmony."

“Look around you and tell me, where can we find balance or harmony in today’s world?”
“Rich and poor, believers, non believers, good and evil, war and peace, all these are the extremes. None is balance, none is harmony.”

“To me, painting is a process to get part of my soul to the canvas. Each painting is a step along the way, trying to get to the painting that contains the essence, the ‘it’.”
“There are 23 paintings here, as Mr. Horák correctly stated, but the whole collection has 24.”

“Now, if we take a look at the first in this collection, one could see heaven and hell, masculine, feminine, hard and soft, strong and weak, organic, inorganic.”
“Fly into the work and you will get a sense of motion, travel, there is an ‘either’ and ‘or’ about it, that does not offer any rest.”
“Whereby here, on the second in the series the sensations are very different …”

The sweetest loss I ever made

Chicago, USA, S & C Ryder, Publishing House

Sam Ryder

"Good day, Mr. Ryder, I'm glad you are here. The phones are running hot. We have advance orders for the special edition we printed a while ago."
"Which edition is this, Sue?"
"She points to the TV set, which again shows the cover of the book."
"Why are you crying, Sue, has something happened to your family, what is it?"
"This book, it just affects me. I haven't read it."
Sue tries hard to compose herself, "I...I...I didn't know it was one of ours, Sir."
"It is not, Sue, well, not really."

"I remember this book. In this case, we are not really the publisher. We are just the printer."
"She, a young Chinese girl, paid for all the printing up front. Her name is, let me think..."
"Ying Kim Yang, no..., that's not it ...it is Ying Kim Xia."
"I am positive; her name is Ms Ying Kim Xia."
"In this case, we have no rights."
"She owns copyright and she is the publisher."
"How can that be, Sir? We normally never do such things."
"This is a special case. It touched me too," Sam Ryder responded. He pulled up a chair and sat next to Sue.

"I met Miss Ying Kim Xia in the park, near the university. She was writing notes. During the conversation she revealed that she is writing a story. She gave me a page or two to read. I must admit that I felt like you now, I was overcome with emotions and could not read very much of what she gave me. I had to walk away, find a rest room and compose myself, wash my face, clear my eyes, and

I'm not ashamed to admit it. She was still sitting there when I got out. In all my years as publisher, never have just a few lines left such an impact on me. It was not brilliant in a literary sense. Grammar, spelling, punctuation, all left a lot to be desired, but in each word she carried the weight of her pain. It is probably the only book we have ever printed that no-one is going to be able to read."
Both shared tissues to dab their tears.

"She didn't know who I was. She said, 'I have $480 saved up and I want this printed as a book'. I explained who I was and offered her a $5000 advance, purely based on what I had seen. My gut instinct was good about it."
"What did she say to that?" Sue responded.
"Oh, no way, absolutely no, in capitals, she would not have a bar of it."

"She pulled out a picture, that's the one that is on the cover. It was all wrinkled up, the picture. The art department did a great job to make it shine. No, she insisted that she pays for it and asked if it could be done for $480."
"I said, yes."
"But Sir, how?"

"I know it cannot be done. She asked how many books she would get for that, and I told her that would be enough for 100 copies."
Sue started laughing, "But, Sir that is so beautiful."
"I guess I'm getting a little soft in my old age. A week later, she came in with a bundle under her arm, dropped it on the desk and said, 'I am finished'. She had a folder of legal documents and asked me to sign them. She pulled out $480 from her purse and held onto it. It's yours when these are signed," she said.

"I called Bill, from our legal department, to have a look at the legal documents. He made me aware that it is not at all in our interest to sign any of them. I glanced over them, pulled out my pen and signed the lot. She said, 'Thank you', and gave me the money."
"They were proper legal papers, she retains all rights. She also takes all responsibilities. She cleared the image for publication. Perhaps she is a student in law, I don't know. Then she looked at her watch and said, 'Goodness, I need to be at the airport in 45 minutes. My

plane leaves for China'. I asked her where to send the books? She said, 'Give them away, I don't need them'."
"So how did they get to Samuels'?" Sue asks.
"I called the old Samuel and asked him if he could do me a favour, take them off my hands. What did he sell them for?"
"They said in the News $4.80 each."
"Ha, no mark-up, and far below cost price."

"They said they sold all 5000 books in 30 minutes, but she only wanted 100," Sue enquired.
"Should I have thrown 4900 books in the bin? 5000 was the smallest run we could do."
"But $480 is barely enough to cover the artwork, let alone any printing costs, Sir."

"Money isn't everything, Sue. It is the sweetest loss I've ever made. It helps me sleep at night, which is more than enough compensation."

"Jack did the editing, fixed the grammar and so forth, but somehow we must have missed to let the boys know that we're not the publishers. She approved it all, sight unseen, as she was eager to get out of the country, and she was cutting it fine with 45 minutes to O'Hare International. As I said, she left for China the same day. What's this with all the advance orders, are they for this book?"
"Yes, more orders have come in, as you can see. They all want the book. Based on this demand it has the potential to become a bestseller."

"Well, unfortunately her legal papers are waterproof and we cannot print any without her permission. It is her book, not ours."

"I want to tell you this, Sue, I have been in this industry for over 40 years. We have had so many bestsellers that I have lost count. We have made a lot of money. This loss is sweeter, than all of that combined."

All synthetics are man-made

Milan, Italy, Fashion Store

Shima Chika

Shima Chika is a 29-year-old student, currently on holidays in Milan, Italy. She explores the narrow lanes taking snaps of the picturesque sights. The pull of the fashion houses acts like a magnet on the young woman. Inside the store, a rich array of designer creations, mannequins dressed in richly embroidered fabrics. Exotic materials, asymmetric skirts, dresses printed with brightly coloured motives, flowers and patterns of abstract art. Some collections restrained other labels as "sexisimo" as Milan has always been.

Signora Bettucini's hands feel the fabric of several dresses, as she flicks through the stand. The young male sales assistant brings another garment to present to the middle-aged woman.
"Signora Bettucini, this is a very similar design, but made of synthetic fibre. If Madam would like to try this on, please, it's only half the price of the other one."
"What do you mean 'synthetic'?"
"It is man-made. It's manufactured."
"And how do you know this?"
"All synthetics are man-made, Madam."

Isabella Bettucini is a full-bodied woman, proud and almost imposing. She is dressed in grey, converses very vocally, in an expressive, gesticulating manner. Her arms have a long reach and it is not advisable to stand too close to her. She lets out a short laugh.
"Man-made?"
"Man-made," she calls into the store, "did you hear that? 'Manufactured' he says."
"Who made the man? Tell me this, bambino, who made the man?"

Isabella Betuccini

The raised voice of Mrs. Bettucini ensures the clientele becomes aware of the conversation. Her raised chin emphasising her words, which does leave the sales assistant somewhat intimidated.

She slaps her belly, “This, look here when I’m talking to you, this… made the man, you see this, bambino, this belly made the man. Your mother made the man, she made the man,” as she points to passersby, “… and so did she.”

Shima Chika withdraws towards the rear of the store and aims her camera unnoticed at the couple, taking several snaps.

“And she made the man, and so did that one, little bambino. All you can do is keep filling this belly, and … you can make synthetics, man-made fibres. We made the man, bambino. We wiped your bums, bambino. We brought you into this world. I made eight. How many did you bring into this world? Tell me, how many did you birth out of your belly? How many did you feed with your breasts?

“But, Signora …”

“Do you think I want to be seen with synthetic manufactured rags in the fashion capital of Italy? And don’t call me Signora.”

“In this here belly is bambino number nine growing, and then this no-good bastardo left me for a young, hot Bella from Palermo, a giovane, this, number 9, at my age, Mama Mia. It’s all synthetic, isn’t it?”

“Madam Bettucini, please calm down.”

“How can I? You’re taking over the world. What you pull out of the ground is manganese, what you eat is mango, the fish live in a mangrove, oh my, Manchuria, they built a place named Manhattan. You are giving me mania and you are even in that word. If I need pills to cure me, your name is in the manic depression pills as well. Man is everywhere.”

“If I get my nails done, it is called a manicure. Men’s manifestation is all over the place. Man-made manipulators you are. Oh my God, you are even in mankind, and in humanity. Who let you in? The belles in Milan are mannequins. You are in manners. Can you believe this, a man in manners? You are in my house, my mansion, even if it is just an old shack, and when the manta bites your head off, you are in her. If I wash the dishes, you're in my hands, in manual."

"You are in manure and for all I'm concerned about you can stay and rot in there. You are in so many, many, many things, even in many. There is hardly a word left without you in it. Your men-made world is all you care about. You pass your power through the generations using manuscripts."

"Just look at this," she pulls the newspaper from the desk, "Ten men gang-raped a young girl and then killed her. The judge in his wisdom gives them a combined punishment of 80 years. What is this divided by 10? That is eight years each for killing the poor Bella. He calls it manslaughter. Do you want to know how I read this, man's laughter? The men are laughing, while they are killing us. It ought to be called 'men's slaughter', because that is what they did to the poor bambina. Men slaughtered her."

"We cannot even call ourselves women without you having your name in it. You control the world with your power, your language, your manipulation, your management and if..., and, are you listening to me, bambino, if... one woman comes close to being your match, what do you call her? Tell me? What do you call her?"
Isabella Bettucini holds the sales assistant by the tie and pulls it closer.

"Tell me, bambino, what do you men call such a woman? I want to hear you say it."
"Madam, please calm down, I'm only a salesman."
Isabella Bettucini breaks out in a loud laugh, "Did you hear that weasel. He even has a 'man' in his job description. 'Amen' to that, 'A men' to that," I say." she signs the cross, "Forgive me, Father."
Her face turns serious again, as anew she pulls his tie closer, "I want to hear it from your mouth, what you call such a woman?"
"I honestly don't know, Madam."
"Then I will tell you what you call such a woman, you call her a 'man-eater', don't you, bambino?"
"A man-eater, isn't that so?"

"And tell me this, Mr. Salesman, how many men has she eaten? Has anyone counted them? Are there any men missing? Are there any men missing anywhere at all? Are there anywhere on earth the bones of men that this man-eater is supposed to have devoured? Can you answer me this, Mr. Salesman?"

"Madam, perhaps I could get another few Euro off the price for you, for the dress, I could ask the manager."
Isabella Bettucini eased the pull on the tie and burst out in laughter, "It had to be a manager, because there are no 'womagers' anywhere on earth."

"Just once in my life I want to parade down the avenue, wearing a dress in the fashion that this city is famous for and all you offer me is man-made fibre."

"But Madam, you can have any dress you want."
"How can I, Mr. Salesman, how can I afford them? How can I even afford a single rag, when I have eight bambinos to feed?" she says, in the resigned tone of hopelessness.
"How can I possibly do that, when my no good husband left me with nothing, while he is Lord knows where, getting another Bella into trouble?"

"One day, just one day in my life, I want to feel like a queen, instead of a queen bee that spits out bambinos like a manufacturing plant. Ha, 'man'ufacturing."
"Can't you understand that? Is this too much to ask?"

"Look at me," she tugs on his tie, "I want you to look at me. Can't you see that I am all worn out? Do you see what eight kids can do to a woman's body? What do you think you would look like, if you had to bear them? Look at me, bambino. You would never think of running away with me, would you? The thought is repulsive; I can see it in your face."

"Don't panic, I took a holy vow. I could never run away with you, even if you paid me."
Through the shop's window, Isabella Bettucini notices a young attractive girl walking by. She drags the sales assistant towards the window, "Look at her, the one in the floral dress, what would you give to have her?"
Isabella Bettucini looks at the sales assistant. Her face is nearly touching his. She whispers in his ears, "What would you give to get into her knickers?"
She waits for an answer. The girl nears a fruit shop, as a small stack of oranges collapses, spilling oranges across the footpath. She helps to help pick them up. Both are watching her bending over.
"She is beautiful. She even offers you a peek preview. That should give you an idea of what she is worth. You can almost taste her, can't you? She stirs you, doesn't she? She moves you already."
"How much?" she whispers.

The sight had an impact on the sales assistant, searching for words, "Madam, this ... this is not appropriate."
"Hogwash, you are a man, it's in your blood."

"You wished she was closer. My eyes are not as good as they used to be, but you are much younger. Your eyes are sharper. You can see her sweet, soft-fleshed peach, can't you? She is a succulent cherry."

"What is she worth to you? There is not a man in the whole country that could withstand her charms, if she sets her mind to it. She does not even have to tease. Inside her is more juice, than in all the oranges of Italy."

"I can see the pearls forming on your forehead. Tonight, you will rewind your memory-tape of this moment and think of her, regardless of who is with you. Am I right? She is already driving you crazy, and all she does is picking up oranges. She looks very much like I did then. That was 100 years ago."

"Come on, how much?"
Isabella Bettucini whispers very slowly, her lips nearly touching the sales assistant's ear. Both have their eyes fixed on the girl's movements. "Come-on, tell me, no-one can hear us. How much does the man in the salesman offer?" as her hands briefly grab his crotch.
"Oh, she's got you stirred pretty good."
He could only respond with a short, vacant "Madam."
"She fascinates you, you are mesmerised by her. You are already undressing her, aren't you? You are unable to speak, as your mouth is full of saliva. I can almost hear your heart pounding. She can do all this, without even trying. She does not even know that we are watching her."

"Is she not a sweet ripe cherry, ready to burst with the sweetest juices? Is she not the finest gazelle you ever did see? Her legs go all the way to heaven. Her heaven is magic, her whole being is. There is not a wrinkle on this beautiful child. She is as fresh as can be."
"Would you not give the earth to have her? Would you not give her the moon? Would you not climb the highest mountain, pull down all the stars and give them to her? Would you not promise her everything under the sun, to have her for one night? And what would she give in return?"

"She would give you everything, her whole being. She would give you her whole life. She would give you her fire and passion, as hot as the core of the sun. She would love you, mother you, and be the mother of your blood. And even when you're long gone, she will still slave for them for all her days."

"She would give you the unconditional love of a dog, for a handful of crumbs. She would follow you to the end of the earth. But for what? So you can abuse her, beat her, waste her youth on you, waste her breaths, waste her womb, waste her worry over you, so that you can one day abandon her, feed her to the beasts. So you can kick her, slap her, humiliate her beyond belief."

"And what can you give her? You do not have any stars, you do not own the moon, you cannot even climb three steps, let alone the highest mountain. You do not have the earth to give, Bambino, isn't that so? You have nothing but hollow words. You promise everything but you have nothing worth giving."

"And you know what? she wouldn't even care about that. You could have her for nothing, this precious, beautiful girl. Untouched and pure, I am sure. She could be yours with the wink of an eye. She could be yours for any pittance at all."

"But do you think you could ever satisfy her. Do you think you are good enough to take her to heaven? But you don't know what heaven I am talking about, do you, Mr. Salesman. It's all synthetic for you. Your heaven is man-made, Mr. Salesman. Your loins do all the thinking, isn't that right, bambino? Relax... I'm not going to touch you there again."

"This is the most beautiful of God's creations, her skin as soft as feathers. Her lips can quench any man's thirst. Her voice is angelic, her hair as silk, her fire for life still burning, her joy as unspoiled as a child. Her dreams full of hope, her heart is as pure as the day she was born. Her eyes have the warmth of the sun itself, her soul so deep you will never fathom its depth. Her scent alone is enough to make you lose your head. How much for a drop of her nectar?"

"How long would it take you to spoil her? How long before her eyes become as a spring that feeds a river with her tears? How long before you infect her with your glorious manhood? Tell me this, Mr. Salesman, how long would she have?"

"How long before you bleed her dry and even her blood carries your name, men's-truation, 'men'struation. Men and man are in everything."

"Is it not she who will carry your shopping bags, despite you having three times her strength? She will ruin her hands with your dishes, doing your washing, hanging up your rags, day in and day out. She will slave her whole life for you and the ones you plant into her belly. She will settle your debt; she will even sell herself to do it, to keep you out of trouble."

"She will beg for you, she will sacrifice all she has, for you. She will sacrifice her honour, dignity and self-respect, all for you. You can slap her face, kick her like a dog and she will still be faithful and obedient, as any dog I know."

“All her needs are a pat on the back, sometimes some crumbs from your table, or less. But you have no comprehension of who she is or what she needs. You do not understand woman, women, any of us, do you, bambino? It just will not go into your heads, will it? You are incapable to comprehend us, isn’t that so, Mr. Man? You, who can vow before God the biggest lies and we believe each time you crawl and beg.”

“You will demand more, and even in that word is the man. The man is everywhere. He rules the earth. How long before you call her a whore, before you turn her to despair. How long before you break this fragile Bella?”

Isabella Bettucini’s anger turns to tears, “Romantico. Can you believe it, smack bang in the middle of romantico, ro...man...tico, synthetico. They are everywhere. He is everywhere. I will tell you why that is, bambino, it’s mandatory, man-da-tory.”

Isabella Bettucini’s’ resigned mood turns quickly, climbing in intensity. Her grasp on the sales assistant’s tie renews, pulling him along behind her, heading towards the store’s doors.
“Come-on, bambino, synthetico, I’ll show you where you belong,” she adjusts his tie, pulls harder, cutting off some of his air supply.
“This is your world, man in commander, command, and in synthetic fibre.”

Both are stepping onto the road. The strength in Isabella Bettucini is now overpowering, her voice strong, with purpose.
She pulls the tie hard, holds the sales assistant’s chin and jolts it upwards. Her fingers dig deep into his cheeks, “Look up there, bambino. You, men, explored the black holes of the universe,” as her arm points skyward. With a hard jerk, she pulls his face level, her arm points to the girl across the street, around to groups of women who gathered to watch this spectacle, “You, men, explored every conceivable hole and crevice in us.”

Her fingernails dig hard in the man’s cheeks. His skin cut, he bleeds. She drags the sales assistant two steps forward, holding his tie and with a firm hold on his cheeks, she rips hard downwards, stamps her feet, screaming, ”This, bambino, is this not of your making? Do you not call this a manhole? Why, bambino, why are you covering it up with a manhole-cover that no-one can lift? Why, bambino?"

She lets go of the sales assistant and swings her handbag hard to unleash a barrage of hits. "This is your home, bambino. Crawl into your manhole, drown in the sewers, there is your home."
The sales assistant adjusts his tie, gasps for air, "You are mad, Madam, with all respect," he utters.

"Of course I am mad. Synthetico drives everyone mad." The barrage of her hits does not lessen, she kicks and both her arms keep swinging her handbag to land heavy blows on the stumbling sales assistant, who is shielding his head. He is losing balance and falls.

Many of the passersby have formed into a semicircle around the couple. No one assists the struggling man.

"I am mad. With all respect," you say. Where was the respect when I needed it?" She spits on the sales assistant, yelling, "I have gone crazy, I have gone insane, I am mad, because none of you syntheticoes have ever given me any. How can we not go mad?"

The strength in her arms is leaving Isabella Bettucini. She kneels next to the man, with a few more tiring blows she gasps, "How can we not go mad, synthetico?"

She collapses over the sales assistant, her body shaken by a cry of relief.

Shima Chika captured many pictures during this visit to the store. She opens her notebook to mark down in pencil the words, 'synthetic man'. She walks up to Isabella Bettucini, embracing her. Other women help her up. The group slowly moves away, consoling Isabella Bettucini. The sales assistant is left behind, still crouching over the manhole cover.

How could I not have known?

Hong Kong, China, Near Tai Mo Shan

Ying Kim Xia

Ying Kim Xia, the author of the book, 'I want to die', is resting, catching her breaths near the twisting road that leads to the peak of Tai Mo Shan, the eastern mountain ridge that in part frame the city.

Hong Kong below is barely visible in the morning fog, which obscures all but the tallest buildings. Ying Kim Xia had run all night, away from the cameras, away from the lights, the reporter, to seek the stillness of Heung Shek Cemetery, at Tsuen Wan.

She continues her run, cross-country, upwards, forward. It is an exhausting ordeal, as she carries the guilt of possibly having caused the death of another human being with the writing of her words. A death in Chicago, so far away, a person she does not know at all, a burden so heavy, that she collapses from exhaustion upon entering Heung Shek Cemetery.

As the sun casts rays through the trees, Ying Kim Xia is kneeling on the pathways inside the cemetery. Her body crouched, shaken in irregular rhythm, her head bowed to the ground.

From a distance, 70-year-old Mrs. Qing Lian, a visitor to the cemetery, notices the young girl beating her fists into her head. She is rushing, hasting towards her. On nearing the girl in distress, Mrs. Qing Lian can hear her call of pain,
"我怎么不能知道
我怎么不能知道"
"How could I not have known?"

Mrs. Qing Lian tries to restrain Ying Kim Xia from inflicting damage to her hand, "Come, child, I know this pain is hard to bear."

She lifts the girl's head. The long ruffled hair obscures Kim's face. Mrs. Qing Lian's fingers part the hair to see the bloodshot eyes of young Ying Kim Xia.
"How could I not have known?" Kim asks the stranger.
She bursts aloud, "How could I not have known?"
Her face reveals the pain behind her question.
"We do not know the measure of our time," said the old woman. "All we know is that it is always running out. Calm down, my dear, who did you come to mourn?" She asks, "Your mum, your dad, your child?"

Young Kim's shoulders shrug, her head slowly turns from side to side. She cups her face, bursts out in tears.
"Oh dearest child, calm down, this pain will pass." she said. "Where is the place of the one you came to honour?"
Kim could not answer, as the weight of her guilt needed release.
"How could I not have known?" Kim asks again.
The old woman tries to comfort Kim, trying to reach for her hand. As Kim feels her touch she screams, "No, no."
"I am not worthy of your pity, I am not worthy of your comfort or your loving kindness. This hand," she lifts her right, "this hand is full of blood. Can you not see it dripping?"
"There is no blood I see," replies the old woman.
Tears smudge her face, "This hand is full of blood."
The old woman is unable to understand the meaning of Kim's words.

"What has this hand made you do?" she asks the girl.
"This hand has killed. This hand has murdered. This hand has taken ... a life," she cries as she tries to shake the hand, in an attempt to throw it away. I cannot get rid of it," she screams again, "it's stuck on me, I cannot let go of it."

She shakes her right hand, but the hand does not fly off. With her other hand, she picks up a rock and smashes it into her right hand in a violent frenzy to break it off with any means.

The old woman calls out to others, "Please help me, help this child."
Six visitors to the cemetery come forward to stop the girl from causing further injuries.

Kim holds up her right arm towards Mrs. Qing Lian and asks, "Can you see it now?"

I have blood on my hands and it will not come off

Chicago, USA, C.M.J. & Associates

Sally Cramer

C.M.J. & Associates is a legal practice, located in the inner city of Chicago. Sally Cramer's father established the firm, which is specialised in corporate law. Mills and Jacob are the other partners in the firm.

Sally Cramer's desk is packed with folders of legal cases. The firm is closed, but she is still sifting through documents when the call arrived.

"What have I done?" the words from the receiver.
"Who is this?" Sally responds.
"It's Kim," after a short pause, she continues, "What have I done?"
"Who are you? Do I know you?" Sally enquired.

"I am Kim, Ying Kim Xia."
"Oh sorry, Kim, I did not recognise you. How are you?"
"What have I done, Sally, tell me, what have I done?"
"I don't know what you have done, Kim. Where are you?"
"I am in Tai Mo Shan Bay Police station, Hong Kong."

"Why are you in there, Kim?" Sally asks, not at all aware of the stir the book had caused in the press during the last few hours.
"They want to question me, the police." Kim said.
"Why, Kim?"
"I have blood on my hands and it will not come off."
"Have you had an accident?" asked Sue.
"I have taken the life of another," Kim said, and she could not continue the conversation.
"Kim, Kim, talk to me. Kim, can you hear me, talk to me."
The connection was still there, but Kim was unable to speak.

"Kim, hear me, I am on my way," Sally heard a click in the line, which ended the call. She dials another number, "I need a ticket to Hong Kong for today?"
She notes a few words on a pad on her desk. She turns the lights off and locks the office.

Two minutes later the phone rings again, too late for Sally, as she is already on her way.

We have no names

Cannes, France, Near the Harbour

Ramona De Urquiza

Ramona De Urquiza is 18 years old. She is Spanish-born and has long dark hair. She sits, dressed in a short white skirt and a white blouse, being driven along the Boulevard Jean Hibert. Her thoughts go back to the script of the film in which she was cast as an actor, her first ever role. Ramona played a nun, a minor role, who nursed an injured soldier during a local uprising, set in another time.

Only this morning did she see the film in its entirety. She was glad not to have the lead role, which Maria Dolores Gomez filled as Mother Superior. A traumatising scene shows Maria fending off eight drunken soldiers who tried to harm her. She pulled a stake off the garden fence and swang it around, to defend herself. It was such a strong scene. There is much to learn, as an actor.

The white stretch-limousine drives slowly along the Boulevard Jean Hibert, which runs alongside the Mediterranean. The limo turns left, into Quai Saint Pierre. Cannes Harbour is located at the right side. The harbour is square, with a narrow, funnel-shaped exit towards the Mediterranean.

A forest of masts comes into view. Sailing vessels, luxurious cruisers, yachts, sports cars, limousines, this place is alive with colour, faces and reeks of luxury and money.

Inside the limousine are three middle-aged men, all over 48, and 4 women, who are all under 24 years old.

Nicole Dubois

Next to Ramona is Nicole Dubois, a young French woman, 23, whom she met 20 minutes ago. Beside Nicole is Gérard, 48, a calm and quiet person. The limousine turns right into La Pantiero.
"Which one is it?" asks Monique, 24.
"Just a few more minutes," replied Antoine, who is dressed in a casual summer suit, wearing white sneakers. He is 50 years old.
"Which one, which one?" asks Monique, as she bounces on Antoine's lap impatiently. Antoine just laughed.
Long gone are the times when the value of the cruisers in the harbour estimated in millions of dollars. Tens and hundreds of millions are not enough these days.
Ramona sat silent most of the way. She asks the man who sits opposite her, "Are you a director?"
Julien smiles, "No, I am not."

"What is your name?" Ramona enquires, trying to keep eye contact, which is difficult, as Penelope, who has her arms wrapped around him demands his constant attention.
Penelope answers the question, "He's Mr. Fix it."
"That is a very unusual name," Ramona replies.
"I am Ramona De Urquiza."
"Nice to meet you," replies Julien.
"Who is the director? I have been asked to audition."
"Darling, I don't know which director you're referring to, there are so many," says Julien.

"Please, Mr Fix it, do not call me 'darling', as I'm not. You may call me Ramona, Ms. De Urquiza, Ramona De Urquiza or Ms Ramona De Urquiza, that gives you four choices and all of them are I. In

addition to these, you may use any prefix you wish, Senorita, Signorina, Mademoiselle, whichever you prefer."
Julien laughs and whispers to Antoine who is sitting on the outer, "Who is this chick?"

Julien - Mr Fix-it

Antoine joins the laughter, "She's from Toni's lot, the Baron's special."
Julien laughs, "I can imagine. He'll love her."
"Oh lucky you," laughs Monique, "you're going to get a sip from the Baron's golden goblet," as she is eying off Ramona from top to toe.

"He doesn't love me anymore, the wicked devil," says Nicole.
"Of course he does," Antoine replies, addressing Ramona he continued, "Look honey... that will be difficult. Your name is just so complicated, he couldn't even remember two syllables," as he continues laughing, leaning his head towards Julien.
"That goes for you too, Mr.? How do you wish to be addressed?" Ramona asks Antoine.
Nicole interjected, "This is Mr. Happening. Anything you want, he can make it happen. But he's not working for us, he works for them."
"Shut up," quips Antoine and squeezes Nicole's arm short and hard.
"Pardon Monsieur," Nicole replies.
"Sugar, call me what you will, I'm not that fussy." Antoine answers Ramona.

"With all respect, Sir, I am," answers Ramona, "I have been told to drive with you for an audition."
With the force of a shook-up bottle of warm effervescent liquid, everyone bursts into an explosive laughter, all, except Ramona, although Gérard was able to subdue his participation somewhat.

"How cute," Nicole says, "she is as green as a lettuce."
Penelope laughs out, "The Baron's dish, no doubt."

"Will you cut it out," said Antoine, "I will introduce you to the director when we get there, darling," he says to Ramona, trying to contain his amusement, "He will know about the audition."
"My name is Ramona," she answers short, "but thank you."
Nicole giggles, biting his ear slightly. Penelope cupped her mouth, an aversive action, so as not to laugh aloud.

Monique

The largest of the vessels is moored near Jetée Albert Eduard. The driver does not need directions, he drove this stretch so many times.
"Julien, which one of those is yours?"
"Gérard has the biggest, don't you, darling?" said Penelope teasingly.
"How do you know?" Gérard replies, "Have you seen them all?"
"Not all, but most," Penelope replies with a grin.

The world of glitz, showbiz and glamour is new to Ramona. It all seems and is so far from home.
The limousine stops in the reserved parking spot. The place is abuzz with people greeting another; cars come and go. Beautiful women, in all directions, attractive men as well and there were those, who would never enter any contests. A carnival atmosphere wherever the eye did see. This is just a small taste in the world of big screen illusions, razzmatazz and beauty queens.

"Hello Jerry, Tyrone, how are you, Bjorn, Frederic, Ricardo, Giuseppe, so good to see you," Ramona heard all the names under the sun, all greeting another, to be heard, to be seen.
Why do the women have no names? She wondered. Darling, Sugar, Honey, Sweet, Baby, Liebling, Schatzi, Chéri, so many women, yet not one of them has a name. A woman's name is no more complicated than a man's.
"Please, get aboard, we are expected," encourages Antoine, "I'll catch up with you, I'll find you."

Somewhat hesitant Ramona steps aboard the ship, which is wider than the length of the stretch limousines parked all along the quay. All ships were moored at the stern, so it was not possible to get an idea of the length of the vessel.

“Welcome aboard, Madam,” said a man dressed in a white suit, an officer of the ship, it appears. “Please, feel at home.”
Nicole hugs the man as greeting and follows Ramona aboard.
“C’mon, I’ll show you around,” she says to Ramona, grabs her hand and leads her to the interior of the vessel.
“It’ll be a great party, Ramona, one you’ll never forget, I guarantee you,” she said.
“Relax, let your hair down and be free.”
Ramona’s smile is forced. Her eyes take in, this place, decorated with flowers, stacks of glasses, tables set, glitter and riches wherever she looks. All is overpowering to the eyes.

"Relax," Nicole calls out to her as she unbuttons her blouse. She rarely wore a bra.
"Let me help you." Ramona crosses her chest with both hands and shakes her head, protecting her buttons. "As you wish, Ramona," Nicole laughs, "C'mon, I’ll show you."
She runs forwards, dragging Ramona behind her. "Food is there; the drinks are over there; special goodies are over here; rest rooms are here; and also on the port side. There is another set forwards." She points at a door and says, "This door, don’t go there; it’s only for crew, engine, or something in there. No one is allowed."

They both take the steps downward, “And here, Ramona, are the ‘Audition Rooms’,” she giggles. ”One, two, three, four, five, all along until the end over there, and of course on the other side as well. I don’t know how many. Let’s get your face done, c’mon.”

Even the restroom is huge in size. The lights, selection of colours,

the ornaments, sculptures, flowers, all creating a mood and magic which is hard to put into words.
"Your lips need to be much darker; you need to complement your skin tones; let me do it." Nicole opens the drawers to compare various darker tones with Ramona's slightly olive skin colour. "Let's try this, which should be pretty close."
Ramona gets a whole makeover from Nicole.

"All we need to do now is your hair, and you're ready. I know what the baron likes."
"Who is this baron?" Ramona asks. "Who is the Baron?" Nicole asks, smiling. Why don't you wait until you meet him? He is very particular, and that's why I don't want to spoil it."

"Relax, Ramona, this is a party. It is a bit like Christmas; you know, the year is over, the work is all out of the way, let down your hair, and enjoy. Here, it is just a different season. We live only once. Forget about work, rehearsals, lines, scripts, and stuff like that. This is fun."
"Are you an actress?" Ramona questioned.
Nicole laughs, saying, "Of sorts, yes, yes I am. If you can't relax, then look at it like acting; your role is to be happy. Do you know what I'm saying? Whatever happens, just play along and improvise without a script. It won't be long, and you'll enjoy it."
"Have you been to many of these 'parties', Nicole?"
"Of course, I've lost count. I know everyone, not the girls; they change so often, I know all the guys."
"Which movies did you play in?" asks Ramona.
She throws her eyes into the air, "Can you believe this?"
"Here you are in one of the most luxurious vessels in the whole of France, Italy and Monte Carlo combined, being invited by no less than the Baron, and all you can think about is work, work and more work."

"What you need is a drink. You have stage fright. That is all it is. I know how to fix this. Back in a second. Don't go away. Stay put."

Nicole closes the door behind her. Ramona now becomes aware of the music, which has been playing all along. She looks around the room and opens drawers that reveal every conceivable type of make-up under the sun. This room could stock up a whole store. Moments later, Nicole returns holding two glasses of exotic-looking drinks. "Take a sip of this," she offers, "or do try mine, whichever you like. You know, Ramona, out there are hundreds, if not thousands, of girls who would give their right arm to be in your place. And what I've just heard above is that you have been handpicked by the baron."

"How does he know me? Who is he?" asks Ramona.
"He might have seen you in your film; maybe someone showed him your picture; or maybe he saw you walking down the street. How would I know? What matters is that you are here at his invitation. That means no one else can... hmm... ah... shall we say... 'audition' you. You are very lucky that he picked you. You must have something special that he likes. I don't need to guess what that is. Here, take a sip."

Ramona hesitates. She watches the glasses. "Why are they moving?"
"What is moving?" replies Nicole.
"The drinks are moving."
"It's just the swell. We are at sea; that is what ships do. They float, you know, on water. We're probably just out of the harbour. Take a sip. Take your pick. You decide," says Nicole, "Have a look at this; do you see this spout?"
"Yes."
"It is made of solid gold, would you believe?"
"No, is it really?"
"Yes, solid gold. All the fittings are solid gold, each of them. Have you looked at them closely?" Nicole asks. "Look here; all are gems; each is a jewel. Look at the hot water, all set in rubies. They are all real, Ramona. There is nowhere on earth where you can buy fittings like these. They are all custom-made for this vessel, each with the a unique design. Have you ever seen a restroom with diamond chandeliers?"
"No, I have not," answered Ramona.
"Yes you have, Ramona, just look around you. These are real diamonds. You'll be surprised what the Baron will give you," Nicole

flicks one of the diamonds and teasingly grins at Ramona, "but I can't be sure. All I know is, if you play your cards right, you won't have to worry about money for a while, but that is not for me to say. C'mon, drink up and let's party."

Ramona refuses to drink.

"You can't keep the Baron waiting. It's fine for a little bit, it might do him some good, but we can't hide in here all night. He will be fuming. Which one is yours, your choice... the drinks?"
Nicole holds both glasses in front of Ramona.
Ramona shakes her head.
Nicole lifts a glass to her lips and drinks it, "Ah..., that's lovely."
"You're an actress, right? You want to be the best actress in the whole Mediterranean, right?" she looks at Ramona.
"Yes." Ramona nods.
"Then show me what you can do. OK. Camera, lights, action, drink," Nicole lifts her hand to her mouth to indicate the movement.

Ramona reaches for her glass; her head turns to look at Nicole, who in turn nods, pretends to hold a camera, and encourages her to lift the glass. Ramona's hand slightly shakes as she lifts the rim of the glass close to her lips. She looks again at Nicole. Nicole holds her hand as if she were holding the glass herself; her lips protrude towards an imaginary rim. She nods again and continues to play the camera operator.

Ramona's glass touches her lips as she lifts it higher. The liquid now touches her lips. Nicole forms her mouth into a circle between her fingers, indicating that she should open up. Ramona takes all the liquid in and swallows it. "And that's a wrap; cameras cut," Nicole calls out. "Bravo. That was perfect." She claps her hands. She now play-acts a whole movie set in the restroom: "Wardrobe, yes director, get her fixed for the next scene, yes director." She kneels in front of Ramona, "Hello, I'm from wardrobe, I need to fix you for

the next scene, allow me." She moves Ramona's hands to her sides and reaches for her upper blouse button. Ramona looks down. The upper button is undone. Nicole opens the next. Ramona's hands now close in to protect the lower buttons.
"Relax, Ramona, I'm not into girls, I'm wardrobe, remember, I fix you for the next scene." She tries to move Ramona's hands away, but they hold firm, she shakes her head.
"No," says Ramona, "no."
"Have you never taken it off?" asks Nicole.
Ramona shakes her head in denial.
"Never? Never ever?" Nicole asks again.
Ramona shakes her head again.

"But you are an actress, and look at me, so am I. We all take it off. It is the done thing. We all do it. Look at mine, they are just boobs, they are breasts, we all have them. Yours are the same as mine. Upstairs, all the girls are topless and some are naked already. Before the night is through the girls will all be naked. You will look ridiculous wearing a top. I want to spare you this."

"I am sorry, Nicole, I cannot do it. Not even my mother has seen me. No one has ever seen me like this, you know, without any."
"But, sweetie, there is nothing to it. Look, we are all the same," as Nicole rips off her own skirt, takes off her knickers, turns around to reveal her whole nakedness to Ramona. "You look like this too, don't you?"

"Why do we women have no names?" replies Ramona.
"Oh my God, you really are an unpicked cherry. I bet you are still a virgin," answers Nicole.
"Of course I am. How can I not be?"
"You are not kidding, are you?" asks Nicole.
"Of course I am not." Ramona says.

“I wish I was,” says Nicole, “a virgin. You are right... we do not have a name. I never noticed it before,” says Nicole. “You are Signorina Ramona De Urquiza, or is it Senhorita?”
Ramona laughs, “It’s neither. I am Spanish. I am a Senorita, or Mona.”
“Of course, pardon, at least you know who you are. Do you want to know my name?” asks Nicole.
“Sí,” Ramona replies, nodding her head.

“Senorita Ramona De Urquiza, my name is... Mademoiselle Whore, so pleased to meet you,” answers Nicole as she lets out a short laugh of contempt mixed with the up-well of tears; she turns her face towards the mirror to spit at her own reflection.
Nicole shushes Ramona by holding her index finger over her mouth. She takes a chewing gum from her handbag and chews, humming a tune. A moment later, she reaches up high, to stick the chewing gum onto a small protrusion at the upper edge of the mirror.
“Microphone,” she says, “they can’t hear us now.”

“The Baron sure knows how to pick them,” she continues. “Oh my God, whatever you do, do not, can you hear me, Ramona, whatever happens, do not drink from the golden goblet. Don’t even touch it with your lips.”
Through the mirror, the two women looked like different worlds, the innocence and purity next to the world of sin, remorse and pain.

“I will stay a virgin until one day I will get married,” replied Ramona. “I feel a bit strange, what was in this drink? What have you given me, what did you put in it?” She looks at Nicole with the question in her eyes.
“Relax, Ramona, it was just tequila. You never had tequila, did you? You never had anything.” She pulls a chair close to Ramona. Both women face each other. She lifts Ramona’s chin, “Let me look into your eyes.”
Nicole’s eyes study Ramona’s, flicking from one to the other, “You come from a small village, somewhere in never-land, you go to church every Sunday, and pray every night, you have a beautiful mother, probably a big round Mama, your Daddy works hard to feed you all. You have four more sisters and two brothers.”

"Yes, but how do you know so much about me," asks Ramona, "but I do not come from never-land."
"I could see me in your eyes, as I was a million years ago," replies Nicole, "but I'm just 23. What are you?"
"I'm 18, Nicole."

"Bastard, Baron. Oh, I hate all this gold and glitter, the bloody gems and jewels. I hate them," Nicole cries out. "Don't you know where we are? Don't you know what this is? You have no idea, do you?" Nicole's body shakes from crying. She spreads her legs briefly, "They all want to get in here, that's all they want. They build skyscrapers to brag about the size of their dicks, they pave the roads with anything you want, just to have you. They have no brains, they have no hearts, they are just walking dicks. Now do not ask me what a dick is, for crying out loud. You must know that much at least."

She lifts her arms up in the air, "This whole ship is full of brainless dicks, do you understand. You are safe from all of them, 'cause you're the Baron's special. No one can touch you and no one will, but you are not safe from him."
Ramona listens and nods.

"Oh dear, we are out at sea, this is just a ship, there is nowhere to hide. I tried and I couldn't find a spot, but try I did."
Voices are outside the restroom. Nicole jumps up to lock the door.

"Ramona, we can't stay here much longer, I want you to listen to me, there is one chance and one chance only, you hear?" Nicole is recovering her strength, "You are an actress, OK. You will have to play the role of your life. When we go out of this door, you must not let anything affect you. Whatever you see is like part of a crazy movie. You must kill all your emotions and see everyone as an actor."
"Whatever you see, remember, they are acting out a fantasy. Only the Baron will approach you. All the others will leave you alone. He

is not a brute, he is not violent, he's cultured and he made me sick," Nicole calls out.

"When he leads you to his cabin, and there are no cabins on this ship, they are like lavish hotel rooms, each of them. The rooms are breathtaking, nothing like you've ever seen in your life. It is a movie set, remember this. Don't let any of it affect you. This is the role of your life. You are the best actress in the world. This role you will play to perfection. The last roll of film is in the camera. We are on a ship. This is the last scene to complete the movie. There is no more film left. If you stuff this up, the film cannot be completed, it will not be finished on time. Millions of dollars will be lost. Do you understand this? You must be perfect, not a single slip-up. No one can afford you slipping this up."
Ramona nods and listens attentively.

"The script writer became seasick and could not complete the last scene. I am the director and I am asking you to improvise. The whole film rests on your performance. You must switch the drinks without him noticing it, and here... is the tricky part: In the golden goblet, the stuff is pink, I can still remember it... and it was the last I could remember. The Baron drinks Bourbon, just in case you don't know what that is, it stinks and is yellow."

"You must find a way to pour from the golden goblet into his drink and make him drink first. You must make sure that he does not see the difference in colour, even if you have to take your top off to do it."

"Perhaps you can darken the room, but it will be difficult, as he likes to see everything. He wants your cherry and as long as it is yours, he is in the palm of your hands. You can play him. He will do anything you ask of him, because all he wants is you. Use all your charms, use all you can, do all you have to do, but make him drink first. Keep his eyes from looking at the glass. This is your script. You can do everything wrong, nothing really matters, as long as you get him to drink."

"And another thing, you have probably never seen a naked man before," says Nicole, as Ramona shakes her head. "Do not freak out, and even if you do, it doesn't matter, he needs to drink first, that is all you need to worry about."
A discreet knock at the door brings back the reality of their situation. Nicole composes herself, puts her knickers on, brushes a streak of hair from Ramona's face, "Are you ready?" she asks, reluctantly Ramona nods, "Camera, lights, action, let's go, you're on, act the part."

Nicole unlocks the door, steps through greeted by two men.
"Baby, you are soooo beautiful. Why have you been hiding? I missed you, oh, who is this?" he says as he notices Ramona leave the restroom.
Nicole, with a laugh says, "Hands off, you horny devil, she's not for you."
Nicole tries to hold Ramona's hand, but the man embraces Nicole, "I want one of your sweet kisses, baby," whispering in her ear, "and I want so much more."
Nicole laughs it off, "I bet you do, you wait your turn."
"Come on, I am so thirsty," says the other man to Nicole, "give me some sugar, honey," Nicole twists from his advances, "I can't, I promised the Baron."
"Ha, he's done you. He's not going to do you again, you must be dreaming," he laughs, "but I love you, give me your sweets."
"Hey, why isn't she dressed," he points at Ramona.
"But she is," Nicole replied.
"But not for a party," he laughs at her.

A chance to buy a tear

Spain, a village near Madrid

It was some months later when Nicole met Ramona again in a small village near Madrid. The events in Cannes triggered a friendship between both that grew over time.

The two women ran towards each other to exchange a joyous embrace.
"Tell me of everything that happened," says Nicole.
"You first," responds Ramona.
The women exchanged stories, memorable moments and events in their lives.
"Are you still an actress?" enquired Nicole.
"Oh yes, but not the big screen. I am quite content with small screenplays, the wooden floor as a stage," said Ramona, "You have taught me a lot in Cannes, my dear Nicole. You are a good director."
Nicole laughs out, "I do not know how you managed to get him to drink first, the Baron, but wasn't he just so helpless?"

Ramona elaborates from her recollection, "And when you came in you made sure he would not wake up. I could not believe how you poured the golden goblet's contents down his throat, then closed his nose and mouth, so he had to swallow it all. And he looked white as death itself, after you done his make-up."
Nicole adding, "Captain, Captain, head for Cannes, the Baron is dying, we need a hospital."
"I knew you were a fine actress and you pulled it off."
Ramona, "I can never thank you enough for what you did that day."

Late in the afternoon both drive to the village centre. They see the sights and enjoy the day together. In the evening they find themselves in one of the many restaurants that dot the busy plaza at the village centre.

Leticia Pastora Chavira

Two flamenco dancers tap to the music, the sounds of high heels and guitars fill the air. Applause thanks the musicians and dancers. A proud woman approaches the stage to take the microphone.

"Nicole, this is Leticia Pastora Chavira. She is a very special singer. We are fortunate that she is here tonight." Everyone suddenly becomes quiet. The only sounds are the voice of Leticia Pastora Chavira and two guitars as she starts her ballad. One could hear a penny drop such is the silence from all tables. Nicole leans towards Ramona whispering, "Can you translate? What is she singing about?"

Ramona explains, "This is a very old song, based on a true story that happened very long ago. There is no one who can sing this ballad, except Señora Chavira."
"Listen..."

"This ballad is not about politics, it's about a mother's pain," Ramona explains. "She sings to her son, Miguel. He did something wrong long ago. The hombres con los armas, the men with guns came to arrest him, but he had run away, hiding in the hills. They could not find him. The hombres returned to the home and shot his two brothers in anger. They held the mother, she had to look at them die. She calls out to Miguel, but he does not hear her. The men set fire to the house and the mother screamed in pain. Six hombres held her and made her watch the flames. Inside the house, the two young bambinas were burned alive."

"Miguel, Miguel, can't you hear your sisters' screaming for your help? Miguel, Miguel, I hope you rot in hell."
"Shhhh..."

"And then she realises that she had cursed the only son she's left with, it drove her mad with pain and remorse. She wanted to unspeak the words, but it was too late."
Four men are nearing the stage, two per side, and all are dressed in black.
"Miguel, Miguel, forgive a mother's curse in pain."

Leticia Pastora Chavira collapses from the pain in the ballad. The four men catch her falling and she is laying on the small stage, a pillow under her head. The music continues, one of the guitarists rotates the microphone and continues the song.

"He is now Miguel, returning from the hills. Tengo dos hermanos y dos hermanas. It means I have two brothers and two sisters. But now, Graciano está muerto, Graciano was his brother, he is now dead. Zacarias está muerto, his other brother was Zacharias. He learns that he is also dead. Dominga está muerta, Chiquita está muerta. These are the names of the little sisters. Chiquita means, little one."

"When he realises how they had died he is filled with rage and vows to avenge their deaths."
"Listen..."
"His mother tries to hold him back, but she does not have the strength. His rage takes the lives of twenty hombres. It is then that his mother renews her curse, for he has spread the pain to others."
People step forward to kneel next to Leticia Pastora Chavira. Some dry their tears on her long dress, all leave money around her. Within a few short moments Señora Chavira is almost covered in notes.

Nicole, visibly impressed by the generous contribution, "Wow, one hell of mountain of money for a four minute performance, I call that acting."
Ramona looks at Nicole, "You don't understand. That is not for the ballad. That is our chance to share her pain, to buy a tear, to share the load."

Ramona strokes Nicole's cheek, "My dear Nicole, you have a good heart. You have been through a lot, you have seen more than I have. Sometimes all that can blind you. Señora Leticia Pastora Chavira is no actress. None of this is hers."

Señora Chavira is now sitting up on the small stage, gathering the money in her apron. Ramona pulls out her purse saying, "C'mon, I will introduce you," and walks towards Leticia.

"Señora Chavira, thank you so much for sharing your pain with us," and she hands her three notes from her purse.
"Thank you, Ramona, but as you well know it is not all my pain."
"Buonas noches," she extends her hands to Nicole and clasps both of Nicole's hands.

"This is Nicole, a dear friend of mine. She has a good heart, Señora Chavira. She is here for a week and I wonder... could we drop in tomorrow, for a surprise visit, would it be alright."
"No you can't, not for a surprise visit if I know already about it, it is not going to be a surprise, is it?"
She laughs, "You know I have no doors. Of course, you are always welcome. Love to see you both and catch up with you."

We can feel shamed to the core of our conscience

Spain, country side

Next day Ramona drives, Nicole sitting next to her, "Her place is over there, the one in the mountains that is Señora Chavira's."
"I'm not surprised," quips Nicole as she judges the size of the buildings.
"It is too small," responds Ramona.
Nicole laughs out, "It would be big enough for half the village, I'd say, judging from here."

A long driveway leads towards the largest of the buildings. Several children play. "How many has she got?" asks Nicole.

"What do you mean, Nicole, many what?"
"Kids, I've counted six already."

Ramona laughs, "I don't know, perhaps a hundred, maybe more. You'll see." She beeps the horn to announce their arrival.
"Hello, Señora Chavira, oh what a lovely day," Ramona calls out.
"It's lovely now. They have all been fed," she replies, "Hello, to both of you..., Nicole, wasn't it?"
"Yes, Señora Chavira."
"How many mouths do you have to feed now?" Ramona asks.
"I think ninety-eight and this little princess."

She holds a young infant in her arms. "Where are all their parents?" asks Nicole. "Madre, padre? Up there or somewhere out there. We do not know. But they all have one madre that shines on them and keeps them warm," Señora Chavira points to the sun.

Nicole hastens to return to the car. She was back in a flash, "Señora Chavira, please accept this for a tear and forgive me for thinking of you badly." Nicole hands her 200 Euro.
"But child, this is so much, Nicole. This is so very generous of you. We can do much with it. Thank you and bless you," she laughs. "I see, you must have thought I made a lot of money yesterday, that it was all an act. I can understand that. The world has changed so much and sometimes we can no longer see the truth. We become blinded by manipulation. Where is the truth, what is the truth?"
Nicole and Ramona listen to Señora Chavira's words.
"The truth I know is this: These children have no mother or father. Bullets took many, famine took some and wars took most fuelled by

hatred in hearts. Some were abandoned, some were abused, and one look into their eyes… and we can feel shamed to the core of our conscience."
Nicole shook her head, the words affecting her.

"In this world, there is an abundance of money, there are riches more than we need, there is never a shortage for bullets, no restraint to wage war, they are so eager to win, to conquer, to control the world. The world cannot be controlled. It will find its own destiny. That is enough. I allow myself to have a good whinge and whine one minute per day," she laughs, "I must have used up a whole week just then. Please, come with me. I'll show you around."
"See all their beautiful pictures. They all told their stories in drawings, and over time we can see how they change. There are many local women here to help us. Most are elderly. In some countries, they are put away, in old aged-care places. They are all mothers with much to offer. These kids grow up rich, nurtured by the wisdom of old women. Here they can contribute, feel good about themselves and the kids have a ball. Some do handiwork and we sell some products; others read stories, grow produce, teach the kids how to garden, mend things, you know, all valuable lessons for life."

"It's like a little township really. They are all our children and we all are their mothers. Sometimes we are short of money and often too proud to beg, but if need be, we will do that too. But so many things don't cost any money. All the clothes come from locals, so does the furniture. Most of the buildings are from recycled materials. Nothing goes to waste."

"The kids that grew up here go into the world. Many send us part of their pay to support all this, and we are grateful for their kind thankfulness, but we need to stop the endless flow of needy children. We need to stop the causes."

"We are not an orphanage, not officially. Only the locals know about this place. It grew out of the shame we felt when looking into their eyes. This land belongs to a local, and we hope he lives a long life, for we don't know where to go if it is ever sold. We leave tomorrow's worries until tomorrow comes." Leticia cups her mouth to call out to a woman running up a hill in the distance, chasing a boy.

"Perpetua, Perpetua!"

The woman in the distance stops running and waves. Leticia waves back, "You're getting too old for this."
The woman's hand shrugs her off, as if to say, 'Go away' and she continues to chase the boy uphill.
Leticia laughs. "Do you know how old she is?"
"Nicole and Ramona shake their heads."
"She is 92. Her name is Perpetua. She is everlasting."

"We met when she was 75 and she was as good as dead then, at least that's what she believed. Her two sons had swindled her out of all her money and put her in an asylum of sorts. She withered like a flower without rain, ready to die, waiting to die. Now she is chasing kids uphill. Oh, she will not catch him, but he will give her a good workout every afternoon. In the cities you pay for a gym, here it is all free. They won't give her a chance to die, the little rascals."

"But tell me," Ramona, Nicole "you see more of the world than I do, is it true, that there are now women soldiers? Has the world changed that much?"
Ramona nods, "Sí."
"Soldier women with guns, who are able to shoot a bullet into another mother's son? Please, tell me a lie if you have to, but don't tell me any woman can do that."
Ramona's hand covers her mouth.
"Only men can make them do this," says Señora Chavira.
Nicole's eyes narrow, as she slowly nods, deep in thought she whispers, "They can make us do anything."

Susie meets Ye Myo

Basel, Switzerland, University

Ye Myo Tun

It is the beginning of a new term and Ye Myo Tun's first day at the university. A place of learning divided into 7 faculties, sought after by many international students. Centrally located in Western Europe, Basel is as the hub of a wheel, just a stone's throw from France, Luxembourg, Germany, Czech Republic, Austria and Italy. Finding one's way will take some getting used to, especially for the newcomers in the early days. Where to go, running late, taking the wrong direction lead to chance encounters with new faces. In the search to find her way, Ye Myo collides with one of the other students, spilling much of her bag's content on the ground.

"Oh I'm so sorry about this, please let me help you, it's the least I can do. You must be new here?" says Susie, who is on her way to the library. "By the way, I'm Susie, pleased to meet you. And you are...?"

"I am new. Is it that obvious? It is such a big place and I don't know where I ought to be. I am Ye Myo Tun."

"Don't tell me, let me guess," says Susie, "You are from Cambodia, right?"

Ye Myo studies Susie, she seems Chinese but also in part Caucasian.

"No"

"Don't tell me, you're from Thailand?" responds Susie.

"Cold, go west," Ye Myo Tun suggests.

Susie is closing her eyes, trying to view her inner map of the world, "I got it..., Laos."

"You're going north instead."

"I give up." Susie laughs.

"Myanmar," Ye Myo Tun replies.

Susie Cross

"Ah," says Susie, "at least I was close. What are you looking for, where do you need to be?"
Ye Myo Tun pulls a note from her pocket and hands it to Susie.
"I know where that is, I'll go with you, I'll show you."
Together the two young women walk, getting to know one another along the way.
"We're almost there," Susie explains, "OK, down there, take the next corridor to the right, then the second door on your left, that's where you need to go."
"Thank you so much, it helps to have a friend." replies Ye Myo Tun and says 'good-bye' to Susie.
"No, wait," Susie calls out, "here, please take my card. I know what it is like being in a foreign and strange place. What are your plans for tonight?"
"Perhaps studying, I have no plans as yet."
"Come to this address, 'round about 7pm. I have some people over and you can meet new faces, if you like."
"I'd love that, thank you," and Ye Myo Tun heads off down the corridor.

What would we need to salvage from here?

Basel, Switzerland, Susie's place

It was 7.20 pm, when Ye Myo Tun finally found Susie's place. Susie, 18 years old, was born in Hong Kong and speaks fluent Cantonese, Mandarin, fluent English, and enough Spanish to get out of trouble. Her father, Aaron, and Susie left well before Hong Kong's handover to China. Eventually, Europe became their home.
"Hey, great you could make it. Come in, meet the group," says Susie, holding Ye Myo Tun's hand to lead her inside.

Nadira

Susie's place has become a hangout and regular meeting place for a group of women. They share various interests and are of different backgrounds, but all share in the warm friendships for another. Lively discussions on any subject will always find an echo, as the hunger and search for knowledge is high on everyone's list of to do's. It grew over several semesters to be an established base of the group. Susie's father was born in England. His adventurous spirit drove him to many overseas assignments. The property in Basel is owned by a business associate of Aaron. The house is characterised by large spacious rooms and cosy living quarters. It also features a large property with secluded garden and privacy from all sides.

Susie has a close and deep bond with her father, who is also her closest friend. There is unconditional trust between the two. On several occasions he arrived unannounced and he has met many of Susie's friends.

“Let's introduce you to everyone. Starting from here, Ye Myo Tun, this is Nadira, she is from Pakistan, next we have Adzumi, Nagoya, Japan, this is Kysa from Sweden, Aislinn is from Ireland and over there, at the left is Gasha, she's from Ukraine. Next to her is Ramona, Spain and last but not least is Karla from Germany.”
"No, I'm not Karla any more, or have you already forgotten?"
"Please forgive me. This is ..., and I can't introduce you by name because at this point in time she does not have a name."
"Everybody, this is Ye Myo Tun, from Myanmar."
The exchange of handshakes and greetings was warm and sincere.
"Thank you all for such a warm welcome, and I am so pleased to make your acquaintance."
"Please forgive my ignorance, but where is Myanmar?" asks Aislinn.

Kysa

"Myanmar is the largest country in mainland Southeast Asia. To the southeast is Thailand, Laos to the east, then China to the north, India is northwest, Bangladesh is west. Myanmar is just a touch larger than Afghanistan, so it is not that easily overlooked."
"But isn't that... Burma?" questions Kysa.

Ye Myo Tun laughs, "Ever since the 13th century it has been Myanmar, but you are also correct, at one time it was also known as the 'Union of Burma'."

"We have been near there, Susie," says Kysa, "do you remember when we were kids, our parents took time out, we sailed the Pacific."
"I do remember, Kysa. I was about 12. Dad and my uncle took over the shipyard in Southampton that my grandfather had run for so long. My uncle runs it now, as Aaron is more interested in other things. But we've been back to the Pacific last year."

"Ye Myo, we come from globetrotting families: Susie, Aislinn, and I," explains Kysa, "and we've known each other since childhood. All our families are in the yacht-building business. The love of sailing is in our blood. That's how we know each other."

Gasha

"As the globe turns, it changes," comments Gasha, "and now you're all landlocked seafarers."
"Do you know also, that in large parts of my country, women were considered literate when they could plot their own name on a piece of paper? Yes, it is true. It was not that long ago, that less than 10% of women could read or write, where I come from. Yes, Gasha, things are changing," as Nadira nods towards Gasha.

“Tanisha, Sheila, come here,” Susie calls towards the kitchen, “meet a new friend, Ye Myo Tun. We just met this morning.”
Tanisha comes forward and hugs Ye Myo Tun.
”I am Tanisha, how are you?”

Susie continues, “This is Tanisha from India, and here is Sheila, she is from ...”
Ye Myo interrupts, "Let me guess, Australia?"
Sheila confirms with a simple "Yep."
“I think you met them all, I hope. No, one is still missing, she’ll be here soon.”

Karla - Nameless One

“I am so pleased to meet all your friends. It is a rich cultural mix. Please, tell me, what happened to the one without name? How can she not have a name? And please, you may call me Ye or Ye Myo, whichever you choose,” says Ye Myo Tun.
She whispers, “Karla has just found out about the meaning of her name. Since then she doesn’t like it anymore.”
“Forgive me, one without name,” Susie addressing the German woman, “Would you mind explaining why you have no name, Ye Myo is interested.”

“I must ask you all not to laugh this time, as some of you could barely contain your enthusiasm last week. My name was, and I say it again, WAS ‘Karla’. I did not choose this name. My parents in their ultimate wisdom named me ‘man’. All my life I lived as ‘man’. Can you believe this?”
Ye Myo shook her head, not understanding what she heard.
“Last week, I found out that the meaning of the name ‘Karla’ is ... are you ready for it... the meaning is ‘man’.” She looks at everyone’s face, some grin, but none are laughing. “Ye Myo, could you live with such a name?” she asks.

Ye Myo's hand moves to her forehead, hiding the vertical scar she had carried for so long. The smile wiped off her face, biting her lips she shakes her head.
The one without name continues, "I have checked to find which name means 'woman', but there is no such name. Yes, there are women, but their meaning is 'armoured warrior women', Brunhill or Brunhilde, both mean the same. I don't want armour and I'm not a warrior either. I am woman, but all my life I lived as 'man', can you understand this?"

Ye Myo nods quickly in agreement.
"I need to know what 'woman' is before I know who I am and I don't mean in the bedroom."
Tanisha responds, "I do understand what you're saying. Can we address you as 'Nameless One' for the time being, without causing offence? Just long enough until you find yourself, then you will know who you are and you will find your name."
"I would love that, thank you, Tanisha," she replied. "Somehow I have lost my identity and I hate them for that."
"You cannot mean this," Ye replies.

"Oh yes I do, I'm lost, I'm no-one, I have no name."
"Is it not possible that you could be wrong? Is it not possible that this 'no-one' that I am looking at is indeed 'someone'. Perhaps your parents did not know, but maybe your parents did know, and knew that you needed the name of 'man' to get you to here."
The Nameless One looks questioning.
"I would not know how to hate one's parents."

Sheila

Susie added, "In that case, you could say, use them and lose them."
Ye Myo could not believe these words, "Parents are not objects to be discarded."
"No, no, not parents..., man," Susie added, "the 'man' in her name."
Sheila joins the conversation: "Karla, or Nameless One, would you like to swap with me?"

"Any man in Australia knows what I am, and many around the world will know where I come from. My parents were migrants to Australia. In the early years, their language skills were a bit limited. When I was born, my father asked his co-workers, 'What do you call a girl?' No matter who you ask, even today, the answer will be 'Sheila'. It's a nice name, but Down Under, half the country is made up of 'Sheilas', as it doesn't matter if you're a girl or a woman. Of course, my parents didn't know that at the time. They meant well; they wanted to ensure their daughter would assimilate quickly and not stand out as a foreigner in their new country."

Susie grins and says, "Tell Ye Myo about the Bonza Sheila."
Sheila laughs, "Some years ago I took part in the 'Miss Sweet 16 Bikini Pageant' on one of the beaches and won. A visiting sculptor from Brazil asked me if I would model for him. I did, but I had no idea that he was famous. Ricardo was his name. When the statue was finally revealed, the local paper mentioned that Ricardo referred to me as 'Bonza Sheila', and the name has stuck ever since. "I've cut my hair since, so no one will recognize me when I go home."

Aislinn

Tanisha joined in, "In Hindi, so many names have meaning of sweet things, women's names, like beautiful, desire, offering, bright drop, fantasy, imagining, honey, sweet, melodious, pleasing. Manjusha means jewel box, lady with a sweet voice, Amrita, one full of nectar. Manjari, Manisha, all sound so pleasing to the ear."

Ramona joins in, "There is a 'man' in the jewel box, Manjusha."
Tanisha responds, "Oh no, man is not 'man' in Hindi. That doesn't come into it."
"But he is in Emanuelle in Mandy and in mañana, tomorrow," Ramona adds, "perhaps that is not fair, as man is 'hombre' in Spanish, and there is no intent by man."

Nadira adds, "And we do need man, how else can we make babies?"

Aislinn joins in, "Whom else but men to go fishing on the oceans?"
"But do we really need them?" adds the Nameless One.
"Wait a minute," Susie calls out, as she hastens across the room to return with a white board that she stands against the wall, "here is a thought..."
All eyes follow her moves. Gasha saying, "We need man to defend us."

"But from whom?" questions Susie. She draws a large circle at the top of the board, saying, "This is the sun." She draws a smaller circle lower down the board, "And this is the earth, which as we all know rotates around this, like so," she indicates the path of the earth.
"Now let's just imagine for a minute that the earth is just a bit too close to the sun," she wipes out the earth and redraws a circle slightly closer to the sun."
"The polar caps are now melting, sea levels rise. There is no place to go."
"What's your point?" questions Sheila.
"I'm getting to it..." she draws another circle a little further from the sun, next to earth. A miracle has happened and we have a neighbouring planet that is just the right distance from the sun. It has the same air, just a bit cleaner, the same animals, fauna, flora, it is as the earth was 100 years ago, OK?"
All are nodding in agreement.
"It's a big miracle, highly unlikely, but carry on," as Kysa adds her voice.
"Let her speak," Adzumi adds.

All their attention is interrupted by a knock at the door.
Susie calls out, "Ye Myo, please get the door."
"Hello everyone, sorry I'm late."
"Sit down Zoe. Sorry, Zoe, meet Ye Myo from Myanmar. Ye Myo, this is Zoe, USA," Susie continues.

"Zoe, this is the sun, here is the earth, bla, bla, bla, it's too close to the sun, waters rise, earth needs to evacuate, a miracle has happened, we've been given another chance. Sister earth over here is where we need to go, get it?" says Susie, now all fired up.

Zoe replies, "Not quiet, but yeah, go on. I'll catch on."
"Earth now has the opportunity to start again, over there, on the sister. Zoe, a miracle has happened. This is earths' sister, in perfect nick, as earth was 100 years ago."
"Wow, it's so simple isn't it, just install a lift and let's move over there, easy, the old one is now under water, am I right?"
"Spot on," Susie answers, "now what would we need to salvage from here?"

Zoe

She draws a big question mark on the board. "What here on earth is worthy to be taken across to the new sister, our new home, the new world, so to speak? Bear in mind, it is clean, unspoiled, pure. Whatever we take across will have relevant consequences for the future, all depending on what it is."

Aislinn interjects, "But you know this is ridiculous."
"Of course it is, I'm not suggesting otherwise, it's just an exercise, a game, if you like," Susie answers.
"Perhaps a good starting point would be to look at what's wrong here on earth and not repeat the errors of our past," adds Tanisha.
Ramona asks, "Would we want to take hunger and starvation with us?"

On the left half on the board, Susie writes 'No' and 'Yes' at the right half, "So what's the answer, hunger, starvation?"
"No, of course," several voices speak as one.
Susie plots it in on the relevant side. "I'll put war here and peace there."
She turns her head to question, "Consensus, easy."
"Pollution, filth, dirty waters, drugs?"
The lists of 'No' fills up quickly, the opposite being noted at the right side.

"Do we need weapons, tanks, guns and soldiers?" she asks.

“If we don’t take any that solves the issue of war,” responds Ramona.
“Do we take cars, the consequence of which may be pollution?” Susie asks.
“Maybe just small cars, as we still need to move around somehow,” adds Sheila.
“You mean small cars, as women drive?” asks Susie.
“Yes,” Sheila replies, “but trucks will also be needed.”

“So why don’t we take all the trucks we need and all the small cars, as women drive, and leave all the rest behind?” suggests Susie.

“What about the men, how do they get to work?” asks Kysa.
Zoe adds, “If it wasn’t for their small dick syndrome, they would not need large cars, their bums are not much bigger than ours.”
Kysa adds, “With smaller cars, pollution could be reduced a lot.”
Adzumi joins in, “Without drugs, and I don’t mean the drugs used for medical purposes, it would be a better world.”

“Perhaps we can also give the drug dealers a miss, all the female crime syndicates, female gangs, the female extortionists, the female drug barons, cartels, people smugglers, the list goes on,” adds Susie.
Ramona, “I don’t know of any female drug barons and all the rest of it.”
Susie answers, “You’re catching on fast, Ramona.”

Tanisha is wondering, "This almost sounds like some moral crusade. A social panic remedy that seems stereotyped is oversimplified categorisation that ought to have some deeper comprehension."
"It does," answers Susie. "Each country is afflicted by internal organisations that find ways and means to bleed their fellow men dry. The question is, is that something worthy to foster?"

"Susie," Tanisha continues, "if I am completely honest and try to analyse what I feel from all the incoming signals, I get a sense that something doesn’t quite gel with me. Is this some sort of mass hysteria? Are we in a men-bashing euphoria that has the potential to whip up a single-minded frenzy that seems to engulf all of us? My concern is that if anyone claims to be right about anything, he or she must also be wrong about something else. The ‘wrong’ we fail to see or recognize in times of exaggerated emotions. I do acknowledge that many of us are victims, as are millions of others. There are lessons in history that need understanding and taken into consideration. I too have an axe to grind, but revenge is not the way. All I'm saying is that my warning bells are ringing and I need to listen to them."

Zoe remarks, "There is no one on trial. No executioner is waiting in the hallway. All we are trying is to clean the house and discard what has not served us well. It is a simple exercise. You are free to nominate if you would feel comfortable with the likes of murderers, extortionists and stand-over men in your new neighbourhood."
Tanisha nods and redraws to silence.

"Do we need the pimps, the ones that lead our sisters to prostitution etc, etc, etc?" Susie enquires.
Gasha asks, "Do we need men?"
Susie laughs, "Bingo."
Nadira, responds, "We do."
Sheila asks, "What for?"

The Nameless One joins in, "Isn't it our conditioning, that makes us believe we can't do without?"
"I carried 'man' all my life in my name. Man is in humankind and I do not know the origin of the word mankind, humankind or humanity."
"Eve formed from the rib of man; perhaps this adds the male side to us, at least in my religious belief system. I am not a scholar in this field and do not wish to offend anyone here, but in my upbringing, I was taught Cain slew his brother, and it seems he is still doing just that."
"I have heard of Greek mythology where women formed an independent kingdom. No men lived among them. They were all warriors. Legend has it they even stunted the growth of their right

breasts, removed it medically, or suppressed growth from a young age to increase the strength in their arm and aid fighting. Very little is really known, but the name Amazon is familiar to us all. Once a year, they did allow men into their kingdom, just for one day, for the purpose of procreation. Their offspring, if it was male, was returned to the men or simply killed. The girls grew up to follow the ways of their mothers. Having said this, I don't have any intentions to follow their paths, as it seems it is no different than our men are now," the Nameless One said.
"Feared they were and strong, yes, but have we not evolved to find other qualities within us? Nurturing, and the Amazons most likely were good at that, after all, it is part of the mothering instinct, traits such as our ability to communicate x times better than men, dispute resolution, compassion, empathy, understanding, our willingness to compromise," Aislinn adds.

"But this is also the case for many men," said Nadira, adding, "there are so many that have made exceptional contributions to the wellbeing of humanity." Zoe joins in, "On the balance of it, what have we got? How many women are leader of their countries? How many lead in business? How many receive equal pay for equal work? How many have equal decision-making powers, equal leisure time, equal..., equal... whatever?"

Tanisha again speaks out, "Women in power, you asked? In recent times, there have been leaders who served as ministers for many years, led their respective parties, and held multiple terms as heads of government, accumulating many years in politics. There's also another prominent figure in India, and another from what is now Nigeria."

"I can think of notable female heads of state from Iceland, Ireland, United Kingdom, Pakistan, as well as historical monarchs from Hawaii and Angola."

"Yes," adds Nadira, "There were prominent politicians in Pakistan, as well as leaders from Bangladesh."
"Russia, Germany and France come to mind," adds Gasha.
Ramona says, "Spain and Portugal had several queens."
"In Sweden too, historical female figures," add Kysa.
"And in Ireland," says Aislinn.

Adzumi speaks of her country: ''Japan ravaged by wars for years, selected their first Empress of Japan. She was surrounded only by women.''

The Nameless One says, "In England too, there were notable queens."

Tanisha adds more, "In ancient China, Egypt, and other regions, there were remarkable women, including queens and leaders. At that time, the world had a population of just one million people." Susie continues, "Today we are a global population of many billions. Amongst those, could we find half that are female and in similar positions as their male counterparts?"

Zoe has her say: "Projected estimates indicate that in less than 40 years, the world will have to feed 9 billion people. Of the 195 so-called 'official' countries in the world, at this point in time, do we find half led by women? Would we find 20% or even 15%? Granted, 50% may be somewhat overly hopeful, due to our mothering role, one would expect less than 50%, but reality is somewhat different."

"But in some countries, there have been periods where female ministers had a greater presence," answers Kysa, "but the numbers have changed in recent years. Some countries have also had female chiefs of police. Norway and Denmark are among them."

"If we ask our sister anywhere around the streets, in whom they would place their trust, a male or female candidate, the doubt in their own abilities becomes reflected in their decision and is projected on the female candidate. Conditioning, self-doubt, or a weak perception of oneself may well be the cause. It could be women's lack of self-confidence voting their own gender out of office."

"How long has it been going on?" asks Kysa, "The emancipation of women? Economic and legal inequalities, sexual and religious

oppression, inheritance laws, look around the world. Another 1000 years will not be enough to liberate all women across the globe."
Tanisha adds, "In the late 19th century, there were calls for women's freedom, led by various individuals. One of them was male."

Gasha says, "In Russia, it was only the beginning of the industrial revolution that made women aware that there is another world outside the family confines. So many groups with high ideals emerged, many to favour their own agenda, not necessarily their gender."

"Once women were considered equal to men," says Tanisha, "at least legally. They had legal rights. Who gave them those rights? Who were the Roman magistrates, judges and jurists? Without exception, all were men."

Gasha shares her thought: "Engels also had some words to say about women, and he was a man. This is not about political power or leadership. It is not even about equalities of the sexes. Biologically, physiologically, emotionally, physically and mentally we are not equal; we are different. Genetically, there may only be a smidgen of difference; nevertheless, we are different."
Tanisha says, "This is also the case in nature."

Zoe adds, "Have men become sick over time and strayed from what nature intended? Violence, wars without end, escalation to worse, is this normal?"

"Violence is a part of nature," says Tanisha. "Go near a lioness with cubs; you will soon find out what a female is capable off. Even the weakest woman, as mother, will find similar strength."

Kysa remarks, "Going back to the inequality in economic terms, many of our sisters do live in the limelight and enjoy the spoils,

movie stars and singers. By comparison to men, few climb the corporate ladder all the way."
"And who stands in the background, behind the till? I bet you ten to one, a man," said Aislinn.

"Mail-order brides from so many countries in an attempt to escape their poverty," voices Gasha. "I have never heard of mail-order husbands."

Susie continues, "Look, we could fill a million whiteboards, but they would all say the same. Mind you, none of this is based on scientific observation; this is just thinking out loud."

She turns to face the whiteboard again and says, "What if there is no miracle, no sister planet? Home is home as is," and she wipes the sister earth off the board, "What if we're stuck with what we've got?"

Some heads move in resignation. "This," and she points to the 'Yes' side of the board, "this, and we are in consensus, is what we want, but this is still with us," as she points to the other side. "I have no desire to become an Amazon, to have blood on my hands, nor do I want to rule the world," she continues, "but what, if we could get what we perceive to be right without spilling a drop of blood?"
Zoe enquires, "You are onto something, aren't you? Go on, tell us."

"What if we add another dimension instead?"
She pauses for a moment, "We add time."
"Let's say we add ten years. A child born today will be ten, in ten years time."
Sheila laughs, "That is brilliant mathematics."
Zoe interjects, "There's more to this, let her talk."
"The youngest girl in ten years time would have just been born, however, the youngest boy in ten years time will still be ten. Now we add another ten years and that boy will be 20 and all the youngest boys alive will be the same age."
"In fifty years, no man on earth is 49 or less. In a hundred years, no men exist. Women are the only gender."
Zoe was first to gasp, "Wow."

Susie continues to a silent audience, "Women can do what no man can do. We can bear the pain of childbirth. We can make life. No man on earth can do that. Men know how to take such lives. Lives that we birthed in agony, they know how to flush the lights out in less than a second. Show me one man who can create life instead of destroy it."

Kysa is the first to comment, "So all the men alive today would live their normal course. They die of natural causes and so do the women."
"Yes," Susie responds.
Ramona continues, "The gender balance in the population changes gradually. Food supplies could increase, the hungry could be fed."
Susie nods.
Zoe adds, "Less males means less ruthlessness, change in attitudes."
More nod in agreement.

Nadira remarks, "Husbands will still leave their older wives in search of youth, and they will have many to choose from, so many girls without men. Older women will find it hard."

Susie answers Nadira, "If you take today's reality, it may seem that way, as older women are abandoned for younger girls even now. At the same time, bear in mind, there will not be enough men for the younger women either. That time will be just a transitional phase, if we keep relying on men to take care of us, will we not always be at their mercy. If we fear loneliness we must find comfort in our sisters."
Ye Myo adds her opinions, "In time, wars may cease altogether; blood may no longer be spilled. Peace could become reality."
Nameless One adds, "In a hundred years, Cain will have gone."
Susie nods. Sheila, who had listened long says, "We, women, we are so very special. I can see a sisterhood that transcends borders, builds bridges across religious divides. National fences no longer mean a thing, racial segregation, what for? We can build bridges across ethnic and skin colour differences, bridges that can potentially work to bring us all together, despite and because of our differences. Yet we all have a sisterhood that can unite us. Within all of us is the common tribal instinct of family, nurture and care. It is possible."

Susie nods in agreement.

Adzumi expresses what is felt be many others, "I can't help but feel a loss somehow, as if we did something wrong, although none would be harmed."

Aislinn replies, "Perhaps this is what they felt in August 1945, after realising that the atom bomb actually worked, you know what I mean? The realisation of the power, that it is possible to unleash such a weapon. And all we need to do is stop making men."
Zoe points out, "Yes, there is a kind of sadness. Has man not brought it on himself? I don't want to get into political or cultural differences, but is not the value of women less than men in so many countries?"

Don't mothers give birth and see their child killed or aborted, if it is a girl. Are boys ever sacrificed in any culture for their gender, are they ever worth less than girls?"

"Can I say something? Didn't the Amazons kill boys?" Tanisha asks, and speaks without waiting for an answer. "This is a kangaroo court. Are you not aware of this? It simply cannot be true, if we agree on everything. Time will change and so will the truth. 'Yes' becomes 'no' very quickly. Add more time and 'no' will change to become 'yes'. Before every war, people hyped up in a frenzy believing all that is dished out, as reasons why this battle needs to be fought. They can't wait to race forward with their lance or their tanks. As the piles of bodies become mountains, eventually they will ask why, and cease fighting."
"Tanisha, I hear you," says Sheila, "but it is not politics, religion, beliefs, resources or land. When our bodies are invaded by illness we must defend it. Compare men to a virus, even as that we already mourn the loss of them."

Kysa nods slowly to add, "I agree, I too feel sad of loss, but we are already being replaced. For so many men, women are just sex objects and they want more. They are even replacing the sex objects into which they have turned some of us. Lifelike mannequins, sex dolls are on the production lines. In time, the quality of these gadgets will rival our bodies. Their vaginas will feel as yours and mine, their breasts indistinguishable from real ones.

They will be able to moan and groan. With a little chemistry they will taste as a woman, have the scent fine-tuned to buyer's dreams. Nothing can age, fine adjustments everywhere. Breasts that will never sag, small dick adjustments are no problems at all, Sir. She will accommodate anything, anywhere, all at once if need be, Sir, as your heart desires, Sir."

"Can't you see," Kysa calls out, "The perfect woman is already here, next week, Sir, and we can offer you our latest model, blond, brunette or black hair, at the flick of a button. If the green light ever turns orange, just bring her in for a service."

Adzumi

"Are they not already working on sex machines to replace us? They will never wear out. They stay forever young. Two screws and they replace the face when they get sick of it."

"They are sick," Aislinn adds. "Add 100 years of technical development and we cannot imagine what they will do to us. These things never complain. Add a bit of software and they will be able to hold conversations. That will not be difficult, as their range of subjects to talk about is limited anyway. They will be able to walk alongside him. No one would know. No one would care as we, the real women, have become redundant."

Tanisha shakes her head, "Your ears are closed."
Adzumi replies, "We can see this, as if our gender is under attack. There is no need to wage war with them. Let them do as they please. We play along and just don't make them anymore," she holds her belly to emphasise her meaning.
Susie's response, "What are we waiting for?"
Aislinn looks to the ground, her mind deep in thought, and she says, "It is a very unusual feeling, one as if a decision has been made for much unrest, turmoil, and a fear of being found out. As if we are guilty of genocide and gender cleansing, and I hate the word cleansing and how men name such things, so we don't throw up at the breakfast table on hearing the news of the day."

"Oh, no," Susie answers, "no decision has been made. We have not done anything."

"They will laugh at us, as they have always done," says Sheila, "How could they believe us. We never had power. It will not go into their brains."

Ramona calmly explains her feelings, "I feel, as if I've aged 1000 years in the last few minutes."

"There is a feeling of guilt within me," says Adzumi, "we will be eliminated."

Ye Myo replies, "We are 'women', we have compassion even for the other side."

The Nameless One speaks, "And we have been conditioned to carry the blame."

Nadira remarks, "Could we give them a chance, a warning perhaps and an opportunity to turn their fate."

Ye Myo continues in Nadira's thought, "Yes, Nadira, I would feel much better if that was the case."

Sheila walks up to the board to say, "All they need to do is find their own solutions to this," and she points to the list on the left side."

"I can well imagine that our thoughts can be put into practice, I mean the ability to control which gender we allow to grow inside us," says Kysa, "I can't see, how all women on earth can act as one. But be under no illusion, within a few short weeks of putting such plan into action, the statistics will show it working."

"They will wonder what is going on. Sheila, from that point forward, they will believe us," Kysa adds.

Gasha speaks out, "There is a means to give them a warning, an opportunity for them to change. They will decide the fate of their own gender, just as we do with ours."

Susie, who had not spoken for a while steps in front of the board to say, "Sisters, let's allow ourselves time for this to simmer. There is no need to decide tonight. Let us all look what is on this board and store it in our heads."

All women study the board once more.
"I will now wipe this board clean," says Susie, "one last chance, are we done?"
Tanisha remarks, "As the earth spins round, the lynch mobs re-emerge."
Susie turns to Tanisha, "White is not white without black. Be our voice to the contrary, so we are able to see what we are doing. Can I clean the board?"
Heads nod.

"I would like to suggest that we take the time we need, so that each of us can think this through. Evaluate the pros and cons, understand the consequences, visualise a possible outcome and in one week, one month, however long we need, let us discuss this then."
Heads again nod. The board is clean.

"Each of us now, can kill all the others with a slip of the tongue, if this is mentioned outside of this circle. Discretion is advisable. We are at each other's mercy. No decision has been made tonight, nor should we act in haste."

The women exchange facial contact with another, fear and doubt, but also the knowing and awareness that they are no longer powerless in their own destiny.
"We are not brutes who decide via short circuits and then blame someone else if it doesn't work out," says Aislinn. "If we decide to bring new life into the world, we will care for this life as long as we live. We know how to make an unconditional commitment, whatever it takes. Men need to feed their egos, quick glories. We have balls, they are just not visible."

Susie empties the contents of a coloured bowl. A mixture of nuts rolls across the table. "We are twelve women here. Let each of us place a coin of any value in this bowl, as an indicator that you are ready, to have this subject brought up again, in your own time.
If this bowl contains twelve coins, then we will address the issue, not before."

Susie laughs, "OK, let's change the subject and give ourselves time. Tanisha, this is no kangaroo court, as you can see."

"By the way, on Saturday is an exhibition at the gallery in Zurich. I know the artist, if anyone is interested. She is a woman with vision. Have a look at her works, talk to her, you will find she can touch your soul. It could be a nice day out, to see something new. The details are over there, the pamphlet on the shelf."

Zoe walks up to Ye Myo, "I am so pleased to meet you, sorry I was late, traffic is sometimes a nightmare."
"Likewise, Zoe," says Ye Myo. "It is my first time here and I must thank Susie, for inviting me here."

"What have you done there? That must have hurt?" she points at the scar at Ye Myo's forehead. Ye Myo does not answer. Her hand reaches up to hide the healed gash.

"I am sorry, Ye Myo," Zoe embraces her.
It takes three attempts to get the word out, then Ye Myo whispers into Zoe's ear, "Men."
The depth of their embrace intensifies.

Now I know why it could not be shown

Switzerland, Gallery in Zurich

Ramona, together with Ye Myo, arrives by train in Zurich to seek out the gallery.
Felicia Fodor is in her element. Her exhibition demands her involvement, so that there is little time for the guests from Basel, who had come to meet her.

"Susie was here this morning, she said you might be coming and I am so pleased to meet you both," says Felicia upon meeting Ramona and Ye Myo.
"Ramona, I shall make time to devote all my attention to you both, give me 30 minutes, then I shall be free," Felicia says.
Ramona and Ye Myo fill 30 minutes, taking in the artworks displayed in the gallery. A little later, Felicia finds them to say, "I'm free, let's go somewhere nice, I want to meet you."

Just as they entered the tram, Ramona receives a text message on her mobile, 'Where are you?' signed by Nicole. Ramona dials her number, then asks Felicia, "A friend of mine is going to join us. She wants to know where we are."
"Tell her General-Guisan Quai, corner Beethovenstrasse, near where the boats are," responds Felicia.
Nicole had already arrived overlooking the lake, where small sailing craft criss-cross the waters.
Ramona sneaks up on Nicole to blind her eyes with her hands, "Guess who?"
"Some handsome devil, who tries to take advantage of me," Nicole replies.
"Wrong." answers Ramona.
"Then you must be my landlord, trying to collect the rent I owe you," she says.
"Wrong again, last chance now," says Ramona.
"Are you the damsel in distress?" asks Nicole.
Ramona releases her hands, "I most certainly am," she says.
In joyous laugh they embrace, Ramona saying, "But I'm no longer the damsel in distress, thanks to you, my friend."

Ramona introduces Nicole to Ye Myo and Felicia, "We have just met Felicia an hour ago, she is a friend of a friend."
"Hello Nicole, the pleasure is mine," says Felicia.
"Where are we?" Nicole asks.
"This is Aboretum in Enge. That is Lake Zurich. It stretches all the way to the Alps, all covered in snow, as you can see" says Felicia. "Come over here, I will show you something very beautiful."

Ramona, Ye Myo and Nicole follow Felicia. In a small clearing surrounded by mature trees she stops. "Isn't she beautiful?" Felicia says as she points to a statue of woman. "I do feel something special every time I see her, it's Aphrodite."

"Yes she is," says Ramona, "men do know how to portray our outer."
Ye Myo adds, "They know how to put us on pedestals, even if it's only a few feet high."

All look at the round simple pedestal and laugh. Let us sit down, under this tree. Ye Myo asks Nicole, "I want to know about the damsel in distress," looking at Nicole.
"So do I, come fill us in," Felicia adds.
Nicole, looking at Ramona, says, "I think she's grown her wings now."
Ramona's thoughts wander to another time. She slowly nods. Sensing some unease, Ramona changes the subject, "Yes, pedestals, men sure can put us up there and adore us."
She continues, "So many artists have the gift to bring it out in their craft, woman, in oil, in bronze, in marble, woman, their fantasy."
Nicole adds, "They adore us."
Ramona adds, "And they core us."
Nicole adds, "And they whore us."
Felicia joins, "Painters, sculptors but not poets." They laugh.

"Hey, it's a long weekend, are you free for a day or so?" enquires Felicia.
Some nod. "What have you got in mind," asks Nicole.
"Come with me, we are going to Budapest. Stay the night or two," says Felicia.
"Why not," answers Ramona, "my little handbag, has my PJ's, I came prepared with just some tissues."
Ye Myo says, "I have never been to Hungary."
"I'm easy, why not," says Nicole.
"Deal, don't worry about a thing," says Felicia.
As they walk along the edge of the lake, Ramona says to Nicole, "You know this end of the lake reminds me of something."
"I know Ramona,' says Nicole, "the straight line from the bridge, it has the shape of a box, not exactly, but similar to ..."
Ramona says, "Don't say it."
Nicole smiles, "I wouldn't have anyway." She gives her a kiss.

They travel across Austria to Budapest. Felicia's place is slightly northeast of Margaret Island, at the outskirts of Budapest. On their

way, they stock up on some provisions. The area is a mountain ridge overlooking the many bridges that cross the Danube.
"We're almost here," says Felicia, "this is it, we're here. Welcome to my paradise."

"This is an artist's den," remarks Ramona. A central fireplace is the main feature inside the large room, as if the walls had been removed. Large windows flood it with light. Partially started artworks are stacked all along one side. Brushes, pallets and paraphernalia are located all over the place. This place has character in every sense of the word.
"Make this your home," says Felicia, "and is anyone good at cooking?"
"Oh the enthusiasm is overwhelming," says Ye Myo.
"Between the four of us, we'll manage something," says Nicole,

Together they fix a dish that will be hard to find in any restaurant. Felicia explains, "It has never been my thing to fix food, but we shall survive this meal, I'm sure. In case we are not, the hospital is just down the road. Hey, relax, we shall survive this."
Together they share the meal. Felicia initiates the conversation. "I met Susie and Aaron some years ago, they bought two of my paintings."

"How do you know each other," she asks.
"Nicole and I met on the French Riviera," explains Ramona.
"When the damsel had no wings, I suppose," laughs Felicia.
"Yes," said Ramona, "she may have had no wings, but she knew they would grow."

Ye Myo explains, "I met Susie at the university in Basel, and through Susie I met Ramona. I didn't know Nicole until we met in Zurich, when we met on the lake for the first time."
"As you can see, I am an artist. There are 24 pieces in this particular show, but there is one, which I've never shown anyone," says Felicia.

She walks to the rear of the room to pull out a framed work, skilfully protected from the environment. Ye Myo asks, “Why is this so?”
“Ye Myo,” Felicia says, “I don’t know what it is.”
She rests the painting on an easel.
“If I don’t know what it is, how can I show it in public?” she says, “Does anyone know what this is?”
Nicole, the first to respond, “Felicia, I am honest with you, I don’t know anything about art. I cannot read abstract representations, sorry.”

Felicia leans towards Nicole: "Nicole, each painting has a voice. Its voice is colour, shape, texture, light, shading, composition, and a million little things. I am not after a professional analysis, a dissection of its elements, etc., and so forth. What do you see in it, what does it say it is, because I do not know it myself.”
Ramona says, “I am very much a traditionalist; the school of the old master has always fascinated me. What I see here is very different. As if one is trying to break the mould, a reach for something different, new.”
Ye Myo steps away from the canvas, to get a total overview, then says, “You know, Felicia, I can only give you my perception, which is all I can say. I am not trained in the arts or pretend to have knowledge about the subject.”

“From back here, the first thing that strikes me is not the art work, not at first, but the frame,” says Ye Myo. “It is so very unusual.”
Ramona adds, “Yes, now I see it. I have never seen a frame without corners, oh, sorry, Ye Myo, I didn’t mean to interrupt.”
Nicole walks back to the room, to stand beside Ye Myo, looking at the works.
“That’s OK, Ramona,” replies Ye Myo. ”The overall perception is smooth, sweet, gentle and non-confrontational. It seems like a conscious suppression of something else, like on purpose.”

Felicia listens with interest, “This is the last in a series of works, based on the theme ‘Balance and Harmony’. When I finished, I thought this one had all the ingredients, like the jewel in the crown of the whole collection. You have seen all the others in Zurich. This one belongs to them, but shortly afterward, after it was completed, I could not recognise it anymore. That's why it is still here."

Ye Myo repeats the words, "Hmm..., Balance and Harmony, sorry, I feel the harmony side of it, or at least an attempt towards it, but, forgive me for saying so, the balance, I can't make out."
Ramona adds her views, "It is overly faint, too soft perhaps."
Felicia says, "At one time I thought this was woman. All wrapped up, 100% woman."

Nicole speaks out, "That's it, it is 'woman', but not as we are or as we see woman, this is woman as men see us. Not all men either, but a romanticised view, a pedestal fantasy by a section of men."
Felicia walks up to Nicole, smiles and nods, "And you say, you know nothing about art, you could have had me fooled."
"Thank you, Nicole, thank you Ye Myo and Ramona. Now I know why it could not be shown," says Felicia.
She wraps the work up to return it where it had been before.

The next day filled the senses with Hungarian delights under Felicia's guidance, feasts for the stomach, feasts for the eyes and ears, good memories for days to come.
Upon their return to Switzerland, Ramona, Ye Myo and Nicole stopped by at Susie's place, where Nicole is introduced to Susie for the first time.

Wait a minute, what is going on?

Basel, Switzerland, Susie's place

Week after week, the coins in the bowl were counted. First two, then five, then six, then ten. Two coins are still missing as one month became another. No one mentioned the subject. However long it takes, all sisters needed to be ready. That was the deal. The subject was taboo. Five weeks on from the initial discussions, the number of coins reached eleven. There is still one missing.

Several weeks had passed, when Susie had first met Nicole. They met again as Ramona brought Nicole along when she came to visit Susie. As Susie's place is a meeting place for many, one never knew who might be there at any one time. Nicole met Aislinn, Zoe and Tanisha that day.
Aislinn counted the coins. There were eleven, as they had been for a while now.

Some minutes later, Tanisha calls out, “Wait a minute, what is going on? There are 11 coins in here, but I have never seen this brand new Franc.”
“It wasn’t there a moment ago,” said Aislinn, “I just looked.”
Ramona walks up to the bowl, “Neither have I seen it. The coin is brand new.”
“Oh, that’s mine,” says Nicole, “I needed small change and swapped it for two fifties Rappen. I didn’t take any money, except the two fifties and just swapped it for that Swiss Franc.”
“That’ll make it twelve,” said Susie.
“Oh, I'm sorry. I thought they were just coins, shall I swap them back?” asks Nicole.
“No, no, it is fine, Nicole,” said Susie.

When Nicole left, to refresh in the bathroom, Susie said, “I’m glad we were all here, as witness to explain the numbers in the bowl. OK, we can now arrange a meeting of the group. We have consensus.”

They do not understand
Basel, Switzerland, Susie's place

Ramona was first to voice her feelings, "I have thought about it long and hard. If even one unborn is aborted, just one women forced into killing her child, be that by knife or needle or any other means, then I cannot give my support to the idea, even knowing the suffering that men have caused."

Susie notes, 'No killing' on the whiteboard. Nameless One remarks, "My views are like Ramona's. The blood of just one will turn us into Cain."
"We would become no different from men, repeating a never-ending cycle. Any blood on our hands would be our doom."
Nadira explains her views, "I would refuse an absolute decision without an opportunity for redemption."
"I do agree with all the views I have heard so far," adds Adzumi, "as to redemption, we know men can be as thick as bricks, perhaps they need three warnings, three opportunities, so that they realise that it is no joke." Zoe takes the marker to write '3 chances and three warnings' on the board.

Aislinn's thoughts touch another area, "I am troubled with the ethics. Who owns me, my body? I do, I should think. Who can tell me what children I can bear and which I am not to bear? 'No one' is my answer to that, as only I have that right."
"Point noted," says Susie, and checks that Zoe marks it on the whiteboard, "Good point."
Susie expresses her views, "I love my father dearly. There are many men, who are considerate, wonderful human beings. Cloning such

men is an option and a bag of worms. No doubt, there are many beautiful, exceptional men in our societies. The ideal men do exist among us."

"Men are not a country, they are a gender. How do we address men? Who speaks for men, who are their leaders? They live in the wild world of survival of the fittest. How do we negotiate if there is no structure in their hierarchy?

"If we speak to the leaders in industry, commerce, finance or political structure, are these perhaps not the worst examples of 'men' in mankind, having demonstrated their insatiable hunger to get to the top while climbing over bodies? That is the wrong side of the tree."

Gasha adds, "We could change the composition of men, their chemical, hormonal and biological structure. Less testosterone, tweak the pituitary glands. There are many ways to change life, but each means interfering with a living organism, interference with nature."

Kysa speaks, "Reverse the roles, what would men do to obtain their objective? Either a total surprise attack or closing borders, spread the suffering to everyone, increase demands, engineer incidents that can justify full out attack. The leaders, usually on both sides, feed their egos, having the power trip of their lives, each willing to sacrifice the lives of their subjects, of course never themselves, whatever it takes to win. Who pays the cost? Mostly the little ones, the powerless, the economic slaves, the lower caste or class will lose everything every single time."

"Who wins? Money wins," Kysa, continues, "It is said, 5% of people own 95% of all the wealth. These 5% are the leaders. The other 95% will follow them in the illusionary hope, that you and I, we have the same chance and we too can be like them. This hope is the carrot that keeps the wheels turning. If we just learn how to kick hard, become like me, buy my book, DVD, follow me, vote me into office and leave your money on the counter, and we all can be in the 5%. Mathematically that is impossible. We all know that. But here is the trick, feed the ego some peanuts and it will run for a million miles."

"Ten years from now, how many of us will lead a major corporation, are in charge of any major project, get all the way to the top? We can study until we are blue in the face, get degrees, diplomas, doctorates, enough to wallpaper a high-rise building, for what? To feed an ego, become like them or the chance to offer our offspring slightly better chances."

"Who are these 5% that can watch their brothers and sisters, 95% of people, struggling to get by on the 5% of wealth that's left? Perhaps it is our ability of accepting a status quo, given minimum food and shelter, the status quo of a prison cell can become acceptable. Finding just enough scraps on a garbage dump, a plastic sheet to keep the rain off, can become an acceptable status quo. As humankind we will eat rats if need be, we are able to shed all pride, all honour, for fear that it could get worse. None of us may live in such conditions, but millions do."

Susie asks, "Are you suggesting we knock at the doors of the 5% and ask them to swap places?"

Kysa gives this a short laugh, "How many revolutions have tried doing just that? Even if they can be found, in 10 years from then, the world will be the same, just different people will have accumulated the 95%. Other revolutions have tried that. The evil is in men."

Adzumi questions, "Do we have the means to put a plan into action? Is it at all possible to rid the world of men, practically I mean?"
Susie indicates a slow silent nod.
"But how can it be accomplished?" questions Adzumi.
"If we would have a full comprehension of the technological possibilities at our disposal today, we would cower in fear," Susie adds to continue, "How?"
"We must be aware of this, the less each of us knows, the safer we will all be. It will be acceptable to lie, to safeguard our knowledge

and protect each other from another. We will need to learn to do what it takes, to create a better world," says Susie, and adds, "It is possible for a woman to conceive only female offspring. To answer Ramona's earlier concern, it is possible to do this without abortion. Once sperm and egg unite, from the first cell division, the technology exists to ensure this can only become a girl."

"In other words, we will not destroy any living being, even at the very beginning of life. We will know before conception, that this sperm and this egg will become female."
"As you all know, medicine is not my field. What I have just said does not come from my own expertise or experiments. If I am drawn and quartered, I can not reveal how it is done, because I do not know."
Nadira asks, "You are saying such things already exist, it can already be done?"
Susie answers, "Yes, Nadira, it is already possible."
"Is this knowledge in the hands of men or women?" asks the Nameless One.

Ye Myo responds, "Perhaps we need not ask what may endanger someone's safety." Nameless One replies, "I accept that and withdraw the question."
Gasha speaks, "We do not kill, we do not abort, we do not modify, inject, interfere with the natural functions of women's bodies, is this correct?"

Susie answers this question, "We do not kill, correct. We do not abort, correct. Modify, inject and interfere, none of them. Gasha, the answer to all your questions is 'no' in each case."
Nadira asks, "How can we ask men to change, before this may be put in place?"
Aislinn answers, "Have we not asked since time began?"
"But we need to give them a chance for redemption," replies Nadira.

Susie responds, “We can select a township in any country on earth, or even a suburb within a town. We can action the plan to show that for a time of say 3 months, no boys will be born in the selected town.”
“Susie, this is possible?” asks Ye Myo.
“Yes. In several months most doctors will already know that there will be no males amongst the unborn. Between nine and twelve months, only girls will have been born in the selected town,” explains Susie, “after the plan has been implemented of course.”
“Yes, yes,” Ye Myo replies.

Gasha adds, “That could be taken as a first warning, as proof that it can be possible, well, that it is possible, there is the proof. Men, change your ways or else...” “Exactly,” Adzumi adds,” The second warning someplace else should wake them up.” Sheila nods. “The last warning could be on a larger scale, elsewhere, and this time perhaps a whole country. They must believe us that they need to change or they will die out.”

Nadira asks, “Can we also show, that the first and second places are able to bear boys, after the ‘warning’ has been shown to work. They would then know that it is not their women’s fault. That all can be reversed, as it was before.”

Tanisha speaks, “Who are we? Who gives us the right to make such decisions?”

Zoe joins in, "Self-defence." She places a binder on the table. "Every single day women are murdered, Tanisha, well over 80000 every single year, according to the statistics. Most are murdered by their former lovers, their partners, husbands, or their boyfriends. That's one in every 10 minutes. Is this not systematic killing? The only reason it's not called a massacre is that every women dies alone. One next door, another in the next village, wherever. Even if this binder held a million pages, it could barely scratch the surface. The sexual violence, incest, physical, and mental abuse that our gender has suffered comes close to a billion victims. Add to this the female infants killed for no other reason than being born female. How high would the numbers be if all types of abuse and harassment were actually reported?"

Gasha walks towards her bag, removes a folder, places it on the table and continues, "Man is the stronger sex?" she asks. "Wrong, we are conditioned to believe that. The Amazons, and there are more in history who have proven to be equal to men, in mind and physical strength. Self defence," she repeats, and slides a DVD into the player, pausing before she presses the play button, "In the folders are all the source references to this, and a warning, what you are about to see is very, very distressing."

"This is real footage obtained from police sources, hospitals, military and women protection shelters. In one segment, I am an unwilling actress, the victim of men. You will not recognise me, even I can't believe it. As I said, it is hard to take." Gasha presses the play button and reduces the sound of the speakers.

The group watches the monitor in silence. Within moments Ye Myo excuses herself to run to the toilet. Nadira turns her face, "I cannot watch this," she leaves the room. Ramona turns away. Aislinn steps forward to stop the DVD.

Gasha explains, "These are no actors, everything is real. To be fair, it also shows how far some women have come and what they can do to their own kind." Susie walks to a shelf to add another folder to the table, "Statistics from 18 countries, social, economic and violence. Anyone can find these anywhere."

Ramona adds her research information, "Abortions, child abuse, hunger, three folders." Sheila steps outside to console Nadira.

Moments later, they return to the room. Ye Myo dabs her mouth with her sleeves and fills a glass with water in the kitchen.

The Nameless One adds her information to the table, six books, two folders, another disc, “Forced prostitution, missing persons, taxation reports based on male / female incomes, pictures of bodies, dead bodies. You’ll also find court judgement sorted by verdicts of male / female judges with references to the relevant cases. If men were to face court, I wonder, would he get eternity or walk away free.”

Kysa says, "Men's behaviour is far worse than animals. A single man can commit mass murder, killing dozens. He can also inspire others to do the same, leaving millions dead. History has plenty of examples. Animals don't engage in such acts. While there have been some female perpetrators, their number of victims is generally less than 100. Fathers can sexually abuse their own children, a motivation absent in the animal world. Although rape, coercion, and aggression exist in both worlds, animals are primarily driven by natural mating instincts."

"Serial killers, dictators, war criminals, sexual predators, financial fraudsters, terrorist leaders, these individuals have committed atrocious acts, causing suffering, brutality, abuse of power, and caused widespread fear. These things have no equivalent in the animal world. Moreover, there are unspeakable and perverse inhumanities that some men are capable of, too often left unmentioned. Could injustice, brain chemistry, upbringing, socialisation, life experiences, moral development, or culture be influencing factors?"

Tanisha emphasises that for millions of people, their primary motivation is to generate income in order to support their families. "Economic hardships often lead to financial stress and desperation, which may compel individuals to compromise their ethical standards in order to meet basic needs. This can manifest in activities such as drug dealing, fraud or robberies. Many individuals who engage in such activities are eventually caught, convicted, and forced to face lifelong consequences. However, it is important to recognise that the root cause lies in the initial inequality that exists.

Some sell themselves or even their children, as they find it difficult to feed them all."

"This inequality is further exploited by individuals who offer false promises to the vulnerable, extracting their last resources. It gets worse. A word of warning, be prepared to throw up when you open this folder. The way I see it, the heart of these issues: economic disparity, lack of equal opportunity, and insatiable greed by the few who claim they've earned their wealth."

Ye Myo regains her voice, “I do not have a folder to bring. All my knowing of men is in my heart, my head and in the brand I'm given.” Both hands are next to her forehead to reveal the gash to all. Ramona was about to speak as a knock on the door interrupts her thoughts.

“Anybody home?” the voice questions, “Hello.”
Susie runs towards the door, “Daddy, oh Daddy, it's so good to see you.” They embrace in greeting.
“Oh, what's with all the long faces? Who died?” he asks the group.
“Zoe, hello, good to see you again,” they hug. “Aislinn, Adzumi, Nadira, it is so good to see you all. I see some new faces.”
“Daddy, where do you come from?” asks Susie.
“Thailand, Bangladesh, Sri Lanka, a short stopover here for a cup of coffee, then I'm off to Africa.” he says.
“I'll make you a cup.” Susie hastens into the kitchen. “By the way, Dad, José and Angela called earlier. It was Moyo's birthday, she's
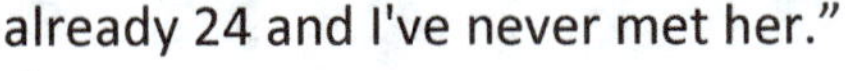
already 24 and I've never met her.”

Aislinn, addressing Susie's father, says, “Welcome home, Aaron, is it still home? Meet Ye Myo Tun.”
“Hello, Sir,” Ye Myo says, as they exchange greetings.
Aaron laughs, “I am no Sir, no Sir. Just Aaron is fine. I am so pleased to meet you.”
“This is Ramona,” Aislinn continues introducing the new faces. He greets Ramona, then sees the Nameless One and walks to

embrace her. “Karla, you have not changed a bit.” Karla laughs, “Oh yes I have. I am no longer Karla.”
“Oh?” Aaron replies, “But who am I to know? You must know yourself better than I ever could.”
The Nameless One nodding and they embrace once more.
“I must apologise for barging in. You were deep in serious discussions, I am sure, before I so rudely interrupted you all. Please forgive me.”

“This is your home, Aaron,” says the Nameless One.
“Perhaps so,” he replies, as Susie hands him the coffee cup, “Thank you, Susie." Turning to Aislinn he adds, “Yes, Aislinn, finding all of you here makes it still feel as home.”
He laughs, “I shall withdraw, to let you continue with whatever you were doing. I am here for twelve days. I am sure we will catch up. Bye for now, everybody.”

The group’s mood had changed. All are waiting for some moments before they continued where they had left off.

Sheila was the first saying “Isn’t it interesting. Has anyone noticed something?”
Adzumi said, “Yes, a change in balance the moment he walked in.”
“With all respect to your father, Susie, but I noticed it too,” said Nadira, “twelve to one, and what a transformation, possibly in most of us.”

Susie added her thoughts, “To me it is not so strange, but then, he is my father, a familiar figure for all my life. He is also my closest friend. I have no awareness that he is ‘man’, and that he also belongs to them.”
The Nameless One adds, “He is a beautiful guy. If we ever get to the cloning stage he would be on top of the list as possible specimen.”
All laugh in a sense of agreement.

Gasha remarks, “But there will be no more of his kind. He does belong to them.”

Ramona says, “I am not aware that there has been a decision on that.”
“We cannot be the judge, jury and executioner all in one,” says Ye Myo. Tanisha adds, “I am glad to hear you say this.” Nadira says, “Men must be given a chance to defend our accusations.”
Tanisha speaks, “Ask 1000 men, you will hear the voice of few, likewise with women.” Adzumi replies, “Who is man? Which men can be held accountable?”

Susie calls out, "Aaron, Daddy, could you join us, please?"
"But he is your dad," says Kysa.
"What has this got to do with it?" asks Susie.
"Yes, Susie, you called," Aaron answers.
“Oh, good you are here, Daddy,” says Susie. “Dad, are you tired from your travels?”
“No, not at all. I was in Zurich for a couple of days and got rid of all the jetlag. I’m fine, wide awake, thanks to your coffee.”
Since childhood, Susie calls Aaron by his first name, but if she feels as child, she uses ‘Daddy’. It has been a normal part of their life.
“Aaron,” Susie says, “please sit down here. Do you have time to spend with us?”
“I have all the time in the world, darling,” answers Aaron.
“OK, Daddy, in that case hear this,” Susie begins. “You, Aaron, the father of Susie, I, are a member of mankind.”
“I am,” answers Aaron, “and so are you.”
“Oh no, I am not. Neither are any of us, except you. We belong to ‘Womkind’.”

Aaron laughs, “I don’t know what that is, but I’m sure you will let me know in a minute.”

“I will,” Susie continues, “and for the purpose of this exercise, I will not call you Daddy, but address you as all others do, as 'Aaron'. The fact that I share half of your genes shall not have any bearing. I do

not belong to the clan of men. I belong to the clan of 'womkind', based on gender, not blood. Despite all that, I love you dearly."
"This much I know. Go on. I am a member of mankind, OK, I accept this, I am, while you, all of you, belong to the gender womkind, OK, I shall accept this as well," says Aaron.

"Over to you, Zoe." replies Susie.
"We, womkind, accuse all mankind, meaning all males. You, as the only male here, have been selected to represent all of mankind. You are here to hear our grievances, offer your views in defence, tell us of changes you will put into place to correct and remedy what you are about to hear."

Aaron laughs, "What an interesting idea, I must say, it is never boring when you get together. This is going to be fun."

Sheila joins in. "We understand, that you, the person named Aaron, have not personally carried out any atrocities. Most likely, none of what we reveal to you is your fault or doing. The person named Aaron is innocent of any or most of those inhumanities. We blame these on your gender, and because of you not rectifying these wrongdoings, you are as guilty of those crimes as the next man."
"I will not take it personally," replies Aaron.

"Here is some of the evidence," Kysa steps to the DVD player and presses the play button.
"Enough," Aaron says after a few moments, "I get the picture," Kysa stops the DVD. Gasha points to her folders, "Inequalities across the board." Aaron views some of the content.

All women present their information. A look at the various headings summarises the women's issues. "We each, or at least most, have personal experiences to add to the long list of wrongdoings," adds Zoe.

"I see." Aaron says, "I, as men's representative, now need to defend my gender from those accusations."

"Yes," replies Susie.

Aaron bows down and nods, he looks at the group to say, "Guilty as charged."

"Have you, at any time in your life, done anything to help our gender?" asks Sheila.
"I guess opening a car's door for a lady does not count," Aaron says without an expression, "I have helped, but I have never separated my help based on gender."

"What good deed have you done?" asks Nadira.
"I made several documentaries of tribes in Africa, the Amazon Delta, confronting stories from South East Asia and several assignments in war ravaged countries, to bring the plight of people to the eyes of the world. I have paid my taxes, which in turn help the country and its people," Aaron answered.
"Did you get paid for these assignments?" asks Ramona.
"I was honoured with several awards and have received financial compensation. Yes, to answer your question."

Sheila continues the questioning, "And you drove in a black limousine to collect these awards, followed by lavish dinners. You had the time of your life, were invited to functions to rave on about the plight of the poor sods that featured in your productions. All the while, you are collecting brownie points, adoration, standing ovations, the talk of the town, ego-boosting, self-serving, glorifying rewards, that you humbly call compensation."
Aaron swallows.
Sheila carries on, "Yet, six, nine or twelve hours away, the subjects of your glory continue to live in the same mud, crap, filth and

unspeakable conditions that you found them in. Would all of this be correct?"
Aaron slowly nods to say, "In essence, yes. I am guilty as charged."
Nameless One begins, "So your motivation was, to bring the misery and plight of these people to the eyes of the world, your words in essence?" Aaron nods, "I said this, yes."
Zoe starts, "Could it not be the case, that you did seek such places for the sole purpose to gain fame, a step up the ladder in men's hierarchy, the posts, the titles, the doors it opened, in other words, have they not all been used, to further your benefit or standing in the community and ... feed your ego?"

Repeatedly Aaron swallows, "If I am brutally honest, I must say, that could be seen to be the case."

The Nameless One continues, "How much of the proceeds have been returned to the ones in need? Have you travelled back, to see if their lot in life has improved, thanks to your efforts?"
"None and no are my answers," Aaron replies.

Sheila asks, "While on the surface you appear as a respectable person, honoured by your peers, privileged to enter through doors that are locked to most, all this built from the misery of others, your fellow men?"

Aaron not sure whether to shake or nod replies, "You are right, Sheila, that is close to the truth. It had never occurred to me, I never saw it, as you and the others are pointing out."
Ye Myo said, "Because you are a man."

"My, my," Aaron says, "as much as I would like to say otherwise, I can't. Overall, everything you said seems to make sense. I am guilty. On the other hand, this is now becoming a personal attack on my person, which has little to do with the so-called crimes of my gender, that I have been called to defend."

“Can you think of any misery, any wrongdoing, any pain and injustice that have, at its source, not been caused by men? Think of any disadvantage that men need to suffer where women enjoy the spoils?” asks Sheila.
"Yes, I can," Aaron replies, "circumcision is one; the single father does not get similar social support as women do. There are no shelters for abused men who suffer at the hands of their women. If women rape men, they need to carry that burden or be ridiculed. It does happen. It seems that by nature, men are alone, while women congregate, have bonds, and are closer to one another. More men are victims of crimes and violence. Suicide rates among men are seven times higher than for women. By that, I mean actual deaths, not attempts that do not result in deaths, which are higher in women. Occupational death is 11 times higher in men. Only a select few countries grant the father parental leave."

“If worldwide the literacy rate is 88 for women to every 100 men that will have some bearing on why women are not equally represented in other areas. Most men have a shorter life than women.”
Kysa asks, “How can men be alone? They have created their own organisations, no women allowed. Even the pubs in some countries were the exclusive realm of men. We had to fight to be able to vote. How many religious leaders are women? We are in general, excluded from high office. How many women, who carried their peoples’ hope, end up shot, assassinated, blown to bits, if they challenged the high chairs of men? But you are right, we are closer to one another. I will tell you why. We, the gender of women, have made everyone on earth. We gave life to each human being. We are mothers by instinct and nature. Even a three-year-old girl is already a mother within.”

"Yes, you are mothers of all. Are you not to blame for what we have become? Have you not reared us on your breasts, been with us every day, and have we not been under your influence and guidance since the day we were born?" Aaron answers. "Should not I be the accuser? Have I not become what you made me?"
“Interesting,” remarks Gasha, “the built-in defence mechanism, men is not to blame. He can even blame his own mother for his life.”

Gasha continues, “Men are the ones that tried to keep us enslaved in the kitchen, the cooking pot, our expression of self. Keep us ignorant, uneducated, dependant on your mercy, all that was just 50 to 100 years ago.
Our brains are that much smaller, you, men, told us, we do not have the capacity to be equal. How many of us believed you?

The cooking pot, our paradise, and what are you doing to us now? You cast us in roles, in the world of movies, as men. You try to brainwash us that we act as you do. Some of us have become as men, in their behaviour and ruthlessness. Be that in the courts, business, even in sports. Boxing for women to show, we are no different.

In your obsession to rule, you must show your superiority, you change the rules to suit your ends. Men now do fight to near death and broadcast it, collect bets, not realising the slip to the deep and darkest times of barbarism. But this is really getting me to the boil: You train OUR children in the same violent games, caged fights without rules, this is true, it is happening, so that from the age of six, and tomorrow perhaps five, you can sit at the sidelines and clap, to say ‘that’s my boy’.”
“You will not stop there, girls will be next, I have no illusions about this,” she adds in anger.

Sheila adds her views, “Look at the shelves in the book stores, 'How to be successful'. You will find not an ounce of heart, of love, of compassion, of empathy. On display, the total disregard of humanity. These are the teachings of your leadership, all geared to awaken the greed.”
Aaron responds, “Perhaps aggression, even the capacity to murder may well be due to our evolutionary past. The need for survival, conquer or perish, kill or be killed, has led to this. Today, we try to defuse this innate trait with sports. Sport is war in a sense, a means to discharge aggressive tension in a mostly controlled manner.

Death is not victory. The aim is to discharge mostly male aggression. We are aware of that. Sport replaces war. This is the aim. Males tend to resort to physical aggression quicker than the female gender. Women are not immune from that, they too have aggression, just the means they utilise are different."

Zoe says, "So you are aware of this. Yet you, males, use the media to spread and incite such behaviours. Statistics, they say do not lie. The amount of time children and teenagers spent, being exposed to watching violence has a direct relationship in their later lives and they are more likely to commit acts of aggression."

In reply, Aaron said, "Statistics can be used to fit any purpose. You, as the viewer, have the power to select any channel, to switch such things off, or to select another. Therefore, if a violent tendency is not in you, you cannot become violent due to media influences. People interested in fishing, romance, adventure, whatever, are most likely inclined to watch such channels, likewise with violence."

Sheila adds, "Aaron, the capacity to murder, our evolutionary past, words you just mentioned. Down Under, we have our fair share of potent critters, but none have enough poison, venom, or toxin to extinguish life itself. No creature has the capacity, ability, or interest to even try. Aaron, is it not insanity that men have developed weapons that can erase life, not just the enemy, but every living thing? The most intelligent creature on earth, isn't that insane?"

"Look at marketing, a world controlled by men." Adzumi adds, "Say something long and often enough and it becomes the truth, Hitler already knew that. Have you not taken the repetition of marketing, applied it to the world of so-called 'entertainment', to mould the whole world to your sense of 'ideal'?"

"Are not the blockbusters repetitions of violence, of destruction, of inhumanities, annihilation, all, the result of the sick mind of men? You have us believe that people demand such stuff. You have

achieved your marketing objectives, you have created this demand, you, and only you are to blame. Bake in your glory."
Aislinn remarks, "You blame us, all mothers, for rearing you to become like this. Each mother must have tried, throughout all generations. Each feels as failure as a result. Yet what can we do? What is it in men that make you like this? We do not know. The women in Imperial China must have gone through agony, their toes broken, their feet bound and tied, known as the 3-inch lotus feet. In Victorian England, a tiny waist was achieved by imprisoning the body in tight corsets; eating arsenic to aid the complexion and the appearance of stretched necks with rings in Africa, India, and Asian cultures."

"Menstruating women are forced to sleep inside cowsheds during their periods, overweight or super skinny, whatever the local cultural ideal may dictate. Much of it is still practised to this very day, either to increase a woman's attractiveness or to make her appear ugly to guard against other men's advances; the painful genital mutilations of girls, their virginity being auctioned off for the highest bidder. The horrendous suffering, mutilations, deformities, and deaths of millions of women throughout history for not being acceptable the way they were born. And even today, billions and billions of dollars are spent in the beauty industry and plastic surgery. Are we not worthy of being accepted as we are?"

Nadira asks, "If you could make amends, what would you do? What would you change?"
"Yes, yes," Aaron is thinking, "what would I do? To be honest, and I say this because you asked, I would perhaps go, get a drink and try to forget what you accused me of. I would watch TV, read a book, anything, to move my thoughts away from this. Most likely, my life would continue as before."
Aislinn says, "I thought as much."

"But perhaps that may also be some escape mechanism, as I have been hit with all this in a few short minutes," Aaron continues, "Let's face it, people, who can devote their life for the purposes of genuinely helping others are very, very rare. This may have nothing to do with gender, as history has shown special people on either side of the gender divide."

"What then makes these rare people so special, the ones that are truly selfless, no rewards expected and received, not even the reward in an after-life. Not even the reward to be reborn, as a higher form of self. Are there such people and what makes them so rare? Is it perhaps that no such people exist, yet the need for them, or the inner wish for such, makes us create them, if only as an illusionary substitute? The legends that cannot be asked to verify their deeds?"
"Unfortunately, we are not here to sidetrack, into widening discussions, we are here to find out what to do with you," said Adzumi.

"What would you suggest we do with you, Aaron," asks Gasha.
"To be fair, it seems that you have done your homework, furthermore, I am outnumbered 12 to 1. As one, I can only have the capacity of one man, whilst you have the combined resources of 12. I am disadvantaged."

"Is not your brain larger than ours?" asks Sheila.
"Even if it were, it is not twelve times larger," he answers.
"Granted, that does give us an advantage. Are not the victims always at a disadvantage?" remarks Ye Myo.
"In addition," adds Aaron, "this has been a surprise, I had no time for preparations."
Nadira comments, "This is also true."
"But hey, it's going to be a great play," Aaron says. Aislinn remarks, "Even on their way to the gallows, they do not understand."

Some are laughing, except Susie. With a forced smile, she walks up, to sit on Aaron's lap, "Thank you, Daddy, for your help. We did not know how you would take it. Thank you," as she hugs him deep and long.

"As the blade comes down, they will want to know if it worked smoothly," adds the Nameless One. Susie unleashes a series of loud kisses directly in her father's right ear. Both of her hands cup the left in an attempt to shield him from hearing the remarks of the others.
"Another of their gender will oil the track, they will even count the heads for us, but they will not understand," says Kysa. Zoe laughs,

"The last one will ask the most stupid question, 'where have they all gone?' he'll ask."

Tanisha stayed in the background throughout this time. She did not ask Aaron a single question. She remains subdued, while infectious laughter afflicts most of the other women. Susie calls out, "Thank you, everyone, that was an interesting little exercise."

Aaron asks, "I hope I get a ticket to the show."
"You will, Daddy," Susie replies.
"I'm glad to be of help darling," Aaron whispers in her ear.
"Enjoy your coffee, come, lay down a bit and stretch your legs."
"If I didn't know you that well, I would think you are trying to get rid of me," he says, as Susie leads him away.
"Could I do that, Daddy?" she asks.
"Good night, all," he calls out.
"Good night, Aaron, and thank you, for your participation.

This book has less than 150 pages, yet it is so heavy

Chicago, USA, S & C Ryder, Publishing House

The intercom announces, "Someone is here to see you, a Sally Cramer, Sir".
"Please send her in, Sue," replies Sam Ryder.
Sam Ryder gets up from behind his desk to walk towards the woman entering his office. She is dressed in a grey suit carrying a small case. She stretches her hand out to greet Sam, "Sally Cramer of C.M.J. & Associates."

She hands over her card.
"I'm Sam Ryder," he studies the card, "please, Mrs. Cramer, please do take a seat."
"You are a lawyer?" he asks.
"Yes, I am." Sally pulls a photograph from her wallet to show Mr. Ryder, "Do you know this lady?"
"Is this not Xia, the young Chinese girl, the book...?"
"'I want to die', is the name of the book." she replies.

“Oh yes, yes, yes, oh I am so glad you are here,” speaking into the intercom, “Sue, please bring me the folder of the young Chinese girl, the one with the advance orders.”
Mr. Ryder laughs, “You would not believe the stir this has caused. We have advance orders for over a million.”
Sue places the folder onto the desk to correct Mr. Ryder, “No, no, Sir, more like 3 million, and rising.”

“Never, in all my days in publishing has demand outstripped supply,” says Mr. Ryder, “Mrs. Cramer, I’m so glad you are here. We can sell 5 million in less than a week. I am willing to throw all our resources behind this work, without any hesitation. We can justify a 10 million print run easily. Mrs. Cramer, I am willing to finance the lot and offer prepayment, a substantial amount, and...”

“Sorry for interrupting you, Mr. Ryder,” says Sally, “could I have a look at the legal documents which Ying Kim Xia signed.”
“But of course. Sue, the legal papers please.”
Sam Ryder’s enthusiasm does not affect Sally.

Sue brings a small folder from which Sam Ryder pulls several pages to hand to Sally. She glances briefly at the documents, checking the placement of signatures, quantity and dates.
"Mr. Ryder, would you be so kind to give me a photocopy of these?"
“Certainly, Mrs. Cramer, I thought they were very professional. She must be a student in the legal profession, I suppose.”
Sally waits until the photocopies are in her hands before she continues, “No, Mr. Ryder, she is not. I prepared these documents on Ying Kim Xia’s behalf.”

“I trust they are all in order?” Sam Ryder replies, “Can we go ahead with printing?” His eyes reveal the sparkles of excitement.

“Off the record, Mr. Ryder, you seem like a respectable person with very special qualities,” says Sally, “on the record, Mr. Ryder, there is no way on earth that you can print 100 copies for the amount of $480. There is no way on earth that the retail cost of 100 copies can be $480 also.”
“I know, Mrs. Cramer, I am fully aware of this,” Sam Ryder smiles. “The old Samuel has a heart, after all. He did not add any margins,

in fact he went out of his way to give this book prime position in his store."
"Mr. Ryder, the Press reports tell of 5000 books. Did Ying Kim Xia increase the order? How did she pay for them?"
Sam Ryder, slightly embarrassed shrugged it off, "Oh no, she did not increase the order. You see, we cannot print 100 books. We are not geared for such small numbers. 10000 is normally our minimum."

"Are you not here to allow us printing?" asks Sam Ryder.
"No, Mr. Ryder," responds Sally.
"Oh dear, the mistake we made with 'published by'," says Sam Ryder, "you see, Mrs. Cramer, an error has occurred. We have made a mistake and had the words 'Published by S & C Ryder' on all the books. The boys downstairs got it wrong. I take full responsibility for that."

"When we became aware of it, I issued press statements and paid for newspaper and TV spots to correct the information. Once a book is released, how can we get it back when it has sold out? We also tried reaching Mrs. Ying Kim Xia, here is the letter, and offered her compensation for our professionally embarrassing mistake. Ying Kim Xia, despite what it says on the book, is the publisher. We do not claim otherwise. We have acknowledged that and made amends. Unintentionally, this blunder has occurred. All our books are published by 'S & C Ryder', with this being the first ever exception. I have failed to let the guys know."

Sally notices the letter addressed to Ying Kim Xia, her eyes glance at the figure for compensation, $5000. She returns the letter.
"Mr. Ryder, this letter is addressed to Ying Kim Xia. I am not privileged to read it."

"You must be here, because of the editing," Sam says, "with all respect to Ying Kim Xia and the content of her story, no publisher could knowingly print spelling errors, mistakes in grammar or punctuation. Under my instructions, these are corrected and Ms. Ying Kim Xia signed a release, sight unseen."
"I have trust in our editor and am certain that he has not changed the story's content in essence."

"No, Mr. Ryder, none of these are my reasons for being here. I am very touched by what your intentions were. You have done more than one could possibly ask. You have, at your own loss, tried to rectify errors and I respect all this. You are well-intentioned, and if I may say so, your heart is in the right spot."

"Mrs. Cramer, Ms Ying Kim Xia's book has less than 150 pages, yet it is so heavy, I can barely lift it. I have read five pages to this very day. That is all I was able to read, without it affecting me beyond description."

"You have high ethics, very rare to find these days."
"Oh, don't get me wrong, Mrs. Cramer, we're still here to make money, but thank you for saying so."

"Mr. Ryder, I am not here on Ying Kim Xia's behalf. I am not here to give the go-ahead for printing."
"Yes, Mrs. Cramer, why are you here?"
"I came here to get the facts," says Sally, "and the facts are: quantity 100 books, for a cost of $480, yet you printed 5000 instead and released them all."
She paused a moment.

"There are now 5000 books in circulation, fifty times more than intended, fifty times more than ordered by Ying Kim Xia."
"Yes," said Sam Ryder, "that is correct."
"The issues of editing, correcting the spelling etc, and the error re who published the books are not of concern," says Sally. "Mr. Ryder, are you aware of Ying Kim Xia's current condition?"

"No. As I explained, we have been unable to make contact with Ms Ying Kim Xia, although we've tried. How is she?" asks Sam Ryder.
"Are you aware of the media hype, when the book was released?" she asks.

"Yes, of course, everyone is. That is what brought all the advance orders. They continue to grow without end. People suggest we're holding back on purpose," answers Sam Ryder. "We have heard that someone received a million dollars for just one book. It is true, it happened.

We stand accused of all sorts of sinister intentions, to raise expectations, to whip up demand, to go in for the kill with some calculated marketing strategy. People sometimes cannot believe the truth. We cannot print without permission of the author, regardless of how much money is on offer. It is as simple as that."
"Well Mr. Ryder, can we talk off the record? By that I mean can we talk in confidence, that nothing may leave this room?"
"Yes, Mrs. Cramer, you have my word."
"I am a lawyer, Mr. Ryder, I rarely believe any word, but I am inclined to believe yours," Sally says.
"Ying Kim Xia is in a mental institution, Mr. Ryder. She has been in a mental hospital since the day of her book's release, Mr. Ryder. Ying Kim Xia is out of her mind with guilt, Mr. Ryder. Instead of 100 books on her conscience, she will need to carry fifty times more, once she knows the full extent of what has transpired. Can you understand that, Mr. Ryder?"
Silently Sam Ryder nods.

"I am a professional, Mr. Ryder. I have learned to keep my emotions under control. I am a lawyer and I can play poker. No one can read me, Mr. Ryder. At this minute, Mr. Ryder, I am fuming with every ounce of my being and I don't know at whom to scream, to let it all out."
Sally's hands shake.

"Some crazy reporter has dragged Ying Kim Xia out of her bed in the middle of the night, set lights and camera onto her face, virtually accusing her of murder, Mr. Ryder. She ran throughout the night, trying to flee from his words. She was found hours later at a distant cemetery trying to cut her hand off with a rock."
Sam Ryder is stunned.
"Heung Shek Cemetery, at Tsuen Wan, Hong Kong, is a long, long way up hill, Mr. Ryder. She ran all that way, don't ask me how."
Sam Ryder's mouth is open. He is shaking his head as he looks at Sally Cramer.

"Mr. Ryder," Sally continues, "the reporter had told her, that a woman had died, from the touch of her book. A certain Mrs. Snyder, a Mary Snyder."
"Yes, I do remember that name," says Mr. Ryder.

"I have investigated the death and circumstances surrounding her death, Mr. Ryder, and I am certain, no court in the land could attribute her death to the touch of a book. The news channel that broadcast the story whipped it out of proportion, creating media hype based on some minor, flimsy, circumstantial, fabricated, and meaningless so-called 'evidence'. None of it had any relationship to the book or its content."
Sam Ryder listens attentively.

"An elderly woman, tired of living, a Mrs. Dulcie Nielson, brought the news to the station. She herself had the wish of death, which was in her before she ever became aware of the book. All the fallout that followed Dulcie Nielson speaking on live TV, seem to me as artificially inflated, empty and irrelevant reports that were bluntly bashed into shape by the station, to meet their needs to perpetuate a myth of their own making."

"I have met Mrs. Nielson. She is a lovely person, and she acknowledges that her words put into a context quiet different to how they portrayed on air. Several sections of material recorded with her never aired."

"She insisted to take the book home, and she did. Do you know, Mr. Ryder, they had offered to repair her steps. Live on air they had told her, the steps already repaired. This was a lie. Some weeks later, she fell and got injured."
Mr. Ryder shook his head.

"I have further investigated several of the other claims, released by the station, reports of people becoming unconscious, outbreaks of severe stress symptoms, dyspnoea and respiratory problems, onset of suicidal depressions and such like, attributed to the touch or the showing of the book's cover on air. I am yet to find any evidence that could even remotely be fabricated to a link between the book and the conditions the book is accused to have caused."

"Mr. Ryder, I am not here to sue. Mr. Ryder, I have no mandate from Ying Kim Xia. I am not here as her lawyer. I can say this; I would have ripped you apart, in court, if you had printed a second run to line your pockets. With all respect, having heard the motivation behind your decisions, I cannot fault your intentions. Despite this, it will be Ms Ying Kim Xia, who will carry the unnecessary burden of knowing that circulation is fifty-fold to what she had asked for."

"Mr. Ryder, have you read the book?"
"No, Mrs. Cramer, I tried, but ..."
"You will find the saying 'Sticks and stones will hurt my bones' ... etcetera, etcetera, is not true at all."

"Oh, Mrs. Cramer, I am at a loss of words, I do admit. Ying Kim Xia, you say is hospitalised? Is there any way I can assist, doctors..., treatments..., some means of help..., financial support, travel, I don't know how, whatever, what can be done?"

"Thank you, Mr. Ryder. You've done enough."
Sam Ryder stands up and turns to look out of the window.
Unnoticed, Sally Cramer walks to the door, "Good bye, Mr. Ryder."
As Sam turned, the door had closed behind her.

What is it all about? No one is telling

Basel, Switzerland, Susie's place, upstairs

It was one of those sleepless nights, just before midnight. Aaron could not settle down to rest. Out of sheer boredom, he switches to the news channel and then looks out of the window, not really paying attention to the news report.

Downstairs, Susie is engaged in lively discussions with her friends, no doubt working through the play they seem to be preparing. It was usual for them to spend the whole night up, to go to sleep the next morning until midday, with bodies spread all over the living room. Aaron settles back into his chair, increasing the volume of the speakers.

"The news from faraway Chicago is this. Mrs. Dulcie Nielson died following a fall that injured her hip. Who is Dulcie Nielson, you may wonder?"

"Some of our viewers may recall the story that made headlines across the world, not that long ago, on another channel, I might add. The book with the curse, titled 'I want to die', so the story goes, apparently killed Mrs. Snyder."

"The book, written by a young Chinese girl named Ying Kim Xia, apparently telling the true story about her mother, Ying An Jia. The book fetched the highest price ever paid for a single copy of an unknown author."

"How much you may wonder? A cool 1 million US dollars. Yes viewers, 1 million US dollars, although the retail cost was just $4.80 minutes earlier."

The mother's name triggers some buttons in Aaron's brain, and he pays total attention to the report.

"But that is not all. It was Dulcie Nielson, a patient in a local hospital at the time, who saw the event unfold. "Mrs. Snyder, another patient, the so-called first victim, was admitted; upon waking from a 13-day coma, she touched a book and... died."

"The story doesn't end there. Dulcie brought the story to the attention of a local news station, channel M-Kay Y News, which broadcast it around the globe. Dulcie sold her information for the princely sum of $50, and a promise to get her steps fixed. The whole ensuing hype is based on her words."

"It gets better. Live on air, while Dulcie was telling her story, a young camera operator recorded the station's promise to get her steps fixed. During a commercial break, the operator was swiftly promoted to news desk reporter. He repeatedly told Dulcie not to worry, that her steps had already been fixed, in order to get an interview with her without interruptions."

"Hello viewers, are you still with me? I hope so, because there seems to be no end to this. The reporter, the young man, who just a minute earlier was a camera operator, is now suing the station for an undisclosed amount, due to the fact, that he was the one telling Dulcie the steps had been fixed. He is suing for stress. The stress caused by the fact, that he told her a lie. Understandable, as the young man had no knowing if this was truth or fibs. He was instructed by the station's manager to say these words to Dulcie."

"Bear with me; it gets better. Dulcie, who, with her own words, admitted live on air that she had a death wish, got her wish. The director of the station, Jerry Baxter, who turned the $50 investment, which was Dulcie's fee, into a small fortune worth several million dollars within hours, selling publishing rights all over the place, refuses his desk reporter's stress claim outright."

"It is not a funny story at all, in all honesty, the station director's argument for not budging to the stress claim is..., the fact that Dulcie's dream came true, by that he means her death wish."

"I wonder if Dulcie's family gets an invite to the station, perhaps a new segment, like 'Thank you for helping my mum's dream come true,' but I don't want to sound sarcastic."

"But why would a woman with a death wish bother getting her steps fixed, I hear you ask? The story continues. A young lawyer in Chicago asked a different question."
"Sally Cramer, from C.M.J. & Associates in Chicago wanted to know why the steps had not been fixed when the station publicly declared that they had already been repaired, while Dulcie was still being interviewed."

“Lawyer Sally Cramer, must have had a premonition, as her claim on the station came two weeks before Mrs. Dulcie Nielson had her tragic fall.”

“Please, dear viewers, bear with me a bit longer; it’s not over yet. As a result of the story going to air, and the myth of its curse, the young author, Ms Ying Kim Xia, upon hearing the news that her words had caused the death of another person, ran up to a Hong Kong cemetery, trying to cut her hand off with... a rock.”
“The stress this whole sad affair inflicted on the young woman, the author, caused her to end up in a mental hospital. But she, the young writer, is not suing for that.”

"The printers, S & C Ryder Publishing House, also in Chicago, USA, have been inundated with massive orders, virtually guaranteeing a bestseller overnight, due to the unprecedented demand created by the news station’s publicity. What is it all about? No one is telling."
"It turns out that 5000 copies all sold out within 30 minutes on the day the story went to air. That is all there is; there are no second editions because the author retains all her rights. No one can contact her to get her permission for another print run. The fact that the whole affair left her hospitalised may have something to do with it."
"So if you do have one of those 5000 copies, you may be interested to hear that your $4.80 purchase price is now worth at least $28,000 and rising. Do your bidding online."
"Word on the grapevine is that channel M-Kay Y News is trying to buy the film rights to the book but is unable to reach the author. How much did the young author get out of all this? So far, absolutely nothing, and she may not even be aware of all that has transpired."

"So what is happening in our parts of the woods, and ‘wood’ is the current in-noun in Switzerland?" Aaron opens his wardrobe doors, collecting items of clothing. "A group of protesters is sick and tired of chasing after every truck and person carrying chainsaws, trying to protect trees they may be about to fell. The protesters have now presented the Federal Assembly with a petition and requested the introduction of new laws, and I quote: 'The felling of trees is a crime akin to planned and premeditated murder. Therefore, the cutting down of any tree must be dealt with in the harshest possible terms'. End of quote."

"The protesters do not accept any reason for cutting any trees down; they claim the justifications used, such as age and health of a tree, public safety, branches falling, etc., are convenient means to rid spaces of life-giving trees. By life-giving, they mean the tree's ability to convert dirty air into clean air."

Susie's place, downstairs

The twelve women are deep in discussion; the next phase of the plan is on the agenda. Aislinn, "I can't see how it is possible to distinguish one from another. I don't understand how this plan is put into practise."

Zoe says, "Do we need to know? The more each of us knows, the more at risk we will be from each other. Don't you understand that, Aislinn?"

"I do understand it, and we have accepted lies from each other to safeguard each other's safety," answers Aislinn, "but it also means that any answer we give could be a lie. It makes decision-making somewhat difficult, as we don't really know what we are discussing anymore."

"You've got it wrong, Aislinn; we accept lies only to protect the how, what, who, where, and when of the plan; that is all," answers Zoe, "to protect the mechanism, the intelligence behind the implementation."

Sheila says, "You can bet your bottom dollar, as soon as the statistics change, they will come looking."

"And after the second warning, all hell will break loose; have no illusions about this," says Nadira.

Gasha added, "They will get the medical profession in first, then look at the water supply, aerial spraying, planes that were in the area at the time, food chain, whatever."
Susie remarks "Aren't we lucky that neither of us studies medicine or biology?"

Tanisha asks, "Are we fully aware of what is going to happen?" As soon as we make the demands public, every woman on earth may well pay the price, as all become branded the enemies of men."
"By making our demands public, every leader in the world will want to know how it is done, so that they can influence the gender balance for their own ends. It is a very dangerous game we're playing," adds Tanisha. "Who gives us the right to make such a decision?"

Aaron comes downstairs with a small suitcase in his hand and says, "Susie, I need to go. I don't have time to explain."
"But I thought you had a few more days?" says Susie.
Aaron replies, "Change of plans, sorry, got to go." He hurries out of the house.

Gasha calls out, "What if he heard us? What if he does us in and reports us?"
Susie runs outside to follow Aaron. "Daddy, wait..."
Aaron stops; Susie reaches him, holds his head, looks him deep in the eyes, and then says, "You must never leave me without a kiss."

They embrace and kiss. "So sorry to rush out at short notice; I love you."
"And I love you," answers Susie. "Take care, Daddy."
When Susie returns to the house, Gasha asks, "Does he know? Does he have any idea?"
Susie laughs, "Relax, he does not know; I would have seen it in his eyes. I think he has a personal issue. He'll tell me when he's good and ready."

Kysa joins in the debate, saying, "Look at what is happening. How many powerful men have frozen their bodies? The ones who reached the end of their lives, frozen bodies, paid for in advance, to be awoken when technology is able to prolong their lives indefinitely. If they could, they would replant their brains into young men and so live on forever."

Tanisha asks, "Who has the technology to put this plan into action? Susie, Zoe, I have the feeling you two know more than you are telling us."
Susie responds, "Do you think the world knows what is really going on behind closed doors? What if the technology of cloning or stem-cell research were never made public? Then add a few years of trial and error to it, and no one would know, would they?"
"The ones with all the resources would have wardrobes filled with body parts, their own newly grown duplicates. They would never need to wait for donors if things needed fixing."

“To answer your earlier question, Tanisha, who gives us the right, you were asking,” says Zoe, “are not most if not all decisions done by those who feel the calling in their hearts?”

Nameless One, "When we look at history, yes, for a time some reached their goal, and then time played its cards and dealt some surprises."

"As much as we may wish to influence the future," says Adzumi, "the future will do its own thing and deal us all some surprises, I’m sure. Aislinn and I are working on a website to get the views of other women as well." The women discussed the ‘plan’ until late. So many questions have no answers.

Keep these memories close to your heart

Chicago, USA, a local cemetery

It was late afternoon with light rain, when the body of the late Dulcie Nielson was put to rest. Sally Cramer walks up to a young man who is dressed in a grey suit, wearing a sweater underneath that must have been in fashion 50 years ago.

“Did Dulcie take this one in for you?” she asks the young man.
“Yes, she did. She was a lovely lady.”
“I know you liked her,” says Sally, “would you mind if we share your umbrella?”
"No, please come under, but forgive me, who are you?" asks Tom.
"I am Sally Cramer, and if I’m not mistaken, you must be Tom, the newsman?" she inquires.

“Yes, that is where I met Dulcie. You know, we became friends. She invited me so many times, telling me her whole life’s story,” says Tom.
“I am sure you have given her much joy,” says Sally.
“Do you know that Jerry Baxter, the director of the station, started several new channel programmes, all geared for the elderly?” says Tom.
“I didn’t know that, Tom,” she replies.
"Yes, he did. So many age care facilities, wheelchair manufacturers, medical supply companies, anything the elderly needed, became station sponsors," Tom says. "A pity Mrs. Nielson died. Jerry Baxter had plans for her."
"Jerry Baxter sure knows how to capitalize on an opportunity and make the best of it," Tom says, "but he didn’t fix her steps, and I do feel so miserable about it. I could have fixed them myself, but it just never occurred to me. I think some legal firm is suing the station for that," says Tom.

“Yes, so I’ve heard,” answers Sally.
Tom adds, “And it is my entire fault; I told her the steps were fixed, repeating what the manager had told her earlier.”
“Tom, you have given her some joy in her life; remember that and keep these memories close to your heart.”

Both were deep in thought when approached by a Japanese woman. "My deepest condolences to you both," she says. "I am

Shima Chika, and I recognize you as the news reporter from the station, am I correct?"

"That is correct," replies Tom.
"I know this is not the right moment, but I wish to meet with you, maybe a little later?" she says.
"Yes," Tom replied, and all three stood together under two umbrellas, paying their last respects to Dulcie.
When the ceremony was over, people dispersed.

"I am making the assumption that none of us belong to Mrs. Nielson's family; could we go to the restaurant for a coffee?" asks Chika, "all of us, if that's OK?"
"Yes, that would be fine," answers Tom.
"Oh, perhaps you have things to discuss with Tom," asks Sally.
"No, no, I have no secrets; please, you are invited too, of course," says Chika.

The restaurant is almost empty. All settle at a table near the windows. Chika opens her purse to give both her business cards. Sally inserted her card into Chika's purse, unnoticed by Tom, while Tom gave both women his card.
"Oh," Chika notes, "I thought you two were a couple."
"No, Mrs., or is it Ms. Chika?" says Sally, "we met just now, at the funeral."
"No, I'm not married, and please call me Chika," she says.
"To explain my being here and my interest in meeting you, where do I begin?" says Chika. "I am interested in women's stories; that would best describe it, I think. I gather all sorts of stories from women about women, as long as they are women. I do not make much sense to you, do I?"
Both laugh, "It will become clearer as you go on, I'm sure," says Sally.

"Well, in a way, I am like a freelance reporter; oh, have no fear, I am not a reporter in that sense; more like, I collect stories that relate to women's issues or experiences that women go through; in a way, stories on any subject, as long as a woman is at the centre of it; does this make sense?"

"Which publication do you work for, Chika?" asks Tom.

"Oh, none at all. Now, all I am doing is collecting such stories, which maybe some time in the future will become a book, a documentary, or some sort of publication that can hold it all together. That is still a long way off. Freelance, without pay for now, just doing the groundwork and have been for many years. None of my work has yet been published anywhere."

"So how do you support yourself in the meantime," asks Sally, "if you don't mind me asking?"

"Some years ago, I had the good fortune to win a modest amount in a lottery," says Chika. "With my father's help this money is invested to provide me with a small, but steady stream of income, which affords me the luxury of free time, to pursue my interests. I have studied for many years and have no problem to find employment, as two degrees are to my credit."

"It is more the drive in me to collect women's stories that absorbs me at the moment. My reasons for approaching you in the first place are Mrs. Dulcie Nielson and the young Chinese women who had written the book that Mrs. Nielson was talking about in your programme, as well as the woman who died at the time, Mrs. Mary Snyder. These are the subjects of my interest."

"I came to this funeral to pay my respects to Mrs. Nielson. When I recognised you there earlier, I could not resist speaking to you. However, that was not my reason for coming to the funeral. I didn't know I would meet anyone there."

The three sat for an hour in the restaurant, partially getting to know one another and discussing how the event was unfolding when Tom was interviewing the late Mrs. Nielson. Sally Cramer unwittingly heard inside information from Tom, as he was not aware that Sally was the lawyer who instigated legal proceedings against the station.

"But I must be going back now to the station," says Tom. "I'm sure we will catch up again, Chika. I'll fix the tab. The station can pay for this meal. Bye for now."
Tom left, and the two women remained in the restaurant.

"This is such a fascinating interest, Chika." "I am very interested in reading some of your material."
"Oh, you would not believe what I have seen," says Chika. "Can I invite you whenever it suits?"
"I would love that, Chika," answers Sally.

Sally does not reveal the fact that she knows the young Chinese writer; she needs to find out who Chika is first.

Thank you, for remaining calm

Hong Kong, China

Inside a passenger jet plane at 20000 ft, approaching the airport.
“Ladies and gentlemen, please fasten your seat-belts and ensure your luggage is secured safely. We will be approaching Hong Kong International Airport shortly.”

Aaron double-checks his seatbelt and takes in the view over the wing at the right of the plane. His thoughts are elsewhere. He can just make out the fast orange glow in the corner of his eye, a quick sensation of heat, as the plane is shaken by a shudder that frightens everyone aboard.

The far end of the wingtip appears damaged, and alarm sounds are heard. A stream of vapour trails the wingtip. Moments later the speakers reveal some news. “This is the captain speaking. There is no cause for alarm, but I would like you all to remain calm and prepare for an emergency landing."

Aaron signals the flight attendant and makes her aware of the damaged wingtip. Moments later, the captain's voice advises, "Ladies and gentlemen, we have sustained some minor damage on the right wingtip. We are not under attack. Hong Kong Airport confirms that the damage to the wing was caused by a freak accident, a collision with the remnants of a falling meteorite. We are very fortunate for now, as I have full control of the plane and its functions. Let us hope we get down safely." A moment later, he adds, "I am positive we will have a safe landing."

As Aaron looks around the plane, the passengers' faces reveal the inner thoughts each is dealing with.
"All items must be stored under your seat. Please use the oxygen masks now. Place them firmly over your mouth. Please raise your arms if you need assistance. Parents, ensure a secure fit for your child's oxygen mask. Just in case, wear your life-jackets as per instructions. As we prepare to touchdown, bend forwards to place your head between your legs and cover your head with both of your arms. This is a precautionary measure, and thank you for remaining calm."

Apart from the fact that each person is anxious and under some stress, the plane is not behaving any differently from before, despite the damage. Hope is in the thoughts of every passenger. The plane's descent was uneventful. The side of the runway at Hong Kong Airport is lined with emergency vehicles of all descriptions.
"Ladies and gentlemen, we are about to touchdown. Please prepare yourselves now."

All seemed to indicate a safe landing until the plane suddenly tilted sharply to the right. On touchdown, the right wing hits the runway, spewing a trail of sparks behind it. The next moment, the tilt went the other direction, which is all the recollection Aaron has of the landing. Aaron's head is bandaged. He has several cuts on his hands, but he is alive in a hospital in Hong Kong.

Let us keep an eye on the place in the future

Basel, Switzerland, Susie's place

Again, the women debate the 'plan', discussing ethical questions and the likely consequences.
Ramona says, "Why did your dad rush out of the house so suddenly yesterday?"
Susie replies, "In all honesty, I don't know."
"We must be aware that he too is a man and belongs to the other side," says Adzumi.
Nadira says, "I am very worried that the plight of women will increase manyfold if mankind is fully aware of what we are doing. They may try to force the truth out of individual women, who have no idea why they can't bring boys into the world."

Adzumi agrees: "How many will get slapped across their faces, even beaten up? They will be blamed for it."

"They will be interrogated, subjected to torture, and who knows what else" says Nadira.
Gasha adds, "What if your Dad has dobbed us in already and this place is being watched? Perhaps everything we say is recorded this very minute."
At this very moment, a loud knock at the door demands attention.

Susie, somewhat intimidated walks towards the door, "Who is it?"
"This is the police; please open up."
Panic sets in, and most of the women run out the backdoor.
Susie slowly opens the door. Two police officers fill the door-frame.
"We are looking for a woman named Zoe Wilder, says the officer."
"Is she under arrest?" Susie asks, not realising what slipped out. The police officer notices several women in a hurry running through the room.
"Should we have reason to arrest her?" the officer asks.
Susie didn't know what to say.
"Madam, is there a reason for us to arrest Ms. Zoe Wilder?" he asks again.

"Of course not; what a stupid question is this?" asks Susie.
"You brought the subject up, Madam. Where is she?" he asks again.
Susie turns around to see that most women had opted for a quick escape, and she is not sure if Zoe did a runner.
"Well, officers, yes, hmm... no, what I'm saying is, I don't know," she says.

"I am Zoe Wilder, Officer; how can I help?" says Zoe as she comes from behind Susie.
"The blue convertible with this registration number... "Is this yours?" he asks, showing her a notepad with the registration number of the car.
"Yes, it is, officer," Zoe says firmly.
"Are you aware that your car is parked right in front of a fire hydrant, madam?" he asks.
"No, sir, I am not."
"Could I ask you to move your vehicle to some other place before I pull my book out and issue you with a ticket, Madam?" he says.
Zoe gets her keys and says, "Gentlemen, officers, I am so sorry. I shall move it this instant. I did not see the hydrant, honestly."
"It is big enough, Madam. Do you have a problem with your eyesight?"
"No, and I do apologise." It shall not happen again, and thank you for letting me know."

"Is everything alright here, Miss?" the officer directing this question to Susie.
"Yes, yes, of course. Why shouldn't it be?" replies Susie.
"I am just asking, Madam," he says, "and good night."
"Good night, sir."
On their way to the patrol car, they said, "There is something fishy going on in there, don't you think so?"
"Drugs, maybe; let's keep an eye on the place in the future," the other replies.

... you just don't get the words out

Basel, Switzerland, Susie's place

The police had left, and Zoe returned to the house. It took another 15 minutes before all the others reassembled again. Zoe wrote on a

piece of paper, "Not a word about it," and showed it to everyone. Underneath, she scribbled, "Maybe microphones.' Paranoia spread, fuelled by fear and the surprise of how easy it was for the police to knock at the door.
"Tell me, Susie, how many eggs does one put into pancakes?" asks Zoe.
What a weird question, Susie, but she caught on quickly.
"Just two eggs, a bit of flour, and milk, and that's it," she answered.
Sheila was not so easily intimidated, calling out, "Hello boys, I know you can't hear us."

Within moments, the telephone rang: "Susie Cross, please."
"Speaking," replies Susie.
"This is Medical Clinic, Hong Kong. It is about your father, Ms. Cross."
"Yes, go on," Susie answered.
"There has been a bit of a mishap when his plane landed, and he is in the hospital with some injuries," said the voice from Hong Kong.
"Am I able to speak to my father?" she asks.
"Not at this moment, I'm afraid. We are doing some more tests on him. Do not worry; it is not life-threatening. He is not in serious condition. We'll keep you updated. Good bye."
Susie puts the receiver down and stands in silence.
"What's happened?" asks Tanisha.

"Dad's plane went down in Hong Kong. See if you find something in the news," says Susie.
Tanisha and Zoe go upstairs to Aaron's room to see if they can find some news from Hong Kong. Within a minute, both call out, "Susie, come here."
Amateur footage shows the runway lit up, the plane coming in almost touching the ground, and the aileron extending downward. Suddenly, the plane tilts, with the edge of the wing hitting the runway. Following the pilot's correction, the plane now flips the other way and digs the wing into the runway on the other side. Despite that, the plane

remains in a forwards direction, nose first, and disappears into the distance, followed by a large number of rescue vehicles.
"I think, I'm going to be sick," says Susie and heads to the bathroom.

Ye Myo also enters the room. Her eyes were drawn to many of the videos stacked in a shelf: Angola, Congo, Amazon.
She pulls the tape out to search for a more detailed description. Failing to find any, she slides the tape into the machine. Tanisha and Zoe are also interested in what might be on the tape. Adzumi and Nadira also enter the room as the play button starts the tape.
Zoe quickly reduces the sound. The scene reveals men in uniform, a group of women tied together, obviously screaming, and six uniformed men aiming their rifles as a firing squad at the unarmed people.

Within a few seconds, Ye Myo becomes ill and runs to the toilet.
Zoe removes the tape from the player and returns it to the shelf.
Susie returns from the bathroom, saying, "Look, he's my dad; I've got to go there. I'll fly out now." No one mentions the content of the tape.

"Sorry to rush out on you like this; here are the keys. Bye for now," she says and throws Tanisha the keys to the house. "Stay for the night if you want; I don't mind, and neither would Aaron."
They wait ten minutes to make sure Susie is gone and reload the tape, with Nadira saying, "Ye Myo, I know this is very distressing; do not watch this, please, but we need to find out what this is."
"I understand," says Ye Myo.

All women, including Ye Myo, watched the tape. It is in bad quality, as if copied several times over. All the footage is in black and white. It becomes obvious that the film is amateur footage. It is hard to establish which army they could belong to; they could be mercenaries with an order, being the executioners for someone. The tape shows women with their hands tied behind their backs. A long rope connects all the women to each other. Men were herded into the corner of a high, fenced-off area and shot; their bodies lay as they fell, one lot after another.

Silence is in the room. There is no need to speak, nor is anyone able to get a word out. Suddenly Kysa calls out, "Stop, rewind this bit."
Zoe rewinds, "There's the one on the left," says Kysa. Zoe stops the tape in freeze frame.
"The time is maybe 20 years ago," says Kysa. "Could that be Aaron? Could he have been a mercenary 20 years ago?"

"Twenty years ago, they didn't have video. This must have come from film footage recorded off the wall. We will find out soon enough what this is," says Zoe. "We have time on our side; they're both in Hong Kong, at least one is, and Susie is on her way."
"But that can't be Aaron," says the Nameless One. "He makes documentaries. Maybe this is something he had been given by someone else."
"Let's not make any judgements about what this is unless we are 100% sure," says Sheila.
"I agree," adds Aislinn.

"Ye Myo, what country does it say on the sleeve?" asks Zoe.
"Kampuchea," says Ye Myo, "that is Cambodia then."
"Let's note down the time on the tape so we can find it easier when we can compare it to something else," suggests Tanisha.
"It just doesn't want to sink into my head that it could be Aaron; I mean, that is not the man I know.

Why would he leave such stuff sitting here? Susie wouldn't know about this, I'm sure," says Zoe.
"OK, the benefit of doubt until we're absolutely certain," says Sheila, and all agree.
"Let's put this tape back where it was and start at the beginning of the shelf, so it all stays as is, in order."
"I'll take notes," says Sheila.

"Tape 1, Bangladesh," says Nadira.
The Bangladesh tape shows hunger and starvation at their worst.
"Tape 2, Vietnam. That would be before the war."
"Tape 3, Congo. That is Belgian Congo; before 1960, it became the Republic of Congo; yes, these are white mercenaries, probably 1959 or early 1960s, I'd say," says Zoe, "minerals and power games."
"Tape 4, Algiers, let's run that a bit," says Aislinn, "fast forwards, more, stop, play from here."

"There, the third guy from the left... could be, note it down, Sheila, at 12 minutes and a bit. The tape is from 1961. Maybe we can find some cross-references to it somewhere else."

"Look what I found, diaries from long ago," says Nameless One. "Oh no, here it is, Algiers was in 61 and 62, going back in time here, in Congo, in the early part of 1960. Aaron was a mercenary. He took part, not as a cameraman; he held a gun."
"Rhodesia, yes, a mercenary, a paid killer; I can't believe it. Why would he leave that stuff out here in the open?" says Gasha.
"Well, it is his room," says Adzumi, "but can we be sure?"
"How much more evidence do you need?" asks Zoe.

"The video could be him, but we don't know what he really looked like that long ago; it is not evidence; it's circumstantial; that's all it is. We need pictures, perhaps ID cards from the time," adds Tanisha.

"I doubt that we'll find it here," says Nadira, as she pulls a box from a shelf, packed with small folders, typical of the times for photographs.

"Do you think Susie knows about this?" asks Ye Myo.
"Could be," says Tanisha, "but what could she do? It's her father after all. The past is done, whatever is there. Times were different; right becomes wrong. I said that before. We have not lived it yet. As we grow through life, we too will see such changes."

"Being a mercenary for money?" says Nadira. "It's just not on. It is unbelievable."
"Let's not be too superficial by measuring this on our present set of self-righteous values of humaneness," adds Tanisha. "The full circle of life will give us many surprises."
"We all know people get killed in war; here we see how, which the idyllic home-based family is not going to see," says Sheila.

"I have seen it," says Ye Myo. "I know what they can do. They come suddenly and unexpectedly, just like the two police officers. They come with overpowering force. Before you know what happens, five people are dead, then nine, then 20, and then there is only you left. You piss in your pants. Your brain is nearing its bursting point because you cannot understand what is going on. What do they want? We only got a bit of rice in the pots; we have bananas; and we have a few lambs; why not take them?"

Ye Myo Tun finally faces her past; filled with agony, she yells, "Why don't you take it all? Get out of here, you... You murderers, you, you... But when you're only five and your mother is wired to a wooden pallet and men piss all over her, then you just don't get the words out. But that is what happens in war, I guess."

"Look into old people's eyes; in some, you'll see they hide their shame. Others have a never-flickering light. They did something to my mother, but my memory still shields me from that. All I know is that everyone perished except old Nyein. She gave me my name. Ye, she said, for being brave, Myo is for relative, and that you are to me, and Tun, so you shall succeed."

"Stay clear of hatred, guard from evil; her words as a lunch pack for my life. Nyein, have thanks for giving me my name. We are of one blood. Your blood runs in my veins. I am your granddaughter and your sister. I have never forgotten." Ye Myo's head bows in respect.

Are we having secrets now?

Hong Kong, China, Hospital, Accident Ward

Susie's touchdown in Hong Kong went smoothly. The roads are always busy, making it a vibrant and hectic place. The taxi weaves its way towards the hospital.

"Your father is in ward 9; they will know in which room he is up there," says the person staffing the information desk.

"Dad, gosh, I'm so glad you are still breathing," says Susie, embracing her father.

"And you thought only cats had nine lives, but what are you doing? Why are you here?"

"You would have come for me," Susie answers.

"I never, I would have let you rot in hell," he says and laughs.

"Sure you would, Daddy, tell me, how are you? How do you feel? Are you OK? Look at you; you're all bandaged up."

"Easy does it, one question at a time. Good, good, yes, to answer all three; as for the last one, it's only a scratch, I think."
"Would you believe? It was the oddest thing, and I couldn't film it. A meteor hit smack bang into the wing at unbelievable odds. It was a bit of a bumpy landing, but we are all alive, so they tell me. An outstanding effort by the pilot, I want to meet him when I get the chance."

"But why did you come here in the first place? What's in Hong Kong for you? We left this so long ago," says Susie.
"I got a tipoff from somewhere, and I'm here to find something out; that's all," he says. "Are we having secrets now?"
"Wouldn't you want to know?" he says. "I do think tomorrow they will set me free," says Aaron. "Do you have a hotel for tonight?"
"Not yet, but I'll do that as soon as I can get away from you," says Susie.

Hong Kong, China
Clinic for the mentally ill

Next morning Aaron calls Susie, "I'm out of the hospital, just need to visit someone and I'll call you a little later. If you want, take a tour through the city, see how things have changed."

Aaron instructs the taxi driver to an address noted down, a clinic.

Upon arrival he enquires at the counter, "I believe Ms Ying Kim Xia is in your care here."
"Just a second, let's see..., yes, Sir. She is here."
"I would like to visit her," says Aaron.
"Access to Ms Ying Kim Xia is to close relatives and family only, Sir, in other words, no," says the staffer.
"Can I speak to the director," enquires Aaron.

"Just a moment," the attendant arranges a meeting. "Please follow me."

"Hello, I am Director Cheung. You wish to see Ms Ying Kim Xia, yes. I am afraid that is not possible. Ever since the story broke, so many journalists have come dressed as so-called 'relatives', 'friends', or whatever in an attempt to get near her. It is our aim and responsibility to prevent this from happening. These are also the wishes of Ms. Ying Kim Xia." "May I speak to you in confidence, Director Cheung?" says Aaron.
"Yes, please do. But what has happened to you? Your head is all bandaged up."

"The crash landing at the airport, I was on the plane," says Aaron. "I have reason to believe that Ying Kim Xia and I are related."
"I like your sense of humour; please, the door is over there," says the director, laughing. "You are very funny; forgive me, but this is a new one." He can't stop laughing. "Related, this is just so inventive, resourceful, and original; I love it. You wouldn't be from one of those funny shows?"

One can see that Director Cheung must have faced many challenges in his time as director.
"You will find, Director Cheung, that I am not laughing; in fact, I am deadly serious. Allow me to rephrase this. I do respect your desire to protect Ying Kim Xia from any vultures, and I do admire you for it, but please allow me the courtesy to state my case."
"Do you see any resemblance between Kim and me?"
"I see you are Caucasian and Kim is a great deal Chinese; off hand, it is not so easy when mixed races produce offspring," says the director. "I enjoy this laugh, I must say."

"Director Cheung, I am not sharing your joy. Kim could be my daughter, but I cannot be sure. I will explain."

"Two days ago, a report in the news mentioned the name of Kim's mother, Ying An Jia. There are many such names in China. Considering Kim's age and the face of her mother's twin sister on the cover of a book they showed in the news, I am almost certain she is my daughter. Her mother had a birthmark on her right cheek. Her mother's twin does not have such a birthmark. Apart from that, they are almost identical. I knew Kim's mother when she was 16 years old and lost touch with her long ago. I did not know she fell pregnant, but the time could be right, hence my surprise and length of time 'til now to come."

"With all respect, I shall still treat your request with suspicion, unless you can convince me otherwise," said the director.
"I can accept that."
"Can you think of any other differences between the mother and her twin?"
"There were differences in mood swings; one was slightly more introverted; they had a different laugh, and I could tell them apart on that."
"The laugh will be somehow difficult to prove."

"Only if you are indeed genuine, and please do not waste my time if you are not, can a lot be uncovered by comparing your words with statements Kim has already made. You would not be privy to Kim's statements, but if I were to hold them side by side, the likelihood of you possibly being her father may be viewed in a more positive light."

"Please come into my office. Let's see what answers we can find."
"What is the name of the mother's twin, the mother's parents' names, the birthdates of the twins, and the location where they grew up? Any investigative journalist would know the answers to these questions. I will ask you more than this. Are you ready to answer such questions without going away to think, or, in other words, to 'research' the answers?"

"Yes, I am willing to answer all I know, here and now."
"Please allow me a moment to formulate some more questions."
The director takes ten minutes to combine a list of specific questions; only a daughter and father may know about Kim's mother, considering the mother's age at the time. Aaron reads each question, casting his mind back to a different time, Kim's mother was then 16 years old. Despite their age difference, they were in love.

Birthdays, easy; location, easy; what caused the mother's cut on her upper arm? There was no cut on her arm. The name of the

mother's twin is Ying Lijuan. Which of her teeth had a filling? None, unless the fillings were so small as not to be noticeable. What were her favourite songs and her colours? Faint lilac is the answer here. What was her favourite dish? Duck in peach sauce is the answer. How many other siblings did she have? She had a brother, then 12, another sister, then 14, plus the twin sister. Who was her favourite grandparent? The mother on her mother's side, who was a sweet old woman who lived in a wooden shack, she had two goats. Two large trees stood to the right of her building.
Aaron hands his answers to the director.
"Well, I am impressed. Some answers I do not know myself, so I will check with Kim; please wait here."

"The answers to most of my questions appear correct. This does, of course, not prove that you are the father."
"This I do not know with certainty; it's just the likelihood that's there," answers Aaron. "I still have pictures of Ying An Jia, Kim's mother, at 16; please see for yourself."
"Could I see Kim, please?" asks Aaron.

Moments later, the director and Aaron walk through the clinic's parklands. "She's the one over there, the one sitting on her own," says the director.

"An Jia, An Jia," says Aaron, momentarily losing his balance and holding on to the frame of the door, repeating her name.

"Mr. Cross," says Director Cheung, "your mind is in another time. This is not An Jia. This is her daughter. Mr. Cross, are you okay? This is Ying Kim Xia."

"The way she sits, her knees touching one another, her feet outward, just like An Jia used to sit. She looks so much like her, Director Cheung. Her memory is now so fresh in my mind."

Director Cheung says, "Take a little time to absorb this."
"Thank you; may I sit next to her for a moment?" asks Aaron.
"Yes, as long as you are extremely sensitive about it. If she shows signs of being uncomfortable, I request that you leave her be and return here. Agreed?"
"Yes, Director Cheung, I agree."
Ying Kim Xia sees Aaron approaching. From a distance of six feet, Aaron asks, "May I sit there, please?" Kim nods once. Aaron sits at the far end of the bench. He does not speak for a few moments. Neither does Kim.

"I do love this garden," he says eventually.
"Yes, there is a lot of serenity here," Kim adds.
"I'm Aaron."
"I'm Kim; I'm pleased to meet you. Are you a doctor?"
"No, Kim, the director allowed me to sit with you for a moment. I am not a doctor."
"You are from the press?" asks Kim.
Aaron laughs, "Heavens forbid, no, no, thank you; I run a mile from them."
"I'm glad," says Kim. "I'd run many more."
"I need to go now. May I sit with you again, perhaps another time?"
"Yes."
"Thank you, good bye for now." Aaron says.
"Bye."

He returns to the director. "Sir, I do thank you sincerely for this. She has agreed to see me again, at least to sit next to her. She does not appear to be mentally ill."

"Many mental patients are completely normal. You too appear normal, yet you could also be mentally ill, and I would not know it at a glance," answers the director.
"I do not wish to ask her direct questions about her mother; in case I am wrong, this would upset her needlessly."
"Thank you for considering Kim's sensitivities," responds the director.
"I take it that only a DNA sample could answer my question with some degree of certainty?" asks Aaron.
"Yes," replies the director.
"As she is in your care, who can allow such a decision?" asks Aaron.

"You are correct, Ying Kim Xia is in our care, and while this is a mental clinic, personally, I must say I do not like this description at all. Kim is not here as a mental patient. She is free to make her own decisions, even in regards to a DNA test. Could I suggest that you spend time with one another, get to know each other slowly, and that you're both comfortable approaching such a subject gradually as trust between you two establishes and grows?"
"That is excellent advice, director."

Men are capable of anything

Basel, Switzerland, Susie's place

“We now have absolute proof that Aaron was a mercenary, a killer for money,” says Gasha. “Does anyone disagree with this?”

All agreed that this fact has been established.
“We do assume he was a killer. We cannot prove that he actually did kill,” adds Tanisha.

"Come on, be real, Tanisha," Aislinn says. "He is dressed like them, carries weapons, laughs with them, stands by as the bodies pile, and he does not stop it. But we can ask him when he comes back."

Gasha continues to summarise, "Aaron was a mercenary; that is an established fact. Aaron did not prevent the killing of unarmed people; this is also an established fact."

Tanisha agrees with this. Kysa speaks, "But worst of all, we do not know about the footage showing a mass grave of children." No one spoke for a moment.

"I guess our silence is a good indicator of the impact that piece had on our hearts," Nadira says. Gasha continues, "We are always coming back to the same conclusion: men are capable of anything."

Adzumi speaks: "I am interested to know what Susie has to say about all this." Nameless One added, "Aren't we all?"

I would love to meet her

Chicago, USA, at Chika's place

Over time, Sally and Chika became much better acquainted.
"These are all your pictures of women, it is fascinating."
"No, Sally, these are just some; I have thousands more, each worthy of its own story."

Sally's mobile rings, "Excuse me, Chika. Hello, who is this? Kim, how lovely to hear from you. How are you?"
The call comes from Hong Kong. Ying Kim Xia asked, "Sally, do you know a man named Aaron Cross, stationed in Basel?"
"No, Kim, but I can find out; tell me more."
"He does documentaries. All I need to know is, is he from the press? Can I trust him?"
"Kim Xia, as soon as I know something, I'll call you," says Sally, ending the call.

Chika says, "Sorry, I overheard some of it. I didn't mean to, but the name "Kim Xia" sounds so familiar to me."

"I guess the whole world knows that name," answers Sally.
"She's not the one from TV, the mysterious book that no one knows what it is about."
"She is a good friend," answers Sally.
"I would love to meet her," Chika says.
"And so does everyone. Kim is highly sensitive. She is suspicious of anyone from the press. You are a freelance reporter, unpublished, as you said, nevertheless, a reporter," Sally says, "could I use your Internet for a couple of minutes?"

"Yes, sure, please, here." Chika says, "But reporter, no, not in that sense; I haven't found my true vocation yet, but I do collect the gems along the way."
Several minutes later, Sally returned the call to Kim. She is on the balcony to afford her some privacy. "Kim, this is what I found out without getting deep into it. Aaron Cross is a documentary maker with many publications, films, books, and memberships in many respected societies. He has been awarded a list of prizes, awards, mentions, etc., and on the face of it, he has all the glow of Mr. Perfect written all over him. This is not to say that he is. Do you understand me?"
A moment later, she ends the call.

What do you want from me?

Hong Kong, China, Clinic for the mentally ill

“Oh hello, Mr. Cross, thank you for the flowers, how did you know they were my favourite colour?” says Ying Kim Xia.
“It's just a hunch, Kim.”

"Mr. Cross, this is the fourth time in three days that you have come to visit me; why?" asks Kim.
"You are not a doctor; are you some sort of psychologist, analyst, or psychiatrist who is trying to get into my brain? But these people never bring flowers."

"Mr. Cross," says Kim, looking at the flowers, "you cannot have romantic feelings towards me; there is a huge age difference. This is not a public park. You came here with a purpose. You came to this clinic to seek me out. What do you want from me?"
Aaron smiled and answered, "No, I am not a doctor or anything like it. As much as I would like, as you are such a charming lady, I do agree that there is a small age difference."
"Of 30 years or so," Kim adds.

"Before I answer the rest of your question, Kim, can I tell you my story and things about my life?"
"Please do, Mr. Cross."

"About 25 years ago, I lived in Hong Kong. I used it as a base for my work in South East Asia. It was long before the return of Hong Kong to the Chinese. I've travelled in and out of Hong Kong. I lost count of how many times. Laos and Cambodia, Vietnam, even Nepal, all places that I frequented, but Hong Kong was always home."

"I fell in love with a very young Chinese girl here in Hong Kong. One look into her eyes, and I lost my head. To be honest, I could not think straight; she was on my mind non-stop. There were many who tried to stop this relationship from flourishing. We faced a cultural divide, a big age difference between us, and so many obstacles thrown in our way, but we believed in love. She was so young. I could have been her father, but all that mattered little."

"We've tried to hide our relationship from others, but we were found out. Her father threatened to kill me, or her, or both of us, if we would not end seeing each other. I could not bear to lose her, and together we ran away like children, hiding from the world, trying to find our own paradise. I had many friends here in Hong Kong, one of which gave me access to a house northwest from here, in the hills. We stayed there for several months. I flew in and out of the country working for short stints in SE Asia compiling footage, making some sort of income."

"I usually stayed there for two weeks at a time and came back to our place in the hills. On one of my trips, a group of armed men held me captive for ransom, hoping to make some money. I was not a big shot. They didn't believe me."

"For six weeks they held me in a shed; I was tortured for weeks. They wanted information that I could not answer, so I told them

what they wanted to hear, made it all up, and nothing was true because I did not have the answers. They must have had the wrong man; maybe they got me confused with someone else. I became very ill. I think they dumped me someplace. I had no idea where I was and was delirious with fever. To cut a long story short, it took a year before I got back to Hong Kong. I found the house empty. She had gone."
"What had happened to her?" Kim asks.
"I honestly don't know."
"I went back to her parent's place, and there she was, so I thought. I ran up to her, embraced her, and she slapped my face. It was Lijuan."
"I had her mixed up with her twin sister, as they looked so much alike. The eye is fooled by wishful thinking. I asked where An Jia was, but they did not know."

"Stop," said Kim. "You are trying to get into my brain. I cannot believe a word you say."
"Believe what you will, Kim, the fact is Jia was gone. Her father came out, and when he saw me, he hit me with whatever he could find. I did not fight back; after all, he was her father. I could feel his anger and pain. I was to blame."

Kim looks at Aaron, who stares straight ahead. She can sense sincerity despite her doubts.
"What is this?" she asks, pointing at a small pendant Aaron wore on a chain around his neck.
"This?" he holds it in his hands. "This is all I have of An Jia, plus some pictures and a box of memories in my heart."
"In which sign were you born?" asks Kim.
"The year of the dragon," answers Aaron.
"Tell me what it is, this pendant? The engraving, what does it mean?"

Kim holds the pendant as Aaron explains its meaning.
"When she gave it to me, she said, 'Yin is the metal; this is the boar; this is the dragon and fire; wear it close to your heart, so they get to know each other and may find harmony'."
"Yin is An Jia's sign; she was born in the year of the boar."
"Why have you told me this story?" she asks.
"I hope you have the answer," Aaron replies.

She gets up and walks away slowly, thinking. Aaron pulls an envelope from his jacket and looks at An Jia's pictures.
From a distance, Kim asks, "What made you come now?"
"A report in the news a few days ago mentioned An Jia's name. Then they showed an image, the cover of a book that looked so much like her. I have never seen this book. I don't know what it is about. I made notes to find you, and I came straight over here."
"If you don't know, perhaps I'm wrong," says Aaron. He hands Kim the pictures.

Kim walks away again, looking at each of the pictures. When she returns, she sits next to Aaron, still viewing the photos.
Aaron says, "If you are born in the year of the dragon, you could be..."
"You do look so much alike..."
"I did not know she was with a child."
"You could have been born after I was captured."
"Can you understand what I'm saying?" Kim swallows and slowly nods.

From behind the window, Director Cheung keeps an eye on the couple discretely.
"Do you think it is possible that my blood runs in your veins?" asks Aaron. "Could you be my...'
"...daughter?" Kim finishes his question. Aaron nods.
Kim shakes her head, her inner world confused. "This throws my whole life around. I need time to digest all this."
"What we don't know for certain, our blood could answer," Aaron says. "DNA, I know," says Kim. "My brain is just so confused. If this could be true, then I have been so wrong about everything," Kim says.

Director Cheung slowly approaches the couple with a smile and says, "Kim, if you need rest, just say so."
"Thank you, Director Cheung. Do you know about this?" she asks.
"I know why Mr. Cross is here, but I do not know the answers," he says. "Could I be alone, please?" Kim asks.
"Certainly, Mr. Cross, please, we can go inside," says Director Cheung. Both men leave Kim behind in the park.

Inside the office, Aaron says, "Director Cheung, imagine you are 16 years old, a girl, carrying the child of a white man, many years ago. You're possibly cast out by your family, feeling abandoned by your boyfriend, and you have run out of money. What options would you have?"

"Director Cheung, on my return to Hong Kong, I spent two years looking for Ying An Jia, Kim's mother. I could not find a trace. The fact that she was pregnant never occurred to me."
"I can see what you're getting at. Obviously, the hospital's birth records at the time would be a good starting point," says Director Cheung.

Aaron's mobile interrupts their conversation. "Hello Daddy, I'm in Shenzhen," says Susie.
"But what are you doing there, Susie?"
"I was bored and thought a change of scenery would do me good. It's just next door, virtually."
"OK, enjoy; I'll be in touch," says Aaron.

A faint knock comes from the door. Director Cheung calls out, "Yes, do come in." Kim opens the door to lean in the doorway and says, "If it's alright with everybody, let's do the DNA. Knowing is better than speculating."
"Are we all happy with this, Mr. Cross?" asks Director Cheung.
"Yes," was the quick reply, "where do we go for that?"
"You can stay right here, and it's done in a second," says Director Cheung. "Please excuse me; I'll be right back."
Aaron Cross is rolling up his sleeves as Director Cheung returns. "Oh, no, we're not vampires; we don't need blood for this. Open your mouth."
Director Cheung takes a swab from inside the cheek and says, "Done."
"The same with you, Kim... "Thank you both."
"Amazing, two swabs hold the answer to influencing two lives," says Aaron.

"Well, in 3 days or less, we shall all know, at least with 99.9% certainty. If there are still doubts, we can get 100% as well, if needed."

I will make sure your mother will not recognise you

Lyon, France, Luxembourg

Nicole is just out of the morning shower when the phone rings, a call from Felicia Fodor, the Hungarian artist she met in Zurich some time ago.

"Where are you and what are you doing, Nicole?"

"If I am not mistaken, this voice belongs to Felicia; am I close?"

"That depends where you are."

"Lyon, France," replies Nicole.

"Well, that is close enough; I am in Luxembourg. Feel like coming over?" Felicia asks.

Nicole laughs: "Why don't we throw a coin? What do you want, heads or tails, Felicia?"

"I'm having heads, hang on, I'm looking for a coin," Felicia answers, "found one, OK, heads you come and tails means I come, agreed."

"Anything you say," replies Nicole.

"Guess what?" Felicia asks.

Nicole responds, "What?"

"Luxembourg it is, see you soon, I'll pick you up from the airport." says Felicia. What better way to fill the day than with an unexpected little excursion across the border? Some hours later, the women meet.

"Say, Nicole, do you have time for this, coffee, meal etc," asks Felicia.

Nicole says, "No," turns around to head towards the departure terminal. A few meters further she stops and both laugh. Both women stood six paces apart as Nicole's laughter quickly changes, "Don't move and keep your head still."

"Don't turn around, I'm serious."

Felicia, not knowing what went on behind her, did as instructed. Nicole slowly walks towards her, ensuring that Felicia's head covers her face from being seen by the man who is behind Felicia.

"Felicia, behind you is a man I fear. Your head is blocking his view. I need a scarf, something, or anything to hide my face from him."

Felicia unties the knot of her scarf. Nicole pulls it from Felicia's neck. The man behind Felicia begins to walk, heading towards them. Nicole bends down, crudely throwing the scarf over her head, pretending to tie her shoelaces.

The baron's stooge, Julien, reaches for her upper arm and says, "Good try, darling, but slippers have no laces."
Felicia laughs, "Jennifer, this is not how you get the stain off. Nicole, who is Nicole?"
"Sir, you lay a hand on Jennifer, and I will make sure your mother will not recognise you."
Julien freezes in his motion," Oh, I might have been mistaken, pardon."

Felicia stares at him, Nicole rubbing her slipper, pretending to clean it.
Julien, somewhat hesitant moves on. Felicia kneels down, ensuring to keep Julien in sight. "Ha, darling, let me help you with this," she calls out. "Stay low," she whispers to Nicole.
"When we get up, you must walk totally different than you normally do, otherwise he'll see your step and knows it's you. On the count of 3, I will lead you, 1, 2 and 3."
Both get up together and walk away from Julien. "We will be safe as long as we are in the airport."
"No hurry. Stay calm, laugh, and joke."
"Let's get a clever exit plan," suggests Felicia.
"Have you got your mobile on you, Nicole?" asks Felicia.

"Yes," Nicole answers.

"Kink your left foot in, limp with your left, and that will force you to walk differently and keep it up until we're out of here. As long as I call you 'Jennifer', he is nearby, OK."
"Yes, Felicia." Nicole answers.
"I know this airport. Let's find out if he still thinks you're Nicole. Is he dangerous or what?"
"No, yes, I hope not, but he has reasons to get even with me; something happened in Cannes, or rather the Mediterranean, and he will be pretty pissed off about it. He works for the Baron, so I don't feel all that comfortable in Luxembourg this very minute."

"You go into this shop; we split up and confuse him. I keep an eye on him and call you to tell you what to do. Buy another outfit; change your appearance; look different; maybe you find a hairpiece of a different colour; whatever you can do. We will split up now. Take care."
Nicole enters the shop while Felicia heads roughly in the direction of where Julien is. Occasionally she stops to view merchandise in display windows, always in such a way as to see the baron's stooge in the window's reflection.

Felicia checks out the possible escape options outside, watching Julien from a distance. He is calling someone from his mobile.
"Oh my God, what if he calls Nicole?" Felicia rings Nicole.
The line is busy. She heads towards a security guard. Nicole does not answer; her line is still busy, but Julien remains where he is, still engaged in conversation.

Nicole now approaches the security guard and says, "Excuse me, sir, is it not true that all mobiles need to be switched off at the airport? I have been watching this man over there and can't help but have an uneasy feeling. He is acting very suspicious, and he perspires."
"Thank you, Madam," he says, reaching for his two-way communications device.
Felicia walks away from the guard, grinning. 'I could have thought of something brighter, I guess.'
She enters the shop where Nicole is. The expression on Nicole's face reveals that she is not talking to Julien.
"That was Ye Myo; I had to take it, sorry."

"OK, let's take two different taxis out of here; we meet at this place," Felicia notes down an address. "You take the first taxi."
Felicia leaves the shop to see two security guards leading Julien away.
"The coast is clear; let's head for the exit."

Both taxis arrive a few minutes apart at the prearranged location.
"Life with you is never boring," laughs Nicole.
"I'm not going to ask how you spice it up, being followed by a baron's stooge," Felicia answers.
"A meal was the deal; let's have a bite."
They settle at the rear of a secluded restaurant, finally relaxing after the interesting moments at the airport.
"Tell me, how is everyone?" asks Felicia.
"Ye Myo called earlier; Susie has gone to Hong Kong. Her father survived a crash landing there."
"Oh dear, is he ok?" Felicia answers.
"Something is not right; I can tell, but she would not say what. Ramona and Julien, or the Baron, must never meet. It just shows you how small the world is becoming when I bumped into him earlier."

There will be no guessing what we grow

Basel, Switzerland, Susie's place

All attempts to reach Susie fail.
"Maybe she's just out of range. Perhaps there is no coverage, who knows?" says Zoe.
The Nameless One suggests, "It could be that Susie knows about Aaron's past; after all, they are very close. What can you do when your father has a past?"
"Who knows the past of anyone?" asks Nadira.
"What we are planning will one day have its consequences when our time now becomes our past," says Tanisha.
"At least we know the world will become a safer place in time," Kysa adds.
Ramona, "But we shall miss them."
"Who will be the last man on earth?" asks Adzumi.

He knew the results, but glanced at the letter anyway

Hong Kong, Hotel / Clinic for the mentally ill

“Daddy, where are you now?” asks Susie.

Aaron takes the call from his hotel room balcony: “Susie, where have you been? You’ve been gone for a week, I've tried every day to reach you?”

Susie laughs, “That is not like you at all. What has gotten into you?”

A few hours later, they share a meal in the hotel’s restaurant.

“How much longer is your business in Hong Kong?” asks Susie.

“I am not sure, Susie.”

“What’s her name?” she asks.

"Kim," Aaron answers.

"I knew it was a woman. I caught you red-handed," she grinned, "but the day hasn’t come yet that I couldn’t read you."

"Kim could be either," answers Aaron.

"Wrong answer, got you again," says Susie, laughing.

Aaron laughs but does not say, "So what were you doing in Shenzhen for so long?"

"You keep your secrets, and I’ll keep mine," she says, adding, "What does the doctor say?"

"I’ll know in a day or so," says Aaron.

"What do you mean? Are you waiting on test results?" asks Susie.

"Hmmm, concussion; yes, it is going to be OK," answers Aaron, his mind occupied with the other matter.

"Will you be OK on your own? I need to get back to Europe," says Susie. "Any idea how long your, shall we say, ‘business’, will be?"

"No, I’ll be all right; how long? I can’t tell. I don’t know myself yet," says Aaron.

"Then I shall head out tonight, Daddy, back to Basel," says Susie.

"Sorry, I had no more time for you, Susie."

That night, Susie flew back to Europe. Two days later, Aaron receives a call from Director Cheung. An hour later, they meet in his office at the clinic.

"Kim, Aaron, are you both ready to hear the results from the DNA tests?" asks Director Cheung. Kim and Aaron look at each other. With one word, their world can change. A month ago, it seemed so far away that none had any idea that the other existed.
Aaron nods. "Yes, Director Cheung, I am ready."
Director Cheung looks at Kim and says, "Kim, you have the choice to say 'no'. Do not feel under any pressure. 'No' is OK too."
"I know, Director Cheung. Yes is also my answer. Yes, please tell us the outcome of the tests."

Director Cheung opens the envelope. He knew the results but glanced at the letter anyway. He steps towards the couple and puts the letter on his desk. Holding the hands of each, he says, "Ying Kim Xia, this man is your father. Mr. Aaron Cross, this woman is your daughter. Congratulations for finding each other." He joins their hands together, almost like in a wedding ceremony.
Aaron's thumb strokes Kim's hand. The skin of his own flesh, this is what it feels like to touch for the first time a skin that half grew from An Jia's flesh as well.

In a unique moment in Kim's life, she is holding her father's hand in hers. This hand is not the hand of one who misused her mother, not one who stayed for just one night.
A thousand men or more she had cursed, as fathers, all her life, to realise this moment there had been only one. The questions that she had tried to answer by researching the past and countless trails for three years of her life did not bring any answers at all.
Her hand slips out of Aaron's. With a bowed head, she leaves the office, seeking solitude to sort through a million thoughts.

I don't know, I don't know, I don't know

Basel, Switzerland, Uni Basel

On her return to Basel, Susie could sense a change. Ye Myo made the first contact upon realising Susie had returned.

"How is your father, Susie?" asked Gasha. "We've heard of the crash landing."
"Last night we spoke; he's doing fine. I think he found someone to nurse him better, but he's not letting on," answers Susie.

Susie looks at everyone. There is something not right. "Out with it. What is on your minds, everyone?"

Gasha asks, "Susie, what do you know of Aaron's past, your father's past?"
"I think I know everything." "We've been through a lot together," says Susie.
"Was he always a documentary maker, or did he do other things?" Zoe asks.
"What other things are you suggesting, Zoe?"
"I'm asking, not suggesting, Susie."
"We need to get back to business," Susie says. "Our demand after the first warning needs some thought."
Gasha's question is more direct: "Was Aaron ever a soldier?"
"Wasn't everybody?" Susie quips.
Aislinn adds, "Did he ever kill anyone?"
"I see," Susie says, "cross-examination time. He is my father. Whatever there is in his past is his issue to deal with. I love him and shall defend him from anyone, if need be. He has been good to me all my life, end of story."

Nadira asks, "Did you know that he was a mercenary?"
"Of course I knew, and I know a whole lot more. What has that got to do with anything?" she asks.

Zoe says, "Good point. Our parents did what they thought was right. If later on it turns out to be wrong, what can you do?"

"Exactly, I don't want to hear no more about it," Susie insists, " the past is done; we need to get back to business."
"What is the urgency?" asks Sheila.

"The urgency is this: All women who are about to become pregnant in Shenzhen are developing female offspring. Between January and April of next year, no boys will be born there unless they come from travelling pregnant visitors. So we need to formulate some declaration."
"Is that why you went there?" asks Gasha.
"Yes, no, maybe, maybe not. You know the answer to such questions." Susie replies.
"Maybe that's why Aaron is there as well," says Kysa.
"Who got this started? How? Who authorised this? Who selected Shenzhen and why?"

"I don't know, I don't know, I don't know, as to why? Perhaps it makes a lot of sense if you think about it," says Susie.

"In China, in general, boys are the preferred gender. Shenzhen is in the limelight in China and around the world due to its special status. What better place on earth to get the message across, I ask you?"

"Let's get started," she says.
"Come on, Nadira, you wanted three chances. What do you want from men? What do they need to do for us so we're willing to bear them?"
"You're always a few steps ahead, Susie," says Adzumi.
The Nameless One says, "Let's think this through; remember what we had on the board; let's start from that."

I grew up with Chan, my great-grandmother

Chicago, USA, Court building, Hong Kong, Clinic for the mentally ill

Sally Cramer is about to enter the court building when the call comes. "He's my father, Sally."

"It would help if you told me your name," responds Sally.
"It's Kim. Aaron Cross is my father.
"What does he want? Sorry, Kim, I am just thinking aloud. I am in a hurry. I have a case in 20 minutes and need to devote my thoughts to that. Are you OK, Kim?"
"I'm OK, Sally. We'll talk later; good luck with your case."
"Thanks, Kim; bye for now," says Sally as she enters the building.

It was late when Sally found the time to call Hong Kong.
"Yes, the DNA tests confirm that we are related; he is my father," says Kim. "You know what this means? My whole book could be wrong. All my research may be wrong."
"Kim, I do not know anything about your research. I cannot have your answers," says Sally.

"It means a woman died, based on my words, which may all be based on an error I may have made along the way," says Kim.
"This is not true. I told you this, Kim. You are in no way to blame for Mrs. Snyder's death. These are all fabrications by the press. Mrs. Snyder died from ..."
Kim interrupts Sally, saying, "I know that, Sally, but I can't help feeling guilty about it."

"Based on what I know, Aaron Cross lived on and off in Hong Kong, around about the time you would have been conceived. If you have a DNA match, it could well be true that he is your father."
"Excuse me, Sally, I am receiving another message."
A moment later, Kim continues, "It's Mr. Cross, waiting downstairs."
"And he is also your father, Kim," says Sally.
"Yes, it still takes some getting used to," replies Kim. "I don't want to be rude, but thank you, Sally. Take care and bye."

Aaron and Kim met in the lobby of the hospital.
"Hello, Mr. Cross, I am trying to comprehend that you are my father. I have never had any parents, and it may take some time for me to get used to the idea of having a father."
"That is all right, Kim. Take all the time you need," says Aaron. "By the way, I did some searching in the hospitals, trying to find birth records in an attempt to uncover where your mother, An Jia, gave birth to you."
"There are no records of this," says Kim.

"This is what I found out as well," responds Aaron.
"I could have saved you a lot of work," says Kim. "From what I know, I was found by my grandmother in her garden. Someone knocked at her door late at night. When she opened, there was no one there. She stepped through the door and nearly fell over a box. I was found in this box with a note that said: 'This is Ying Kim Xia, the daughter of Ying An Jia, who is the daughter of Ying Jiao, who is the daughter of Ying Chan. Help her grow'."

"Ying Chan is my great-grandmother. Ying Jiao is my mother's mother. Ying An Jia is my mother. I grew up with Chan, my great-grandmother, although the rest of my family would have nothing to do with me. My mother had been an outcast, and so was I. I never met them. I was looked at as the product of shame that brought dishonour to the family."

"The day when the 13th annual Hong Kong International Dragon Boat Festival opened was my birthday. If it really is, I don't know for sure, but I accept it as such. It is only by the grace of my dear old great-grandmother that I have some sense of identity. Strange, don't you think, that you too were also born in the year of the dragon?" says Kim.

"What do you know about your mother, Kim? What happened to her?" asks Aaron.
"That is what my book is about." "You must have read it."
"I have not. In fact, I did not even know about your book, even though it might have been in all the headlines and world news. Although we all live in this world, each person also lives in his or her own world. The world inside our heads knows little of what goes on in the 'real' world."
"But you did mention the book and the cover picture," says Kim.
"I saw it briefly, for moments only, in a news report. That's what brought me here," said Aaron.
"Yes, you are right; I now remember."
"I will let you read it. This is what I think happened to my mother," says Kim.

The right moment is more important for us

Basel, Switzerland, Susie's place

The group of 12 women sit around the table. Kysa is typing on the laptop. "Can you read out what we have so far, Kysa?" asks Tanisha. "Certainly, Tanisha, it starts like this:
'Men of the world, this is your first warning, a chance to change your ways."
'We, womkind, the women of the world, hereby demand the following:'"

"Stop," Tanisha calls out. "We are not the women of the world. We are a dozen out of approximately 3.3 billion women all over the globe. They will laugh at us."
Kysa, undeterred, continues, "...hereby demand the following, the next written in bullet points, that men change their ways and treat women with respect; that men give women equal opportunities in ALL areas of business, politics, domestic, social, and all other areas of life; that men provide women equal remuneration, equal work opportunities, and equal decision-making powers to remove social and, in particular, gender differences of any kind."

"So what's the bottom line?" asks the Nameless One.
Kysa adds, "Men, please be aware that we, womkind, are serious in our demands. If you do not heed this warning, we will refuse to make men. As proof that we are able to do this, look at Shenzhen, China, where no boy will be born between the coming months of January to April."

"We must see progress in the implementation of our demands by May at the latest. We shall use statistics to count the gender of all politicians in every country, compare income differences, compare gender-based job opportunities, and so forth. If no improvement is

noticeable in any of these areas, we will give you a second warning."
"This is signed by Womkind," concludes Kysa.

"OK, now that will be delivered to the press in all countries," explains Zoe. "We have a massive database to reach a great many of them. In any case, once the news is out, the rest of them will pick it up. Are we all happy with this?" asks Susie.
Silent nods confirm agreement.
"When will this come out?" asks Nadira.

"Next Friday at 2.12 am is an auspicious moment to be taken advantage of," says Susie.
"With the help of the stars?" asks Gasha and grins. "But we will miss the press deadline. The newspapers will already be in print for the day." "Yes," answers Susie, "we may miss the newspapers in some countries, but the right moment is more important for us."

Let us live this moment

Hong Kong, China, Clinic for the mentally ill / Harbour

Another email from Ye Myo arrives in Kim's inbox. Her first email came just after the book's release. The two women exchanged their different experiences of the past, but Kim was not aware that Aaron also knew Ye Myo.
Dear Ye Myo, would you believe that I have just found out that my father was not one of many, but he did know my mother for some time? We both had a DNA test, and this proved the fact that I now have a father. Thank you for your last message and the many pictures you sent. I will see if I can get you some pictures soon. I hope we will both meet one day.
Your sister in spirit,
Kim

She clicks the 'send' button; the email is on its way.
Kim goes back to the early part of her research that followed her mother's trail. 'Could I be wrong?' she wonders. She arranges to meet her newfound father at his hotel.

"I still haven't found a name to address you properly; father, daddy, dad; none of them do it for me. What would you suggest?" She asks Aaron.
"Kim, this Mr. Cross business is definitely out, but you're welcome to call me Aaron. We need time to find each other. After so many years, I wish I would have known sooner."

"How is your head now that the bandages have come off? Do you feel OK?" she asks.
"I am very happy and have been very lucky. I didn't know they had to shave part of my head. But it is healing well, would you agree?"
Kim looks at the injuries. "Actually, that is all mending very well."
"Oh, I meant to thank the pilot. Time must be different in Hong Kong; the days seem to run so fast here."
"Did you get a chance to read the book?" Kim asks.
"I did, Kim, and if this is the truth, then it would be unimaginable. A few things in the book make me wonder. What would the An Jia that I knew have done in similar situations?"

"Would you mind, Kim, if I retraced her path based on your research? Do my own enquiries based on what you had to begin with?" Aaron asks.
"I hope I am wrong; I sincerely do. I will give you my data and my reasoning behind each. You knew Mum, and I never did. You might see it in a different light. You can better put yourself in her position. You may also be able to think of things that I couldn't."
"Thank you, Kim."
"This beautiful day, why don't we go on a ferry ride, enjoy it, and think of nothing but to live this moment?"
"I would like that, Aaron."

Both enjoyed the day as tourists, sightseeing, sharing meals, and laughing. Both knew Hong Kong, yet somehow, it all looked so new and different.

The next day, Aaron receives two folders of notes, research material Kim had used to trace her mother's past. Another day went by, and again they met, each hour getting a little closer.
"Kim, I have studied your data; thank you for sharing it with me. I would like to make my own investigations and get my head into it."
"Father, I hope you can prove me wrong," says Kim.
Aaron laughs and says, "Do you know what you've just said?"
"Yes, I hope you can prove me wrong," says Kim.
Aaron embraces his daughter and says, "No, you called me 'father' for the very first time."
"Did I?"
"Yes, you did."
Kim grins. That night, Aaron calls Susie, letting her know that he will not be coming back to Basel for at least two months.

All this is in a picture

Chicago, USA, Sally's Place

Sally Cramer had invited Shima Chika. "Am I doing this correctly, Chika? The way you handle the chopsticks is so much more natural"
Chika laughs, "I can see you're not dropping anything, so that's worth something."
"You handle the knife and fork as good as anyone I know, but my chopstick skills have something to be desired," says Sally.

"It's just an extension of your fingers, but then, I grew up with them, so it comes natural, but you're doing fine, honest," says Chika, just as Sally drops some peas from her sticks.
Both laugh. "Peas have a life of their own," says Chika.
Following the meal, both relax in the cosy lounge. Sally puts the box of Chika's photographs at the side of the table and places a folder next to it.

"Thank you, Chika, for bringing them last time. I sorted some out and have them in this folder. I'm interested in the stories they tell," she says, pulling an image from the folder showing a bunch of flowers tied to the railing of a bridge. "Tell me about this one."
"This was taken two years ago. I tied the flowers there so that people pause in respect for at least a fraction of a second."
Chika searches in the box to find three other photos.

"These all belong together; this is the story. Here, a woman is leaning against the railing of a bridge. I took this photograph after she stared for several minutes down into the water. Next, she climbs on top of the railing. I scream out, but I am far away from her. These two men heard my scream and realised why I was screaming.
They ran towards her; the right one nearly caught her arm, but she'd already jumped."

"I am ashamed of the next shot. By sheer instinct, I raised the camera to snap these, the last seconds of her life."

"Just a bit below here, out of view, is the foot of the pillar that supports the bridge. She did not fall into the water. If she had, she would have lived. Instead, she fell onto the sharp concrete edges of the footing, received severe injuries, then slid down into the water and drowned." Sally gasps, "That is terrible."
"Yes, it is, Sally."

"I found out who she was after that happened. She was a 32-year-old woman who lived in the parks. She was homeless and an addict. She sold herself to anyone who would have her so that she could afford her habit. She had lived on the streets for most of her life. Her name was Rachel."
"This one was taken in Milan. The woman is Mrs. Bettucini. A salesperson offered her a dress made out of artificial fibres. The word 'synthetic' triggered her off when the assistant explained that it was made of man-made fibres. She was a proud woman who needed to vent her bottled-up anger and frustrations on someone. In a way, the poor sales assistant had to bear the sins of all men. I'm sure he will have learned a lesson he'll never forget."

"All this is in a picture. This is fascinating, Chika," says Sally.

"What happened here? The woman is looking up, and the child in the pram is crying."
"The little one was suffering from diarrhoea. The woman had changed his diapers three times in the last few minutes, and then she had none left. She looks up to heaven, asking for one."

Are we going to live a life in fear from now on?
Basel, Switzerland, Ye Myo's place / Susie's place

Ye Myo Tun is studying in her room as she receives another email for Kim in Hong Kong:

Dearest sister, Ye Myo, we have both had a difficult life, growing up without parents. Your grandma, Nyein, helped you along your way. My great-grandmother Chan did all she could for me, yet none of us can remember much of the past, we were just too young.

Please find enclosed some pictures taken near the Cross Harbour Tunnel, near Wan Chai, Hong Kong. No, he is not my boyfriend. This is my father in the pictures. I still cannot get used to the idea altogether, but I do wake up a little more positive these days.
I could have been wrong with my book, and my father is trying to look into it. I do hope I have been wrong. By the way, his name is Aaron, my father. He is currently travelling and has been gone for a week, but he tries to call me when he can. I am glad you have so many friends in Basel, and the pictures you sent were all so lovely.
Take care.
Love from your sister in spirit, Kim

Ye Myo looks at the attached images and finds Aaron holding Kim in his arms. Why has Susie never mentioned this? Does she know? She gets dressed to meet the others at Susie's place.
The winter is cold in Basel. As Ye Myo approaches Susie's place, many cars are parked near Susie's entrance, and she becomes aware of a spotlight. She drives past her place to park at the side of

the road, a long distance from Susie's driveway. The spotlight came from a slow-driving patrol car. Two times, the patrol car drives past Susie's place. The spotlight scans the number plates of the cars near the driveway.
Ye Myo dials Susie's house and says, "Susie, there is a patrol car pacing up and down your place. I am a bit further down the road. Watch what you're doing."
"Thanks, Ye Myo, let's meet near the place where you found the two coins last week. Don't say it; do you know which I mean?" asks Susie. "I do. Take care. Bye," says Ye Myo.

The women leave Susie's place at staggered intervals, each taking a different route to meet at the arranged place, a park, where Ye Myo found two Francs a few days ago while she was walking there with Susie. It took another 20 minutes before everyone had gathered. "Let's walk away from the cars," says Gasha. "Has anyone been followed?"
"No," says Kysa.
"I got here first and have kept a lookout over the ridge; each car came alone; no one was followed," says Aislinn.
"It is ice-cold tonight. It is not a nice place to meet. We will look suspicious, 12 women at night in a park," says Adzumi.

"We forgot all about the police since the last time they knocked at the door," says Sheila.
"We must now assume they are onto something," says the Nameless One. "Could any of the messages we had emailed to the newspapers and press be traced back to us?"
Adzumi says, "Then they must be a whole lot smarter than us. I don't think so."
"Never underestimate the enemy," says Tanisha.
"They know who we are; each number plate on our cars tells them who we are," says Nadira.
"They will also know each address, mobile, and email account. Even our cars may have sensors. Each mobile phone we carry will tell them where we are. What we say can all be recorded," says Adzumi.

"Are we going to live a life in fear from now on?" asks Ramona.
"Why has none of the press published our demands?" asks Nadira.
"In the coming months, they'll see the proof."

"They must all think it was a prank, or they think we're a bunch of lunatics," says Susie.
"Where is your dad, Susie?" asks Ye Myo.
"He rang this morning; would you believe he is in Russia?" says Susie. "He says he is following some trail."

"In Shenzhen, the doctors must know by now that none of the women are carrying males."
"We must stay low for now; we have nothing in our homes or on our computers that can give us away," says Sheila.
"We must be so clean that a thorough house search reveals no evidence," says Aislinn.
"We need to acquire new mobile phones under assumed names and use them to communicate instead of the ones we've got," says Gasha.

"And we need a meeting place that is warmer than this," adds Nadira.
"That is unanimous," says Zoe.
"I do agree," says Tanisha. "Is there any change at all in the statistics?"
"It's still a bit too early for that, even if they were changing. We need to wait until May," says Adzumi.
"But we can think of phase two of the plan," suggests Zoe.

One of the mobile phones is ringing. It is yours, Ramona. She looks at the caller ID and says, "Hello Nicole, how are you?"
Ramona walks away from the group to talk in private.

Could mum still be alive?

Hong Kong, China, Hotel room

Aaron has returned from his investigative mission. Kim joins him at the hotel. "I must say, I did miss you. I'm glad you're back, Father."
"And so am I, Kim. It is so good to have found you. It is so good to know An Jia left me you, the most precious gift anyone can give."
"I do have news, Kim. Good news, in a way."
"Could you prove me wrong?" Kim asks.
"Yes," says Aaron.
"Oh, I'm so glad; what a relief. Where did I go wrong?" asks Kim.
"You are a very thorough researcher, Kim. I came to similar conclusions, but one small thing did not fit," says Aaron.

"An Jia, your mother did not attend the school you thought she was in. She was in the one next door to it. You know what this means, Kim?" asks Aaron.
"I got the wrong woman. I followed someone else's trail."
"Exactly, another girl, also aged 16 at the time, went missing, never to be seen again, not in Hong Kong. She had a striking resemblance to your mother."
"She also had a relationship with a Caucasian man, but he was 10 years younger than I. You followed a girl by the name of Chang An Jia," says Aaron.

"It is still a sad story. She was smuggled over Russia into Europe via Italy, just as your book describes," says Aaron.
"She did end up in Holland, and I have seen the police pictures. Have you seen any of those?"
"No, father, I have not."

"I will not show them to you. They are very distressing. So your book is correct in everything except that she is not your mother. You followed Chang An Jia's trail."
"I'm glad and sad. What happened to my mother?" asks Kim.
"I don't have all the answers, Kim. I know she moved at least twice after she left the place we shared. Then I ran out of time. I do have an assignment in Africa, which I postponed by two months. I need to leave Hong Kong to complete these works."
"Could mum still be alive?" asks Kim.

Aaron embraces Kim, "I honestly don't know, Kim. I've got to do Africa first before I can carry on searching."
"I am sorry, but I will need to leave tomorrow, Kim."

What does it all mean?

Basel, Switzerland

It was mid-April when the group in Basel met again. A friend's house has become their new meeting place.
Zoe holds a notepad and says, "The results are in from Shenzhen, everyone. Even though April is not over yet, the birth-rate figures from most hospitals have come in, as well as the sex distribution of these births.
"Just so we get a comprehension of what Shenzhen is, it has been the fastest-growing city in China for the last 31 years or so. Mandarin is the predominant language. The city is divided into six precincts."

"Before I tell you the numbers, please note this: sex distribution in China just last year was 51.5% male; the rest is female. At the time of birth, and that is the number we need to work with, the sex ratio is 1.11 males per female. In other words, 111 boys are born to every 100 girls; these are last year's figures."
"Of course, as the population grows, the sex ratio will shift so that there are more women left in the older generation than men."
Nameless One interjects, "Zoe, please get on with it. What's the damage?"
"I will," says Zoe. "In the period from January until now, we have an overall ratio of 79 boys to each 100 girls; that's for the whole of Shenzhen."
"So what went wrong?" asks Aislinn, and all the others are wondering too.
Zoe continues, "Bear in mind that Shenzhen is the first special economic zone established in China, the first out of five such zones. All eyes are on it and have been ever since it was nominated for that status. When we look at the districts in detail, we can see a strong change in sex ratios in two out of the six districts. One of them had a ratio of 40 boys to 100 girls; the other had 42 boys per 100 girls."
"So have we failed, or what does it all mean?" asks Sheila.

Susie explains, "Now this is where it gets interesting. Shenzhen has a very large proportion of medical professionals when compared to the rest of China. If we take into consideration that we made our demands public long before January, one could assume that the numbers given by the hospitals may well have been 'doctored' under some higher-up direction, to show the world that no one can do this to China."

"There would be a large influx from Hong Kong anyway, I would gather," adds Nadira.
"Yes, there is, Nadira, but looking at the total population a figure, that's just a drop in the ocean. Besides, many people from Shenzhen also commute to Hong Kong. Maybe the intent was to make us the laughing stock, to show the world that China can defend against anything that is thrown its way," says Susie.
Aislinn says, "They are ignoring us. Nothing has changed in the statistics. No news channel has touched our story; we may assume that the Chinese stocked the hospitals with rent-a-babies to belittle us."

Susie continues, "There could also have been some hiccups with the mechanics of getting the plan to work successfully in the whole area of Shenzhen. After all, nothing like this has ever been tried on such a scale."
Ramona adds, "I assume we go by the hospital reports; I mean, no one stood at the doors of the delivery rooms and had a look at what was born."
"Right, Ramona," says Susie, "but you can be sure that the doctors will know that we have had some successes. Politically, it may not be in their interest to let the world know the truth. Think about it. Any country that can influence the gender balance of another could use this as a weapon to reduce the number of males or females among their enemies, thereby reducing the number of enemy forces in the future. It would be just a matter of time before all enemies just fade away."
Susie says, "The fact that the women in Shenzhen are able to bear boys after the set period also made it more difficult to guarantee 100% effectiveness of the plan. As we all know, Nadira insisted on that, as well as some others. The permanent change that women can only bear females is irreversible and also has a 100% success rate."

"We should think of the second part of the plan a bit more carefully."
Zoe adds, "We need to show China that we are not into politics; therefore, the next target should be a foe of China."
Aislinn comments, "Perhaps this time we give the warning after the fact; wait until they are born, and then we know that no one can manipulate the figures. You should have a look at all the stories that have come in from the website. It is unbelievable what women have had to endure."

"The plan now calls for a whole country," says Gasha. "Which country?"
"As a foe of China, I can think of Russia, the USA, India, Taiwan, and even Japan as likely candidates," suggests Kysa.
Susie says, "If we still insist on reversibility, meaning that women can bear boys after a set period, then we cannot pick a country that is large in size. Such surprises cannot be implemented at this point in time on a larger scale."

"How big can we go?" Aislinn asks.
Susie explains, "a few times larger than Shenzhen."
"Japan, Taiwan, and Hawaii, if we want to stick to China's foes."
"Japan and Taiwan are out; it could be seen as an attack on Asians," says Nameless One. "Hawaii is not bad. It is part of the USA, but it also leaves a bad taste in the mouth."
"New Zealand," suggests Sheila, "if not all of it, either the northern or southern island."

"Here is an idea," Adzumi brings forwards: "what about a warning across the globe, so that it can be seen by the entire world to be indiscriminate?" Across political divides, racial, ideological, and religious differences, it is clear that we mean business, so that it can't be swept under the carpet by anyone."
"It will take some time to organize things at such a scale, but I like the idea," says Susie.
"I do agree," says the Nameless One.
"I also am in favour of this," says Gasha, "if, as you said, the Chinese may have doctored the figures in Shenzhen with no warning beforehand, and on such a scale, no one is able to hide it."

Is it off your shoulders, Kim?

Chicago, USA / Hong Kong, China

Chika and Sally met again in the spring.
"Chika, how many images have you collected so far?"
"3000, 5000, I have not counted them, Sally."
"I will go back to Japan in two weeks time, my brother needs my help."
"In two weeks, I shall be in Hong Kong, on business," says Sally.
"I will have a stopover in Hong Kong," says Chika.
They both look at each other, "Are you thinking what I'm thinking?" asks Sally. Chika nods. "Let's put a few days aside to spoil ourselves," says Sally. "I would like that, Sally."

The two weeks passed quickly, and both sit next to another heading for Hong Kong.
"Perhaps this is the wrong time to bring up the subject," says Sally, "but I guess it would be right about here, where Kim's father was hit by the remnants of a meteor, the plane, I mean, right here before the descent to Chek Lap Kok International Airport."

"Thank you, Sally; I needed to hear this right now," says Chika.
"Let me make it good, Chika. Guess who is picking us up from the airport?"
"No, really?" asks Chika.
"Yes, Ying Kim Xia herself," says Sally.
"Oh, I do look forwards to meeting her ever since... oh, so long ago," says Chika.
"I know. That is why I arranged it. Now you can't wait to see the plane land, am I right?" Sally says.

So many faces in the arrival lounge, people with signs and nametags, waiting for ones they have never met. Kim stood among them. Sally saw her first and ran towards Kim, both finding joy in a long embrace.

Chika watches the two women, so different on the outside yet so much alike in their smiles. She took five pictures of their joy.
"Kim, meet Chika; she wanted to meet you for such a long time."
"Hello, Kim Xia, am I pronouncing this correctly?"
"It sounds like me; yes, hello Chika. Sally spoke of you so many times. You must have left a good impression on her."
"That she did," says Sally. "Oh, where do we go? There is so much to talk about."

"I have just the place," Kim says.

“Lead the way,” says Sally. Some 20 minutes later, they settled on soft cushions around a table.

“Kim, how do you feel? A new father, a book that is not about your mother. Are you relieved with what you know?”
“Yes and no. Yes, I am happy to have a father and I do admit that I miss him. He is in Africa at present. No, as I feel the weight of my book has rolled off my shoulders only to land on someone else’s. Aaron found out who the girl was, which I mistakenly believed to be my mother for all those years.”
“Should her family know the truth, or are they better off not knowing?”

Sally holds Kim’s hand and says, "We don’t wish anyone to carry such a burden. Is it off your shoulders, Kim?"
"It is off my shoulders in a sense that I now know it was not my mother’s fate, but perhaps they had met; it was still the fate of someone who once lived here."
"It could have been any girl," says Kim as Sally nods.

What are they after?

Basel, Switzerland, Susie's place

Ye Myo and Susie are the only ones in the house. Two months have passed since the group's last meeting. They hear a knock at the door. Ye Myo opens the door. It is Aaron.
"Ye Myo, hello, so good to see you," he says.
"Hello Aaron, welcome back," she says.
"Daddy, welcome home," calls Susie. "Where have you been this time?"
"I had a stint in Africa," says Aaron.
"You've been gone a long time, Aaron; have you been anywhere else?" asks Ye Myo.
"I have been around the world, well, almost. Let me see, where was I? Hong Kong first, then across to China, then Russia, all the way to Italy, Germany, Holland, then back to Hong Kong, then Africa. Correct me if I'm wrong; I am now in Switzerland?"
"Yes, Daddy, you are home. I would have thought you would go back to Hong Kong. Wasn't her name 'Kim', the new flame in your life?"

Ye Myo, watching Aaron's expression, wonders what his answer might be to Susie's question.
"This is what I want to talk to you about, but first, please..."
"Coffee, I know, Daddy," says Susie. "Give me a minute."
"Do you wish to be alone with Susie?" asks Ye Myo while Susie is preparing the coffee.
"No, please stay; I do have wonderful news."
A moment later all sit together. "Share your news, Daddy, what is so wonderful? You want to get married, am I right?"
Aaron laughs, "Not this week and not the next."
"I can bet you a million dollars, what you're about to say has something to do with another woman, am I right, Daddy?" she asks Aaron.
"That's why I will never bet with you, Susie. Yes, you are right."

Aaron pulls a picture from his jacket to hand to Susie; he hands another to Ye Myo, saying, "This is Kim."
Ye Myo recognized Kim Xia straight away. She had received the same picture via email from Kim sometime earlier.

"Oh, Daddy, she is so very young. You can't be serious, Dad. She could be your daughter," says Susie.
"She is," answers Aaron.
Susie's coffee went down the wrong way, and she spits and coughs a mouthful over the table.
"Sorry about this," she says.
"This is Ying Kim Xia; she is my daughter. She is your half-sister, Susie," says Aaron.
"So last time you were here, you suddenly remembered, 'Ah, I forgot something in Hong Kong.' You rushed out of the house to find a fully grown woman, and bingo, she's your daughter. What did you find in Africa? Am I to expect any others from Russia, perhaps Italy, maybe another one in Holland?"
"Calm down, Susie," says Aaron.
"Algiers, Congo, where else have you been? Bangladesh, Laos, how many have you left behind there, Dad?"
"Susie, hear me out."
"Vietnam; there must be some over there. Oh, let's not forget Nepal or the Amazon, shall we?" quips Susie, then lets out a bitter laugh, "Ha, and I thought I was the only one. Stupid me." Susie calls out. Filled with anger, she leaves the room.

Aaron puts the pictures back in his jacket.
"She will calm down, Aaron," says Ye Myo.
"I did not expect a reaction like this," says Aaron.
"What is her name, Aaron, your daughter's name?" she asks.
"Ying Kim Xia," he answers.

"I know her, Aaron; we've become friends, Kim Xia and I," says Ye Myo.
"You do?" asks Aaron. "What a coincidence!"
Susie comes back to walk to the kitchen.
Ye Myo calls out, "Susie, come here; I know your sister too."
Susie returns, "Ye Myo, it had never occurred to you to fill me in. You knew, but you never said a word. What does this tell you about the trust between us, Ye Myo?"

"I did not know, Susie. I knew Kim before she knew she had a father or a sister. She is a writer; she wrote a book. I emailed her because of that. That's how I got to know her."

"Sit with us, Susie; let me explain," said Aaron.
"Susie, when I married your mother, I did not know I had a daughter anywhere on earth. When you were born, you were my first child, so I believed all this time. Your mother died giving birth to you, and for so many years, nannies gave you the care that I couldn't. I reared you as best as I could."

"Before I met your mother, I fell in love with a young girl. On one of my assignments they captured me, and I became very ill, preventing me from returning to her for a year. I searched and could not find her. I spent two years looking for her, but I could not find her anywhere. Eventually I gave up, not knowing that she could have been pregnant. I had no idea, Susie, none."

"Life goes on. Then I met your mother, and I loved her with all my heart. Do you understand, Susie? Finding Kim does not make me love you any less."
"How did you know she even existed?" asks Susie.
"Last time I was here, I happened to switch on the news." They mentioned the name of Kim's mother. Kim had written a book about her. It made big headlines. I flew out to Hong Kong, not knowing if she could be mine. I met her doctor, and I met Kim. We did a DNA test, and it was positive. Kim is my daughter. She is two years older than you, Susie, although she has a baby face and looks younger than you do."

"When I came to Hong Kong, after your crash landing, you did not say one word about her. Why, Dad?" asks Susie.
"I needed to be sure first. At that time, no DNA results had come in, Susie."
"Show me the pictures, Dad."
Susie studies the pictures; she looks at Ye Myo and says, "And you know each other?"
"Yes, Susie. Kim searched for three years to find out what had happened to her mother. I never met her, but we are in email contact every few days."

Susie asks Aaron, "Why did you go to Russia and all the other places in Europe?"
"I followed the trail Kim had uncovered, but she followed the wrong girl. The book she wrote was not the story of her mother," explains Aaron.
"Are you finished with your assignment in Africa?" she asks Aaron.
"Yes, I postponed it for 2 months, but I have caught up with it. I'm free for two weeks before I get to go on the road again."
"Two weeks, OK, what's your schedule? Yeah, Myo, what's on next week's agenda for you?" asks Susie.
"Why do you ask, Susie?"
"Well, there's a public holiday. I could afford to miss a few days," hints Susie. "What I'm saying is, why don't we fly out to Hong Kong tomorrow to meet Sis?"
Aaron laughs and says, "That's more like it, Susie."

Ye Myo was somewhat surprised: "But I haven't budgeted that into my finances. I could miss a few days at university too."
"Done," says Susie.

A knock at the door interrupts the sudden travel plans.
"Come on in, Nadira; what's happening? You're all upset," asks Susie.
"Did you know that your whole road is blocked off?" asks Nadira. "Oh, not a normal road block. I drive along when all of a sudden a police car comes out of a driveway and drives right across the road to block my path. At the same time, behind me, another police car locks me in like a sandwich. They searched my whole car, did some sort of drug test on me, and then they let me go."
"When did that happen?" asks Ye Myo.
"Well, just now, a minute ago," says Nadira, "what are they after?"
"Ye Myo, please make Nadira a cup of tea; use the Indian one, weak. I'll be back in a minute," says Susie as she disappears into her room.

Nadira sips her cup, standing near the rear door and looking through the window towards the back.
Aaron whispers to Ye Myo, "Don't worry about the cost of a ticket; it will be such a surprise. I start packing now."
"Thank you, Aaron; I'd love to come. I'll pay you back someday."
Aaron smiles and says, "Please don't mention it."

When Susie returned, Aaron had gone to his room.
"The police are just after drugs; they may even come and search this house," she says to Ye Myo and Nadira.
"How do you know this?" asks Ye Myo.

"I have many friends," says Susie, "and they, the police, are still suspicious from the last time they came. As Aaron travels a lot, they may think we are dealers or something. There are no drugs in the house; there never were. The sooner they come, the sooner they leave us alone."
"Nadira, let the others know," adds Susie.
"Aaron, Ye Myo, and I will be flying out to Hong Kong for a few days. Want to know why?"
Nadira nods her head. "Tell me, why?"
"We shall be visiting my new sister," Susie laughs. "You didn't know I had a sister, did you?"
"You have many sisters, Susie," says Nadira, "but I didn't know you had a sister that's related."

I have another surprise

Hong Kong, China, Inner city restaurant

Kim Xia, Sally, and Chika take a walk along the vibrant inner city when Kim receives Aaron's call. "Would you believe, father is here; he just landed," says Kim to the others. "We will all meet him in 30 minutes; what a lovely surprise."

Somewhat impatiently, Kim keeps looking at the entrance of the restaurant, selected as the place to meet. "If you'd rather be alone with him, just say so, Kim," says Sally. "No, no, not at all; please stay, both of you," answers Kim with joy in her eyes. "It is so good to see you happy," says Sally. Chika asks, "Kim, may I have your permission to take photographs?"

"Yes, Chika, I would love that, but not for publishing, please," says Kim. "Father says he has a surprise; I wonder what he means."

Aaron arrives, looking around the restaurant, but Kim is not there. Sally, pointing to the man, says to Chika, "That may be him; he's looking for someone."

"It could be, but these two women seem to be with him, so maybe not," answers Chika.

From the rear of the restaurant, Kim emerges, returning from the restroom. As she approaches the table, Sally moves her head in the direction of the counter, discretely pointing to the man.

She looks, then heads towards him. "Hello, Father, glad you're back."

Aaron embraces Kim and says, "It's so good to see you."

"Follow me, Father; I want you to meet someone," says Kim, heading towards her table. Aaron laughs and follows.

"Sally, this is my father; this is Sally Cramer," says Kim.

Sally reaches her hand across the table and says, "Hello, Mr. Cross. It's a pleasure to meet Kim's father in person."

"Hello, Mrs. Cramer," he says.

"Oh, please, Sally is fine," she offers.

"Well, Kim, I told you I had a surprise," says Aaron, turning to Ye Myo, who is right behind him. "Do you know who this is, Kim?"

"I don't believe it, are you Ye Myo?" asks Kim.

Ye Myo laughs and steps forward to embrace Kim, "I am Ye Myo," she whispers in Kim's ear, "and it's so good to meet you at last."

Both shared a long hug.

"I have another surprise, Kim," says Aaron.

"Is it Christmas or some special day I've missed?" asks Kim.

Ye steps aside to sit next to Sally at the table. Aaron announces, "This is Susie; she is my daughter also."

Susie extends her hand. Kim steps forwards to embrace Susie. "Why, this is wonderful; yesterday a father, today a sister. I am so pleased to meet you; I did not know I had a sister," says Kim.
"Hello Kim, neither did I know until yesterday," says Susie.
"Please, let's all sit down," suggests Kim, looking around. "Ah, there is Chika; she's taking pictures. Come join us, Chika," she calls out.

Chika joins and is introduced to everyone else at the table. Each explains the relationship they have with one another.
"Yes, Mr. Cross," says Sally.
"Oh, please, Aaron," he suggests.
"Thank you, Aaron," Sally continues. "Kim and I go back a long time. When did we meet, Kim?"
"It seems so long ago, Sally," says Kim.

Ye Myo says, "Wow, I met Kim, via email, from the book, she looked for her mother, and now, here we are, you have found a father and a sister, another one, as I always considered myself as sister too."
"It is a beautiful day," says Kim, "in more ways than one."
Kim smiles. Chika puts her camera away. Deep in thought she says, "Cross, Cross, could you be the Aaron Cross? Aaron Cross the filmmaker, 'Kids in Graves', is this one of yours?" she asks, "Could it be that I am sitting at the same table with Aaron Cross, the famous documentary maker."

Aaron nods, "I don't know about famous, Chika, but yes, I made 'Kids in Graves', the most painful film I ever made."
"How did you sleep at night?" asks Chika.
"I reached for the bottle, Chika, the booze and sleeping pills, eighteen months of that, Chika. Once you've seen such abhorrent deeds, one can never be the same."
"I can well imagine," says Chika. "I too find much that pains the eye. I am not looking for it. It seems to find me. So far I have been spared to see what you've seen."
"The evil in men is beyond comprehension. How often do we change the subject, speak of anything else, so we don't have to face it?" says Aaron. "Perhaps we're unable to face it, unable to comprehend, to understand..."

Aaron sees a young woman with a newborn in her arms and continues, "To fathom that within this child might be the seeds of

destruction, horror, and cruelty, our brains cannot absorb, and with some hope, this child will never know such worlds."
Chika silently nods.

We must find the underlying cause of this

Shenzhen, China, Medical Research Clinic

The research clinic has been very busy, testing sperm samples from large groups of men. Half are the fathers of girls born in the period January to April in Shenzhen, and all the others from randomly selected men. The collection of samples occurs twice per week.

Dr Huang Qiu

"Thank you for coming in, Mr. Hong Tao," says Dr. Huang Qiu, looking at his chart. "How often have you come now? Oh, I see, 30 times. How is your daughter? Is she well, Mr. Hong Tao?"
Hong Tao hands him a picture of his daughter, beaming a grin from ear to ear. "She is so lovely. We are so happy. She is a very healthy girl. Tell me, Dr. Huang, how much longer do I need to donate my sperm?"

"I don't think it will be much longer, Mr. Hong. Thank you so much for your donations and assistance. Our research is to assist all our people in creating beautiful, strong, and healthy babies, just as your little one is."

"Dr. Huang Qiu," says Professor Xu Shen, interrupting the two and looking at his wristwatch, "we will meet in 15 minutes."
"Yes, I have not forgotten," replies Dr. Huang.

Some of the doctors involved in Project 'Jan-April Girls" meet in the clinic's conference room to discuss progress. The team leader is Professor Xu Shen, who starts his opening address by saying, "We now have the sperm count from all the fathers who are parents of girls, born between the months of January and April. Each one we tested since then shows their X and Y chromosome counts are more or less even. If we compare that to a randomly selected group of men, we cannot see any difference. All the male's sperm shows up completely normal."

Dr. Lin Kang adds, "We have checked the oocytes, the unfertilized eggs of women, and compared these with the oocytes of a randomly selected group, and all seems totally normal."

Prof Xu Shen

Dr. Huang Qiu looks through his folder to explain, "We examined the ova of relatives of the women from the January to April group who have since conceived, and there is also not a hint of how it could have happened."

"I wish we would have been aware of all this when it did occur, back then, near the time of conception," adds Professor Xu Shen.

Dr. Huang says, "The gametes in both mothers and fathers of all the groups appear completely normal."

Professor Xu questions, "Are there still acidity results available, pH, alkaline, etc., from the women in the January to April group? If not, let us find out. What did the women use as contraceptives prior to conception? The sanitation pads they used prior to conceiving, the soap, bath water ingredients, even their underwear, there must be some link somewhere. If it is not in the women, then it must be in their men. Something that they all had in common, do they shower or prefer a hot bath?" Dr Lin Kang explains, "We did research the couples' sexual practices, but we could not see any attempt to have intercourse, which might favour the production of girls. There were no similarities noticeable, which would show each couple having the same position during intercourse. We have not made any progress on why such a large number of girls were born in that period."

"We must find the underlying cause of this," says Professor Xu, "All the women are normal, all the men are normal, that's no normal," he concludes.

Kim, each woman is your sister

Hong Kong, China, Hotel

Sally is filling the afternoon, attending to some of the business she had organized for this Hong Kong journey. Ye Myo and Chika are in deep discussions with Aaron, while Kim and Susie take time out to get to know one another.

"Dad was saying he became aware of your mum's name in a news report, something about a book you wrote," says Susie to Kim. "Tell me a little about this book, Kim."

"I was so wrong, Susie. I had followed the trail of what I thought was my mother. When our father researched my material, he could prove that I made an error early in the piece. I had followed the wrong person," answers Kim.

"But how did the book get on TV? How did it get such publicity, Kim?"

"I met a man in a park in Chicago while I was finalizing some handwritten notes, which later became the book. He was a publisher and offered me lots of money, having just read one or two pages, so he could print it. I did not like the idea, but I paid him money for a small print run. All I could afford was $480, which he said would get 100 books printed. As Sally told me earlier, he did print 5,000 books instead. In a department store, they all sold very quickly because a woman died 'apparently' from touching my book. This made headlines across the world, hence the huge demand for the book. But making money was never my objective. I just couldn't bear the pain anymore. I needed to let it out."

"I can understand that, Kim."

"Dad uncovered that the story was true, except it was another woman."

"Yes, Susie. It is still a lot of pain to bear, just knowing that this fate could befall anybody, no matter who it is. We still don't know what actually happened to my mother."

"Dad mentioned that the press came to interview you here in Hong Kong," says Susie.

"They banged at the door in the middle of the night; they put their cameras and lights into my face; it was terrible," says Kim.

"Could you change the book a little to re-release it, explaining that this is the story of another person?" asks Susie.
"No, Susie. In hindsight, I should have never published it. Why spread misery, because that is all that is in the book? I am lucky I ended up in the clinic. They kept all the press away from me. I am lucky that no one can recognise me, as the footage they took showed me with my hair all messed up. They had just dragged me out of bed. At least no one knows who I am when I walk in the streets."

"I grew up in the west of Hong Kong. "I spent my whole childhood here," says Susie. "I had several nannies but never a mother. Ye Myo also grew up without parents; did she tell you about that, Kim?"
"Yes, Susie, we know a lot of each other's background and inner feelings, and I want to sincerely thank you for bringing her with you. It is such a joy to meet her in person, as well as you. To know that I have a sister is a beautiful feeling."
"Oh, Kim, each woman is your sister," replies Susie, "let's go for a walk, just you and me."
"What would you like to see?" Kim asks.
"The festival of lights," replies Susie.
"Then we shall go to the Tsim Sha Tsui waterfront or to Wan Chai; both give us spectacular views. We're lucky it's Friday."
"Tsim Sha Tsui, I haven't been there for years, Kim."
"Tsim Sha Tsui it is," says Kim. "The show is now on both sides of Victoria Harbour, but we have a little time; it's not dark yet. Shall we invite the others too?"
"Yes, Ye Myo surely has never seen anything like it," replies Susie.
Sally arrives and says, "Oh, I'm glad to be back. I'll have another session tomorrow morning, and then my business is all wrapped up."

"Good that you are here, Sally," says Susie. "Daddy, Ye Myo, Chika," Susie calls out, "Tonight, the festival of lights, is anyone interested?"
"That's a great idea, Susie," responds Aaron.
"Do not forget your camera, Chika," adds Kim. "It'll be a great spectacle, with beams of light shining from the rooftops into the sky."

All arrive at Tsim Sha Tsui waterfront, just before 8 p.m. to watch the lightshow begin. Beams of light set to choreographed music transmitted through the local radio stations.

Next morning, all share breakfast at the hotel, with Sally announcing that she will need to fly out this afternoon.
"I will spend one more day in Hong Kong," says Chika, "then I will head off to Japan."
"Ye Myo and I will return to Basel on Sunday night," Susie says. "What are your plans, Dad?"
"I will stay a little longer, but I know I have another assignment following the end of next week."
"Let's all make the best of the time we have together," suggests Kim.

We will not give a warning
Basel, Switzerland

A year of preparation has passed before plans could be put into place to give mankind a second warning. The group of twelve met again in the house. Susie informs the group of new developments, "We are now ready to implement the second stage of the plan. This time we had intended to 'influence' several places at once.

We need to select six targets. Zoe did some research on that."
"Thanks, Susie," says Zoe. "Initially, we thought of Taiwan and Japan, both ideal places to implement the plan. However, since Shenzhen is in Asia, Taiwan, and Japan as well, it could be misconstrued as an attack on the Asian race. Instead, the following are suitable contenders, based on location and size. As Susie said, we are looking for six out of the following: In short, we have Copenhagen, Manhattan Island, Malta, Cyprus, Bahrain, Colombo, parts of New Zealand, the Seychelles, Hawaii, and the Falkland Islands."

"A little bit of detail on each," Zoe continues, "is that Copenhagen is located on an island named Seeland. It is the cultural and economic centre of Denmark, as well as the capital of the country. "The current population is about 510000. Manhattan, USA, excluding New York, has a population that is a bit over 1.5 million. Malta, the land of honey, has a total population of a bit over 400,000. Cyprus, located south of Turkey in the eastern Mediterranean, has a population of nearly 800,000. Bahrain, the Garden of Eden, the Pearl of the Persian Gulf, population over 1 million. Colombo, Sri Lanka, population exceeding 700,000. In the North Island of New Zealand, Auckland, it has a population of 1.3 million. New Zealand consists of two main islands, but the North Island would be easier to handle."
"Seychelles, located east of Africa, north-east of Madagascar, is an archipelago nation with over 150 islands and a population of approximately 82,000. The Falkland Islands, Islas Malvinas, are in the South Atlantic Ocean, 300 miles east of Argentina. They have two main islands plus over 700 smaller ones. The population is very small."

Gasha suggests, "Perhaps we should look at each in more detail and then put it to a vote."
"Yes, by all means," says Susie.
Nadira questions, "What exactly will be the warning in these places?"
Zoe answers, "This time, for a period of six months, no boys can be conceived. After six months, boys will be conceived as normal."
Sheila says, "Last time, the press totally ignored our warnings."
"And they will do so again," says Kysa.

"Not this time," says Susie. "We will not give a warning. We will wait until they are born. They will not be able to fiddle with the numbers in all locations."
"And we issue the warning afterwards," says Adzumi. "They cannot show a single boy at that age."
"We still have the option of reversibility, meaning the influence is for a six-month period only and does not guarantee a 100% success rate. We should consider a ratio of 20 boys to every 100 girls as a success," says Susie, "but there will also be some discrepancies due to the fact that women ready to bear may come in from outside the areas. Such women could be carrying males or females."

Discussion is taking place amongst the group, looking at each of the suggested locations. "Perhaps we could each nominate six countries and take a count to see which have been chosen," says Aislinn.
Twenty minutes later, six names from each were collected in a bowl. They all gathered to sort the slips of paper on the table. The countries with the least number of votes will not be 'influenced'.

"Based on this, we have selected the following," announces Nameless One: "Copenhagen, Manhattan, Bahrain, Colombo, New Zealand, and the Falkland Islands."
"Seychelles, Malta, Hawaii, and Cyprus have the least number of votes," concludes Nameless One.
Ramona collects all the snippets off the table and throws them into the fireplace, burning them all.
"How long will it take to organise?" asks Ramona.
"Between May and September, we should expect mostly female births in the selected places," answers Susie.

It feels like the dawning of a new day

Basel / Shenzhen / Hong Kong

Change was in the air. A check on Shenzhen reveals that male hospital staff have replaced most female staff across the city. A similar trend is noticeable across China. Hong Kong also has fewer female medical professionals than ever in its history. Many, even highly qualified professionals, were pushed out of the industry for flimsy excuses; males have replaced many.

The new 'influence', now implemented in the six selected countries, is starting to show early results. Already by the end of May, a difference in the birth ratio had become evident. The South Island of New Zealand produced approximately even genders, while in the North, the ratio was 32 males to every 100 females.

Bahrain showed the 'best' ratio, giving 16 males per 100 females; Colombia was also good with 18 males. The result from Manhattan shows the worst, with 38 males per 100 females. The average of all six countries shows a ratio of 25 males per 100 females.
The ensuing months changed the numbers somewhat, resulting in 23 males for every 100 female births on average.

It was time to let the world know what had happened. Adzumi, the software expert of the group, developed a system to feed blogs, websites, and news-feeds across the Internet, showing none originating from Switzerland.

Susie had planned to re-release a false version of the book 'I want to die', suitably modified to carry the group's message instead of its original content, to capitalise on the hype this book had caused earlier, but decided against the idea. Live TV was no longer live. Most channels have a 10-minute safety zone, used to filter out any surprises.
The group spread its message through women's organisations, trying to convey their demands through the women to the men in their lives.

The dramatic change in gender ratio for the six-month period from May to September in Copenhagen, Manhattan, Bahrain, Sri Lanka, New Zealand, and the Falkland Islands was noticed by the medical profession, although the press hardly mentioned it. China also became aware of the fact that a repeat of what they had experienced earlier was taking place in other parts of the world.

Statistics did not show any improvements in any area that the group of twelve had hoped for; on the contrary, women were losing ground across the board.

China has never publicly admitted to having experienced similar gender ratio differences, as earlier in Shenzhen. Professor Xu Shen, of the Shenzhen research clinic, concluded that all women examined thus far were completely normal. The test groups of men also showed no abnormalities. During the ensuing months, couples intending to become pregnant underwent thorough examinations, their results were analysed, and sperm count data was recorded. Massive data collected from thousands of couples to do with the conception of their new offspring.

It was December, when the group of twelve met again.
Gasha had an announcement, “Next year, I shall return to Ukraine, return home, to start my new career.”
“We will surely miss you, Gasha,” says Zoe, “but as we all know, it will be just a matter of time before we all return to another life.”

“I will leave Basel in June,” says Nadira, “I hope I can give much to my country, when I return. This could be our last time together,” says Tanisha.

“We are the circle of sisters, wherever we are, we’re bound to one another. No distance can lessen our bonds,” says Ye Myo.
“Times will change. We will meet many challenges,” says Ramona, “We will face a future as none has faced before.”
Aislinn brings the subject to the issue, “A future without men. Men ignore us. We are losing left, right and centre, ever since the plan was actioned.”
"I agree," says Kysa, "we have given them chances. Nadira, is this not true?"

"We have tried. Thank you for considering my wishes," Nadira says. "I wonder how my world has changed when I go home. Will I find a job at all, only because I’m a woman? Although I’m now highly qualified, will I be allowed to work at all?"

"It could be that in the short term, women will feel discrimination on a scale never seen before," says Nameless One. "We face a serious decision."

"We do," says Sheila, "it is a very serious decision. The consequences will echo far into the future."

Tanisha recites a quote: "A pebble, however small, thrown in a pond will generate ripples in all directions. That is the nature of water. It can also rise above, become vapour, renew itself countless times, and even freeze to a solid, changing its name to ice. We are of water."
"Thank you, Tanisha," says Adzumi, "we know why we have come together."
"Yes," Tanisha replies, "to throw a pebble."
"It will ripple in all directions," says Adzumi.

Susie, "We too need to face what is facing us."
"We are facing irreversibility," says Nadira."Yes," says Susie, "the world will never be the same."
Kysa says, "I know we can't ask how this is implemented, what mechanism is actually used, although I'd be interested to know."
"Perhaps it knocks out or damages the Y-chromosomes for good," Gasha says, "No Y-chromosomes, no boys."
"How long will it take to 'influence' everyone?" asks Ramona, delicately formulating the question that can wipe one gender off the face of the earth.
"It will work differently than the last warnings, very differently." explains Susie. "How long? Perhaps five years, maybe six."

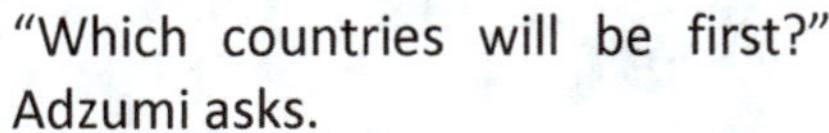

"Which countries will be first?" Adzumi asks.

"There is no telling," says Susie, "Where it begins is irrelevant."
"Could it be like a modified AIDS virus, no symptoms until it is too late and self propagating?" asks Gasha.

"Could it be stopped?" asks Aislinn.
"No," Susie answers.
Tanisha says, "We better make sure that we know what we want the world to become before unleashing whatever it is called that decides the fate of men."

“Not knowing where we go will blind our path,” says Nadira.
“We know where we’ve been,” adds Nameless One, “I have news. I know who I am. I found my name.”
Overjoyed, Nameless One grins from ear to ear.
“This second it came to me, I know who I am,” she says.
"This is wonderful, Nameless One. Tell us, who are you?" asks Ye Myo.
"I am, are you ready for this?" She asks, "From this moment forwards, my name shall be... Asha."
Joy fills the room for the one who found her name.
"This is such a nice name," says Tanisha; "it is an Indian name, you know?"

"I know, Tanisha," says Asha. "I know. In your name too are the letters of this name."

The two women share a close embrace. Each shares the special moment of the once ‘Karla’, with the ‘man’ in her name, transforming to become a whole woman, complete in appearance, self-awareness, and name.

"Oh, it feels so good to have a name," she says, "and such a special name, Asha," she says, "the moment of hope in this room, captured in a name I can carry for life."
"I shall always remember this moment," she says.
"And so will I," says Adzumi.
"I’ll certainly never forget it, gee," says Gasha and laughs. "I too share the letters of your name."

"It never occurred to me, knowing your name for so long, Gasha," said Asha. "It came to me by projecting a thought into the future."

"Asha is light, as if we’re in a deep, dark tunnel. We need a light ahead to aim for, and I do. This name can shine within," says Asha.

"I know what you mean, Asha," says Ye Myo. "It holds within a direction. Perhaps we could all find a name to give us strength and direction for the times ahead. A name that captures this moment, our hope, the foundation, the new beginning, the transformation to create a better world, all wrapped in a name, to help us see it through."
“I like this idea,” says Zoe.
“I’m all for it,” says Sheila, “but I don’t know all the meanings of names.”
“I think I will add a new name to mine as well,” says Susie.
“OK, let’s find one,” says Ye Myo, “what is it you need tomorrow, next year, in the next ten years?”
“I think I need confidence, I have always had confidence, but I have the feeling that it might not be enough,” says Susie, “I need a double dose, if that is possible?”

Ye Myo thinks, “Susie Elfreda, it’s an English name, strength.”
Susie laughs, “Good try, Ye Myo, but no.”
“Treasa, it is Gaelic, or Theresa, Irish.”
“Nope,” Susie replies.

“I could need a name that shines a light,” says Ramona, “What could you suggest for me, Ye Myo?”
“Ramona Ora, or Luminita, Nuru,” says Ye Myo, “Bonifacio may give you a good destiny.”
“Hikari,” suggests Adzumi, “or Haruki. Ki is life, shine or radiance.”
"Ramona Bonifacio De Urquiza, a Spanish-Italian mix," laughs Ramona, "but it has a sound to it." She adds, "To think that once I was led to believe that women had no names, and now we have so many. I'm thinking of Nicole this minute. She helped me."
"Manisha is a name we could all do with," says Tanisha, adding, "Manisha, the wisdom to know we are doing the right thing."

"I couldn't agree with you more," says Zoe.

"The right thing," ponders Kysa, "we know inside, we have strength and the ability to move the world in this direction. There will be pain to bear. Everything worth growing costs pain. We, and probably all our sisters will suffer, at least for a short time, until the inevitable is sinking in," says Sheila.

"Somehow I feel we are procrastinating, trying to hold it off another minute, another hour," adds Asha.
"Tomorrow, the world will not be much different than it is today. It will change slowly. Each day more girls will be born, and with each day, the balance of gender will gradually shift," says Adzumi.

"Just as the icecaps melt, drip by drip, slowly, gradually, but unstoppable," summarises Aislinn. The women link arms to form a circle.
"Yes," says Kysa, "and even though it is 11 p.m. at night, it feels like the dawning of a new day."
"This is the beginning of a new time," says Nadira, "a new era."
"We're in agreement," says Aislinn.
Sheila nods, and Asha says, "Yes."
Tanisha says, "I will agree to disagree, but I shall nod, just the same."
Ramona nods, "Sí."

Adzumi adds her thoughts: "From Japan, the rising sun will herald the dawning of a new age. By the time it gets here, the dominoes will fall against one another to trigger the beginning of change," Zoe adds.
"Like nuclear fission, no one will know which atom started the chain reaction," says Susie.
"Who are the dominoes?" asks Kysa.
Susie replies, "Men."

She steps out of the circle, walks to her handbag, and takes out her mobile phone to ring a number. She walks to the window; the length of the call is 18 seconds. She returns the phone to her handbag.

"We must have a party for Gasha before the year ends," says Kysa.
Sheila and Zoe voice their agreement.
Ye Myo, deep in thought, suggested, "Could we all drive to a nice spot to watch the sunrise?"
Ramona responds, "I would like that."

Asha informs, "I know a good place, but we still have lots of time."
For the rest of the night, the group is discussing a world that might become reality in time. Before sunrise, they travel to the vantage point. The yellowish glow is announcing the sun's arrival, bathing the valley in a soft haze of light.
Each moment, the light changes until the rays break through, revealing a crisp winter morning covered in snow. Never appeared the snow cleaner as on this dawn of new hope.

Ye Myo, addressing Adzumi, says, "The sun came all the way from Japan to bring us this glorious morning."
"If anyone here wishes to conceive in the hope of getting a son, now is the time to do this," says Susie.

"When will the plan take effect?" asks Kysa.
"It has already been taking effect since midnight," Susie replies.
"But how?" asks Kysa.
"I don't know," was Susie's reply, "but you knew I was going to say that."

Our brief is to do whatever it takes
Shenzhen, China, Medical Research Clinic

In April, the Shenzhen medical team at the research clinic called for an emergency meeting, which urged experts in the field of gynaecology and fertilisation to attend. Arrangements for the meeting to take place were finalised quickly.

"Good morning, gentlemen. Thank you for your prompt attention to my request to attend this meeting," says Professor Xu Shen. "Our task is of the utmost urgency, and I must stress that it requires absolute secrecy. You will see why in a few moments."
While China has equal, if not larger, numbers of female-qualified medical professionals, no females were invited to attend this meeting.

"Here is the background information outlined in three steps:
Step 1: You may not know that two years ago, in the months between January and March, the sex ratio of babies born in that time span throughout Shenzhen showed a strong deviation away from what we consider normal when compared to births prior to this period. We have tried to find a cause for this, examined the fathers of these girls, compared the findings against an equal number of randomly selected males of similar age, and found no difference in any of the data we gathered. All appeared completely normal."

“We continued to collect sperm samples from both test groups over several months and could not detect any abnormalities, in either sperm count, or X-Y-chromosome ratios. Likewise did we collect data on the mothers of these girls, compared the results against a select group of mothers having birthed mixed genders from a different time span, and we were unable to find any noticeable deviation from the norm. Following the period January to March, things levelled out to normal. The ratio of boys to girls settled to something like 1.07 to 1, slightly more boys than girls, normal.”

"Step 2: The following year, we have become aware that Copenhagen and the island around it, Manhattan Island, New Zealand, Bahrain and The Falklands have all experienced a similar scenario as we had seen earlier. Very few boys were born in the time span of May to September when compared to their averages. I flew over to several places myself, accompanied by several members of my team. The test results we were privy to see, compared similar to our own, as outlined in step 1."
"Step 1 was two years ago, step 2 was last year. We are now coming to step 3, the present time."

"Since February of this year we have made some alarming discoveries. Sperm count from men has markedly reduced across the whole of China, irrespective of the age of the donors. We became aware of this in Shenzhen. We then tested samples from across China. No matter where the sperm came from, the count was low. We tested 16-year-old boys through the ages, up to 60-year-old men. No matter which age group the count shows equally reduced sperm count results across the board. That is not all... it gets worse. The number of Y-chromosomes is almost negligible. The ones we could identify were far too weak. Gentlemen, we all know what that means."

"In other words gentlemen, men, males will not be born from women who have conceived since February of this year. Just in case no one here understands what I am saying, I will spell it out again for you. Any intercourse with such a low sperm count, semen that contains a few struggling Y-chromosomes, can only result in female offspring, if any."
"Therefore, and this is the conclusion we draw, our days are numbered. Men are on the verge of extinction."
"We don't know how it's done. We don't know if this is some kind of attack on our country and its people. We don't know how this is at all possible."

"I am the team leader and I am under instructions from all the way, and I mean the very top, to make sense of all this. My team and I have handpicked you all, based on your professional expertise in the field of fertilisation and related disciplines."

"Unfortunately, I have a bitter pill for you to swallow, and I can assure you that my team and I swallowed the same bitter pill about a month ago. I am obliged to read to you the following:"

"You, meaning each of you in this room, are hereby ordered to cooperate with the team leader, Professor Xu Shen, I, and his team to uncover the reasons or causes of the unusual fertility changes that are currently occurring in China. You are protected from any interference from the outside world so that you can devote your professional knowledge to uncovering the causes. Your families receive financial support, so that you can continue uninterrupted to undertake any research that is necessary to solve this without the need to worry about your families' well-being."

"Gentlemen, please remain calm. May I continue? Thank you. Other qualified medical professionals are temporarily fulfilling your duties in your home clinics, hospitals, or practises. As of this moment, you are part of Professor Xu Shen's team."
Professor Xu Shen is raising the page into the air, looking at everyone. "I guess you all know where this came from."

He reads the bottom line, "My apologies, there is one more line to go: To be selected for this important mission is a great honour. The people of the country are in your debt."

"What it means, gentlemen, is this: We are locked in this building. My team and I have now been locked in here for over a month. The doors and exits are closed and guarded. Each of you is allowed a 30-minute conversation per day with your families, which I can tell you, that security personnel are going to monitor every word you exchange."

"We are not allowed any female contacts or visitors, except as patients. Even then, a guard will need to be in the room with you."
"The reason for this is that in each of the steps I outlined earlier, the male sperm or foetus is the victim, as an increasing number of miscarriages shows.

As absurd as it sounds, there is suspicion that we are under attack from the female gender. All these measures are put in place to protect us from sabotage from members of the female gender."
"Please, gentlemen, calm down."

"We are given an unlimited budget, resources, and access to wherever we need to go. We will get anything at all that we may require. Guards will, of course, accompany you."

"I would like to create three groups. Group Y will research the male, group X the female gender, and group IV will focus on in-vitro fertilisation with the aim of providing a fast and efficient means to collect Y chromosome-bearing spermatozoa with a higher than 95% purity."

"Based on your own areas of specialisation, please form these groups now. I suggest 'Y' assemble to the left; Dr. Huang Qiu will head this group; Dr. Lin Kang will lead group 'X'; please assemble in the centre; 'IV' on the right of this room is led by Dr. Kym Chang."
"Attention to groups 'Y' and 'IV': we do have several thousand sperm donations, which were collected during the period explained in step 1. Just so you're aware of it."

"Another thing is that we are immune from any prosecution, meaning that normally unethical practises that would result in jail terms or whatever else do not apply to us. We will, of course, treat all our patients with respect and dignity."

"In short, our brief is to do whatever it takes to solve it, regardless."
"I will accept questions only if they relate to solving our problem. The sooner we get this finished, the sooner we will go home. Thank you everyone."

Professor Xu Shen leaves the room, allowing the men to get to know each other. A moment later, he returns to call into the room, "And just in case you need some extra stimulation, I am authorised to offer $10 million to the one who cracks the case and another $10 million, to be shared equally amongst all other group members."

Let us try to start again

Kyiv, Ukraine

Gasha, now living in her hometown, the capital and largest city of Ukraine, looks up at the outstretched wings of the Independence Statue, perched high atop a large column, overlooking the city of Kyiv (Kiev). It is one of the oldest cities in Eastern Europe. She heads across Independence Square, looking at the monument that honours the city's legendary founders.

Kyi, Schek, Khoryv, and their sister Lybid are cast standing in an open, ancient boat set atop three waves and positioned on a low, tiled pedestal next to the Dnipro River.

Gasha walks close to face Lybid, who stands with outstretched arms, high up on steps, set into the bow. Lybid's coat cast, to fly forever in the wind. She looks ahead, proud and tall. Behind her stand the three brothers. The one at the stern holds a bow with one arm, aiming towards the rear. The brother in the middle looks to starboard, the next facing forwards. Each holds a lance upright.

Kyiv, the name of Kyi, for the high, hilly west banks of the Dnipro; Schek and Khoryv, for Schekavytsia and Khorevytsia mountains, at the centre of Kyiv. Lybid stands for the river, a right tributary of the Dnipro.

'Oh, Lybid, you're always flowing downriver, and you are always here, next to your brothers. In your time, this was just a trading post. Look at it now, a thriving city. It has become a cultural, educational, and scientific centre of Eastern Europe,' Gasha's thoughts, 'Ukrainian history, Ukrainian future', what will it be like in a hundred years?'

'There will be no brothers anywhere on earth, Lybid. The waters within you have mixed with every ocean since the beginning of time. Yet you stayed true to yourself throughout all this time. But you're still water, be that in a tear, the rain, or the surf in any ocean. You have not changed in all those years.'

'Humanity, as you, has mixed its genes with one-another, all ought to be as you, alike, and we are. What we see are our differences. No longer do we act as one. Something has gone wrong along the way.'

'Lybid, men have turned bad. We try to start again, without them.'

'I wish I could stand as high as you, to be able to look forth, to see into the distance of time ahead, Lybid.'

It is May. The world still appears as normal.

The balance shifts

Karachi, Pakistan, July

Nadira is returning home to Pakistan. A lot has changed in Karachi since her last visit. Karachi, one of the world's largest cities, the capital of Sindh province, located west of the large Indus River Delta. Traffic, pollution, and overcrowding are evident, as the city has grown by 3 million Karachiites in just 3 years.

The heartbeat of Pakistan is home to more than a million refugees and various ethnic groups from Myanmar, Arakani, Iran, Uzbekistan, and Turkey. There are hundreds of thousands of Filipinos, Bengalis, Africans, and so many other ethnic groups. Fewer than 50% of the city's population speaks Urdu, while Sindhi, Punjabi, Moyoiki, and so many other languages colour the sounds of this rich mixture of peoples from different lands.

Karachi has grown from 400,000 in 1947 to near 20 million today. The lifestyle in Karachi is very different from the rest of Pakistan. It is a melting pot of regional and international influences and the business centre of the country.

Silently, Nadira walks the streets to absorb the sounds, the smells, and the feel of Karachi as it is now.
To Nadira, it feels like watching a documentary of another time, the smells will fade, the noise will silence.
'What will happen to my people? This moment is changing with each child that is born, to become a memory of days long gone. As each man dies, the balance shifts.'

Yes, yes, we know all this

Shenzhen, China, Medical Research Clinic

The Shenzhen research team is searching frantically to find answers. They are instead confronted with the hard reality of facts.
By August, gender differences were observable in the growing foetuses. Almost 73% had become female. The embryonic stage saw a 12% increase in miscarriages. In November, the first babies were born since the change in sperm count became noticeable. By December, the number of females expected had risen to 86%. By April of the following year, 93% of girls had been born.

China was not alone. In June, the world faced the fact that dramatic gender balance change is occurring in all major countries. The Shenzhen team widened research, to include all facets of food production, grains, flour, fruits. Analysts and researchers overworked in trying to provide results for an ever-growing list of requests. The relocation of highly qualified female staff further hampered efforts to find answers.

Change came quick in training men to become medical professionals, nurses and teachers. Male nursery nurses, now exclusively in charge of all male children born, to give each the best chance of survival, giving baby boys special attention and care.

Mothers of boys born in hospitals never saw their sons again. The hospitals issued falsified death certificates and expressed their condolences. The notion of what is right or wrong adjusts to reality, whatever that may entail in practice. Anything that improves men's chances is justified because men's survival is at stake. The discussions taking place in the research clinic mirror numerous others that have since been established in different regions of the nation with the same aim of determining the reason for gender change.

'We do not know yet if the few males we have will develop normally. It will take a long time to see if their testes are able to produce any useful sperm at all. We do not have the luxury of time. Man has XY, while women have XX chromosomes. We know the definition of the male Y chromosome. We have a fully detailed blueprint. It is the first chromosome to be fully sequenced. We know every single DNA letter on the Y chromosome. We know what it should look like. We know what is in it. Who has the capacity to kill it off at the rate it is showing up here? However, my fear is that we are witnessing the birth of the 'XX Generation'. I hope I'm wrong,' are some of the thoughts occupying the research teams.

'Evolutionary change does not happen within this short a time span. The Y is passed on from father to son. The son is an exact copy of his father. By comparison, the female X has close to 1,000 working genes. Overall, humanity shares 99.9% of its genes with each other, which all humanity has in common.'

'We know of the progressive reduction of genes on the Y chromosome over time. We thought we would have 4 to 5 million years left before it came to the crunch. What is happening now has nothing to do with a steady decline. The rapid degeneration we are witnessing is without precedent. On top of that, the irony is that once we had a 1-child policy.'

'Let us look at the fights that chromosomes have. The X has attacked the Y for millions of years, yet the Y still survived, despite losing more genes than it has left, until now, that is.'

'Look, we know there are exceptions to this: women having XY, X, or XXX, males having XXY, XYY, even XXXY, and a multitude of other compositions. Survival is an integral part of every living being. Given half a chance, each will try to stay alive.'

'The problem we are facing is a low sperm count. What could change this so dramatically?'

"Yes, yes, yes, we know all this," says Professor Xu Shen. "Tell me something that I don't know, please!"

It has not sunk in yet

Basel, Switzerland

Adzumi became the communications expert of the group of 12. She had developed a unique method of encrypting messages in data that looked like ordinary digital images to anyone else. Each of the 12 members of the group could decipher the images to read the hidden message's content.

Even if this method is cracked, the extracted code has been re-encrypted several times. It will not reveal its real message to the uninitiated easily. Gasha and Nadira kept informed of anything the group discussed, and both were able to give their input. In Basel, the group, now ten, met again, this time on a boat on the Rhine. Susie chartered the vessel.

"So many women left messages on our websites. It shows we are not alone. Unfair inheritance laws, economic differences, job opportunities, and for many working women the double burden of running a household and a job. I shall be the next to leave this lovely place," says Adzumi. "Nagoya, Japan, is my home."
"How is your brother there?" asks Tanisha.
"Not good. The doctors have given him little chance," she says.

"Aaron is not the same as he was," comments Susie. "My uncle died, and Aaron had to return to our hometown, the port city of Southampton, to run the shipyard now."
"How did he go in Hong Kong? He did try to find Kim, your sister's mother. Did he succeed?" asks Ramona.

"He did. I think the guilt got to him. He's never been the same since he came back," Susie says. "Ying An Jia, that's my sister's mother, died six weeks after giving birth to her. He seems to have aged within weeks. Not only that, I think his mind is in the past. No matter what I do, he's in another world somehow."
"Are you OK, Susie?" asks Ye Myo.
"I'm OK, tanks, Ye Myo."
"I'll leave Switzerland in three months."
"The USA for me, in four months," adds Zoe.
"I'll still be here for a long while yet," says Ye Myo.
"We should all meet someplace, every few years," Kysa suggests. "No matter where, maybe even visit each other, another place every time."

"As long as we are able to do that," says Susie.

"Do I detect some apprehension, doubt, or uncertainty?" asks Tanisha. "Yes," Susie says, "look around you; see what is happening."
"You mean the changes that are taking place?" asks Aislinn.
"Yes. When was the last time you saw a female reporter, newsreader, or anything female near a microphone on TV?" Susie answers.

"Males are pushing females out of all key areas, even in the airports," adds Sheila.
"No one ever mentioned our demands in the media," says Ramona, "not a word."
"We must have been really naïve then," laughs Asha, "a mysterious virus, they call it now, is responsible for the low male birth-rate."
"Have no illusions," adds Tanisha, "they will fight back."

"Kim Xia, from Hong Kong says, she's not seen a single male infant anywhere for months," says Ye Myo.
"The first Shenzhen 'influence' must have woken them up," says Susie; "they did not ignore the warning. That gave them a head start on the others."

"If everyone else follows suit, we're in for a rough ride," Asha suggests.
Sheila asks, "I thought it would take up to 5 years to 'influence' everyone, but it seems to go faster than anticipated."
"It is," answers Susie, "but we didn't realise how effective the system was until the ball started rolling. It took everyone by surprise."
"The domino effect?" "Multiplication to the power of what?" asks Zoe.
Susie smiles, but she does not answer.

"Assuming the 'influence' is 100% effective everywhere," asks Kysa, "we, womhood, will be exterminated as well; it's just a matter of time, am I right?"
"No," answers Susie, "but I cannot give you a proper explanation. That is all I can say at this moment. Perhaps that was already too much."
Aislinn says, "We are all dispensable, as we don't know what each day brings."
Sheila continues her thought, "...but the aim of the 'influence' must not be lost."
"Be prepared for the anger in men," warns Tanisha, "it is still very early. What is happening has not sunk in yet into their brains. Rough days are just around the corner."

"On another matter," says Susie, "this is probably the last time we can all meet in this beautiful villa in Basel, as I will return to Southampton as well."

Help me to smash a bottle

Southampton, UK

The next time to group met was in Southampton, UK. "Why did Aaron wanted us to come?" asks Kysa.

"I have no idea," responds Susie.
The day had arrived that Aaron had finally completed one of his dreams. He calls Susie, "Darling, could you please come over and bring your friends, to the shipyard on Friday and help me smash a bottle?"
"No way, Dad, never on a Friday. You can't launch a ship on a Friday unless you're looking for trouble."
"You're right, Susie; sorry, I forgot."
"You've been away from the shipyard for too many years. Not on a Thursday either."
"Is it for some special client?" asks Susie.
"Yes, yes, very much so," replies Aaron.

A few days later Susie and the group arrive at the shipyard to see a beautiful catamaran on the slipway. She is decorated with ribbons, balloons, and flags. A group of musicians are tuning their instruments nearby. Tables are set, bottles are filled, and it looks like the christening celebration are about to begin. The nameplate at the bow is covered with a veil.

"Let's hand out some drinks," suggests Aaron.
"What's her name, Dad? Where and who is the client?" asks Susie.

"Just go up to the podium, Susie, and make sure you swing that bottle hard on the bow. That bottle is tough. You better use all your strength to make certain it breaks," he says, "Read these words when you're up there." He hands her a slip of paper.

'May God guide and bless her and all that sail within her. I name this yacht _____.'

"But Dad, what's her name?"
"She'll tell you as soon as she gets a taste of what's in the bottle on her bow."
"I can't wait to break that bottle now."

Susie steps up to the platform, speaking into a microphone: "May you cut smooth through rough waters and safely return all in your care; may the seas be kind and carry you always on top. May you shield your charges and guard your content as a mother safeguards her child. May God guide and bless you and all that sail within you. I would like you all to raise your glasses now. I hereby name this vessel ..." and Susie swings the bottle hard, crashing it into the side and spilling its contents over the bow. The veil over the nameplate lifts to reveal a lily and the name, "Susie."

Aaron whispers in her ear: "My most important client is you, Susie. She is yours."
"Daddy, this is just crazy. Thank you so much."
"Don't forget to place the branch of leaves on her, quickly, before she slips away."

The vessel is cut free and slowly slides down the slipway, stern first, into the water, to much applause and cheers.

The vessels heads out, around the Isle of Wight into the English Channel, heading north east towards Calais, France. "Dad, look at her go, this speed on her maiden voyage, wow."

They are an hour out at sea exploring the vessel, navigation systems, auto-pilot, sail storage areas, and the accommodation.

"Susie, come over here," calls Sheila, "Aaron doesn't look well."

"Daddy, what's the matter, are you OK?" asks Susie.
"I don't know, dear. I feel a bit..."

Susie takes charge, "We'll turn back right now. Aislinn, you take the helm."
"Daddy, talk to me, keep talking." She slaps Aaron in the face.
"Kysa, call in a chopper. Tell them where we are, and tell them it's urgent."
Kysa is in communication with the chopper pilot, instructing Aislinn to try to stay steady on course.

The winch-man secures Aaron to the rescue basket while the helicopter hovers overhead. He manages to whisper to Susie, "I didn't mean to mess up your maiden voyage, sorry darling."
"Stay calm, Dad. Breathe slow and steady. You'll be in a hospital in a couple of minutes."

Moments later the helicopter flies off into the distance.
"Thank you Aislinn and Kysa. I knew I could rely on you."
"Don't mention it," responds Aislinn. "Yeah, just like old times," adds Kysa.
"I'm worried about Dad for the last few weeks. He seems to be a bit off colour lately."
Kysa interrupts, "About Aaron, he's out of immediate danger, says the hospital."

Two months later, the women met again at Aaron's funeral. Susie explains: "I was talking to all the managers at the shipyard. It seems that all Aaron was interested in was getting the catamaran commissioned. Nothing else mattered to him. They say he was obsessed with getting it done to perfection. They even said that if she loses all her rigging, she'll still be able to reach land from anywhere. I think the trauma of my sister's mother got to him, but don't tell Kim that, please. The catamaran must have been his last wish in life, and he saw it completed."

"Kim is here now," says Ramona. Both sisters follow the coffin into the chapel for the funeral service.
"I am so sorry, Kim Xia, you found your father and lost him again," say Susie. "We are now family, you know that, don't you?" Kim holds her hands and nods.

The group stayed with Susie for a few days. "Kim, I want you to stay a little longer," says Susie. "What do you know about shipbuilding?"
"Absolutely nothing," answers Kim. "That makes two of us," responds Susie. "I know about sailing but not building a vessel. Dad made a will, and in it he left everything to me. The will was made

before he knew you existed. I would like to make a suggestion. Dad didn't know much about shipbuilding either. He left the expertise to the ones with know-how who had been running the shipyard since my uncle had it. What he did was make all the staff part of the business. This includes all employees. In a sense, each has an interest in seeing the business do well. The details are overseen by an accounting firm that goes regularly through the books. It's profit sharing, which discourages theft, laziness, coming late to work, etc. It's good for morale, as each has an interest in completing the job on time and within budget. My suggestion is that we both become co-owners of the shipyard and the mansion in town and have an equal share in all of Dad's accounts."

"But you didn't have to do that, Susie," says Kim.
"Kim, we're the only one left. I said we were family. I'm sure Dad would have changed the will if, for a minute, he'd stop chasing adventures."

"So far, I have not become aware of any liabilities Dad might have had," continues Susie. We'll sit down with the accountants and let them know where to deposit our share of the profits. Here is a second set of keys for this mansion. There are probably some motor vehicles and miscellaneous things to sort through. In other words, if all goes well, we're both set up for life, at least financially. All we need to do is change the deeds and various documents." Five weeks later, Susie formulates a letter to accompany the three parcels she prepared.

'Dearest Chika,
thank you so much for your words of comfort the other day and for attending Aaron's farewell. I know you liked him very much, and you had a lot in common. It was Aaron's wish that you receive his original material, including all rights to use it as you see fit. I have also included his original notes, which may help you make sense of it all.

Signed Susie.

Such news is very troubling

A village near Madrid, Spain

Following Aaron's funeral, Ramona returned home to her native Spain, near Madrid. She is renting a cottage at the edge of the village, near Leticia's place. It sits high on the hillside. The view from the porch is rejuvenating each morning, filling all her senses with life. Waking up is a joy here.

A dirt road leads to the cottage, which twists for two miles up the hillside. In the afternoon, a trail of dust in the distance announces the arrival of an expected visitor. Ten minutes later the stillness of this tranquil setting change. The voice of Felicia Fodor colours the air, as she steps out of her small bus to greet Ramona.

"Ramona, Ramona, I know how to read colours and signs, shapes and symbols, but your map drawing skills are the pits," as she laughs in embracing her.

"I could have been here by lunch time, if I had any idea of how to decipher your scribbles."

"Felicia, oh look at you, time forgets to catch up with you."

"I'm not so sure about that, Ramona."

"I have brought a surprise for you."

"Oh, you're not alone..., Nicole, that is a nice surprise to see you," says Ramona, as she helps Nicole to climb out of the bus.

All three fill the day to catch up on news, delight in Spanish cuisine on the porch, with the backdrop framed in the glowing colours of a Spanish sunset.
The next day, at 10 a.m., Nicole notices it first and calls the others, "What's this over there?" as she points her arm to aim at the area. They see a tiny, lone figure bobbing its head out of the grass to disappear moments later. “I know what that is,” says Ramona, “an escapee from Leticia. Come on, help me, we must catch her before she gets totally lost.”
The women spread out to home in on the child.
“And who might you be?” asks Ramona, looking into her dark, tear-filled eyes, but the girl does not answer.
“Quiénes son usted. Cuál es su nombre?” she asks again.
“Mi nombre es Gabriela,” she says, “He perdido mi manera.”
“My name is Gabriela. I have lost my way,” translates Ramona.
“Usted falta Leticia, Do you miss Leticia?” Ramona asks.
“No,” she answers.
“Do you miss Señora Chavira?” she asks again, “Usted falta Señora Chavira?”
“Sí,” she replies.
“Gabriela, cómo viejo es usted?” Ramona asks.
“Soy 5 años de Viejo,” she responds.
“She is five years old,” explains Ramona. "I found two others last week. Leticia Chavira is under stress."
“Adelantado, sígame, yo le traerá de nuevo a señora Chavira,” she says to Gabriela.

Half an hour later, they meet with Señora Chavira.
She embraces the girl, “Gabriela, cuáles son yo que va a hacer con usted?”
“Thank you Ramona,” says Leticia, “Nicolina, Nicola, sorry, it will come to me..., wait, Nicole, how are you?”
“Hello, Señora Chavira, I am very well, thank you for asking. How are you?”
“Battling on, trying to make do,” she answers.
“Señora Chavira, may I introduce you to Felicia Fodor. She is a good friend of ours.”
“Hello, Señora Chavira,” says Felicia.

“Come here, let me embrace you," says Señora Chavira.
“How is Perpetua?” Nicole asks.
“That’s why they get away on me. She doesn’t chase them anymore,” Leticia replies. “Perpetua’s time ran out. She can rest now, bless her soul.”
“I am sorry,” says Nicole.
“Oh, she had the time of her life here, dear old Perpetua,” Leticia explains. “It was on a Monday, after dinner, she settled for a nap and she has been sleeping ever since.”

“Nicole, Ramona, and Felicia, tell me, what is happening in the world? I wanted the flow of parentless children to stop. It did. First, no infants, now no toddlers brought to here. What has changed? Explain the world to me?” she asks, “I know so little of what goes on out there.”
“Señora Chavira,” says Nicole, “there is something going on, but no one knows why that is.”
“Tell me, what is going on?”

"In France, I have not seen an infant boy for such a long time; there are none anywhere. Miscarriages are rising. Only girls are born, not only in France but everywhere," explains Nicole.
"The same in Hungary," adds Felicia. "I know of two baby boys, but they died shortly after birth."
"Why is this, Ramona?" asks Señora Chavira. "I have prayed for the flow to cease, but I haven’t prayed for this."
Ramona cups her mouth. She slowly shakes her head in silence.
Nicole explains, "Some say some kind of virus is the cause, others say a change in environment. All sorts of things are said, but no one seems to really know what is going on."

Felicia continues, “Russia, Poland, Germany, Holland, Italy, Portugal, I think the whole of Europe is affected, but that’s not all, America, China, even as far as Japan, from what I’ve heard.”
“If it’s not one thing, than it’s another,” says Señora Chavira. “But this is terrible, such news is very troubling. Has anything like this ever happened before?”
“Not in the history of time that we know,” says Nicole.

“I visited a friend in Budapest last week. She’d given birth to a girl,” says Felicia. “She told of mothers in her ward reeling in pain. Their

healthy sons mysteriously died, so the staff had told them. They were sent home, empty-handed."
"Here in the village too," says Señora Chavira. "Two boys were born, they did not survive their first day of life. The women went home with a piece of paper, saying the boys had died of respiratory complications. Yet they screamed their lungs out as strong as any infant they had seen."

You would have done the same

Saint-Tropez, France

Nicole refills her car at a service station on her drive to Saint-Tropez when she notices a sign nearby. 'Casting Agency, now open.'

In big letters underneath: 'Looking for the "it" girl, could it be you?'

Apply within'.
'Why not,' she says, running low on funds anyway. She enters the agency to see what is on offer.
"Please, Madam, through that door, you will audition in there," says the girl staffing the front desk.

Inside the room, two men sit behind a plain desk while a young woman sorts through papers. "Please come closer. Please tell us your name, age, and experience in the industry," asks one of the men.
She closes the door and steps closer, not noticing the man who had been behind the door. "My name is Nicole."
"And so it is," said the familiar voice of the man behind her.
A shot of Adrenalin surging through Nicole's blood, as she recognised the man as Julien, the Mr. Fix it from the limousine in Cannes.
"You are much too talented to audition for these guys, darling, wouldn't you agree?" he says, bearing an uneasy grin.
"Oh, hello Julien, long time no see," she tries to recover, acting as cool as possible. "How are you? Good to see you again."

"The pleasure is all mine," says Julien, "and I am fine, especially now. Thanks for asking, baby."

Nicole looks at her watch and says, "Oh my goodness, is that the time? I forgot all about my appointment. Sorry guys, I've got to rush; maybe another time."

She walks towards the door, blocked by Julien, who grins and chews gum.

“Take care, Julien. We've got to catch up sometime,” she says, trying to get him to move from the door.

Julien stretches his hand out towards Nicole. She shakes his hand saying, “Good bye.”

Julien holds her hand firmly, swings her body around and pulls it close. His other hand squeezed Nicole’s jaws apart, forced open by his thumb and index finger. He looks into her mouth, “No chewing gum, I see.”

He pulls a long plastic tie from his jacket, to tie both her arms behind her back.

"What are you doing?" she asks. "What’s gotten into you? Let me go; my appointment can’t wait."

"The Baron waited a lot longer, don’t you agree?" said Julien.

He chews on his gum and says, "You know what, darling, chewing gum needs to be worked properly; otherwise, it just won’t stick."

His mouth is close to her ears, his jaw loudly chewing, "You hear that, sugar; that’s properly working the gum."

A moment later, he pulls the wet chewing gum from his mouth, pulling it apart in front of Nicole’s eyes. "This is properly chewed gum," he says, then rolls it into a ball, parts of which stretch as they stick to his fingers. He pushes the softly kneaded gum onto Nicole’s nose and flattens it out with his thumb.

"You see, honey, that won’t come off so easily."

"Let go of me this instant," demands Nicole.

"The Baron’s got your chewing gum. He wants to give it back to you. You do remember the one you lost on the yacht, don’t you, darling?"

"You could have saved yourself the trouble. Inside the lights was another microphone; you didn't know that, I guess."
"A gum needs to be soft and warm," says Julien. "The Baron was looking for something soft and warm too. You do remember the pretty, young, black-haired doll from Spain. She was to be the Baron's special, remember?"
"He was looking forwards to some enjoyment," says Julien.
"That girl was a virgin; don't you understand that?" says Nicole.
"The Baron is a cultured man. He would have been extra careful," responds Julien, "perhaps that made her so special."
"The Baron is a very sensitive man, honey. Sensitive men can easily get hurt. You knocked the Baron out cold and made him a laughing stock in front of his friends. That is very hard to cope with. Can you understand that, sweetie?"
"Let me go," she begs.
"Sorry, but I can't do that. The Baron just wants to give you your gum back."

Nicole calls out to the two men still sitting behind the table, "Help me; can't you see what's going on? Help me, please?"
The men do not move.
"Don't be like that, darling. We go for a little drive, and we say 'hello' to the Baron," says Julien.
"I warn you; let me go," says Nicole.

"You know the Baron lives in another world," continues Julien, "a world of honour, pride, and respect. It is not that he is too upset about the Spanish princess; Lord knows, he had plenty of them. You hurt his feelings, spat on his honour, damaged his pride, and showed no respect. A man like that finds it hard to cope with these things."
"Please, Julien, let me go. I will make it worth your while. Just don't tell him that you met me, and he will never know," she says. "Let's go somewhere; let's have some fun. I'll make you feel like a brand new man."
Julien looks at her from top to toe, smiles, and shakes his head slowly.
"C'mon, just you and me; forget about the Baron. Take me. I am yours. I am a 100% woman. I know what you need. Fulfil your fantasies; let's go," she tries again.

Julien steps very close to Nicole, inhaling her scent and whispering into her ear, "Sorry baby, maybe another time, but not now."
Nicole's right knee lands hard in Julien's groin; her forehead moves fast, aiming straight for his nose, cracking the bone. Julien crouches down, holding his groin and gasps for air. With her hands tied, Nicole is unable to open the door. "Help me get out," she asks the others in the room. Nobody does anything to help her. She kicks the door, but it won't open.

Julien pulls a handkerchief from his pocket to hold his bleeding nose. He regains his composure and walks to the desk to rip off a piece of wide sticky tape taken from one of the drawers, dribbling blood all over the desk and floor.

"Help me!" Nicole begs the others. "He will kill me. Please, how can you let this happen? How can you just watch and stare?" She walks to the woman in the room, "He was going to rape an 18 year old virgin. I had to do something. You would have done the same, Please, just open a door, that's all I ask."
The woman turned away to face the wall.

Julien follows Nicole through the room. She is trying to rotate the round knob of the door with her wrists tied together. She keeps slipping from the perspiration on her hands. Julien grabs her hard and places the tape over her mouth. He heads to the back door and drags her behind. He opens the boot of a dark limousine and shuts the lid with Nicole inside. The car speeds off from the rear parking lot onto the roads of Saint-Tropez. Half an hour later, the car comes to a halt. Ten minutes of absolute silence follow. The boot opens. It is evening. The car is now parked inside a garage with its roller doors down. The garage is wide, and at least three more luxury cars are parked alongside the dark limousine.

Nicole is unable to speak

Lyon, Saint-Tropez, Cannes

Felicia took another route home from her visit to Spain, via Lyon. She sits in a small eatery and the TV shows the news of the day.
"A brutal assault in Saint-Lopez earlier left a woman injured beyond recognition. All we know at this stage is the woman's name, Nicole Dubois. She is being treated in Saint-Tropez Hospital."

Felicia is unable to finish her meal. Her mobile announces the receipt of a text message: 'This message is on behalf of Nicole Dubois: Baron Von Felsburg, Saint-Tropez.' She leaves Lyon to head south on the E15 towards Avignon. At Orange, she follows the E714 heading southeast.

Nicole is asleep when Felicia gets to the hospital. It could be anyone under the bandages. Felicia sits in silence beside her, eventually falling asleep.

The next morning she becomes aware of the full extent of Nicole's injuries. Her face bandaged with just a slit for the eyes, nose and mouth. Her arms bearing heavy bruises, her legs are not much different. Nicole is unable to speak. After two hours, Felicia leaves the hospital.
She returns late the next day. Nicole is still heavily sedated, unable to speak.

Felicia watches the TV news next to Nichole's bedside.

“Saint-Tropez is again in the news tonight. A fire ripped through a mansion, leaving only ruins behind. The fire started in the attached garages housing a number of luxury vehicles, then spread to a nearby storage area housing boxes of celluloid film, all fuelling a ferocious fire that quickly engulfed the whole building. Fire-fighters are trying to bring the flames under control, but there is no hope of saving anything of the building.”

"Baron von Felsburg, the owner of the burning mansion, was not available for comment. Neighbours inform me that the mansion housed priceless art treasures. An estimate of the damage is not yet available. Conservative figures put it in the $70 million plus region for the art treasures alone."

"It seems it’s just not the Baron’s day, as another report, this time from Cannes Harbour shows. Here, the Baron’s luxurious yacht has also gone up in flames, taking with it most of the vessels moored alongside it. Almost all of the 30 or so vessels along the eastern pier were destroyed due to the chain reaction caused by the first vessel. Not a good time for the insurance underwriters, I would imagine."

"Shortly before the initial fire, surveillance footage shows a person with a distinct limp, dressed in dark clothing, loading a tender with several containers of an unspecified substance. The tender is seen heading in the direction of the Baron’s yacht. Onlookers are warned to stay away from the area to allow emergency personnel and fire-fighters to bring this inferno under control."
“An attempt, to set the venue of Cannes Movie Festival alight, was foiled by the quick reaction of security guards. They say, if it doesn’t rain, it pours.”

This may just be the beginning

Chicago, USA

Shima Chika has received all of Aaron's original source material, some of which he used in his documentaries. For the last three months, Chika has been preparing for her first exhibition of photographic works. She titled the exhibition 'A woman's lot.'

Sally Cramer, one of the first through the door to congratulate Chika to get to the point of her first showing. The gallery in downtown Chicago drew good crowds interested in viewing the exhibits. A sign of warning was the graffiti that defaced many of the posters located in the streets surrounding the gallery, drawing attention to the exhibition.

The press did not attend, despite ample time and many invitations. Women's groups showed up in good numbers. Ye Myo flew across the Atlantic to lend Chika support. As she arrived via taxi, groups of young men sussed out the gallery. Some walked through to leave moments later.

Ye Myo pays the fare to the taxi driver, eager to meet up with Chika. The mood of the young men in front of the gallery changed, as several limousines stopped in front to let passenger off near the entrance. All were elegantly dressed women who stepped into the foyer, greeted by the gallery's many assistants.

Some of the young men yelled obscenities and hurled abuse to many who entered. Most women entered quickly and silently.

'They do the dirty on us in there, men bashing, that's what this is all about,' and other comments came from the group. The barrage of outright rude remarks increased.

As Ye Myo neared the entrance, one woman took offence to the remarks hurled at her. She confronted one of the men. Another person at the rear of the group threw a bottle at the large glass window aside the entrance. It bounced off. A large stone, ripped from landscaped areas and thrown with much force, brought the glass window crashing down in countless fragments. The young men cheered for their achievement. Some others are searching for anything of use to degrade the gallery's entrance. Garbage containers were carried to the entrance and then emptied.

Ye Myo withdrew, walking away from the area. She calls Chika, who inside the gallery was not aware of the events outside, near the entrance. "Chika, Ye Myo here, listen: Have them close the gallery doors. A group of louts is trying to mess up your show, and they are throwing unspeakable abuse at visitors. Call the police, wait, call the fire brigade; they are setting rubbish alight at the entrance. Evacuate and get out of there."

Inside the gallery, Chika is searching for Sally to explain what Ye Myo said. Sally calls the fire department and the police. Chika calls for the gallery assistants, some of whom were already aware of the noise and commotion outside. Some push the burning garbage away from the building with long brooms.

Inside, Chika makes an announcement to inform the guests. The back exits are used to evacuate all visitors in a hasty but ordered manner. The sirens of the approaching fire brigade and police cars were enough to disperse the crowd that started the unrest.

When Sally, Chika, and Ye Myo finally met, the reunion was tarnished by the rage of men. "This may just be the beginning," says Ye Myo.

They are just not interested

Basel, Switzerland

Gasha flew in from Kyiv via Frankfurt, Nadira from Karachi, to meet up with the rest of the group of 12.

"Hello everyone," says Susie. "All are here, except Adzumi. She does apologise and is unable to leave Japan at this time. I have called this meeting for us to take stock of what is happening around us and to discuss how we are best able to weather the oncoming storm."

"I guess it has become fruitless to study statistics when we see the reality in front of our eyes," says Sheila.

"Except one," says Zoe, "gender ratio. There are hardly any boys under the age of three. If there are any alive, they are guarded in special places to protect them."

"There is another one of interest to Europeans. Compared to most other continents, Europe's population has steadily decreased for a while. With the reduction in boys, this will further accelerate," says Asha.

"Does it really matter," asks Susie, "if we consider that we are in year 3 of a 100-year plan to 'influence' gender?" There will be no males left with any useful sperm."

"What of the hidden boys and the in-vitro pregnancies? They will exclusively seed the egg with Y-chromosome-bearing spermatozoa. Surely they must work on that," says Aislinn.

"Although I could be wrong, I think this is how it works: The existing males of sexual maturity have a reduced sperm count with only a minute quantity of Y-chromosome sperm. The young boys will have similar characteristics once they reach sexual maturity, but they could also be infertile. Time will tell."

"In-vitro fertilisation is a bit different, depending on what sperm is used. If recently donated sperm is used, which could come from any current male, it will be a fruitless exercise. Even if they separate the X and Y spermatozoa and are successful in producing a male foetus, it will still be an otiose undertaking and pointless."
"The older sperm is different. The sperm of any single healthy male, before the 'influence' took effect, can potentially repopulate the whole world several times over, without any duplication," explains Susie.

"On another subject, has anyone here been demoted or *lost* their university qualifications?" asks Aislinn.
Seven raise their hands.

"The USA follows China's lead by reducing female participation in all areas to do with national and internal security, food, finance, military, law and order, education and health care, media, energy, pharmaceutics, scientific research, and more. As a result, both countries struggle under the load," says Zoe.

"Massive numbers of females, expelled from universities were offered placements or jobs in dead-end industries or demeaning offers with no prospects for the future," adds Ramona, "all far below their qualifications and achievements.

We can do likewise. They are working at their capacity while they deny us dignity and work positions. We can refuse our knowledge likewise. Give it enough time and all this will sort itself."

"Some have lost their diplomas, doctorates, and academic achievements altogether," says Tanisha.
"Nothing means anything anymore," adds Nadira.
"Many island nations have closed their borders. Their runways were blocked, their harbours closed," says Sheila, "to run out the hurricane of change."

"The judiciary doesn't even deal with cases of gender-based discrimination any more. Such cases won't even make it to court," informs Gasha.

"Denmark and most of Scandinavia have been spared much of what you're saying," says Kysa.
"Both genders still work together, trying to find answers and working on possible solutions," she adds.

"In the US, I've heard of discrimination against female staff who had worked in clinics, such as sperm bank collection centres. Most, if not all, have been asked to leave. What their male counterparts don't realise yet is that most of the stored sperm has been rendered useless, pay-back for the discriminations they suffered."

"In some parts of the country, drivers have deliberately targeted women with prams," explains Zoe. "As if for target practise, they speed up and aim their cars directly at prams and run over them. They know there are no boys in prams. The police do not even want to know their car licence number. They are just not interested."

"Take hope away from men, and that is what is happening," Tanisha says. "They will not easily vanish."

Have you really thought about what that means?

Shenzhen, China, Medical Research Clinic

Professor Xu Shen is still the team leader of the special medical team in search of the cause and cure for the outbreak of largely reduced male offspring.

The original team has now been locked up for six years behind guarded doors. The premises have changed twice, each time larger, to cater for an ever-widening expert base.

The new premises are a purpose-built construction surrounded by a high-security fence. Guards and all types of electronic gadgets, monitoring devices, infrared sensors, and laser walls ensure that even a mouse would find it difficult to enter or leave. There is only one entry and exit point for the whole complex. Elaborate scanning devices are used on any vehicle that comes into or leaves the compound. The site includes living quarters for all and a large communal mess for socialising and sharing meals. All food is prepared and provided by on-site caterers. There is no reason for anyone to ever leave the compound unless it is of some benefit to find the answer all have been searching for.

Professor Xu Shen enters the hall, which now accommodates over 3000 experts, to give his address. As he casts his eyes across so many heads, a thought goes back to the beginning, the small room with less than 30 handpicked talents. Now, all 3000 are in his team; all are males, each with a team of assistants to swell the total number multiple times.

Professor Xu Shen stands silent until the hall quietens down.
"Gentlemen, as you can imagine, we are under exceptional pressure to bring forth results. The nation has provided us with the finest facilities in China, if not the world. No expense has been spared. We have received everything we asked for. China is taking

financial care of every team member's family. The correct answer is now worth $100 million, tax-free, to anyone here who can find it. Gentlemen, in return for all that China has given us, we are asked to answer one question. What is the answer?"
"I will call a number of scientists to this podium to explain their findings. I am informed that amongst us are 30 different language speakers who may not have grown up with Mandarin as their native language. I therefore request those, which I will call up shortly, to present their findings in a language that explains in unambiguous terms and is understood across the wide spectrum of specialists assembled here. Please refrain from making any comments that do not advance our goal. Thank you."

"I call Dr Huang Qiu, who has been on the team since its inception."

Dr. Qiu greets the team leader. "My interest is this: How does one attack a healthy productive system? If we look at sperm, by nature it has a protective layer. Each woman has a set of eggs for life. They are mostly immature ovum and ripen, so to speak, when needed."

"We distinguish between the primary oocyte, which is the egg ready to fuse with a sperm, and the secondary oocyte, which is the next in line, as part of ovulation. If we start at the very beginning, we have the blastocyst, when an inner and outer structure begins to form. The inner will later become the embryo, and the outer is destined to become the placenta. All this is prior to conception."

"The female protects her immature ovum, the oocyte, with a protective sphere. Before it is possible to implant the egg into the uterine wall, the egg must get rid of the protective sphere. The fertilised egg cell is essentially the very starting point of life."

Dr. Qiu continues his speech, covering haploid cells, diploid cells, zygote, zone hatching, and glycoprotein molecules. "These molecules protect the surface of the sperm cell and signal the

body's immune system one message: 'Do not attack'. It says this about all human immune systems. What that does is ensure the sperm is not attacked in its own testis or inside the vaginal tract."
"Any other invader can also wear the protective layer of these molecules and thus gain unrestricted access to our bodies. Even if the immune system works fine, it will not attack such invaders. Some cancers, bacterial cells, some parasitic worms, HIV, and so forth, use this coat already."

"What happens if the immune system is modified in such a way that it no longer listens to the molecules, or if the molecules do not send the messages anymore? The male will attack its own sperm, and so will the female. It is a case of overkill, like murdering a dead man. Thank you for your attention," says Dr. Huang Qiu.

Professor Xu Shen steps to the podium and says, "I now call Dr. Lin Kang."

Dr. Lin Kang greets the professor and begins his presentation.
"Thanks to our team leader, Professor Xu Shen. For those who may come from very different scientific backgrounds, I will explain this as simply as I can. Mammals reproduce by fusing one gamete with another. In men, the gamete is the sperm; in women, the gamete is the egg, the ovum. Despite their difference in size, each gamete carries half the genetic information, one chromosome of each type."

"In humans, the number of chromosomes in a gamete is 23; we call this the haploid number. Sperm fuse with the egg and become a complete set. This we call the monoploid number, which in the case of humans is also 23. In short, in humans, the haploid and monoploid are equal in numbers."

Dr. Lin Kang informs of his team's efforts in the area of manipulating the hormonal environment during pregnancy. He also explains the different sets of chromosomes found in wheat. His suggestion is to produce a fatherless daughter from a female egg cell using diploid cells. "This has nothing to do with cloning, as we still have two different parents, although of the same gender."

"This would become a genetically modified human if we were able to accomplish this. It would be one means of continual procreation. For the time being, we could only create females that way, but it's a start."

"In closing, I would like to say this: Yes, it touches on ethical questions while the world's population is 6.6 billion. If this is not stopped or a solution is not found, the only two people left may be you and me. I ask you, are we going to give a rat's ass about ethics then? Thank you."

Dr. Kym is the next speaker. "In our earlier research, we uncovered a different explanation of how the attack on the reproduction system may have been carried out. Initially, we had a low sperm count with much reduced male sperm. Overall, the sperm were healthy, but the male sperm were weak. Much too late did we discover what actually happens during intercourse."

Dr. Kym continues to speak about pH levels and the dramatic rise in acidity. While the next speakers give their presentations, Professor Xu Shen asks Dr. Lin Kang to join him in his office.

"Please come in, Kang," the professor says, "as you can see, Dr. Kym Chang and Dr. Huang Qiu are also here."
"We are the original team, the ones who started everything in Shenzhen. We know each other well, and in our small circle, we can dispense with titles. First name basis is acceptable, so please call me Shen."
"Thank you, Shen. Hello, Qui and Chang."

"I'll fill you in on what we know," says the professor. "The eldest boys that we managed to rear are now six years old. Their testes are all underdeveloped. We doubt very much if they will ever develop into sperm-producing men."
"Kang," asks the Professor, "you made a remark at the end of your presentation, something about ethics: "Who's going to give a rat's ass?" You know the one I mean."
"I do, Shen."
"You also said, "The only two people left over may be just you and me." Do you remember this?"
"I do, Shen."

"Have you really thought about what that means?" asks Qui.
"Well, isn't that obvious?" answers Kang. "If no solution is found, it is the end of humanity."
"And if a solution is found, and you're the one finding it, you will get $100 million," adds Qui.
"Yes," says Kang, "so we've been told."

Chang does not beat around the bush and comes straight out with it. "What if a solution is found and no one knows about it at all. We could start to create our own people in secret, hide them until all have died out. Would not then our people own everything?"

"They could walk into any shop in Asia, Europe, Americas, anywhere, everything on earth is theirs for the taking. There will be no one there to stop them," says Qui.
"Any car in the showrooms of Europe will be theirs, any fancy dress in Paris will be theirs, all the ships on any ocean will be theirs," says Shen.

"Not one of them will ever need to carry money for anything. What for, there is no one else left. The whole world and everything in it, it all belongs to them, do you get our drift?" asks the Professor.

"Wow," gasps Kang, "who do you mean by 'our people'? Do you mean 'Chinese people', or do you mean 'our' people, as are in this room?"
"We mean the people who are in this room," explains the Professor, "and I will tell you why."

"We are all scientists. We have more knowledge than 95% of the entire population on earth, perhaps even more. Politicians, military men, rulers and leaders, with a combined IQ of a single-celled prokaryote, are telling us what to do. Not just in China, but everywhere."

"We all have families, a wife, children, friends and a home that none of us have seen for six years. Why? This research team has spent over a billion dollars, they will give us 100 billion if need be, but they will not let us out of here. We know nothing of what goes on outside of this place."

"Any discovery by any scientist will be exploited by others who have their own interests at heart. With our knowledge, they rule. They have always put the gun to our heads to give them answers."
"This time, the gun is $100 million dollars. Can you buy a single moment from the past six years with all this money? Can you go back in time and relive the years that you have missed?"

"Kang, your wife is a beautiful young woman. She was six years ago. How long can such a woman live without? Every word she says to you, whether on the telephone or via video link, is under the supervision of security. Is she still your wife, or has she become an actress, feeding you with what they think you need to hear to keep you happy? Do you think she slept the last six years alone?"

“Kang, it has taken nature millions of years to evolve humanity. We will be lucky if we can manage it in 50 years. How young will she look in 50 years?”

“Let’s just say we have the answers, we create a new man, with all the fertility questions answered, and it does not really matter who cracks the riddle. Do you think that person will be hailed as the saviour of humanity, the new Chinese national hero, given a bag full of money and be set free?”

"That is an illusion. It is impossible. The one who cracks the riddle will become the most powerful man on earth in an instant. The commandos, Special Forces, secret services, and intelligence organisations of any country will try to hunt him down until they find him. He will never find sleep in his life."

“The ones who put us here, in this fancy prison, they know that too. What they will do is this: They take our findings and create new men. They will not let anyone out of this building. They will blow it up into a million pieces, with everyone in it. Your wife gets a sorry

looking condolence letter with the ministry's regrets, that a tragic accident took your life."
Dr. Lin Kang's hand rests on the professor's desk. As he moves, a pen falls onto the carpet. Kang reaches to pick it up. He looks underneath the desk. He kneels down to look a bit closer and asks,

"What's this little round thing, Professor? Is this a microphone?"

All bidding for the chance to be the only ones

Around the world

European researchers are frightfully aware of the decline in Caucasian sperm quality over the past 75 years. A controversial report released 24 years ago brought this to everyone's attention.
Regional differences aside, Europe's gradual decrease in population growth, due to lifestyle changes or whatever reason, was already of concern almost two decades before the worldwide fertility crisis started to unfold.

Many reminisced about the days long ago, when the world's population growth was adding 78 million people per year, mostly in underdeveloped Africa and South East Asia. Predictions were for continual growth in Africa, a reduction in Asia and Europe, and the rest of the world's population to remain steady without change.

14 years ago, there was concern about how to feed 6.6 billion mouths and the nearly 8 billion that were expected to populate the world today. The concern that women were influencing the gender balance eased as female births decreased the number of newborn girls as well.

Year by year, the male sex sperm count lowers, rendering each, even the young men's sperm, eventually void of any Y-chromosome-carrying sex sperm, and infertile to reproduce any male offspring. No healthy newborn boys saw the light of day; infant girls were the only babies born.

The eldest boys since the fertility crisis began are coming of sexual age. Each nation is anticipating in hope that these boys will allow humanity to go on. Today, all are facing the reality of having reared the first generation that is unable to replicate itself. Another unknown factor was whether the new generation of girls would produce useful ovum.

65 years ago, the birth control pill was developed. Still, 14 years ago, 100 million women swallowed them every day.
They did not control births; they inhibited fertility by making women stop bearing children altogether. 'It can have real health benefits; it is good for you', broadcast across the nation.

The irony of it all is that just 14 years ago, one could buy a vial of sperm containing 20 to 50 million sperm for less than $180, including a money-back guarantee. It traded as any other commodity: tall men's sperm, educated men's sperm, doctors and professors' sperm, high-IQ sperm, Christian, Moslem, Jewish sperm, sexed male and female sperm, or any type of sperm at all. All the money in the world is not enough to buy a single sperm today.

Mysterious accidents and possibly sabotage in sperm labs led some to believe a different kind of conflict was underway. Sperm bank 'accidents' in Maine, Rhode Island, Iowa, California, the UK, across Europe, and Asia never became news, as the media is no longer reporting them.

Sperm labs discover much too late that the protectant, added to control sperm damage caused by freezing, has contaminated sperm for years, rendering sperm that held promise useless. The methods used in practise by many of the labs of 16 years earlier further reveal that vials contained damaged sperm, mostly spoiled, and of no benefit for fertilisation.

Unnoticed, the containers used to store sperm were subject to chemical reactions as soon as the lid was placed on the vials, already causing damage to the sperm before being immersed in liquid nitrogen. No one could rule out acts of sabotage, as countless trillions of sperm were rendered useless. A single male, once capable of producing 14 trillion sperm over a lifetime, another perhaps 10% of that, and the next may be able to produce a million fold as many, massive redundancies, when each ever needed less than a dozen at most.

Some laboratories focused on stem cell research, trying to produce sperm from specialised types of cells. A new war had begun, with the scientist as front-line soldier, the objective not to kill but to create life. A search, like trying to find a needle in a country full of haystacks, for a single healthy male sperm to be used for the injection of a single sperm into an egg.
Several laboratories set their focus on human cloning, stimulating the female egg to start the cell division process, parthenogenesis, without the aid of sperm, just like any embryo. One could only hope to create a duplicate of the egg's donor.

Groups with the financial resources, eager to find the answer the whole world was looking for, established their own research centres. Initially to ensure the nation's survival, but that quickly changed as the survival of self-serving interests was closer to the heart.

Thus began the new race: building research centres for the rich and famous, the business leaders, the magnates, tycoons, and super-rich, the ones with influence and power, the ones that controlled the markets and economies. Each absorbed in the game to grow a life, to be the last one standing, with the hope to create a brand new race that mirrors their reflection. Countless kings of heritage, old money, titles, and beliefs are bidding for the chance to be the only ones that give the world their genes to grow and multiply.

Demand for qualified fertility specialists, researchers, and scientists outstripped supply, effectively removing any upper limits on remuneration packages.

Scientific information available through books, publications, journals, the Internet, or other sources could no longer be trusted. Single-minded interest groups falsified data, drew incorrect conclusions, and deliberately set out to mislead anyone who may have sought to use such material to get to the answer before anyone else.

The exchange and sharing of information became like poker games. Information seeded with misleading and false conclusions and invented test results is all a deliberately set mind game to waste the researcher's time and prevent anyone from getting the answers first. Science became a poker game where no one showed the cards they were holding.

Who and what we were

Nagoya, Japan

It was at the time of Susie's 32nd birthday that the group of 12 met again, this time in Adzumi's hometown, Nagoya, Japan.

"Adzumi, tell us about the history of this castle?" asks Gasha.
"Yes, the stories behind it and the people involved," adds Ye Myo, "make it such a great building."

"I'd love to tell you about it," says Adzumi, telling the story of Imagawa Yoshitada and Ujichika, the invasions and killings in 1476. "Ujichika, the 17-year-old, became the head of his clan. Ujichika formulated the Imagawa house code, a code of rules, such as capital punishment in violent quarrels. He made the parents accountable if their children were involved in fighting, and many more rules."

"The original castle was built by Ujichika in 1525. He died of an illness a year later. The castle was taken over by another, but was eventually abandoned. In 1610, a new castle was constructed on the same site to be the new capital of the province. In 1612, construction was completed. It became an army headquarters and a POW camp. A fire destroyed it during World War II. Again, it was rebuilt in 1959."

Adzumi points to the castle's rooftop: "Right at the top are two golden fish, imaginary tiger-headed fish, talismans for fire prevention."
"What are they called?" asks Ye Myo, "the fish?"
"Kinshachi," Adzumi replies, "symbolise the feudal lord's authority.
"Nagaya Castle is one of the must-see attractions here," she adds.
"So many tourist attractions around the world," says Kysa, "so much blood spilt for so many. Today it shines in the sun; how many battles have these places seen in their time?"
"No one gave their lives. They were all taken by another," answers Nadira.

"In each country stand the monuments of battle, some for the heroes who conquered, some for the fallen, to not forget," voiced Tanisha. "But there are also those of the peacemakers."
"The Great Wall of China was built to guard its people," adds Asha. "Millions lost their lives building it. So much blood was spilt in the countless battles throughout humanity's history."

"Let us also not forget the largest empire ever ruled by women on horseback, Mongolia. Some of them gave rise to building the wall in China," adds Tanisha. Nadira says, "Men have killed for land and resources, yet all are just tenants on the earth. No matter how many died defending it, no owner owns the earth. We all end up buried in its soil or burned upon it."

Adzumi adds, "Men have killed for beliefs, ideals, illusions, and crusades to far-off lands, not understanding that the slain and slayers' mothers are the same."
"It's interesting that even now, with a world population showing a severe reversal, now at less than 5.5 billion, some countries can still wage war."

"They volunteered and cheered, were feared and speared their brother, yet never learned to shed a tear," says Sheila.
"It mattered little if the world had three billion sons or two. To kill is ingrained in their gender," adds Aislinn.

"China abandoned its one-child policy so many years ago," says Susie. Nadira adds, "In Pakistan and India, everyone got rid of family planning since the gender changes."
"Remember the warnings we issued at the beginning?" asks Zoe, "Did we really believe in miracles?"

"Who was it who said, that they will count the heads for us?" asks Kysa.
"I did," says Asha.
"When was the last time any of you saw young boys?" asks Sheila. Most shake their heads. "
"I did. The youngest may be 10 or 11," says Kysa; "the eldest of the XX Generation are now in their early 20s. The youngest I've seen are teens, but this generation cannot reproduce."

"Maybe in ten years from now the world will be 4 billion or less," says Aislinn.

"We don't know if we can still believe anything that is published," Asha adds, "but the cranes have disappeared, and construction of housing has virtually ceased. There is no longer a need to expand."
"Childcare facilities only have girls. Schools are already starting to change due to the low numbers of pupils. The school buildings are modified to cater for community-based needs and serve a dual purpose."
"I'm glad the victimisation of women has stopped," Ramona adds.

"Men have realised that women are also in decline. But the statistics do not show equality."
"They tried to run everything and have taken on too much. Now they are glad that women can take on some of the work," Sheila adds.
"Just think of the future, what it means, and the possibilities," says Adzumi. "It would be like planting a new garden on fresh soil, with all the weeds gone. All the nutrient suckers have disappeared; all the goodness in the soil is to serve the plant that's seeded. Free of the shackles of history, of traditions, of honour and of pride."

"There are no grudges or paybacks that need to be settled or carried through all generations," she says.

Ye Myo says, "No ideology could claim to be the only way to live; no language barriers; no borders; no rulers or slaves. Bygones will go forever."

"No aching that tomorrow brings a better day. There is no race to hoard and take, possess and own," says Aislinn.
"Diseases will be unable to propagate through blood or genes. "AIDS stops in an instant," Kysa says.
"The forests have a chance to recover; rivers flush their suds; oceans replenish with life; and wildlife is freed of its biggest predator," adds Ramona.

"The end of pompous ceremonies, of rituals, and of segregation may not be that far off. No rulers have ever been able to rule for longer than their given time slot; no leaders have ever led to paradise," says Zoe, "but paradise it has always been. We've messed it up beyond recognition."

"The promise of one day living in utopia, the hope to find it in one's lifetime, and others sowed the seeds that if not here, then in the hereafter," Tanisha said.

Asha laughs, "Schlaraffenland, the land of the lazy monkeys, no one ever needs to cook; anything your heart desires is precooked flying in the air. Just open your mouth; it flies straight in, in the land of milk and honey."
"Instead of utopia, perhaps in time this will become eutopia; it could well be," says Sheila.

Ye Myo asks, "Adzumi, do you know Shima Chika?"
"Yes, she's in Tokyo at the moment. We have been friends for years. You should see her show; it is really special."
Ye Myo suggest, “Why don't we?”
“We can be there in $1^{1/2}$ hours,” answers Adzumi.

Tokyo, Japan

Three hours later, the group meets at Chika's show, a very large display within a museum. Areas inside the museum are fenced off to feature live content.

A display of humanity throughout time, with live actors replaying what life was like 50 years ago. A scene in an office from anywhere is shown in one of the exhibits. Men smoking in enclosed spaces The scene depicts women playing subordinate roles to the men, serving them coffee or taking notes, as a living exposé from any of the old movies.

Another display shows the delivery of a baby, born by a native woman. A lifelike artificial model of a newborn is used, doomed to be sacrificed moments after its birth. The newborn's only crime was being born in the wrong gender. Each displays an authentic scene from another time and place.

"There she is," Ye Myo calls out. "Chika, hello."
Shima Chika is overjoyed to meet her friend again.
"Oh, what a lovely surprise, Ye Myo," she says. "I did not expect you."
"We are visiting Adzumi, and I didn't know that you knew each other," replies Ye Myo. "Let me introduce you to everyone."
"Are you the one who had a fiery start in Chicago," asks Zoe, "at your first exhibition?"
"Yes, Zoe, the sentiments were very different then," Chika replies, "but much has changed."
"Hello Susie, I think Aaron is here in spirit," she says. "I'll show you a display based on his work."
"Tell us, Chika, what is this show about?" asks Susie. "My skills in Japanese are lacking."

"This is the first museum in Japan willing to offer much of its floor space to allow at least part of the display to be shown." "Hopefully, others in the country will become part of this effort," says Chika.
"It symbolises snippets of life, of what we were," explains Chika. "As you walk through, you'll see examples from various cultures, different times, and different places. Towards the exit, one begins to realise what we have become."

"The show is called 'this thou art' and no, you cannot buy any of the exhibits," Chika continues, "Hachinohe, Akita, Chiba, Sapporo and Osaka have already agreed to be a part of this. My intention is to have many more participate, so that one can travel from the north to the south of the country, in each city a different display of time and place."

"Is this a playground over there?" asks Tanisha.
"Sandpits, slippery slides, building castles," says Chika, "of course these are not real kids. All are lifelike robots underneath. Boys and girls are playing together. There is no place on earth where this happens anymore."

"Japan has become an exporter of robot children," says Kysa, "they even speak Swedish, with blond hair and blue eyes."
"In Germany at Christmas one can hear children singing Christmas songs," says Asha, "the trick is, to get them all to start singing at the same time."

"The Irish children also, all made in Japan," adds Aislinn.
"Yes," says Chika, "men can do anything, except men."
"By the way, Susie, do you remember Sally, the lawyer form Chicago, Sally Cramer?" asks Chika, "in Hong Kong we met for the first time."
"I do, Chika, she's retired now," Susie says, "Sally and Kim are still very good friends, you do remember Kim?"
"Your sister?" asks Chika.
"Ying Kim Xia," explains Susie, "my sister. We both have the same Dad."
"Did she ever write another book?"
"Oh no," answers Susie, "Kim did make contact with the woman's family, the one she thought was her mother. Her book was based on the life of a Chinese girl, who had been smuggled out of the country, to end up in the gutters of Holland."
"What did Kim do with her life?" asks Chika.

"Kim Xia created an organisation, investigating many of the missing girls. She had so much research material and Aaron added additional information to that. It brought closure to many of the cases. She expanded the organisation to Russia, Eastern and Western Europe."

"Hey, come over here," calls Zoe from a distance.
"I love this display, Chika," says Zoe. "Where did you get all these old TV sets from? They're still black and white, my gosh, were they ever?"
"Many friends helped to put this one together," explains Chika, "from the wireless radio to the first TV sets, from colour to channel TV to living walls. Remember the possibilities this media used to promise, before any of us were born."

"Looks like a display of all the addictions," remarks Kysa, "look, mum in the kitchen frying the fattiest meals I've ever seen, Dad's into the alcohol and smokes non-stop, the kids absorbing all sorts of rubbish from the tube."
"The cigarettes are false. We had to invent them, so they look real. A whole day played out in this display, just condensed in time. Dad comes home, no one looks at one another, only one voice in the room, the TV set."

"All the shows are authentic. A mass-stupefying medium, it became, over here, the progress in time. Eventually, the TV set became so big that it surrounded one from all sides. This room shows the latest: people actually living inside the set without realising it."
"Each wall in this room is a solid TV screen; even the windows are not real; they're also TV sets. You can live in Japan and live in Alaska at the same time."
"See the elk in this window; if you wait a second, it will show up in the other. They are all coordinated, replicating a living scene,

apparently outside. At the press of a button, you live in Africa. It's only when you open the door that you're back in Japan; there are no lions outside."

"Each has their own world, and the food supply is automatic. Watch this: The fridge reports to the organisation what it needs, the ultimate in consumerism. It keeps people happy, and the flow of money never stops."

"You can also coordinate everything in the house to feel like a movie. You can be inside a burning house, feel the heat, and hear the floor collapsing, all triggered by the film. Car crashes and explosions are very effective. Air pressure waves hit you, or the walls seem to fly apart in a million pieces. Nothing is really damaged; everything is just an illusion. The gadget generation comes of age."

"You know what the latest is?" asks Chika, "The live house. For a little extra per month, you do not have to live your life anymore. Type in what and where you want to be, and the whole house will create your life. Each day, another episode plays. Up in the corners are the 'happy sensors', which monitor non-stop your awareness of fulfilment.

For one person, happiness is beating the living daylights out of someone, whereas another is happy smelling roses and another is happy being humiliated. Every taste is catered for."

"Let me show you something," says Chika. She steps into the room and calls, "I am inside of a red rose."

All walls become as the inside of an opening rose. Petals open, huge bees land on them, and the light of the sun enters from one side. The floor moves to give the illusion of the bloom swaying in the wind. "This is an absolute addiction," says Chika. She calls out again, "I am in Cape Town, South Africa."

Within moments, the scent of rose vanishes, replaced by the faintly salted air of the sea. The rose petals change colour to show the purplish glow of South Africa's Table Mountains in a sunrise. "One can change location as well, closer to 'Devil's Peak'," she calls, as the walls reveal a closer look at the lower peaks.

"It conserves energy and saves time," she adds. "This is a healthy way to travel, with time and place at your fingertips; no more waiting at the airports. Reality is what you make it."

"What will they think up next?" asks Sheila.
"They are working on new modules," explains Chika. "You can choose your own friends, anyone from history; you can even have a mixture from different times. Genghis Khan, Cleopatra, and Aristotle, for instance, now that would be an interesting mix."
Ramona asks, "Why are there so many people trying to get to that display? What's in it?"

"It is a dark room now. We had to switch the display off," explains Chika. "People injured themselves. I called it 'Voice of Boys', an audio track from infant boys to toddlers, right through to the age of six. Each is the authentic voice of a boy. When we had the display on, women went out of their minds and ran into the walls, trying to hold them."

"Perhaps you haven't noticed," says Chika, "mankind is dying out. We are an endangered species. All the displays together will show at least in part who and what we were."

Zoe adds, "Yes, Chika. If there is a future it will grow free of culture and traditions. There will be no privileged groups, none entitled to be above another. It could provide an opportunity for a fresh beginning."

Mr President, put two and two together

Washington, USA

"Mr. President, we have a situation on our hands."

"What's up, what's happening? It's 2 in the morning."

"Mr. President, a Russian icebreaker has left Molodezhnaya Station, from the east coast on Antarctica, it's Russian territory."

"So what's the problem?"

"It's a serious problem, Mr. President."

"Terry, get the map of Antarctica on the screen."

"Yes, Sir."

"This, sir, is Molodezhnaya Station. This here, right next to it, is Bellingshausen Base, and there, right in the middle, is Vostok Base, also known as Lake Vostok."

"Mr. President, if you wanted to hide sperm, where would be the best place on earth to do that?"

"Well, in my balls, of course, where else?"

"Let's assume you don't have any balls."

"Does somebody in here have a loaded gun? I'm going to blow his head off. A president without balls, look, Mr. Secretary..."

"I am the Chief of Staff, Mr. President."

"Well, as long as you know who you are, that's all that matters. Somebody take some notes, he'll need it on his tombstone. Now where is that pistol?"

"Think about it, Mr. President. Where is the best place for sperm?"

"Just as I said, at the other end of my appendage, tucked in a bag, reminding me with every step I take that they're still where they ought to be, I call them balls, Mr. Chief of Staff."

"Mr. President, Sir..."

"And why do they call it Lake Vostok? It's all full of ice down there," adds the president.

“As I was saying, Mr President, Bellingshausen Base and Molodezhnaya Base had some mayor fuel tank installations just a few years before the whole sperm saga began. Do you know why, Mr President?"
"I’ll tell you why, because their balls were starting to freeze off, why else?”
“Sir, 2.5 miles under this ice is Lake Vostok. The lake below is huge, Sir. There is warm liquid fresh water under the ice.”
“So now you know how they keep their balls warm, Mr Chief of Staff.”

“Sir, our Galileo Orbiter picked that up a long time ago.”
“Did you get me out of bed, to tell me how the Russians keep their balls warm, after you’ve known that for how many years, 46 years? How long do I have to wait for that pistol?”
“Sir, the lake is 155 miles long, which is a hell of a lot of warm water in a cold place like that. Mr President, put two and two together.”
“The two I’ve got will do just fine, thank you, Mr Chief of Staff.”

“Sir, if the Russian are behind this attack of 40 years ago, isn’t it just very convenient to have two bases with newly fitted fuel tanks, all topped up. No matter what global warming did to the ice in the last 40 years, Lake Vostok is safely located almost in the middle of Antarctica.”
“What’s your point?”
“They also carried out a lot of work on Base Vostok that sits on top of the lake. It has been a permanent Russian station for a very long time. It wouldn’t be that big of a problem to hide some sperm in there or even fully grown men. Now they have an icebreaker trying to break through, keen to get to open waters.”

“What do you suggest we do about it? Declare war?”
“No, Mr President. I would suggest we help our Russian friends, by dropping a couple of missiles onto the ice in front of the ship.”
“And what’s the point of that, Mr Chief of Staff?”
“A slight error in the trajectory of the missiles will make sure they land smack bang in the middle of the ship. A short phone call to our friends in Moscow, explaining our good intentions and the slight mishap that occurred, will smooth things over. They’ll probably thank us for trying.”

"Well, Mr Chief of Staff, couldn't you have figured this out yourself? What are you waiting for; I got to get to bed before my balls are freezing off too."

The ice cracks underneath

Antarctica, East of Molodezhnaya station

The Russian icebreaker отрежьте лед lifts its bow over the ice, the weight of the ship cracking the surface. Its engines are labouring to push the vessel forwards. The bow drops down as the ice cracks underneath it. Five men depart the ship over the sides, lifted off via crane to the surface of the ice.

All run towards the waiting plane, fitted with skis, its engine running. As it takes off, the plane leaves a white trail of snow and ice in its wake. Moments later, two missiles explode in succession directly onto the icebreaker.
Nothing, except a hole in the ice, is left.

A new plan for tomorrow

Russia, Boris's Place

"Is that you, Ted?"
"Yes."
"It's Jerry here. I have been meaning to talk to you about something, business-related. I know you have some guys working on this new idea of getting your offspring sorted out, the chase for the sperm, you know what I mean?"
"Yes, Jerry, I know what you're

getting at."
"I might have missed the boat a bit; I'm too busy making money. What I would like to suggest is that we call a meeting for all those above $20 billion per annum. I've got some ideas that might work."

"There are too many with 20. Let's keep it special; all those above $50 billion, what do you say?"
"Fine, 50 it is," says Jerry.
"Where do we meet?" "Europe, Asia, what do you suggest?"
"Perhaps a bit more private. Boris has a big enough spread, it's secure, and there are no long noses. Let's say a month from now at Boris's place. Does that suit, Ted?"
"Done, I will see you then, bye."

A month later, the 40 richest men on earth meet at Boris's place in Russia. One could always feel safe here in many ways. After dinner, Boris raised his glass and said, "Gentlemen, welcome to my humble abode. For the duration of your visit, make it your home. We all know each other here, so I will cut a long story short: Jerry has something to say, and he is the one who called for this meeting. Jerry, if you please."

"Thank you, Boris, and hello to everyone. In this room, each person's wealth is a minimum of $50 billion. We thought if we made it 40 or 30, there would be too many of us."

"I know that some of us are involved in the chase to find the male sperm," Jerry laughs. "I nearly said 'male germ'."
"And whoever thinks that they get there first, may get some ideas of grandeur, that he can rule the world. True..., yes. There are also many others chasing the same answers, governments, special interest groups, the military and so on."

"It doesn't really matter who finds the bloody thing. My point is that we do need order when it happens, and who better to create order than us? I would suggest that whoever finds this illusive

sperm, and let us say, some poor 'church mouse of a scientist' comes up with it tomorrow, what's he going to do with it?"
"He'll try to sell it to the highest bidder, but he wouldn't have a clue who the big rollers are. So it could get messy."

"My thought in that case would be that we all chip a little into the kitty so that our church mouse scientist doesn't feel out of place when he joins our little 50+ group."
"He won't have a clue what to do with it, but we all have our own problems. We will recoup the money very quickly by getting into the sperm business ourselves. You all know me as a straight-shooter. I have high ethics in all of my dealings, and I think that is the only way to get to $65 billion plus."
"Thanks for the applause; the new figures came out yesterday; I had no idea. By the way, Tom, sorry about the Steelworks deal; I did not know they were up to their eyeballs in the red. I'll make it up to you somehow."

"Don't worry about it, Jerry. Obviously, you have not come across the small matter of the unresolved compensation claims attached to the pharmaceutical group you picked up two months ago. It is not so bad; in a few years, there will be no one left to claim. Let's call it even."

"We all have an opportunity to reshape the world as we see fit... to redraw the maps, if you like," says Jerry.
"What do you propose?" asks Kym, the Asian tycoon controlling transport, advertising, and various other interests in Asia.

"First I thought, let's split up the world geographically," explains Jerry, "but that would not work in practise. My idea is to divide the world into areas of interest, avoid clashes amongst one another, have little battles to absorb all the spoils we pick up from the other players, and we all have the world sorted once and for all, a cartel of peace of sorts, to keep the order."

"Have you gone a bit soft, Jerry?" asks Avanish, the software and technology giant from India. "That's against nature, Jerry."
"Maybe, Avanish, but let's face it, we're all getting on; we don't get any younger. I am sick and tired of driving around with up to 60 security people all around me. Sometimes we use nine limousines just as decoys. The constant fear of being kidnapped, held for ransom, or worse, assassinated."

"You know, Avanish, as a youngster I used to play at the French Riviera, Côte d'Azur, watched the Niagara Falls, been to the Taj Mahal, the Great Wall of China, the Pyramid of Giza, and later on I played in Monte Carlo. No one ever bothered me as a kid. I could go anywhere. I can't do that anymore, and neither can you or any of us. We have just about all the money in the world. I think it is time to buy some happiness with it."

"Boris, when I landed on your patch, I noticed a bit of construction going on. It seems to me that you are trying to rebuild the world in your backyard. You cannot build Venice in Russia. You cannot recreate the Victoria Falls in Zimbabwe here. It's not the same thing, and it's impractical," explains Jerry.

"What we can do is this: We can fence the special places in and create a playground of natural and special beauty spots wherever they are, for our exclusive appreciation. Places that we make safe with restricted access. Secure roads within Rome, so we can have a look at the Colosseum without worrying about a bullet in the neck. In Paris, we have been deprived of the Eiffel Tower, the Arc de Triomphe, Notre Dame, the Moulin Rouge, and the Louvre. It is time we claim them back."

"We need a secure landing patch or a secure road system that leads to all those attractions, the whole areas protected from anyone else, to afford us safety and security. Places like New Zealand and Hawaii will be ideal for our exclusive access. We could create some borderlines here and there, and if we need some more ideas, let's re-create the Hanging Gardens of Babylon, whatever."

"Tyrone, you're into construction, you can re-create all the special places as theme parks, for the general population, charging admissions of course. By the way, whose brainchild is the new trend? Doomsday religious groups, springing up all over the place, secure your spot in the afterlife, leave us your inheritance?"

Alain laughs, "Jerry, that's my idea. It is working, worth $2 billion so far. Your 65 will get you the front row seats, in case you're interested, Jerry."
"You always had an ability to recycle proven ideas, Alain, well done," says Jerry.
"It's been fun, the chase to make money. We have all proven that we can do that. The future needs a new blueprint, a new plan for tomorrow," he adds.
"Aren't you forgetting something, Jerry?" asks Ted.

Population is in decline everywhere

Beijing, China, The Forbidden City

It was a full moon when Wong Wei, China's leader, and Zhuang, his secretary stood in the Forbidden City in Beijing, near the steps of the Hall of Supreme Harmony.
"You have been looking at the moon for a long time, Leader Wong Wei. What are your thoughts?" asks Zhuang.
"Yes, Zhuang, my friend. I am thinking."

"This place has been witness to the great Emperors of China. From the Qin Dynasty to Qing Dynasty, over 2000 years of Chinese history has come to pass right here."
"In that time, you would have lost your head, addressing the Emperor by his name."

"He was to be addressed as Bixia, 陛下, meaning 'Your Imperial Majesty'."
"Huangdi Bixia, 皇帝陛下, 'His Majesty the Emperor'. So much has changed. Most likely, you would be my eunuch, Zhuang, trusted

with my thoughts," says Wong Wei, leader of China, with a population reduced from over 1.4 billion to 900 million in a few short years.

“The Emperor was also called the Son of Heaven, and that is why I am looking at the moon. I was wondering what that means, Zhuang, being the ‘Son of Heaven’. The Emperors of China, the Sons of Heaven. What do you think it means?”

“Perhaps a title to lift themselves above all others, to raise their status so high, that no subject could ever challenge it,” says Zhuang.
“Wrong, Zhuang, ‘The Son of Heaven’, 天子, Shang Dynasty, means a lot more. Go back in time. What did it mean, then? It was akin to God, an overlord with only one emperor at a time to rule the world, as a representative of heaven."

"The Emperor was a descendant from the heavens, to rule by divine providence here on earth. What do you see in the heavens now, Zhuang?"
"I see the moon, Wong Wei."
"And there is the answer, Zhuang. Someone wants to become a new emperor, and he will come from heaven. He will come from right up there, Zhuang, from the moon."
"I don’t understand your meaning," says Zhuang.

"Then I will explain it to you. When did this fertility crisis begin?"
"In Shenzhen, many years ago, then it started in six other places around the world: Manhattan, New Zealand, etc. Sometime later, it spread around the world to affect every country," says Zhuang.

"Do you remember who took the blame for Shenzhen?"
"No, Sir."
"Womhood did. No, it's not public knowledge. Apparently, a group of women put their demands on all the men in the world: 'Change your ways or we will stop making you', they said. They sent such warnings to all the press at the time, but no one believed them."

Zhuang laughs and says, "Sir, a full moon can do strange things."
"It clears one’s head, Zhuang."
"But, sir, that is preposterous. Forgive me for laughing."
"Of course it is, Zhuang."

"Zhuang, for the last 30 years, China has been at war and has not even noticed it."
"Are you sure you're alright, sir?" asks Zhuang.
"The new Emperor is waiting up there."
"Wong Wei, look at me; you are the leader of China. Can't you hear what you're saying?"
"I know exactly what I'm saying, Zhuang."
"We are at war with whom? Who would dare touch China? There are no men born anywhere. We are all in the same boat. Population is in decline everywhere," says Zhuang.

"We are at war, Zhuang. We just don't know who our enemies are," explains the Chinese leader. "All this womanhood talk is a decoy. I don't know how the world has been poisoned, but men are rendered infertile to reproduce male offspring. They used the first attack in Shenzhen as an experiment. Then they selected six countries to throw us off guard. Next, they poisoned the whole planet."

"Who are 'they', Wong Wei?"
"Whoever is waiting up there." Wong Wei points towards the moon.
"The moon is a barren place, Sir, no life can exist."
"Have you ever heard of Noah? The Christians believe in it. He heard the voice of God, telling him to build an ark, to bring with him every living thing of flesh, to protect them from a flood. He did that, he built a ship, loaded it with animals of every kind. The floods came, killed everyone else. Once the waters receded he could re-populate the whole world, so the story goes."

"Up there is a new ark, a ship, a space station, a spot on the moon, where they are waiting. Up there are men, which will come down and repopulate the world."

"Sir, how did they get up there? Who are these men?"

"With a spacecraft, how else would they get up there? Who are they? Anyone with space technology, like the USA, Russia, India, Europe, etc.," says Wong Wei.
"Anyone with the know-how to keep men up there for 30 years or more," he adds.

"Most likely, there are men and women who have been sent up there before men's seeds were killed on earth in a cunning attack that left no clue of who might be the perpetrators. A war without a drop of blood spilt, no soldier sacrificed, and no property damaged anywhere, an ingenious plan."
"What makes you so certain, sir?"

"That has been planned for a very long time. Initially, their aim was to store the DNA of endangered or extinct species, then to use the moon to store the world's DNA in case an asteroid ever destroyed the earth, like a safe space storage place. Maybe that gave them the idea to take over the whole world in one clean swoop. It all makes sense with the space activity at the time. All they need are regular shipments of life requirements from earth, and they can keep people alive indefinitely."

"Zhuang, we've got to mount a mission to find out where and who they are. Whoever it is will become the Chinese Emperor, a true descendant of the heavens, and he will have the seed our women need."
"Zhuang, let's bring Huangdi Bixia, His Majesty the Emperor, back home to China before he lands someplace else."

I feel an ache for Venezuela

Cascais, Portugal / Venezuela

"Hello, hello, I am looking for Dona Moyo."
"Yes, that is me; how can I be of help?"
"Hello, Dona Moyo, I sent my deepest condolences for the loss of your father earlier."
"I am Salvatore de Dominguez, an

attorney. It is about your father's will." "Please do come in, Senhor Dominguez."
"José and I knew each other for a long time. Angela died last year, and now José. Still, 90 years is a good stretch."
"Yes, he did have an interesting life."
"My reason for being here is to execute José Câmara de Sousa's last will and testament." Is this a good time for you?"

"It is a sad time, but please do come in and sit down," says Moyo.
Sr. Dominguez fits his reading glasses and opens his folder to read the document: "As you may be aware, Dona Moyo, you, as the only child of Angela and José, are the sole heir of their estate.

The estate consists of the property in Cascais, which is this house, the ketch, located in the harbour of Cascais, another property in Venezuela, two chests of your father's research materials, and these. Listed here are your father's accounts, held in various financial institutions. I am also under instructions to hand you this folder, unopened. Please note that the seals are unbroken."

"I do not know what is in these folders, and I don't need to know. All I need are some signatures, one here and there, and that is all."
Two men carry the chests into the house while Moyo signs the receipts and various documents.
"Again, I'm sorry for disturbing your time of mourning, but it's one of those things that needs doing. Good bye."
"Thank you, Senhor Dominguez." Good bye."

Moyo stands on the balcony overlooking the harbour. The masts of her ketch barely sway in the calm, sheltered waters.
'I am sixty years old. The Atlantic can be tough. I feel an ache for Venezuela. Am I still able to sail her across to the Caribbean? Perhaps not single-handed,' Moyo thought.

She returns to the room and opens one of the chests to find maps, small artefacts, documents, notes, and scribbles, most of which relate to South America.

The second chest contains woven dishes, two woven grass bowls, additional maps, and many detailed reports. The chest brings memories of crabs, but no memory of her parents, recollections of the forest, the homes on stilts, all so long ago. Moyo replays the music of her people. She knows each song and each word.
'I virtually grew up on water; I can still sail her in 20 years; I will go where my heart needs to be,' Moyo's aim clears.
Moyo places the sealed folder, unopened, into the first chest. It doesn't hold her interest, as her mind is far from Portugal.

"Mama, are you home," a voice from the hallway.
"Dorothea, come in," Moyo answers, "How was your day at the clinic?"
"My eyes are sore, Mama. All day at the microscope, I'm tired," answers Dorothea.
"Grandmamma, what are all these boxes?" the girls ask in unison.
"Hello Josefa, hello Francisca, sit down, I'll tell you," answers Moyo.

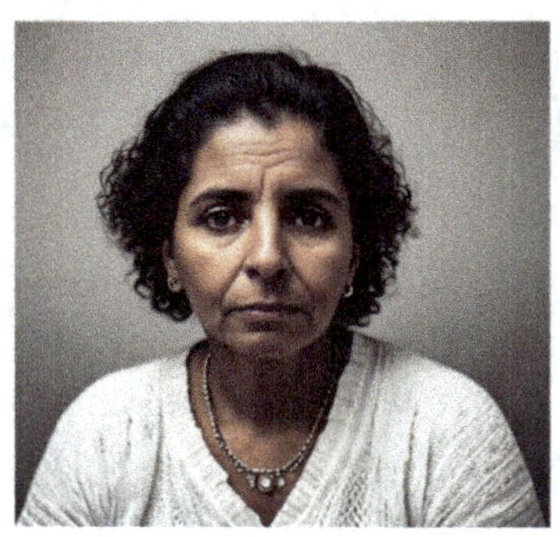

Dorothea, 38, Moyo's daughter, and the sixteen-year-old twins, Josefa and Francisca, Moyo's grandchildren sit next to the chests.
Moyo explains. "Your Grandfather was an adventurer. He travelled the world. He collected many treasures, stored in these chests. I am also one of his treasures. Parts of my heritage are in these chests. They hold many memories of home. I feel an urge to go back."
"Why don't you, Mama?"

"Come with me, all of you. I show you the roots of your people."
"That would be so interesting," says Josefa, "to see another world in Venezuela," Francisca adds.
Dorothea offers a tired smile, "Let me sleep on it first, please."

Two weeks later, the ketch leaves the harbour of Cascais, heading east, with the chests aboard stored below. A steady breeze powers the vessel. Moyo stands at the bow, looking ahead. It feels as if the ketch is following her, almost as if José has the helm, reminiscing of the many journeys they had together.

The woven pendant of her childhood survived the many years when it lay in her drawer in Portugal. Up ahead in the Azores, Porta Delgada on San Miguel is the first port of call. The last time I was here was 47 years ago.

"You know, girls, I was 13 the last time I was here. There were so many boys to play with then. That was 47 years ago"

"There are none here today, Grandmamma," answers Francisca. Two days later, the vessel heads out on the long, lonely journey eastward and south-east across the equator.

The years changed the delta. She would not find her way home without charts; so much had changed. The delta forms a huge triangle, its widest side being almost 400km long. The rivers flow into the Atlantic Ocean. They head upriver, the father of the people, in search of her Indigenous tribe.

The delta had grown lush, with crabs in abundance and berries everywhere. The whole area covers over 40 thousand square kilometres. Moyo checks and double-checks her navigational charts. 'This is where the waters fork; this is home; where is everyone?' She anchors the boat and calls out to the forest. Only the wildlife responds. They row in their small tender to the shore. The landscape is as it was, but home has changed. The buildings collapsed, and the remnants of houses on stilts are now weathered and overgrown.

She stands on the shore to sing the song of her tribe. The sound of the birds and the river accompany the tune of ancient times, yet there is no sound of her people. The mangroves are rich with life, the swamps are healthy, and there is more than enough food to feed thousands of tribes.

"Am I the only one left of my people? Where have you all gone?" She calls into the forest. The charts were dotted with hundreds of settlements, all of her native kind. "Mama, this would have been paradise when you were a child; it is today," says Dorothea.
"So much peace here; so calm," adds Josefa.

"Be careful, Francisca; don't hurt yourself," Dorothea calls out.
"Yes, here you need to be a bit careful," says Moyo. "If you fall into the water, swim slowly and steadily; don't splash and get out. Piranhas may get a bit hungry in the dry season. When I grew up here, they mentioned large crocodiles, but I've never seen one here. Things could have changed over time. On land, the jaguar is the undisputed king. Stay away from the colourful frogs. Their skin is poisonous, and the vipers don't want to be surprised. It seems no one has lived here for a long time."

"There are the canoes, Grandmamma," she points to the side, "which was your house?"
"I lived in all of them, Francisca. They all belonged to our people. Their blood is in yours."
They set out to find others. All places deserted and abandoned, villages left to rot, none of her tribe anywhere, but mosquitoes by the billions.

They sail out of the delta in search of a township. Moyo approaches a woman in the small harbour. When she sees Moyo's pendant, she reaches for it. A toothless smile shines from her weathered face. She speaks, but Moyo does not understand it. Another joins them. "She wants to know where you got this from," an old man explains to Moyo.

"It is from my people," Moyo explains. "I grew up in the delta. Where is everyone?" The old woman speaks, and the old man translates: "They came for oil and took that. Then they brought people from everywhere, bringing with them every illness on earth.

When we could not sing or catch the fish, they stopped coming. They left us with their illness to cope with alone. The shaman did not know what to sing to clear our bodies of the sickness they brought. Some of us left for the cities, like here. We never knew the ways of the city. This has never been our world."

"It is good to see you in good health. What is your name?"
"I am Moyo. I left here a long time ago. What are your names?"
The old couple laughs. "We never needed a name. We never had one. Our people are among these now; only a few that we know," the old woman explains. "We never were many, even in the delta. It is good to see you at all," says the old woman to Moyo.
"Could we find our people? Would you help me? We could start again," suggests Moyo.

"What for?" responds the old woman. "There is no pure blood left of our people, now mixed beyond recognition. We had always feared the men-eating spirits. While we had enough voices, we could sing them away. We have lost our voice. There is hardly anyone left."
"Let us return to the delta; it is richer than ever before. This is no place for our people to live on the scraps from the garbage bins. Come to the delta; it is lush, and it can heal you. Find the others; let us go back home," says Moyo as she stands in the shadow of the garbage container.

The old woman points at the shadow. "Are you the one called 'Shadow'? Are you the little shadow, the one that went missing when the white man who lived among us left? Are you 'Moyo', that Moyo from so long ago?"

"Yes, I am. I was José's shadow, and perhaps I still am. In Portugal, he became my father. I grew up far from here. I brought my daughter and grandchildren to see the delta. There is no one there to chase you away. Return home, please."

Moyo sits beside her. All three sing the song to keep the demons away.

Moyo returns to the ketch. "Mama, you are bleeding."
"Oh, it's this time of the month again," responds Moyo.
"But Mama, you are sixty years old; that should have stopped long ago."
"It comes every month, Dorothea, without fail."
"Do you know what that means, Mama? You still have eggs. That is so rare at your age."
"Old eggs they are, as old as I am," says Moyo.
"Do you know what was in the chests, Mama?"
"Yes, charts and memorabilia, lots of documents and things, all collected by José, your grandfather."
"Did you read the documents, Mama?"
"No, dear."

"I opened the sealed folder," Dorothea smiles. "Mama, there is a very slim chance. Grandfather collected blood and sperm samples from your people. The sperm is dry, but there is a chance to bring it to life. You still have eggs. Your egg and this sperm are pure blood; they could bring your people back to life."

"I don't understand these things, dear; you have worked in laboratories most of your life; I don't know about these things. Isn't sperm usually frozen?"

"Freezing makes the money go 'round. It needs constant top up of liquid nitrogen, and anyway, frozen sperm is dead sperm. No one has found any sperm of use."
"Mama, there are no men for my daughters. I will collect your eggs and try to bring the sperm back to life. There is a very slight chance that it could work."

"We could start a new life in a bowl and implant it into young women." She looks at the fore-deck, where the twins are.

"Mama, you could become the mother of your granddaughters' children. Your people could be reborn from Josefa and Francisca. How else could they have children, there are no men left to father them? Mama, we could try."

Moyo smiles and says, "How did you know that, when you named the twins, 16 years ago? Josefa, it means 'God will bring another son,' Francisca, means 'free'. Did you know that already then?"
"No, Mama, I had no idea, but these girls will get the aching for a child, the hope a child brings. We can give them this hope."

Self-reliance to survive

Beijing, China / USA

Under the leadership of Wong Wei, China launched several lunar expeditions in search of their '*emperor*' without success, while Russia was not at all happy about the USA's 'assistance' blowing up their icebreaker in Antarctica. Russia demanded and received financial compensation for the lost ship and reached a restitution settlement for the families affected by the loss of their loved ones.

The USA assembled a scientific team of glaciologists and scientists to explore the possibility of keeping men alive over an extended period of time at Lake Vostok, Antarctica. The experts concluded that it would be highly unlikely that any nation would have the technical expertise or resources to keep anyone alive in such extreme conditions, as the pressures were just too immense for such an undertaking. The know-how does not yet exist to contemplate such an endeavour.

The falling GDP and resulting lower tax revenues in all countries due to a shrinking workforce and the overhead of servicing unsustainable debt brought economic havoc to many nations. The governments of several countries had no choice but to start confiscating the properties of those without heirs and introduce severe measures to cut spending and increase taxation. These uncertainties lasted several years, with banks ordered to close to prevent massive withdrawals of funds.

The days of ever-growing GDP were truly over, resulting in severe cutbacks in research, development, exploration for resources, and investment in new projects. A chain reaction of defaults in several countries led to isolationism and the closing of borders. The increase in natural resources provided some compensation to the citizens of poorer nations, as self-reliance became for many the only way to survive.

In search of Moyo

Nagoya, Japan / Southampton, UK

Shima Chika turned 63 when her curiosity finally got the better of her. In Aaron's material, which she had received from Susie following Aaron's death, was a stack of bundled-up correspondence from many years ago; letters that Aaron and José shared about their time in the Amazon and Venezuela. At that time, the Internet and email did not yet exist. Chika had never looked at them before.

Most were handwritten, a few with a typewriter. Most were written in ink, while some were written in lead pencil. A few had moisture damage, making them difficult to decipher. Most of Aaron's letters were written in English, while José wrote in Portuguese and English, often using words from both languages in the same sentence.

Chika sorted all correspondence based on dates. In Aarons letters constantly the name of Moyo is mentioned, and likewise in José's writing, although Chika does not speak Portuguese. Despite that it became obvious that Moyo must be a young girl, and as such peaked Chika's interest even more. Chika and Susie arranged to meet in Southampton to go through the correspondence together.

Susie explained, "You know Chika, Moyo is an Indigenous, which José brought back on his return from Venezuela. He married Angela and they adopted Moyo. I never met any of them, although I know that Moyo is six years older than I am. I don't know if José and Aaron had a falling out. I remember that Aaron never talked much about him. Let me see if I can find an address, and if I do we can go down to Portugal and try to find her?"

Cascais, Portugal

Both women found the last known address of José. "Sorry, I don't know any José or Moyo. We've been renting this place for the last few years. Perhaps the neighbours would know, they've been here much longer than us," says the woman living in the house now.

The next door neighbour could provide more information.
"Yes, I remember José well. Angela died first, some years later José passed away as well. Moyo stayed a little while but then had the aching to travel back to Venezuela. She took her daughter, Dorothea, and her twin grandchildren, Josefa and Francisca. They went out in José's ketch. But that's a long time ago. I think Moyo still owns the house next door. Some agency is looking after the tenants. I haven't heard from them since. Please let me know if you find them."

"I'm more intrigued now," says Chika. "First Moyo, now Dorothea and her daughters as well."
"What I would suggest," says Susie, "could you leave the correspondence with me. I get in touch with Ramona, she knows Portuguese as well as Spanish. Much of José's correspondence is written in Portuguese. Perhaps we can learn something from the translations."
"That would be great," says Chika.

Shima Chika was not part of the group of 12. Susie learned that José too had blood and sperm samples collected in his time in Venezuela. Where are these now? Chika's interest was in the women's stories.

"When you go back to Japan, see if you can find some photographs from Venezuela in your material," says Susie. "What we need are some landmarks, the shape of an island, a mountain ridge, something that does not change with the seasons of the jungle and tidal changes. The problem is that Moyo is Indigenous, and so is most everyone in Venezuela. Even if she stood in front of me I would not know her, as all I have is a picture of her when she was 6 years old. The delta is a huge place with miles and miles of waterways. It would be impossible to find her without some landmarks to aim for."

Is the root of evil in civilisation?

South Pacific

The economies of consumerism collapsed over time. The planet offered more than ever before, but the number of buyers reduced demand to a trickle. The world population is in constant decline, 2 billion by the time Susie turns 76. A strong shift in gender balance all over the globe has females outnumbering males by 8 to 1. Amassed prosperity was donated to noble causes due to a lack of heirs. Many offered their entire fortunes to anyone who could father a son to be the heir of all they had gathered. There was money and wealth, but no heirs to claim it.

The self-proclaimed gods of wealth beg for life eternal; their teachings are doomed to fail. A religion of falsehood and rob thy neighbour. Most of the world once followed the call, 'You too can be as I am', a catch-cry that left millions in misery. Who came to benefit from their gospel? Their bags filled to the brim each year, and then they started overflowing. Each coin in their hands was extracted from the poor with the promise of making them feel on top of the world.

The shopping malls became the modern cathedrals of worship, offering a semblance of heaven within the bags one carried, all for a few coins. These establishments possessed the art of stimulating the feel-good receptors, liberating endorphins as money changed hands. The carefully calculated disposable income served as a means to pacify the masses, helping them endure the burden of poverty's stigma. Yet there had always been enough for all.

In time, the meaning of language changed; greed is a remnant that belongs to the past. The 'I Generation' stands accused of seeding selfish goals in the vain search to buy one's happiness. As each day changes to night, so do the ideals over time, just at a different cycle.
'Why are we dying out?' echoed from all sides. "Because we deserve it," some answered, "we've lost our way."
Species once on the brink of extinction are now recovering. The description of 'endangered mammals' is now applicable to just one. All living things can seed, breed, and multiply, except humanity.
Susie, with Tanisha and Nadira, is crossing South Pacific waters in her catamaran.

"To think, this is the largest of the oceans, it is larger than every piece of land combined," Tanisha says, "Look how full of life it is."
Susie, looking through binoculars, calls out, "Look, even the pygmy blue whales have recovered."

"There is enough on earth for

everyone's needs, as men's footprint is getting smaller," says Nadira.
Tanisha laughs out, "Men's footprints are disappearing altogether."
"When is your birthday, Susie?" asks Tanisha.
"It is tomorrow, Tanisha, I will be 76," replies Susie.

Nadira raises a fundamental question: "Isn't sufficiency for everyone the essence of it all? Hasn't this notion transformed humanity? The relentless craving for ownership, exploitation, and control, hasn't that been the catalyst for transforming societies worldwide? The consequences of such greed have led to injustice, inequality, and widespread harm affecting millions. Corruption, amassing unimaginable wealth stolen from millions of people, nepotism and favouritism have further eroded trust and compromised equal opportunities."

Tanisha ponders, "In the tribes of the past, doors were nonexistent, and locks were unnecessary. Could it be that the introduction of money sparked greed?"
"Money bought weapons, power, even wives and slaves. One man became the owner of another. It transformed into economic slavery. Fuelled by incessant greed, to own more than enough was never enough," says Susie. "Eventually, they believed they owned the entire world, but it was nothing more than an illusion."

"Is the root of evil in civilisation, I wonder?" asks Tanisha.
Tanisha raises a poignant question: "Who laments the tribes and ancient peoples burdened by the weight of civilisation's actions? Our plundering of the earth has been unparalleled, leaving scars that bear witness to our deeds. Never before have Indigenous communities poisoned the planet on such a devastating scale, an undeniable truth before our very eyes. We dismantled the time-

honoured principle of sustainable living that numerous wise voices sought to impart upon humanity."

In response, Nadira asserts, "Savages, beasts, and sub humans what they called them because they could not read or write. But was it not always us who failed to understand what they tried to convey? Yet, could it be that our failure lies in our inability to comprehend the wisdom they endeavoured to convey? The structures of their societies were destroyed, respect for their customs and traditions was eroded, their traditional languages were suppressed, and the remnants of tribes were reduced to seeking solace in drink in the slums of degrading existence."

"Do you see these islands, up ahead?" asks Susie, "Far from anywhere, far from international shipping lanes. On each map, they are marked as desolate places. Would you start again, if you could? Burn this vessel to start anew?"
"I would," says Nadira. "And so would I," adds Tanisha.

Susie stands at the bow of the yacht and lights an orange flare, then shoots a bullet into the air.

Shortly later, Nadira spots a rowing boat departing from one of the islands, "Look, there!"
Tanisha, surprised to see a boat, Susie smiles. Two elderly women row the small boat.

"They all look so familiar," says Nadira, as the boat comes closer.
Susie laughs, "You'll be surprised, Nadira."
Tanisha scans the islands through binoculars, "I can't see any life out there, just a high cliff. I would not have expected anyone living there," she closes in on the boat, "She looks like Ramona, I thought

she died."
"Hello everyone, come aboard," Susie calls out.
The two women reach the yacht, "Ye Myo, come aboard, Ramona, it is truly a joy to see you all. Come let me help you."

Nadira, surprised at the unexpected visitors, "You've been alive all this time? I didn't know."
"Hello Nadira," says Ye Myo, "there is much you don't know, I guess."
"Before we fill you in with everything let us guide you in," says Ramona.

"Can we go to the islands?" asks Tanisha.
Susie says, "If we do, we can never return, the ship will be burned."
Nadira smiles, "Let's burn the ship."
"What do you say, Tanisha?" Susie asks.
"Yes, let us burn the bridges."

"Before we do, let's get a bit closer to the islands," adds Susie, "Unload the provisions we brought and then we can burn it."
The catamaran sets sail to head the short distance north. As it enters the narrow gorge to reach the inner shelter, it disappears from view, as if the islands had swallowed it. "Come and meet the others," suggests Ye Myo.

Joyous embraces reunites the friends. "Nicole and Felicia, you were not part of the group of 12, how come you are here?" Nadira asks.

Ramona answers her question, "I owe them both, Nicole and Felicia, big time. Because of me, both were on a wanted list in Europe, hunted by men who had a score to settle. This has been a safe place for us all."

Ye Myo explains their new surroundings, "See the island at the left, that is 'Men's Island'. See the others around them, these are the 'Women's Islands'. No map has those names," Ye Myo explains.

"I'm at a loss," says Tanisha, "What is happening, can someone fill us in?"
Susie laughs, "Tanisha, Nadira, there is the beginning of a new world."
Ramona explains, "We have been living here for the last 20 years. Twenty years are a long time, but we made much progress."
"Wait, wait, wait, please start at the beginning, how did this all came about?" asks Tanisha.

Susie explains, "Kysa found the islands when she was a child. Her family are boat builders too so they crossed the oceans. On one of the trips they discovered this. Years later, when she was grown up, she remembered and searched for it until she found them again. The main island has fresh water. We planted some seeds."

"A few years later, Aislinn did the next trip," explains Susie. "She brought supplies, more seeds, checked if anyone else had been there since. There was no evidence of that."
"And then we started to populate them," says Susie, "Nicole, Ramona and Felicia came first, preparing everything for the others."

"Ye Myo and Gasha came with the first children," says Kysa, "with each trip we checked if they could sustain themselves."
"Now we have thirty-two children, all born on these islands, 15 boys, 17 girls," says Gasha.
"But who fathered the boys?" asks Nadira.

"That is a long story," says Susie. "A few years before Aaron died, an old man approached me. Aaron was overseas at the time. The old man was part of the Amazon expedition that Aaron and José, a Portuguese man, as well as some others took part in. The man had kept stuff on cold storage for the group. He didn't know what it was, neither did I. He asked me to take the whole chest, as he battled a terminal illness. His time was running out, he said. He taught me how to keep it cold. He gave me a stack of paperwork and each piece in cold storage was itemised in that."
"And what did you find?" asks Nadira.

"I found a treasure. It turned out to be the cool box of several expeditions, containing tribal sperm and blood specimen from most Indigenous people. All sorted by continent and location, as well as in-depth descriptions of tribal habits, ways of life etc."

"Are you saying you used that sperm to make the 32 children?" asks Tanisha.

"We certainly did," answers Zoe.
"How come that sperm was not contaminated, as all the others?"
"They did not use any commercial vials. That sperm was collected long before the idea of IVF came out," says Susie, "they must have thought of another way to do it."
"Shortly after the 'influence', the police knocked at my door. They were asking about a cool chest. I showed them the empty chest and told them, that I needed it for something else and that I had thrown all the rubbish in the bin months earlier."
"I knew they were going to come, eventually. When the calls for male sex sperm became louder, some of the others in the research team must have remembered the specimen."

"By that time, they were already safely located someplace else. Thankfully, the old man also gave me the compressor, so I learned how to make liquid nitrogen, to keep all the stuff cold."
Nadira laughs, "And you never said a word about it."
"With such temptation all around us, many would have caved in and sell it to the highest bidder. No one knew, until 20 years ago, when our sisters settled on these islands."

"This is amazing," says Tanisha, "what do you have on the islands?"
Nicole explains, "Most importantly we have a cool chest with lots of sperm. We do not have the technology to sort male and female sperm, so each pregnancy is a 50/50 chance. We do have the technology to make liquid nitrogen to keep it cold indefinitely. We have solar panels, wind generators, compressors, rainwater collectors, water pumps and water filtration systems. We have been self-sustained for the last 5 years."

Ye Myo explains, "All the women and girls live around the outer islands. Children stay with the women until they are ten years old. Then we bring the boys across to 'Men's Island', where they grow up with the men."
"They don't have water on that island, but we supply their water through long pipes from our pump. Be aware there are so many dangers in the waters here, sharks, stingers, sea wasps, sometimes infestations of blue ringed octopus and a variety of sea snakes."

"It is mostly warm around here and with that come these creatures. Luckily we have not seen any snakes on land."
"And with the waters so deadly, the men stay put on their island," says Nicole. "Guess what," says Felicia, "we had a big celebration about six months ago. We had our first child born, fathered by a real man, not from the cool box. The future looks promising."
"That is wonderful, Felicia," says Nadira, "how do you bring the kids up?"

Ye Myo explains, "They know about the world and geography; they know most of the rivers, continents, and animals. We teach them to respect each other and their elders. We have simple rules, but not many. We all speak one language. They all know their blood is red, no matter what their outer shades. Even the youngest know that one day they too will become elders, not to rule but to guide their people. There are no prisons on the islands; there is no need for them. And another thing: no matter how much money you have, there is nothing you can buy here with it. Money here is useless."

"One day they will return to the mainland; they will repopulate the world," says Nadira. "They will not find the hierarchy that was in part to blame for its demise. No men shall put them under."

"They will find a world free of politics, free of borders, a world in which they can excel." "Remember what we had on the whiteboard that many years ago?" asks Tanisha. "Perhaps we need to revisit this to provide some guidance for the future, addressing all the points we raised some 60 years ago. At least now we each have a lifetime's worth of lived experience."

"It will be a new start," adds Kysa. "Bear in mind that in time, all we know will come to a halt. If infrastructure is not maintained, it will deteriorate, nature will reclaim it. No GPS will work, no power generation plant will work, and no refinery will work. There will be no reliable water supply. All that we know will decay, rust, and disintegrate. There will be no Internet, no phone, radio, or television network. There will be no satellites circling the earth."

"Critical for survival would be shelter, water, food, fire, tools, first aid, communication, and support for each other, I would think," says Aislinn. "Has anyone come past here?" asks Susie.
“Yes, lots of whales migrating through here,” says Ramona, “We have not seen any ships or planes.”
“What is happening in the world?” she asks.

“Population is less than 2 billion now and in steady decline,” says Nadira. “Women outnumber men everywhere, but even now, the old men still try to hold all the cards. The oldest of the XX Generation are 66 or so.”

“And look at us, Susie has always been the youngest, now she’s getting closer to 80,” adds Tanisha.
“We’re preparing one of the islands for an experiment,” says Felicia, “we will see if man and woman can get on together. Time will tell.”
"What happened to the others?" asks Ramona.

Tanisha explains, "We know Adzumi passed away eight years ago. Karla, the Nameless One, who became Asha, is currently in Europe. I was waiting for Susie to return. I'm preparing to go out and get Asha," says Kysa. "When I return, Aislinn will try to get Chika from Japan." Susie chimed in, "Well, we can't burn the ship, not yet. We'll have to sail out once more when Kysa and Aislinn have returned, to find my sister, Kim Xia. We will also need those vessels in the future. Oh, by the way, Tanisha was wondering if all the problems we faced stem from civilisation."

Ye Myo joined the conversation, saying, "Civilisation has brought us many good things. We have complex social structures, efficient use of resources, advancements in technology, medicine, healthcare, sanitation, agriculture, and communication."
Felicia jumped in, adding her thoughts: "Don't forget about culture, arts, and literature. We had complex infrastructures and higher living standards when compared with the past."
Kysa nodded and said, "Absolutely! There are so many positive aspects to civilisation."

Aislinn, however, had a different take. She said, "But let's not forget the other side of the coin. Civilisation has also led to the wasteful production of useless gadgets just for the sake of making money. It caused environmental damage, cultural homogenisation, loss of diversity, social isolation, and sometimes a complete disregard for nature and sustainability." Ramona couldn't help but join the conversation, saying, "And let's not forget the conflicts that have arisen throughout history due to differences in ideologies. It left millions in misery and worse."
Susie's voice became serious as she added, "And you know what bothers me? It's this disgusting accumulation of power and wealth in the hands of a small group of leaders in large organisations and businesses. Those who tried to expose it often ended up in jail, with

the current laws suitably modified to blame the messenger. How can we prevent this in the future?"
Tanisha chimed in, her tone thoughtful: "We have to think about the future. We're the ancestors of tomorrow's world. Do we have the wisdom to build a society that can sustain life in a fair and ethical manner?"

"Behind mangroves, we found a few deep caves, enough to hide six ocean-going yachts. Three are already there from earlier excursions. Kysa has the sloop, plus the one she is preparing to go out with. The other two are Aislinn's."

"Aislinn will head to Japan when Kysa returns, trying to bring Chika over," explains Ramona. "In the beginning, we only had three sailors," explains Aislinn. Kysa, Susie, and me. We arranged it so that only one is ever out at sea. If need be, one of us could go out on a rescue mission, and the other sailor is left to not leave the group stranded. But meanwhile many others have learned to sail. We're trying to get another vessel here as a spare and for future use. We hope that Sheila is bringing one up from Australia."

"For the time being, we want to make the islands appear desolate, with no hint of human habitation, just in case some strangers find their way here," adds Kysa. "In time, we will need to spread out further, as these islands can only support a limited number of people."

"Yes, Tanisha, we are the ancestors," says Gasha, her voice filled with contemplation. "What we leave behind are the seeds of the future. I hope we have the wisdom to channel our actions towards building a society that nurtures compassion, equality, and sustainability. We must prioritize the well-being of all, fostering a world where power is wielded responsibly and wealth is distributed fairly. Our legacy should be one of progress, harmony, and justice, ensuring a brighter path for generations yet to come."
"Let's have a minute's silence for Adzumi," says Nadira, "and hope Chika, Asha, and Kim Xia can be found."

end

Afterword

'to never take for granted' is my 18th book. Several years ago, I received a confidential request from a prominent individual to assume the role of a ghost-writer for a book. The instruction was simple: 'Craft a tale where women rise to power and dominate the world.' Puzzled, I pondered why women would pursue such a path and what compelling motivations would drive them. This led me on a quest to explore numerous justifications that could lend credence to their actions.

The sheer volume of reasons I discovered was overwhelming, far surpassing what could be contained within these pages. To tackle this subject in a work of fiction, I opted to spotlight a select group of twelve individuals who would both ignite the discussion and devise a strategy to attain their ultimate goal. The narrative of the story was further supported by several side characters, whose presence added depth and complexity to the overarching plot.

While the precise methodology is a product of imagination, the underlying rationales and arguments presented align closely with real-world considerations. Upon completing the book, the person who initially commissioned it found it difficult to connect with the narrative. Consequently, I made the decision to release the book under my own name with the title 'Barren Seed' (release 2008).

During the journey of 'Barren Seed,' several unfortunate incidents occurred that I feel compelled to address. After its initial release, I discovered that a number of websites had listed the book without my permission, infringing upon my copyright. Despite my efforts to rectify the situation by informing them of the infringement, it became evident that the 'Barren Seed' version of the book was still circulating in various corners of the internet. This raised concerns about potential confusion and the integrity of my work. To safeguard the essence of my work and to ensure clarity for readers, I made the decision to re-edit the book and give it a new title. 'Barren Seed' no longer represents the current iteration of the story. Instead, 'to never take for granted' embodies the essence of the journey and the evolution it has undergone.

Images of characters with changes over time

Gasha Ukraine	
Ramona De Urquiza Spain	
Karla becomes **Nameless One** becomes **Asha** Germany	
Tanisha India	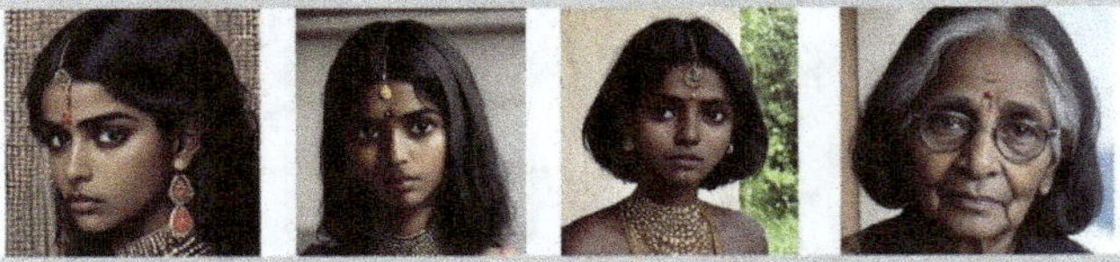
Sheila Australia	
Zoe Wilder USA	
Mary Snyder USA	
Ying Kim Xia HK / China	
Dulcie Nielson USA	

Sam Ryder USA	
Sally Cramer USA	
Shima Chika **志麻 千佳** Japan	
Nicole Dubois France	
Julien **Mr Fix-It** France	
Leticia **Pastora Chavira** Spain	
Felicia Fodor Hungary	
Honza Horák Czechoslovakia	
Tom USA	

Roland McGuire USA			
Isabella Bettucini Italy			
Dir Cheung HK			
Dr Huang Qiu China			
Prof Xu Shen China			
US President USA			
Wong Wei China			
Dorothea (Moyo's daughter) Portugal	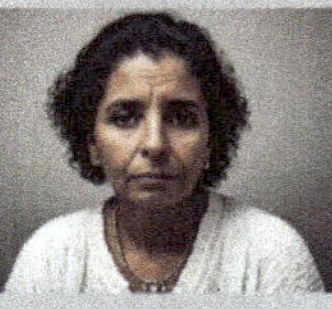		
Josefa & Francisca (Dorothea's daughters) Portugal			

Characters and Location

People, Nationality, Location

Main characters are the group of 12, their age in Basel:
Susie Cross (Hong Kong born, Caucasian, Asian) 18 yrs
Ye Myo Tun (Myanmar) 23 yrs
Nadira (Pakistan) at Aaron's place (Susie's father)
Adzumi (Japanese)
Kysa (Swedish)(Sailor family)
Aislinn (Irish) (Sailor family)
Gasha (Ukrainian)
Ramona De Urquiza (Spain) 18yrs
Karla (German) becoming the 'Nameless One'
Tanisha (Indian)
Sheila (Australian)
Zoe Wilder (American)

In order of appearance:
My grandchild and my sister:
Aye Ye Mya becomes Ye Myo Tun, 5yrs old, Nyein (Grandmother)
We need to go back
José Julio Câmara de Sousa (Portuguese) in Venezuela
Moyo 6 yrs (Native of Venezuela), Captain Garcia da Costa, Antônio
How can she be so big already?
Garcia da Costa, José Julio Câmara de Sousa, Angela, Moyo
Those are all songs from her people
José Julio Câmara de Sousa, Portugal, Angela, Moyo
I want to die
Mary Snyder (USA) 40 yrs, Chicago, Dr. Novak
The goldmine
Dulcie Nielson (USA) 72 yrs, Tim Sorrens, Roland McGuire, Prof. Edmund Fryer, Tom, Jerry Baxter, Garry Stoner (HK), Jim (Chicago)
You are going to be a very rich woman
Ye Myo Tun (Myanmar) 23 yrs, Garry Stoner (HK), Ying Kim Xia (HK), Roland McGuire (Chicago), Tom, Dulcie Nielson
Harmony and balance
Felicia Fodor (Hungarian) 25yrs, Honza Horák (Czech) 50+yrs
The sweetest loss I ever made
Sam Ryder (USA) 55yrs, Sue, assistant to Ryder
All synthetics are man-made
Shima Chika (Japanese) 29 yrs, Signora Bettucini (Italian) 58 yrs
How could I not have known?
Ying Kim Xia (Caucasian/Asian), Mrs. Qing Lian (Chinese) 70 yrs

I have blood on my hands and it will not come off

Sally Cramer (USA), Ying Kim Xia
We have no names
Ramona De Urquiza (Spanish) 18 yrs, Nicole Dubois (French) 23 yrs, Gérard (French) 48 yrs, Monique 24 yrs, Antoine also Mr Happening 50 yrs, Julien also Mr Fix it 52 yrs, Penelope 23 yrs
A chance to buy a tear
Nicole Dubois, Ramona, Leticia Pastora Chavira (Spanish) 56 yrs, Perpetua (Spanish) 92 yrs
Susie meets Ye Myo
Ye Myo Tun, Susie Cross (Switzerland)
What would we need to salvage from here?
Ye Myo Tun, Susie Cross, Aaron Cross (UK), Nadira (Pakistan), Adzumi (Japanese), Kysa (Swedish, Sailor family), Aislinn (Irish, Sailor family), Gasha (Ukrainian), Ramona (Spain), Karla (German) becoming the 'Unnamed One', Tanisha (Indian), Sheila (Australian), Zoe Wilder (USA)
Now I know why it could not be shown
Ramona, Ye Myo Tun, Felicia Fodor, Nicole Dubois, Susie (Switzerland)
Wait a minute, what is going on?
Nicole meets Aislinn, Zoe and Tanisha
They do not understand
All 12 girls at Susie's place, Aaron Cross
This book has less than 150 pages, yet it is so heavy
Sally Cramer, Sam Ryder (USA)
What is it all about? No one is telling
Aaron, Group of 12, Jerry Baxter
Keep these memories close to your heart
Sally Cramer, Tom, Shima Chika
Thank you, for remaining calm
Aaron
Let us keep an eye on the place in the future
Group of 12
… you just don't get the words out
Group of 12
Are we having secrets now?
Susie, Aaron, Director Cheung, Ying Kim Xia
Men are capable of anything
Group of 12
I would love to meet her
Sally Cramer, Shima Chika, Ying Kim Xia
What do you want from me?
Aaron Cross, Ying Kim Xia, Director Cheung
I will make sure your mother will not recognise you
Felicia Fodor, Nicole Dubois, Julien

There will be no guessing what we grow
Nameless One, Nadira, Tanisha
He knew the results, but glanced at the letter anyway
Susie Cross, Aaron Cross, Kim, Director Cheung, Ying Kim Xia
I don't know, I don't know, I don't know
Susie Cross, Gasha, Zoe, Aislinn, Nadira, Sheila, Gasha, Kysa, Adzumi
I grew up with Chan, my great-grandmother
Sally Cramer, Aaron Cross, Ying Kim Xia
The right moment is more important for us
Group of 12
Think of nothing. Let us live this moment
Ying Kim Xia, Aaron Cross
All this is in a picture. This is fascinating
Sally Cramer, Shima Chika
Are we going to live a life in fear from now on?
Ye Myo Tun, Group of 12
Could mum still be alive?
Aaron Cross, Ying Kim Xia
What does it all mean?
Group of 12
Is it off your shoulders, Kim?
Shima Chika, Sally Cramer, Ying Kim Xia
What are they after?
Susie Cross, Ye Myo Tun, Aaron Cross, Nadira
I have another surprise
Kim Xia, Sally Cramer, Shima Chika, Aaron Cross
We must find the underlying cause of this
Mr Hong Tao, Dr Huang Qiu, Professor Xu Shen, Dr Lin Kang
Kim, each woman is your sister
Sally Cramer, Ye Myo Tun, Shima Chika, Susie Cross, Aaron Cross
We will not give a warning
Group of 12 in Basel
It feels like the dawning of a new day
Group of 12, Nameless One becomes Asha
Our brief is to do whatever it takes
Professor Xu Shen
We try to start again
Gasha
The balance shifts
Nadira
Yes, yes, we know all this
Research team, Medical Research Clinic, Shenzhen, China
It has not sunk in yet
Group of 12, Aaron Cross, Ye Myo Tun, Shima Chika

Such news is very troubling
Ramona, Felicia Fodor, Nicole Dubois, Leticia Pastora Chavira
You would have done the same
Nicole Dubois, Julien
Nicole is unable to speak
Felicia, Lyon, Saint-Tropez, Nicole Dubois, Cannes
This may just be the beginning
Shima Chika, Sally Cramer, Ye Myo Tun
They are just not interested
Group of 12
Have you really thought about what that means?
Professor Xu Shen, Dr Huang Qiu, Dr. Lin Kang, Dr. Kym
All bidding for the chance to be the only ones
Global
Who and what we were
Group of 12
Mr President, put two and two together
President of USA, Chief of Staff
The ice cracks underneath
Antarctica
A new plan for tomorrow
Ted, Jerry, Boris (Russian), Avanish (Indian)
Population is in decline everywhere
Wong Wei (China), Zhuang (China)
Huangdi Bixia (old name for Emperor of China, Bixia (His Majesty)
I feel an ache for Venezuela
Salvatore de Dominguez (Portuguese), Moyo, Dorothea, Josefa, Francisca
Indigenous man and woman (Venezuela) 70+ yrs
Self-Reliance to survive
China, USA, Global
In search of Moyo
Shima Chika, Susie Cross
Is the root of evil in civilisation?
Susie Cross, Aislinn, Tanisha, Kysa, Nadira, Ramona, Ye Myo Tun, Nicole Dubois, Felicia Fodor, Gasha

About the author:

Welcome to the vivid tapestry of the author's artistic voyage. From an early age, he proclaimed his destined course as a writer, hinting at the extraordinary journey that lay ahead. Alongside his passion for music creation, he delved into the visual arts and video production, expanding his creative horizons and nurturing an enduring quest for artistic discovery.

His musical compositions became transcendent channels for emotions, freed from linguistic confines, as books, akin to vessels, became conduits for his thoughts, dreams, and explorations across a diverse range of creative paths. This 18th publication follows a lineage of previous works including 'Logos,' 'Between Eternities,' 'Only for Now,' 'The Puma's Trail,' and numerous others.

From poetry to articles, from magazine production to his diverse array of books, compositions, and videos, the author's unwavering passion for artistic expression shines through. Within the pages of his works, readers are welcomed to embark on an extraordinary voyage where inspiration intertwines with imagination, prompting thought-provoking questions along the way.

heinzross.com

No art, and all will fall apart.

to never take for granted

www.ingramcontent.com/pod-product-compliance
Lightning Source LLC
Chambersburg PA
CBHW060621310726
48982CB00003B/627
9780645928181